Nolten the Painter

Studies in German Literature, Linguistics, and Culture

Edited by James Hardin
(*South Carolina*)

Eduard Mörike

Nolten the Painter

A Novella in Two Parts

Translated
and with a Critical Introduction by
Raleigh Whitinger

CAMDEN HOUSE

First published 2005
by Camden House

Camden House is an imprint of Boydell & Brewer Inc.
668 Mt. Hope Avenue, Rochester, NY 14620, USA
www.camden-house.com
and of Boydell & Brewer Limited
PO Box 9, Woodbridge, Suffolk IP12 3DF, UK
www.boydellandbrewer.com

ISBN: 1–57113–312–7

Library of Congress Cataloging-in-Publication Data

Mörike, Eduard Friedrich, 1804–1875.
　[Maler Nolten. English]
　Nolten the painter: a novella in two parts / Eduard Mörike; translated
and with a Critical Introduction by Raleigh Whitinger.
　　p. cm. — (Studies in German literature, linguistics, and culture)
Includes bibliographical references.
ISBN 1–57113–312–7 (hardcover: alk. paper)
　I. Whitinger, Raleigh, 1944–　II. Title.　III. Series: Studies in
German literature, linguistics, and culture (Unnumbered)

PT2434.M35E6 2005
833'.912—dc22

　　　　　　　　　　　　　　　　　　　　　　　　2004026153

A catalogue record for this title is available from the British Library.

This publication is printed on acid-free paper.
Printed in the United States of America.

Introduction

THIS IS THE FIRST English translation of Eduard Mörike's *Maler Nolten* (1832). It is intended to further the rediscovery of a complex prose work by an author whose fame has long resided mainly in his lyric poetry and in his later artist novella *Mozart auf der Reise nach Prag* (Mozart's Journey to Prague; 1854). Mörike (1804–1875) is usually located between Goethe and Rilke as a major force in the development of nineteenth-century German poetry. His *Mozart* novella is ranked with Thomas Mann's *Death in Venice* (1912) as a major contribution to the German artist story. Yet only recently have critics begun to recognize his novel as a remarkably innovative contribution to an emerging modernity in the German and European novel since the late eighteenth century — especially with respect to the Bildungsroman and the artist novel.

Mörike began *Nolten the Painter* in 1827 and published it in 1832. His work on it accompanies his struggle to reconcile his poetic interests with his studies and calling as a Protestant pastor. In 1826, after four years of study at Tübingen's famous theological seminary (the "Stift"), he began eight years of work as an assistant vicar in a series of parishes in his native Württemberg, interrupted only by a brief attempt to establish himself as a writer for the Stuttgart *Damenzeitung* in 1828. Yet even as a student, he was well on his way to developing his lyrical talents and imaginative, myth-making proclivities. In the mid-1820s he devoted considerable energy to creating, with fellow seminarian Ludwig Amandus Bauer, the fantastic figures and stories of the "Orplid" mythology that both young men would later rework poetically — Bauer in two dramas and Mörike with the drama "The Last King of Orplid," which, as a collaborative project of young Nolten and his beloved mentor Larkens, plays a prominent role in the plot and thematic fabric of *Nolten*. He had also written numerous poems, some included in a handwritten collection of verses dedicated to his sister in 1828 (the "Grünes Heft") and later in the first public edition of his lyrics in 1838, many of which he wove into *Nolten*. One is the first of the novel's two dozen poetic inlays, the "Fire Rider" ballad of 1825, which is part of the scenes that the actor Larkens organizes early in the novel as part of his New Year's Eve efforts to steer young Nolten's attention away from the tempting fires of new passion and back to the safe and simple idyll of his engagement to the village beauty Agnes. Another is the cycle of poems entitled "Peregrina," which appears late in the novel as Larkens's poetic recasting of the young title hero's stormy — and never fully described or explained — relationship to his half-Gypsy cousin, Elisabeth. Mörike had composed that cycle in 1824 in response to his own traumatic affair the year before with the mysterious beauty Maria Meyer, a crisis that also inspired the work on the artist story that became *Nolten the Painter*. Maria Meyer, a vagabond intellectual and one-time follower of the Pietist visionary Madame Krüdener, was in 1823 both the object of the young theology student's intense attraction and the victim of his anxious rejection — the erotic side of the attraction disturbingly countering the young poet's desire to envision her as his angel and muse. In 1827, he began work on a short prose piece about a young artist's encounter with the temptingly exotic but dangerous woman. Yet with the work on the first draft from 1827 through 1829, and with additions before 1832, the originally planned "novella" expanded significantly. In 1829 Mörike became engaged to Luise Rau, the daughter of a deceased vicar whom he briefly replaced in Plattenhardt, and with that the fictional account of the artist-Gypsy encounter grew to include the protagonist's precarious betrothal to his "foster sister" Agnes. This expansion also involved the inclusion of still more of the young author's own poems, for five of which the first edition also offered an appendix of musical scores composed by Mörike's brother Karl and Louis Hetsch (the "Musikbeilage zu Maler Nolten").[1]

Critics from early on perceived the resulting work as a problematic hybrid, emphasizing its contravention of expected forms — but overlooking the possible sense and consistency of its critical dialogue with traditions of the novel, Bildungsroman, and artist story. *Nolten the Painter* is a work of patently novel-like size and scope, and it offers an artist as its protagonist. Yet it calls itself a "Novella in Two Parts" and, simply with its initial move from title page to text, renders its promised artist figure a painter in a context that raises doubts both about what degree of skill and creative genius make a successful painter and about the title figure's right even to that reduced title. It promises at the outset the narration of an artistically gifted young hero's *Bildung* — his personal formation and successful integration into the frameworks of the father's world — and often proceeds in psychological detail, striking in this way as a realistic echo of several landmarks of the modern Bildungsroman. Yet after the opening expository sequence, which seems to clarify dark mysteries to reveal handsome young Theobald Nolten as an artistic talent about to continue his ascent as painter and lover, the two main parts of the unusual novella's plot show him repeatedly thwarted in both endeavors and ending in catastrophes that seem brought about by a capricious fate working through deranged figures and supernatural events. In the first part, Nolten produces little as an artist, despite the efforts of his beloved mentor, the actor Larkens, to draw him into collaboration on new genres, and the transition of his romantic attentions from his far-off fiancée to the intelligent and charming Countess Constanze is disrupted as a result both of Larkens's unclearly motivated desire to guide him back into the idyllically safe "Biedermeier" haven of marriage to Agnes, and of Nolten's unresolved ties to the mysterious Elisabeth. In the second part, Nolten's artistic productivity has not progressed past the barely begun painting of a Narcissus, and his reaffirmed betrothal to Agnes is ultimately ruined by his unresolved ties to his diverse and exotic past. His mysterious death coincides closely with the demise of those dear to him and leaves the surviving father figures to gaze, sad and mystified, into the abyss of fate. In this way the story counters the fictive narrator's opening promise of felicitous progress. It even mocks it on the last page by revealing Nolten's failed *Bildung* to have been transcended by and contained in the makeshift Bildungsroman of his Uncle Friedrich. That earlier "Painter Nolten" has progressed from Gypsy adventurer to "Hofrat" (court councilor) only by suppressing his creative and diverse side, but even his shaky reconciliation of art and life is unattainable for the nephew who struggles to live by the ideals of earlier art works.

With these countered or destabilized promises of an artist's formation and integration, *Nolten the Painter* drew mixed reviews that established a lasting conception of it as a flawed work and fostered its relative neglect in studies of the German Bildungsroman and artist novel. It came to be known as a work in which the young poet, out of his depth with longer narrative and hesitant to be seen mounting a challenge to the revered Goethe, had fleshed out a contradictory and ill-titled plot line with thematically extraneous poetic inlays to create an inconsistent work in which elements of psychologically realistic portrayal are countered by what appears to be the author's lingering romantic fascination with notions of demonic, supernatural fatalism. Early reviewers saw in it a "double motivation" of theme that rendered it a contradictory mix of realistic and romantic elements. Mörike's friend Friedrich Theodor Vischer declared it in his review to be one half a Bildungsroman in the tradition of Goethe's *Meister*, a realistic psychological novel, but the other half a *Schicksalsroman* (novel of fate), a mystical novel fostering belief in a capricious fate working through demonic figures. Ensuing critics long tended to lament this shift from psychologically realistic Bildungsroman to fate story. Many also fault the title for promising a painter who in fact achieves little in the way of completed paintings or artistic insight, while others accuse the author of making the work a vehicle for publishing poetic works of his own that have little to do with the main narrative's plot and themes.[2]

In the last two decades, however, critical analyses have begun a revision of this view of *Nolten* as a flawed and inconsistent work. They have done this by focusing on the narrative structure and its link to the text's network of poetic inlays, episodes of fictive narrating and performance, and evocations of several "novels of formation" and artist stories of the preceding decades. These studies have correctly located the novel's alleged romantic lapses — its flights into mythical and poetic recasting of the real problems depicted, or into speculations on the capricious workings of a demonic fate — in the figures rather than in the author. They intimate how even the fictive narrator's entire project of offering a "portrait" of the "painter Nolten" is drawn into the strikingly modern critical dialogue that the novel conducts with the all too idealistic "narratives" to which the various artistic men involved resort in their efforts to impose a heroic and romantic story upon the full "text" of life.[3]

This revised view finds compelling support in further details of the genesis and basics of the text. This is so with the work's formal evolution into a "novella in two parts" and thus with its relationship to trends prominent in the development of the modern novel that flourished with Goethe's *Wilhelm Meisters Lehrjahre* (Apprenticeship of Wilhelm Meister) in the 1790s. *Nolten the Painter* might appear even with its subtitle to admit itself to be an unwieldy mix of simple story and extraneous inlays, and thus to shy diffidently away from competition with Goethe's *Meister*. Mörike was quick, after all, to distinguish his story from an aesthetic or philosophy-of-life novel on the scale of *Wilhelm Meister,* a work he claimed to revere as an "inexhaustible" book, "infinitely instructive" in its artistic composition, which he read at bedtime in order to enjoy the feeling of "bright sunshine" that it awakened within him to impart — as do all great classical works such as Homer and Greek sculpture — a feeling of harmony with the world.[4] In fact, however, essentials of genre and form indicate the critical thrust behind that humble homage, the publication as a "novella in two parts" signaling instead how *Nolten the Painter* intensifies the irony and critical self-consciousness of its illustrious forerunners.

Formally, *Nolten the Painter* adheres closely to the theoretical conception of the modern novel that Friedrich Schlegel developed in the late 1790s as part of his positive response to *Wilhelm Meister.* With its many genres and discourses, with its portrayal of art works within its own art, it achieves the "poetic mix" that Schlegel saw bringing the diverse voices of the modern world to expression and rendering the entire work a piece of "poetry about poetry" that depicts its cherished figures and events while reflecting with its multi-voiced array of lyrical and narrative inlays on the limits of poetic representation.[5] By ending with an appendix in which the author has collaborated with two composers to set some of the inscribed poems to music, the August 1832 edition takes the self-reflexive irony of Schlegel's romantic novel a step further. It adds another dimension to the text's multi-voiced scope and, with its invitation to compare the work at hand to the many dubious collaborative art works that it includes, imparts a still more subversive thrust to its "poetry about poetry." The subtitle "novella in two parts" explicitly invites readers to ponder how this patently novel-like work differs from Schlegel's romantic "Roman," and Mörike's theoretical reflections at this time indicate his novella's more subversively ironic take on the sovereign, controlling narrative authority of the romantic novel that emerged in the 1790s. While completing *Nolten*, Mörike had defended to Vischer his choice of the term "novella" over "novel," favoring the former as a genre that dispensed with the "maxims and reflections" with which the traditional novel's masterful narrator elucidates his story's deeper, underlying idea — a choice of words that, with its explicit allusion to a section of Goethe's *Wilhelm Meisters Wanderjahre,* signals a departure from the expectations of omniscient control in favor of a narrated world that, for all its novel-like breadth, does not yield up an authoritatively stated meaning, that instead offers a recurring and varied idea that the reader must seek out. In his 14 May 1832 letter to Vischer, he proposed a new genre that, neither "novel" nor "novella," would make its simple central story the vehicle for a symmetrical arrangement of thematically related segments that reflect on related ideas from various perspectives. Those ideas bear strong resemblance to aspects of the "novella in two parts" that he is about to send to press, where the many inlays — contrary to long-standing critical opinion — closely reflect themes and problems of the main narrative, above all by depicting its male protagonists constantly taking flight into artistic fantasies that tend more to adorn and transform real problems than to clarify or explain them.[6]

For all their apparent diffidence, Mörike's comments on Goethe's *Meister* provide a point of entry into the text of *Nolten the Painter* that reveals its critical dialogue with traditions of narrative and art. Subtly ironic in their own right, his words of praise about *Wilhelm Meister* as enjoyable bedtime reading are echoed when the novel's opening episode links sunshine, classical art, and Homer in a subversive way. There the fictive narrator appropriates the mantle of Homeric authority by beginning with the sunlit scene of the young hero lauded by the elders of the community. Yet he wields those codes ineptly when he has the afternoon rather than the sun shine down on a scene of heroic promise that soon proves to harbor secrets and problems.[7] Goethe and his *Meister* are then more distinctly present as the narrative unfolds, first when Jassfeld's attitude of repose at Tillsen's recalls Tischbein's famous painting of "Goethe in the Campagna," and then when the opening episode seems to begin where *Wilhelm Meister's Apprenticeship* left off — with a passive title figure assured success by the achinations of a committee of older men who mold his image of success ithin their structures — readers thus invited to expect a critical reappraisal of the earlier work's impression of successful *Bildung*. With the story going on to develop the Nolten-Elisabeth affair as an echo of Meister's relationship to Mignon — and in fact a twisted echo, revealing the young hero unable imply to dispatch and forget the exotic female Other — *Nolten the Painter* emphatically delivers on its opening promise of taking up and rethinking at least one illustrious forerunner.[8]

Background facts and text combine to support an analogous reassessment of the work's apparently contradictory shift from Bildungsroman to fate story, indicating the belief in the inscrutable working of higher powers to be an inclination of the fictional figures that the text presents in a critical light as part of its self-conscious reflections on the illusions and confusions born of traditional artistic activity. Mörike, of course, did alert one reader to the role of Elisabeth as a "weaver of fates,"[9] and he has portrayed the workings of fate as a major thematic concern, an idea repeatedly put forward by the figures and at times even supported by the fictive narrator. This has fostered the long-standing critical view of *Nolten the Painter* as an exemplary product of a transition phase in German literary history bespeaking an early but underdeveloped trend towards psychological and social realism, the novel setting out to give a psychologically realistic account of an artist's development but ultimately resorting to romantic notions of a capricious fate to explain that ideal's unattainability. In fact, however, genesis and text suggest that this prominent theme is part of a critical dialogue with the novel of fate analogous to the one that develops with the tradition of the Bildungsroman and artist story. In this case, too, the novel invites interpretations that focus on "fate" as the central problem, only then to reveal that view to be a self-serving fiction with which figures or narrator uphold their own image and authority. Thus the view of *Nolten the Painter* as a problematic combination of "novel of formation" and "novel of fate" (*Schicksalsroman*) does accurately register the echoes of those two strains of prose fiction. Yet it fails to note the dimension of self-conscious and ironic parody that such echoes involve. Significant in this respect are Mörike's comments to Friedrich Notter in a letter of 2 April 1833, where he claims that his novel is a "portrait" ("Gemälde") of a "willful fate" that "seems" to take pleasure in abandoning favorites such as Nolten, destroying their existence before their purpose in life is fulfilled, with others plunged with them into the abyss. As significant in this comment as the verb "seems" is the use of the term "portrait" or "painting" to describe the novel that the fictive narrator has created. The two terms combine to suggest that the impression of a capricious fate at work to destroy the hero is an illusion born of artistic activity. In addition, the close link of "portrait" and "novel" draws attention to the relationship that emerges from early on between the host text and the various art works that it contains, with the fictive narrator's attempt to offer a "portrait" of a painter named Nolten repeatedly referring to other instances of painting, portraiture, narrative, performance, and poetry that do likewise in distorted fashion.

These self-reflective references weave through the opening sequence of expository episodes — preceding the New Year's Eve events that begin at

x

the Spanish Court — to make it a masterful overture to the entire work, countering the foreground promise of pleasing developments with warnings both about the reliability of the fictive narrator's authority and about questions and problems that will recur to impede the title figure's expected formation and integration as an artist. The fictive narrator's opening account of an emerging "painter Nolten" contains even in this brief sequence several subversive mirrors of efforts by others: above all the "queer" and devious Wispel's performance as a "painter Nolten," likewise the disturbing drawings themselves and Tillsen's secret rendition of them in oil. They all hint at the gaps between complex truths and the version of them that art works might concoct, and Baron Jassfeld's attempts at interpreting these works still more emphatically urge readers to avoid hastily positive judgments where art and artists are involved.

The fictive narrator's official project of narrating the "rapid and felicitous development" that Nolten's fortunes are about to undergo is repeatedly confounded by his drive to exhibit his mastery of facts and details. His remarks are self-contradictory in terms of themselves. They purport to present a successful and deserving painter, yet intimate that he ranks merely among the "proper" ("brav") artists in terms of skill, while his "grandiosity of spirit" is without equal. In addition, they reveal that the surprisingly "rapid and splendid change in his situation," as well as owing much to Tillsen's connections, is accepted with embarrassing speed by Nolten as something earned as his natural due despite these qualifying factors and remaining problems. The surrounding context still more emphatically subverts these positive assurances. It reveals problems in Nolten's relationships both to the men who have facilitated his ascent as a painter and to the women with whom he is romantically involved, with the account of unfolding success quickly passing over several figures — Wispel, Nolten's far off fiancée, and the mysterious woman in his sketches — who will later return to darken the horizon.

The fact that Nolten's entire rise as a respected artist springs from Wispel's masquerade, Tillsen's forgery, and hasty judgments like those of Baron Jassfeld should alarm even first-time readers. While Wispel obligingly disappears at this point, he reappears later to offer a grotesque mirror of Nolten's efforts to play the genial artist and to disrupt the progress of his conventional romances by drawing him back into the homosocial circles that stimulate his art. In addition, Wispel and Tillsen are supplanted by Larkens, who acts both as the embodiment of Nolten's affinity for homosocial collaboration — expressed in grotesque extreme by the ties to Wispel — and as the forger of works that foster Nolten's persona as a properly attractive, gifted, and socially adjusted artist. Larkens's forgery of Nolten's correspondence with Agnes, his sequence of multi-voiced and mixed-genre notebooks that recast Nolten's life and problems as romantic story or poetry all render him a recurring subversive mirror of the fictive narrator, creating dangerous illusions with his persistent efforts to write his young friend into a romantic love story or artist story.

Nor does the ensuing narrative uphold this opening promise of romantic success. Much like the "fishy" man Wispel — with his clammy skin and webbed digits — so too do the "mermaid" and "ghostly organist" of the first sketches refuse to remain under the control of the male artists. Their real-life model Elisabeth turns up to disturb the relationships to the two women that the narrator introduces in the closing portion of this opening sequence. In art and romance alike the "liminal" types, which the sunny opening seems at first glance to dispatch and control so easily, prove in the ensuing episodes to retain a presence in Nolten's life that has not been re-solved simply as a result of his and Larkens's repeated attempts to fit them into artistic structures that romanticize them as agents of a higher and in-exorable fate. In this context, the fictive narrator follows a pattern similar to that prominent among the story's other male artists. He has attempted to create a pleasing portrait and narrative that evoke romantic traditions of Bildungsroman and artist story. Yet the entire text persistently reveals those "paintings" to be an illusory veneer concealing unresolved problems of communication, morality, and identity.

Some years after the mixed reception of his completed *Nolten the Painter* of 1832, Mörike undertook a revision of the work. He worked on it intermittently from about 1850 until shortly before his death in 1875. These efforts resulted in a revised version of the first part only, and the two parts were published posthumously as a "Novel in Two Parts." Yet the two parts of this late and partially revised version are quite at odds with each other, the older Mörike's revisions having cleansed the first part of much that spoke for a dark, delusive, or even queer side of the artist's interaction with tradition and convention.[10] The older Mörike in the early 1850s was a recently mar-ried pastor in need of income and anxious not to jeopardize his professional and domestic persona. He was also a recognized poet eager to secure himself a lasting place in the literary canon with a contribution to that most German genre of Bildungsroman. Accordingly, his revisions to the first part of his "novella" drastically reduce the narrative to its popular foreground line of possible *Bildung* at the expense of the ironic perspective on that ideal that its original version had shared with the salient Bildungsromane since around 1800. Mörike makes changes that reflect or echo the emergence, through the middle of the century, of the "narrative of formation" as a national genre dedicated to upholding the ideal of the gifted male's integration into the prevailing bourgeois order. The alterations also parallel the entrenchment in the strongly nationalistic German studies of the middle and late nineteenth century of a conception of *Wilhelm Meister* and of its author as embodiments of that ideal divest of all ironic awareness of the diversities that do not fit into that narrative — testimony, perhaps, to the growing tyranny of the closet that, even as young Mörike creates his early masterpiece, is evidently in existence as a retreat in the face of the disapproval of the diverse. Gone or drastically reduced in Mörike's revised portion of *Nolten the Painter* are several elements that, in the original version, destabilize the official project of *Bildung:* Wispel's prominent facilitating and mirroring role, for example, is drastically reduced, as are the indications of the faltering productivity and extreme self-centeredness of Nolten's painting, also the confusion and reticence that ruin the relationship between Nolten and Constanze.

Whatever this belated and incomplete turn by the later Mörike might say about his own development and that of the popular Bildungsroman, it does not detract from the significance of the completed 1832 version as a document of the emerging modernity in the era of post-*Goethezeit* realism and of essentials of the development of the modern German Bildungsroman and artist novel. The recent critical reassessment of *Nolten the Painter* helps to reveal young Mörike's kinship with early modernist giants of his own day such as Heinrich Heine and Georg Büchner, with their critical turn, in the 1830s, against a bygone idealism that forces impossibly unrealistic visions of poetic mastery and heroic identity onto the complexly mixed potential of modern reality. A kinship between Nolten and the title figure of Büchner's novella *Lenz* emerges especially with the tendency of both to react with almost nihilistic rejection when their high ideals are disappointed, as with Nolten's reaction to Agnes's alleged unfaithfulness.

In addition, this recent rethinking of the consistency of *Nolten* furthers consideration of its significance as a pivotal or threshold text in the development of the modern German novel since the 1790s — above all with respect to its relationship to the Bildungsroman, that sub-genre flourishing in the wake of Goethe's seminal *Wilhelm Meister,* those novels that variously emulate and alter the account in *Meister* of the gifted young protagonist's journey through exotic encounters and errant adventures on his way to what promises to be positive formation and conciliatory integration in the conventions of the father's world. Mörike's *Nolten the Painter* has long been relatively neglected by studies on this problematic category, excluded from consideration on the grounds that it fails to portray the promised or expected *Bildung* of its hero successfully achieved. Yet running parallel to the recent reconsideration of *Nolten,* the critical discourse on the Bildungsroman has moved to a more discourse-oriented definition that locates the main concern and major commonality of these "novels of formation" *not* so much in their portrayal of a protagonist's successful *Bildung* — a criterion that would exclude most of the acknowledged masterpieces of the category including *Meister* itself and leave only the legion of popular emulators such as Horatio Alger's novels — *but* in their use of the basic story as a vehicle for critical reflection on the problems of living and narrating such *Bildung.*

To this criterion *Nolten the Painter* adheres in a way that involves a marked increase in the level of metafictional self-consciousness. On the one hand it intensifies the ironic perspective on the formation of the artistic hero that is already inherent in those earlier landmark works that it evokes — above all Goethe's *Meister* and Novalis's *Heinrich von Ofterdingen* (1801). On the other, it anticipates a range of works that likewise qualify the expectations they awaken of such cultivation successfully achieved and narrated. It bears comparison in this respect to the monumental contributions to the tradition by Adalbert Stifter and Gottfried Keller, which show the conciliation either withheld (as in Keller's *Green Henry* of 1854 and 1878) or achieved only at an artful and idyllic remove from modern reality (as in Stifter's *Indian Summer* of 1857). It also anticipates texts by Thomas Mann (*Tonio Kröger*, 1903) and Franz Kafka ("Das Urteil," 1912, and *The Trial*, 1912–1920) that still more provocatively counter idealistic notions of ethical and aesthetic *Bildung*.

Nolten the Painter anticipates those later works with its use of episodes of fictive writing and artistic activity to offer a critical perspective on the conventional heroic narrative that it has moved from the ironic background of its forerunners to greater prominence. Like Mörike's novel, Mann's artist novella alludes to novels of formation such as *Wilhelm Meister* and *Heinrich von Ofterdingen* as its protagonist struggles towards the beautifully written conciliation with conventional life to which the story's full text has already alerted readers to view as a facile literary "dispatching" ("Erledigung") of complex realities.[11] Like Mörike's novel, the two Kafka texts begin where conventional narratives of formation leave off — the opening of "The Judgment" strongly evoking the ending of *Tonio Kröger* in this respect[12] — only then to show the protagonist's nicely penned or posed *Bildung* unmasked and destroyed, the hapless hero hounded to his grave for his neglect of the diverse problems and potentials of real life's "intercourse." Where no reader would dispute the modernity of these early twentieth-century landmarks by Mann and Kafka, the foreshadowing of their metafiction in Mörike's 1832 masterpiece is all the more striking for its unsung prescience.

Notes

[1] These scores are reproduced in the fifth volume of the historical-critical edition of Mörike's works edited by Herbert Meyer (Mörike V, 259–75).

[2] Friedrich Theodor Vischer's 1839 review is included in the fifth volume of the historical-critical edition (Mörike V, 67). Regarding the negative reception by subsequent critics see: Eilert 165; Immerwahr 79; Jennings 165; Sammons 211ff.; Sengle; von Wiese 181.

[3] The most extensive and convincing reassessments along these lines are offered by Bruch; Nuber, Schüpfer, and Tscherpel. See also Beste; Bohnengel; Hausdörfer; Horstmann; Park; and Scholl. Irene Schüpfer (139–41) applies Julia Kristeva's differentiation between "narrative" and "text" referred to here.

[4] The praise of Goethe's *Meister* cited here occurs in Mörike's letter of 10 December 1831 to his fiancée Luise Rau (Mörike, XI 239). A year before, Friedrich Theodor Vischer had read a draft of Mörike's novel and praised it as the narrative of an artistic subject's development. In his response of 30 November 1830, Mörike disavowed any such Goethean scope and resolved to remove the term "artist" ("Künstler") from the title in favor of "painter."

[5] Friedrich Schlegel's enthusiastic interpretation of Goethe's *Meister* and his theoretical statements on the novel best suited to poetic portrayal in the modern age occur in his journal *Athenäum* (1798–1801), above all in that journal's 454 "Fragments" and in the "Gespräch über die Poesie" (Dialogue on Poetry), as well as in the long-unpublished *Literary Notebooks* that preceded those publications. His reference to the novel as a "Mischgedicht" (poetic mix) recurs in the *Literary Notebooks* (#4, 20, 55, 79, 120, 185, 582). His description of "romantic poetry" as the "true universal poetry" that combines lyrical outpourings with philosophical and critical reflection and becomes "poetry about poetry" ("Poesie der Poesie") occurs in his "Fragment #116" (Schlegel, *Kritische Friedrich-Schlegel-Ausgabe* 182–83), translated and discussed by Hans Eichner (57–58 and passim) and by Peter Firchow (Schlegel, *Friedrich Schlegel's Lucinde* 175–76).

[6] Mörike's defense of the novella occurs in his letter of 30 November 1830 to Vischer (Mörike, XI 155–56), while his thoughts on the new genre with its various segments expanding and mirroring the main story line occur in the letter of 14 May 1832 (Mörike, XI 281). The close link of the many poetic inlays in *Nolten the Painter* to themes and images prominent in the narrative has been pointed out especially by Herbert Bruch and Gerhard von Graevenitz.

[7] Irene Schüpfer (87–88) notes the slip in the opening sentence, with the June afternoon shining down on the city, and proposes it to be a clumsy echo of so many Homeric openings — which are, incidentally, likewise echoed and twisted in a host of modern works, from Novalis's *Hymns to Night* (1800) to Thomas Mann's *Tonio Kröger* (1912), James Joyce's *Ulysses,* and many others.

[8] Compare S. S. Prawer's 1955/56 article "Mignon's Revenge. A Study of Mörike's *Maler Nolten,*" still one of the most stimulating attempts to awaken interest in the way Mörike's novel takes up and twists Goethe's novel. See also Sigrid Berka's essay.

[9] He refers to Elisabeth's role this way in his letter to Johannes Mährlen of 2 September 1832 (Mörike, XI 321).

[10] Irene Schüpfer (217–35) offers the most concise account of the "cleansing" process in Mörike's revision of the first part of the novel. See also Hennemann.

[11] Benjamin Bennett calls attention to the allusions in *Tonio Kröger* to the Goethe and Novalis novels; see also Gabriele Seitz (108–13). Tonio's beautiful closing letter occurs at the end of a story in whose middle chapter he himself has spoken at length of the capacity of literary men to "take care of" or "dispatch" matters of feeling and love.

[12] *Tonio Kröger* ends with the title figure writing to his Russian friend about his successful conciliation. Kafka's short story begins with Georg Bendemann likewise writing his Russian friend to impart news of his successful displacement of his father as businessman and husband.

Works Cited

Behrendt, Marianne. "Die Figur der Elisabeth in Eduard Mörikes Roman *Maler Nolten*." In *Romantik und Moderne: Neue Beiträge aus Forschung und Lehre. Festschrift für Helmut Motekat*. Frankfurt/M.: Lang 1986. 55–75.

Bennett, Benjamin. "Casting out Nines: Structure, Parody, and Myth in 'Tonio Kröger.'" *Revue des langues vivantes* 42 (1976): 126–46.

Berka, Sigrid. "Kindfrauen als Projektionsfiguren in Mörikes *Maler Nolten* und Wedekinds *Monstretragödie*." In *Goethes Mignon und ihre Schwestern: Interpretationen und Rezeption*. Ed. Gerhart Hoffmeister. New York: Lang, 1993. 135–63.

Beste, Gisela. *Bedrohliche Zeiten: Literarische Gestaltung von Zeitwahrnehmung und Zeiterfahrung zwischen 1810 und 1830 in Eichendorffs Ahnung und Gegenwart und Mörikes* Maler Nolten. Würzburg: Königshausen & Neumann, 1993.

Bohnengel, Julia. "'Der wilde Athem der Natur': Zur Friedrich/Loskine-Episode in Mörikes 'Maler Nolten.'" Wild 45–69.

Bruch, Herbert. *Fascination und Abwehr: Historisch-psychologische Studien zu Eduard Mörikes Roman 'Maler Nolten.'* Stuttgart: M&P Verlag, 1992.

Eichner, Hans. *Friedrich Schlegel*. New York: Twayne, 1970.

Eilert, Heide. "Eduard Mörike: *Maler Nolten* (1832)." In *Romane und Erzählungen: Zwischen Romantik und Realismus*. Ed. P. M. Lützeler. Stuttgart: Reclam, 1983. 165–82.

Graevenitz, Gerhart von. *Eduard Mörike: Die Kunst der Sünde. Zur Geschichte des literarischen Individuums*. Tübingen: Niemeyer, 1978.

Hausdörfer, Sabrina. "Späte Blendung — Eduard Mörikes *Maler Nolten*." In *Rebellion im Kunstschein: Die Funktion des fiktiven Künstlers in Roman und Kunsttheorie der deutschen Romantik*. Heidelberg: Winter, 1987. 241–64.

Hennemann, Doris. *Individuation oder Integration: Mörikes Weg zur zweiten Fassung des 'Maler Nolten.'* Frankfurt/M.: Lang, 1991.

Horstmann, Isabel. *Eduard Mörikes Maler Nolten. Biedermeier: Idylle und Abgrund*. Frankfurt/M.: Lang, 1996.

Immerwahr, Raymond. "Mörike's *Maler Nolten* as a Romantic Novel: The Problem of Unity." In *Echoes and Influences of German Romanticism: Essays in Honour of Hans Eichner*. Ed. Michael S. Batts, Anthony W. Riley, and Heinz Wetzel. New York: Lang, 1987. 63–83.

Jennings, Lee. "Das Groteske bei Mörike: Ein nachromantisches Phänomen." In *Eduard Mörike*. Ed. Victor Doerksen. Darmstadt: Wissenschaftliche Buchgesellschaft, 1975.

Middleton, Christopher, trans. *Friedrich Hölderlin. Eduard Mörike. Selected Poems*. Chicago: U of Chicago P, 1972.

Mörike, Eduard. *Historische-Kritische Gesamtausgabe*. Ed. Hans-Henrik Krummacher, Herbert Meyer, and Bernhard Zeller. Stuttgart: Klett, 1967.

Nuber, Achim. *Mehrstimmigkeit und Desintegration: Studie zur Narration und Geschichte in Mörikes Maler Nolten*. Frankfurt/M.: Lang, 1997.

Park, Jong-Mi. *Eduard Mörikes 'Maler Nolten' im Hinblick auf die Schicksals-frage*. Marburg: Philipps Universität, 1992.

Prawer, S. S. "Mignons Genugtuung. Eine Studie über Mörikes 'Maler Nolten.'" In *Interpretationen. Band III. Deutsche Romane von Grimmels-hausen bis Musil*. Ed. Jost Schillemeit. Frankfurt/M.: Fischer, 1966. 164–81. Originally in English: "Mignon's Revenge. A Study of Mörike's *Maler Nolten*." *Publications of the English Goethe Society*. New Series 25 (1955–56): 63–85.

Sammons, Jeffrey. "Fate and Psychology: Another Look at Mörike's *Maler Nolten*." In *Lebendige Form: Interpretationen zur deutschen Literatur. Festschrift für Heinrich E. K. Henel*. Ed. Sammons and Ernst Schürer. Munich: Fink, 1970. 211–27.

Schlegel, Friedrich. *Friedrich Schlegel's* Lucinde *and the Fragments*. Translated with an introduction by Peter Firchow. Minneapolis: U of Minnesota P, 1971.

———. *Kritische Friedrich-Schlegel-Ausgabe*. Vol. 2. *Charakteristiken und Kritiken (1796–1801)*. Ed. Hans Eichner. Zurich: Thomas Verlag, 1967.

———. *Friedrich Schlegel: Literary Notebooks 1797–1801*. Ed. Hans Eichner. London: U of London P, 1957.

Scholl, Annette. "'Kunst! o in deine Arme wie gern entflöh' ich dem Eros!' Kunst und Künstler in Mörikes 'Maler Nolten.'" Wild 71–89.

Schüpfer, Irene. *"Es war, als könnte man gar nicht reden": Die Kommunikation als Spiegel von Zeit- und Kulturgeschichte in Eduard Mörikes "Maler Nolten."* Frankfurt/M.: Lang, 1996.

Seitz, Gabriele. *Film als Rezeptionsform von Literatur: Zum Problem der Verfilmung von Thomas Manns Erzählungen "Tonio Kröger," "Wälsungenblut" und "Der Tod in Venedig."* Munich: tuduv, 1979.

Sengle, Friedrich. "Mörike-Probleme. Auseinandersetzung mit der neuesten Mörike-Literatur (1945–50)." *Germanisch-Romanische Monatsschrift* 11.2 (1951/52): 36–47.

Slessarev, Helga. *Eduard Mörike.* New York: Twayne, 1970.

Tscherpel, Roland. *Mörikes lemurische Possen: Die Grenzgänger der schönen Künste und ihre Bedeutung für eine dem* Maler Nolten *immanente Poetik.* Königstein: Athenäum, 1985.

Wiese, Benno von. *Eduard Mörike: Ein romantischer Dichter.* Munich: Heyne, 1978.

Wild, Reiner, ed. *"Der Sonnenblume gleich steht mein Gemüthe offen": Neue Studien zum Werk Eduard Mörikes (mit einer Bibliographie der Forschungs-Literatur 1985–1995).* St. Ingbert: Röhrig Universitätsverlag, 1997.

Notes on the Translation

T HE MAJOR CHALLENGE TO TRANSLATING Mörike's novel was the high incidence of included songs and poems, twenty-four in all — plus, encompassing forty-nine pages of the historical-critical edition's 414 pages, the "phantasmagorical intermezzo" of the "Last King of Orplid" with its mix of prose, unrhymed verse, rhyming verse, and its own three inlaid songs. The presence of these lyrical passages ensured that the eagerness to present *Nolten the Painter* as a work akin to more recent novels did not result in the loss of the original's foreignness of place, time, and culture, or of its dialogue with still earlier modes of discourse and poetry. Yet it also put the translator in the uncomfortable position of having to produce English equivalents of German verses by an author recognized as a leading formal and lyrical talent among nineteenth-century German poets. Some of this anxiety was reduced by the fact that the lyrical pieces and the "intermezzo" were all included as the recollections or creations of fictional figures whose artistic skills and enthusiasm the text subjects to critical scrutiny. Yet the translation was still required to reproduce them as poetry that, while retaining the coherence of meaning, themes, and imagery that tied them to the host text, also rhymed and scanned like the original versions. While other translations of Mörike's poem's were consulted (those by Christopher Middleton and Helga Slessarev, for example), the translations offered here are all original, with the exception of that of "The Huntsman," for which the uncredited translation enclosed in the 1975 *Deutsche Grammophon* recording (2530– 584) of Hugo Wolf's *Mörike-Lieder* was considered so felicitous as to be adopted with only minor changes.

A similar resolve to preserve the peculiarities and foreignness of the original prevailed in dealing with other problems encountered in the prose narrative. This was so with Mörike's tendency to shift from past tenses to present-tense verbs in order to convey the suspenseful immediacy of some episodes, a strategy that German and English share but that occurs in *Nolten the Painter* with such frequency as to strike many readers as arbitrary or careless. These shifts have been retained, however, in the belief that the appearance of excessiveness in their usage is part of a strategy to intimate a fictive narrator who is anxious about the compelling and convincing nature of his own story. The same principle prevailed in translating many of the original's sentences into an English style that many present-day readers would find to amount to comma splicing and run-on sentences. In many such cases, the translation converted some commas to semicolons in order to divide independent clauses for the sake of clarity. Yet it chose not to break up such sentences in the belief that the impression of over-long and over-loaded sentences once again expressed the narrator's own attempt to uphold his command of the facts and cover up possible gaps or inconsistencies.

While the original itself contains three explanatory footnotes, several notes have been added to the translation. Many provide information on writers and works cited in the narrative or point out allusions to other works. Others explain obscure terms, idiomatic expressions, or instances of word play that made close translation difficult, while a few draw attention to apparent inconsistencies in the narrative.

Nolten the Painter

Part One

A BRIGHT JUNE AFTERNOON was shining down upon the streets of the Provincial Capital. The elderly Baron Jassfeld was once again, after some time, paying a visit to the painter Tillsen and, as his hasty steps would suggest, with some very special matter on his mind. He came upon the painter, as usual, still at table with his young wife in their small, tasteful but simple dining room, its classical decor fitting quite harmoniously with its customary appointments of everyday use and fashion. They chatted lightheartedly on a variety of topics until Tillsen's wife withdrew to attend to various household matters, leaving the two gentlemen alone.

The Baron took his ease, legs crossed, in a soft armchair and, resting his cheek on his right hand, appeared in the ensuing pause to be lost in amiable thought as he tried to rhyme the painter he knew with the new view that since yesterday he had found forcing itself upon Tillsen's works.

"My dear fellow," he then began, "I simply must tell you just why I've come by. I was recently visiting Count Zarlin, where I saw a painting and had to look at it again and again as if I couldn't get enough of looking at it. When I inquired what master had done it, the Count made me guess, and, guessing, I said 'Tillsen!' — involuntarily shaking my head as I said so because at the same time I felt it just couldn't be you. Then again I said 'Tillsen!' but then said 'No!' for a second time."

These words brought a flicker of consternation and embarrassment to the painter's face; yet he was able to hide these feelings and ask good-naturedly: "Well then! This lovely work of wonder that twice denies my poor brush — what kind of painting is it, actually?"

"Don't play ignorant, my dear friend," the Baron rejoined, rising to his feet with hearty good cheer and eyes shining, "You know very well what I'm talking about. The Count purchased the picture from you, and I have his assurance that you're the man who painted it. Listen, Tillsen" — and with this he took his friend's hand — "listen! I just happen to be a decent fellow, and I don't care to make an elaborate show of caution when I think I know what my friends think and feel, and so that's why I just came right out and told you what I thought when I saw your picture; there's just so much in it that is unmistakably your touch, especially when it comes to color, to beauty of detail, and as far as the landscape is concerned, too. But then it contains — no, it simply *is* something completely different again than what you had been until now; and when I admit that I was surprised and confused to discover in it certain merits that you have always possessed to a lesser degree, I mean it as a criticism of your previous work that you've always heard me make, without there ever being any doubt that I consider you to be an outstanding artist in your own way. In this painting I saw boldness and grandeur in the composition of the figures and, in all, a freedom that, as far as I know, you'd never shown the world before; and what was really a riddle for me was the striking new departure in the poetic mode of thought, in your choice of subjects. That's especially the case with the two sketches of which I have yet made no mention — the ones that you promised the Count you would do in oil.

"Here we have a very strange bent of fantasy; wondrous, fantastic, in part audacious and, in a pleasing way, bizarre. When I see it, I think of the ghostly music in the moonlight, of the dream of the infatuated giant. Tillsen! For God's sake, tell me, when did this immense change occur? How can you explain it to me? We've known and regretted the fact that Tillsen hasn't put paint to canvas in the last year and a half; why didn't you say a word to me these last months about starting your work again? You've been painting in secret. You wanted to surprise us all and, truth to tell, my dear and inscrutable friend, you succeeded in that!" With that the fiery speaker shook his silent listener by the shoulders, beaming with pleasure and gazing deep into his eyes.

"Now, truly," the other man began, quite calm, but smiling, "you leave me at a loss to convince you how astonished I am at your words, none of which I have understood in the least. Neither can I take credit for that painting or those sketches, nor do I understand at all what you're talking about. The whole thing seems to be some kind of joke Zarlin is playing, and one he might better have spared us, at that. Look how we've embarrassed each other. Now you must retract words of praise that weren't my due, while leaving be the faults you've added to our old account. Yet we don't have to let that bother us, Baron; we'll stay, I hope, the best of friends. But do give me, I beg you, a clearer account of these pieces you're talking about."

Jassfeld had heard out the first half of this speech with mouth agape, barely drawing a breath, while during the last half he tripped zigzag about the room and then suddenly stopped still and said: "That devil Zarlin! If that's what he's — no, but it's impossible, I swear by all the heavenly hosts that you're the painter, and none other; and there's no way of assuming that it was only partly your work; you've never in your life taken over someone else's work." Again the painter asked the Baron to describe the works he was talking about.

"So I am to describe to you, at your request, your own work," began the old gentleman, taking a seat, "but let me be brief, and correct me at once when I make a mistake. — The completed oil painting shows a water nymph to whom a handsome youth is being brought in a boat by a satyr.

2

The water nymph is placed foremost in the picture, to the left of her some sea cliffs. Up to her hips in the water, she is leaning forward, pressed against the edge of the little boat, seeking with open arms to embrace the object of her desires. The slender lad is leaning back in fear and reaching out one arm towards her, albeit involuntarily; it must likely be the magic of her voice that attracts him irresistibly, for she is shown with lips parted invitingly, the set of her mouth rhyming well with the desire of her warm gaze. Here is where I saw your brushstroke, your shading, your gentle touch, O Tillsen, and here I called out your name. The nymph's face is almost only in profile; her inclined back and one breast are visible; her wet, blond hair is done with incomparable mastery. Where one wave dips down, a small bit of her scaled fish torso can be seen, and nearby her fish tail emerges from the water. But the monster there below one soon forgets when beholding the beauty of her human half, and the boy falls thrall to the charm of her countenance, letting slip the light scarf still but draped across his shoulders — the wind catching it, it flutters, a narrow band, up into the air. A figure of great significance is the satyr standing by as audience. A muscular figure, he stands in the boat, leaning on the tiller, somewhat to one side, towering, though not completely upright, over the others. A silent passion speaks from his features, for though he had wanted to serve the nymph by kidnapping the glorious youth and bringing him to her, his ardent love for her now afflicts him with unexpected jealousy. He would like to turn in rage from this scene, yet he forces himself to look on, calmly seeking out its bitter pleasure. The whole picture is wonderfully rounded out, the painter cleverly concealing the empty end of the boat, to the right, behind a high growth of sea flora. Beyond all that is a full view of the open sea, observers thus left, like the figures, feeling alone and quite eerie in that hopeless realm. I shall say no more, my friend. Your calm expression divulges your long-time acquaintance with what I am describing to you, and anyway you can at least show, if not astonishment, then surely some well-earned pride in your work — assuming that precisely this show of indifference is not itself a sign of the most towering pride."

"The sketches, if I may ask," responded Tillsen, "what are they like? You've made me very curious."

The Baron fetched a deep breath, smiled, but then went on quite in earnest: "a pen-and-ink drawing, quite well finished in watercolor, in your usual manner. The page in question made a deep, almost terrifying impression on me, especially when I looked at it a second time in better light. A nocturnal gathering of music-loving ghosts is all it is. It shows the grassy knolls and hillocks of a forest clearing, completely enclosed on all sides but one, to the right. That open side reveals part of the plains lying below, glimmering in the mist. Opposite that there rises in the left foreground a watery wall of rock, at its foot a lively spring and in the resulting hollow of the cliff stands a gothically ornate organ of moderate size; on a moss-covered rock in front of it sits, playing, the central figure of the piece, while the other figures can be seen either happily playing away on their instruments, or curling about in dancing lines, or otherwise just scattered about in groups. These wondrous creatures are mostly wearing long, dragging garments of grey or other somber colors, which they have gathered up in order to get about; pale deathly faces, some of them quite attractive, rarely anything ghastly, and rarer still any ugly bare skeletons. Clearly, in order to enjoy themselves as best they can, they've come from a nearby church graveyard. This is suggested by the chapel that is only partly visible off to the right and down a bit — it's cut off from view by the grave barrow in the foreground. On one of whose slumping stone crosses reclines a flute player, strikingly posed, the drape of his robe exquisitely captured. But I turn now to the charming female figure playing the organ on the other side of the picture. She is a noble young maiden, her head inclined, seeming to listen more to the song of the bubbling spring at her feet than to her own playing. Her soulful dark eye rises but dreamily from her inner spirit world; its attention captured by no one object around her, it rests not on the keys, nor on her pretty, voluptuous hand; a melancholy smile hovers, barely visible, about the corners of her mouth, and it's as if this spirit were thinking even at this moment of the possible departure from this her second corporeal being. At the organ stands leaning a youth, dazed with sleep; his features marked by suffering, he holds a burning torch; a large golden-brown butterfly nestles in his cascading locks. Between rock wall and organ, death itself seems to have taken on the task of pumping the organ bellows, for a bony hand and one foot of the skeleton are visible in the background. Prominent among the figures in the picture's middle ground is one group of dancers: two robust men and likewise two women are moving gracefully and artfully, their hands clasping on high, so that here and there bared limbs are revealed, noble and beautiful. Yet their dance seems a slow one, mirroring the earnest, even sorrowful mien of the dancers, while to each side of them and more towards the background life seems more merrily afoot, affording glimpses of cheerful bearing, even of teasing and playful antics. One feature struck me especially. A youth's skeleton in light scarlet capelet has sat down to let another figure take off his shoe, but his leg right up to the knee comes off with it, and the clumsy rascal is laughing himself to death. Then there's another feature: in the foreground by the flute player there's a bush with a gaunt hand reaching out of it, holding a little bird's nest, while an old man is kneeling down so that his small boy, in the light of the candle the old fellow is holding, can gaze into the bird's wondering innocent little eyes; the little fellow is already holding a fluttering bat by the wing. There are several such details, and, really, I could go on describing them. The light, the wonderful interplay of moon- and candlelight; and the way the oil version will capture it, especially in the manner it plays against the green of the forest, is already very effectively evident

4

in every detail and done with great skill. But enough! Confounded if I can describe it all!"

At this point, Tillsen had been sitting for some time distracted and brooding. Now that the Baron's silence had brought him to his senses he rose from his armchair, his forehead aglow, and declared resolutely: "Yes, dear sir, I may tell you now, what you saw was by my hand, and yet" — but here he broke out in forced laughter. "Thank God!" the Baron interrupted him, jumping to his feet in delight, "that's all I need to hear! oh, let me kiss you, embrace you, you most charming fellow! That year and a half of fasting where you let your palette go dry has brought wonders in you to full bloom, called forth a phase in your art whose fruits will astonish the world. Now you'll score success upon success, just you wait and see, since this new, vital springtime has broken forth in your art; and in this hour I prophesy unto you the fullness of your fame, which may well inspire hundreds to turn the essence of their talents to the most noble of arts, though it must force thousands more to renounce it in craven envy. O my dear, modest man, I see you are moved, and I no less so in heartfelt joy. Let us part now in this happy moment with a warm handclasp and not a word more. I shall go to the Count. Farewell! Until we meet again!" And with that he was out the door.

The painter, unmoving, watched him depart. He wanted to start up after the Baron and provide him immediately with the enlightening facts, but an involuntary, sober decision held him back, as if rooting him to the floor. Only after a long silence did he break out, with an almost painful smile, with the following words: "O you deluded, honest man! How pointlessly did you rejoice for me, while so guilelessly exposing my weaknesses. I had to hear your praise, which was due not me but another, and which singled out all that I lack — and shall forever lack — to make me a true painter!" It's the truth, he went on, thinking to himself, the execution of those compositions is mine, and it's not the worst of the lot: it serves to give those inventions their proper significance and meaning; without my contribution the sketches of that poor draftsman might well have passed unnoticed before the indifferent eye. But only in tracking his spirit did my spirit come alive and grow strong, and only spurred by him could I rise to a height of expression that I could never have reached on my own. How paltry, how insignificant did I feel in comparison to this unknown draftsman. How gladly I would cast away all that otherwise has gained me note and praise, to possess the gift to create such contours, such lines, such arrangements. A pencil and the cheapest paper is all he needs to sweep me from the field. If those good gentlemen only knew that it is the works of a madman — a depraved nobody — that they so admire, their amazement would be greater still than when they thought they'd found in me the master. As yet none but me know the true designer of these works. But if, at the risk that he might break his willful incognito, I were nevertheless to claim the fame for his creations, I would find

5

in my own inner awareness a still stronger reason against doing so. For that reason it must come to light — and better now than later — that I am by no means their man.

Roughly so ran the thoughts of this deeply agitated man, yet on the last point he was not quite so firmly decided. While until now he had more or less left the opinions of his friends open, without lending them support, without refuting them — this by holding the middle ground with a two-sided quip — he was thinking now that he could, with no grave harm to his conscience, still hold off a bit longer before revealing the truth, and then, if need be, justify his behavior in duly honorable fashion.

Just then his young wife returned to the room; she noticed that her husband was visibly agitated; she inquired anxiously; he denied that anything was wrong and hugged her with unaccustomed ardor. Then he repaired to his room.

Several weeks went by without our painter explaining the true state of affairs to anyone — save for his brother-in-law, Major von R., to whom he made the following surprising revelation: "It's probably a good year ago now that I was visited in my studio one evening by an unkempt individual, feeble of form and sickly of appearance, a wispy snippet of a fellow, thin as a broomstick. He played himself up as an avid amateur painter. But the giddy long-windedness of the way he carried on and the mixed-up confusion of his conversation about matters of art were as suspect to me as his entire visit was annoying and bewildering. I took him to be no less than a presumptuous chatterbox, if not a downright rogue of the type that commonly wheedle their way into other peoples' homes to thieve and betray. But then how great was my astonishment when he produced some sheets that he humbly announced to be a few modest samples of his own work They were neatly done sketches in pencil and chalk, full of spirit and life, even though some faults in the drawing were immediately apparent. I intentionally held back my praise, wanting to find out more about what kind of man I was dealing with, to convince myself that he wasn't trying to pass off someone else's property as his own. He seemed to notice my distrust and smiled as if embarrassed as he rolled the papers back up again. As he did so, his gaze fell upon a canvas that I had recently begun and that was leaning against the wall, and while just moments before some of his judgments had seemed as trite and laughable as possible, I now found myself surprised by some of the meaningful words he spoke — words that I shall never forget, for they captured in the most accurate way what is characteristic about my style and solved for me the mystery of an error that before I had only vaguely sensed. This remarkable fellow acted as if he didn't notice my astonishment and was just reaching for his hat when I hastened to draw him down at my side and demanded a further explanation. Yet it defies description the way, as I questioned him, the fellow offered up the strangest mix of the most trite and nonsensical

galimatias with the occasionally most piquant flash of insight and percep-
tion — all in his sweetly whispering way of talking. All this, together with
the most unseemly giggling with which he seemed to be mocking both me
and himself, left no doubt that I was dealing here with the strangest instance
of insanity that I had ever encountered. I broke off our discussion of art and
turned the talk to more commonplace matters, and he seemed to take even
greater pleasure in carrying on with his foppishly affectatious behavior. The
elegant airs he was putting on stood in quite laughable and grotesque contrast to his shabby clothes, which consisted of a worn, bright green, swallow-
tail dress coat and a pair of old Nanking trousers. At one moment he would
be picking with a dainty finger at the rather unwashed nap of his shirt, the
next he would be tapping his bamboo walking stick against his narrow back,
while struggling all the while to pull his arms in so as to conceal how
wretchedly short his green coat was. All this awakened my genuine interest
in the fellow, for did I not have to imagine him to be a person who, with his
exceptional talents — perhaps out of injured pride, perhaps from dissolute
living — had come to such ruin that at last only this miserable shadow was
all that remained? And as he himself admitted, those drawings were from a
better, long-past time of his life. When I asked what he was doing at present,
he answered quickly and cryptically that he was subsisting on private means;
and when I gave the vague indication that I might be interested in acquiring
the sketches he had shown me, he seemed, despite his precious smile, more
than a little relieved and pleased. I offered him three ducats, which he pocketed as he promised to visit me again. Four weeks later he turned up again,
and this time dressed in a markedly finer ensemble. He brought along several
sketches, and they — though I'd scarcely thought it possible — were still
more interesting and imaginative. In the meantime I had resolved to accept
no more of his works for the time being until I was totally in the clear about
the legality of such acquisitions — doing this perhaps by having him execute
in my presence a task that I would assign him on some innocuous pretext.
On this point, I had written out my ideas and I also explained them to him
orally, and he immediately hurried off, hoping to be able to show me his attempt in a few days. But who can describe my joy when, on the evening of
the following day, the most noble outline of the figures of the assigned
grouping from Statius lay spread out before me, done, in the whole conception of the idea, far more daringly and ingeniously than the scope of my own
imagination had ever conceived.[1] Many a fleeting comment that the foolish
fellow made also gave me irrefutable proof that the drawing was dear to his
heart and soul. This sketch, too, and in the days to come another and yet
another, came into my possession; but then the strange man suddenly
stopped coming to visit and, in his peculiar way, he had given me neither his
name nor any kind of address. By and by I experienced an irresistible desire
to sketch the pictures anew, in enlarged format and in watercolor, and then

immediately do them in oil, which then soon resulted in the most charming mutual interaction of my style and that strange genius, with the result that it might not have been so easy to decide, when looking at the completely painted tableaux, how to apportion dual and distinct credit for their authorship. To my friend and brother-in-law I might well make this self-serving claim, and perhaps the public will be no less fair to me when at the next public exposition I present those pictures, without in any way denying their double provenance — for it has long been my firm resolve to do so."

"That would suit you best," responded the Major, who until now had been listening with rapt attention, "to my mind, a painter of your reputation would need show but little resignation to be so honest, and in fact people would likely see in your act a certain magnanimity in the whole matter in the sense of your recognizing and honoring an unknown talent. But getting back to this poor wretch: you found no way of tracking him down?"

"No way at all. At one point my servant thought he'd found a lead, but then we lost it."

"It would be a right devil of a thing," the Major exclaimed, "if my tracking hounds let me down on this one! Just leave it to me, dear in-law. The whole story is just too remarkable to leave hanging. You can tell the whole world that I myself am this mysterious fool if in twenty-four hours I can't somehow fetch him up out of some drinking-den, attic, or madhouse."

THOSE TWENTY-FOUR HOURS had not yet passed when it happened that Tillsen was enlightened about the facts of the matter in a way different than he could ever have imagined.

In his absence one morning a well-dressed young man came to call at the Tillsen residence, and the lady of the house led him to a side room where he might, for a moment, await the return of her husband. She herself, though not a little interested by the young man's promising and strikingly pleasant physiognomy, withdrew at once, since it was quite clear to her from the distracted restlessness of his looks that further conversation with him was not in order. After a quarter of an hour, the painter himself entered the aforementioned room. He found the young man lost in thought, his head in his hands, sitting on his chair with his back to him, and facing the large painting that, completely covered except for the heavy gold frame, hung on the wall. The painter, rather intrigued, approached silently, whereupon the young man started up in surprise, while at the same time, clearly having been caught off guard, trying to hide his tears behind a show of pleasant, though embarrassed amiability. "I have come," he then began with good-natured openness, "I have come to see you, honored sir, concerning a most wondrous yet at the same time most pleasing matter. You do not know me personally, and yet you have, as I well know, come to know and, to a certain degree, even view fondly my actual, truest self, such that I now come before you in feelings of unshakeable trust. But let me explain. My name is Theo-bald Nolten and, known to few, I am studying painting here in the city. But now yesterday, among the paintings in the gallery on display, I found one depicting the "Sacrifice of Polyxena" that struck me at first glance as an in-timately familiar image. I felt as if some magic had conjured up before my dazzled eyes a bygone dream in living form. This melancholy princess seemed to greet me as if she were a long-lost sister, her surroundings struck me as by no means strange, and yet the whole was bathed in a light of charm that emanated not from within me but from a higher, from an Olympian power; I trembled, by God! I —"[2]

"What?" Tillsen broke in, "Then you would be — yes, you are the won-derful artist to whom I must apologize for so much —"

"But no!" the young visitor responded, afire with enthusiasm, "no! Who has so much to thank you for! You have revealed myself to me by transport-ing me so high above myself. You have awakened me with the hand of a friend from my dark dream, borne me up to the sunlit heights of art, just as I was near to despairing of my powers. A miserable wretch had to steal from me so that you might have the chance to reveal to me in your clear mirror my true, my future form. So receive then your pupil into your fatherly heart. Let me kiss it, this gentle hand that has ordered forever the tangled strands of my being — my Master! My Savior!"

And so the two men stood some moments in firm embrace, and from this moment onward a vital friendship joined them such as surely is seldom possible in so short a time between two people who have actually only just met for the first time in their lives.

"Allow me, dear friend," said Tillsen, "to come to my senses. I still do not know whether I should be more ashamed or more pleased by your heart-felt words. I shall come to understand you as we proceed. So tell me first of all just what is the situation with that thieving scoundrel whom we must for-ever have to thank for having brought us together?"

"Very well! Listen! After my return from Italy — over a year ago now — on my journey here, where I am a complete stranger — I chanced upon this sniveling fellow, a barber by profession — he called himself Wispel[3] — who offered me his services as my valet, and, my humorous interest piqued by his strangeness, I all the more gladly took him on in light of a certain good-naturedness that struck me about him — along with what one might call his crazy streak of enthusiasm for things universal and his typically barberly high spirits — that I soon enough learned could give way only to the most self-centered vanity; for I'd swear that he stole those rough sketches with no other intention than to play the great man for you."

"Yet he took money for them, didn't he?"

"And even if he did: that prospect probably didn't occur to him until you mentioned it."

"But he played the fool so totally!"

"I very much doubt that he planned to do that — or if he did, it was only after he sensed your suspicious interest. His stupidity was almost equaled by his cunning: he was able on some trumped-up pretext to induce me to do an impromptu drawing that he surely intended for you and that I found intriguing by dint of the pleasingly proportioned subject. If on top of that he was able to deceive you with the appearance of his own erudition, then I can understand all the better why he always found so much in the room to busy himself with on those occasions when I was carrying on discussions with a friend. He may have tossed your way many a badly digested fragment that he picked up this way."

"Oh," said Tillsen, not without a certain feeling of embarrassment, "of course, statements of that sort always struck me as suspicious enough, like hieroglyphics on the market-square fountain, I had no idea where they came from. But he's one cunning rascal, he is! And where is he now, the rogue?"

"God knows. Half a year ago he took leave of me; a few weeks later I discovered the big gap in my portfolio."

"I shall fill that gap back up!" responded Tillsen in good cheer as he led his friend to the covered painting. "I wanted to have this taken away for public exhibition today; yet now it is your property. Let's see if behind this cloth you recognize your old acquaintances."

Nolten held back the painter's hand while confessing that he'd previously not been able to resist the temptation to draw the curtain back a ways, but that then, as if frightened by the ghost of his own mysterious double, he'd let it drop back again without daring to take in the entire canvas.

With that, Tillsen swept back the covering with a flourish and stepped to one side so that he could see what impression the piece made on the painter. We shall say nothing of the indescribable feeling that young man then had, and instead merely recall to the reader the wondrous ghostly concert whose essence the old Baron had earlier described. Moved and solemn, the two friends parted.

THE RATHER LABORIOUS NARRATION of these events had to occur at the outset so as to make all the more understandable the rapid and felicitous development that from this point on now took its course with the young artist's whole life. It may have been a certain faintness of heart or obstinacy, perhaps, a capricious attitude of some kind that led him to keep the light of his talents hidden, keeping, unheralded, his own counsel, until just that moment when he could let them shine forth in their still higher degree of perfection — but one thing is sure: painting in color with oil had previously given him great difficulties. Yet, as Tillsen now found, none as great as our modest friend had made for himself, as it were. Instead, the former found in this matter too that the latter was making the most remarkable progress in

10

his efforts, and he gladly resolved to make favorable report of each individual advance. In a short while Nolten, where skill was concerned, ranked the equal of any proper artist, while in grandiosity of spirit he far outranked them all. His works, along with Tillsen's recommendation, gained him highly valuable contacts, notable among them Duke Adolph, brother of the King, who proved to be a well-disposed patron of his endeavors.

While with all this Theobald himself responded to the rapid and splendid change in his situation with a certain degree of surprise and at the start even some embarrassment, he soon came to marvel almost even more at the ease with which he accustomed himself to his new position and made the most of it. But of course he needed only to accept the respect through which he found himself distinguished before others as something he had earned, in order then to see it as his perfectly natural due.

Through the influence of the Duke he gained admittance to the home of Count von Zarlin who, without any insights of his own and — as word had it — purely out of vanity, had distinguished himself as a passionate friend of every branch of the arts and actually succeeded in gathering round himself a circle of noble men and women devoted to intellectual diversions of all manner, notable among them the reading of fine poetic works. Yet the animating soul of it all was, albeit not of her own volition, the Count's beautiful sister, Countess Constanze von Armond, the young widow of a general but few years deceased. Her charm would have been great enough to dominate the circle of men and prescribe its laws, but the pleasant woman remained content with the gentle influence her personality had on all the eager spirits involved, as was manifest in the intensified enthusiasm she awakened for the topics of concern. Indeed, Constanze seemed at times to restrain her natural vivacity in order to deflect from herself the admiration with which the gentlemen declared her in no uncertain terms to be the queen of the circle. Theobald too felt himself secretly drawn to her, and during the one and one half months in which, three evenings each week, he was allowed to be near her, his glad good pleasure in her company had developed into a stronger degree of affection than he was willing to admit to himself. Her personal charms, her fine and well-schooled intellect, combined with a lively and actively expressed interest in his art, had made him her passionate admirer, and even when his reason, even when the most cursory consideration of the outward facts of the relationships involved would suffice to dash his every remote desire, he would still, on the other hand, repeat to himself in tireless self-persuasion so many a subtle sign of her special favor, all the while never letting himself forget what a clever rival he had to contend with in Duke Adolph, who, when it came to the adroitness and flattering tone of social intercourse, was by far his superior. The Duke's warm feelings weighed all the more heavily on Theobald, the more the friendship between them showed signs of growing cordiality, forcing the latter to struggle to conceal a hidden tension from his unsuspecting princely friend.

In addition, he had good reason to be as confused as possible about growing infatuation, for a long-established liaison still made its silent claims upon his heart, even though he had already, after no small struggle with his conscience, emphatically resolved to spurn that erstwhile tie. The untrammeled happiness that our unspoiled youth had once found in love with a creature of purest innocence had but recently been disturbed by a lamentable state of affairs that had given his sensitive feelings cause to react with a distrust that was as forgivable as it was unyielding. The matter really appeared to have gone so far that he no longer granted the far-off girl a single word or sign, giving her not the least indication of the reason for the change. Disconsolate with grief he quickly steeled himself in the delusory belief that the noble foundation of their beautiful relationship was ruined for good and always and that he would have to count himself among the fortunate if he could, with the bitterness of his injured conviction, poison and kill off every last vestige of longing in his heart. In fact, however, this grievous loss was not without beneficial impact on his entire self; for clearly this experience helped in no small measure to enliven his enthusiasm for art, which from now on was to be the one and only highest goal of his desires. While by and by he was able to gain mastery over feelings of anguish that threatened to consume him, the girl for her part was faring no worse. Agnes still believed she was loved, and she was sustained in this happy belief, as we shall learn, in a remarkable way and without Theobald having anything to do with it, while in the meantime *he* had begun to hope that she would voluntarily dissolve their relationship, for the absence of any letters from her he quite simply took to be a sure sign of her own guilty conscience. It was in this state — of feeling that he was at once only half liberated and also the injured party — that he made the acquaintance of Countess Constanze, which makes all the easier to grasp the ardor with which the portals of his soul turned towards this new light.

THE SPANISH COURT — this being the name of the city's foremost hotel — was on the evening of December's last day, when the finest circles were busily preparing themselves for the masquerade, unusually quiet. In the hinter-most green corner parlor the two brightly burning chandeliers shone upon but two guests, of whom the one was a regular visitor, well acquainted with the world and the ways and customs of the hostelry, a retired civil servant of high rank, and the other a young sculptor arrived in town only hours before. They were conversing, as they sat some ways apart from each other, about everyday matters, during which Leopold — as we shall call the young traveler — found himself at one moment having to conceal his annoyance at the old man's distracted taciturnity and at the next finding himself compelled to look with a certain sympathy at the diseased distortions of his face, at the restless agitation of his hands as in one moment they smoothed out a wrinkle on his fine dark coat, in another mixed a pack of whist cards, or then took a pinch from his agate snuffbox. All this had brought the conversation to an impasse, and, to move it forward again, the sculptor began: "Amongst the artists of this city and of the fatherland, the young painter Nolten, as I note with pleasure, is now said to be attracting considerable attention?"

These words seemed to bring the old gentleman to his senses again. His eyes twinkled brightly from under their grey brows. Yet since he maintained what seemed an expectant silence, his lips busily working as if to formulate an answer, the other went on: "I've seen nothing of his work for three years, and now I'm curious in the extreme to establish for myself what is true about this lavish praise as well as about the vehement pronouncements of the critics."

"You demand of me then," said the old fellow almost mockingly, "that I answer now with a nice phrase, such as: in the middle, perhaps, lies this fine talent still in search of its proper direction — or: of him we hope for the best but fear the worst — or feeble piping of that sort? No! Instead I tell you straight out, this Nolten is the most depraved and dangerous heretic of a painter, one of those break-neck daredevils who turn art on its head because they've started to become bored with walking on two feet; an objectionable show-off strutting his fantasy! So what does he paint? A dismal world full of ghosts, wizards, elves, and those sorts of spooks, that's what he cultivates. He's totally in love with the distasteful, with things that bring no one pleasure. The good, pure milk of simple beauty he disdains and brews a potion that reeks of skullduggery and the gallows; and on that point, dear sir!" (he said with a conspiratorial smile) "have you ever had the opportunity to see one of those fine institutions wherein they lodge those poor devils who, if you follow my drift, are burning a bent wick in their lanterns — well? Did it not occur to you, too, how it would be if, shall we say, the hazy vapor of thoughts that must rise from such heads were to condense upon the ceiling above, what a fresco of figures would have to come to view? What do you think? Nolten has copied them all, heh-heh-heh — copied the lot of them!"

"You seem," Leopold said casually, "if I otherwise grasp what you're saying, more to be faulting the topics that the artist — albeit perhaps a bit too much — prefers to depict, than to be attacking his talent; but now there is no doubt that in his work as easily as in any other it is possible to find successful renditions of the characteristically and purely beautiful, whereas tasteless and ugly forms, the intentional seeking out of repugnant constellations, cannot be expected of Nolten; I know his character from before, and I have come here with a mutual friend, who is also a painter, with the intention of visiting Nolten and taking pleasure in the recent progress of his development."

13

The old gentleman had likely not listened to these words at all, for he went on chuckling loudly and repeating the refrain of what he had said before: "Copied the lot of them, yes, yes, it's enough to make one die laughing! Aye, I have to tell him that every day."

In this moment Ferdinand, the sculptor's traveling companion, came in and, eyes shining, called out joyfully to his friend: "He's coming! He's following on foot! He's still the same good old Nolten, I tell you! Oh, by no means the arrogant, lucky dog that people were claiming he was. Just imagine, he was so caught up in our joyous reunion that he completely forgot he'd been invited by the Duke — with whom he must surely be on very good terms — and he went hurrying down the street to excuse his absence."

After a short time the awaited Nolten appeared, accompanied by another friend. It was a heart-warming reunion, an ever newly astonished, giddy greeting and rejoicing among the three young men. What delight his friends took in Theobald's imposing appearance, in the fine decorum that life in society's higher circles had imperceptibly and subtly imparted to him, although they made no attempt to conceal from him the fact that the robust red of his cheeks, in the span of but few short years, had diminished noticeably. Yet he still looked healthy and fresh enough next to his lean companion, the actor Larkens, whom he was just about to give a friendly introduction when that man, in most amiable fashion, took his leave from the company, closing with the words: "Now do sit down, you happy threesome! With your kind permission, gentlemen, I shall join you soon again, but the first frothy bubbling joy of reunion you really must drain off amongst yourselves! I espy nearby a pair of dealer's hands convulsively fingering the pack, beckoning to me in particular!" And with that he took a seat off in the corner with the old gentleman whom our Nolten only just now noticed and was greeting, not without respect, when Leopold whispered quietly to him: "But tell me, what sort of art expert is he? He has the most remarkable ideas about you."

"Oh," replied his friend, "I can't give you much help there. He's quite a curious old bird, full of his peevish idiosyncrasies, yet for all that full of insight and quite a likeable fellow towards me. He has a good knowledge about paintings, but in that area he's inclined to hold to some one-sided theories. They say that some of my pieces have made him particularly partial to me yet at the same time awakened an undisguised aversion that I can hardly figure out for myself. For it's hardly likely that I've lost favor with him merely as an artist — at any rate he'd be doing me an injustice on that count, inasmuch as by reproaching the fantastic elements in my painting, as he appears to be doing, he is addressing only a small portion of my creations, as if that were to be taken as a reproach at all. Most of my works are of quite a different category than that. I suppose the man has come to take a secret exception to me personally and that, without having the slightest awareness of how, I must have insulted him by doing something that, try as he might,

14

he simply cannot forget — for striking indeed is how, whenever he looks at me, his face reveals his struggle between the sweet and the sour.

That explained to some degree those impassioned comments the old man had made, and there was reason enough now for the three to share news about business, life, and all manner of adventures. They looked back on past events, recalling their sojourn in Italy, where three years before their friendship had come about. At last Ferdinand began: "You'll hardly guess where we were guests just six days ago to the very hour; in which little village, in which parlor, and who was our host." "No!" said Nolten, but an alert observer would have sensed in this subdued negation a very quickly discerning "yes." "Neuburg," whispered Leopold, happy to oblige, while from the other side the name "Agnes" breached Ferdinand's lips. "Many thanks," said Nolten, as if trying to end the matter, concealing his ill feelings.

"What do you mean, 'many thanks'? We haven't even handed over the message we were supposed to bring you!" — and with that Nolten found himself presented with a letter, which he pocketed with a forced show of good cheer — this while trying, with a cautioning glance at the card players, to urge his friends to be silent about the matter for the moment.

"Then," resumed Ferdinand, "let me at least make mention of that charming rustic idyll, of that forester's humble abode, where you lived out your boyhood years with a second father, until the Baron, that good and vital man, your neighbor there in his nearby castle, saw to the fostering of your talents. He is still alive and in fine fettle, that worthy veteran; he and that simple good forester shared affectionate memories of the happy day when, three years ago now, you introduced me to them there when we returned from our Italian journey. Truth to tell, it would have taken little to make those two old men weep like children at the mention of your name, not to mention another pair of eyes, close by, that seemed from the start to want to look their fill of me and my companion, of our clothes and packs, knowing that five days hence they were to come into contact with her beloved. You were once wont to call that girl your fair-haired doe, and how fitting I found this phrase once again! Yes, and she still remains so in the most touching and endearing sense of the word. Oh, how I wished I could have limned her darling figure for you, sketching it with my pencil and stealing it away to you in my portfolio, then, as I watched through the half-open door as she was sitting in the adjoining room at the table to write you a letter, her back to us, barely visible from the side — yet the Baron was just too talkative."

"And so are you," Nolten responded with gruff good humor, standing as he did so to greet the approaching Larkens, who said: "Well, can't you persuade these gentlemen to don themselves in dominoes and spend a few hours being foolish with foolish people? Or shall we follow suit with him over there, the Hofrat, who on such evenings takes his dinner here in the hotel and then has the waiter secure him a room where he can sleep the night five streets away from the masked ball, which, unfortunately, takes place just across the street from his own lodgings. I was thinking, dear sirs, that, before you make the acquaintance of the pleasing realities of our city in the next days, it would be a pleasant diversion for you to repair to the masquerade and there behold the fata morgana of our local humanity — but forgive my clumsy metaphor and follow my suggestion." It took some convincing, but they resolved to go with Larkens and wished the Hofrat a good night.[4]

A THOUGHTFUL, ILL AT EASE — yes, even sorrowful — Nolten arrived with his friends at the door of the large, brightly lit building where life at its most manifold pulsed and teemed. All possible types of figures, for the most part in striking contrast to one another, mingled, turning and shuffling among each other, wordlessly, solemnly, some quite apart and to themselves, some humming softly, heads nodding, dancing. More quickly than he thought, our gloomy-mooded friend, apart from his friends, by and by came to take some grim solace in playing hide-and-seek not only with the masked ball around him but also with his own heart, hardly admitting to himself as he did so what special hope made him scan the passing rows of masked ladies far more carefully than he likely would otherwise have done. Agnes's modest image, which, longing and imploring, seemed to beckon to him from afar, receded ever more into the background of his soul, making way for a very different one that, with each passing turn of the dancing groups, he hoped to see emerge incarnate from the crowd. Constanze! he said to himself, who can help me find her? And yet, how could it be that I should not be able to discern that special creature from amongst these thousand marionettes, seek out that one and only being who even in her most simple natural gesture reveals that inborn grace, that smiling magic that only nature's eternal truthfulness, that only innocence itself can bestow and meld in such easy charming fashion with propriety well-learned. Is not all that stirs and moves her the unwilled, natural expression of the angel that breathes within her bound?[5] Is not all about her naught but aura and spirit? And today, especially today, how good a glimpse of her would do me! Oh, how I would cling fast for three seconds with all my thoughts and senses to that consoling vision, then to hurry away content in knowing that my eye had beheld her, that my foot had touched the same ground she walked upon, that a common breath of air had touched my lips and hers.

Wearied by these and similar thoughts, he at last cast himself onto a window seat when the clock struck ten, reminding him to rejoin his three friends, as previously planned, in an empty room of the house. They all appeared at almost the same time, Larkens with a goodly portion of warm drink. Happy about reuniting again, each brought his own comments from the dance hall, with only Nolten seeming to have seen and heard little or nothing. It was almost comical how he repeatedly answered the one or the other question about some interesting sight with a lame "I don't know" and how finally, to avoid being laughed at, simply acted as if he remembered what they were talking about. "How did you like the King Richard and the Duke of Friedland?"[6] "Very much," he would answer, "well done, upon my soul! But the hunchback king could have been done better." Larkens, cuing the others with a wink, played the rogue, saying:

"There's one little bit you all missed. A giant of a fellow, dressed in old German costume, clearly portraying an old-time student, is plodding back and forth, wearing long spurs and smoking a long pipe; then finally, when he stops standing in a corner, a tiny little fellow comes hurrying up to him, a little chimney sweep in a kind of harlequin costume with black and white checked breeches and waistcoat; he ties up the giant, leans a little black ladder up against the man's broad back, and scampers on up with his scraper and broom, lifts off his scalp as if it were a pot lid, and then, after making all sorts of suspicious grimaces, begins to give the head a good sweeping by pulling out a whole plunder of symbolic ingredients: for example, a convincingly realistic imitation worm of astonishing length, a strangely drawn map of Germany, one whole crown and several broken ones, little daggers, beer glasses, ribbons, and such like. But then he starts packing in other little items — some thought they saw a Greek primer — and then the head was closed back up, and the man, whole again, was given a few taps, not long after which a cheerful, meek, round little priest came crawling out of its ostentatiously gigantic shell."[7]

The friends had a quiet laugh at this typically Larkensian fiction (which in fact was only a veiled jibe at the arrogance of all boisterous students, one of whom just before in the dance hall had let his combativeness make a fool of him), and they all took secret pleasure in the fact that Nolten acted as though he had actually witnessed the whole scene even though nothing even remotely of the sort had taken place.

But meanwhile the attention of the comrades was drawn to a real masked figure that had turned up unnoticed in their room. It was a tall figure, simply garbed in a heavy, coarse, brown robe, a lantern and a staff in its hand, its head hooded. The bearing, dignity, and long white beard all imparted to this masked person something venerable and awe-inspiring. After standing some moments in silence, with neither side uttering a word, the masked figure, in a pleasant voice that, despite its hollow resonance, the discerning ear could soon mark as a woman's, began as follows:

"You know me not, gentlemen, but your appearance tells me that I find myself in no frivolous company. You surely cannot be inclined to spend this solemn night, this birth of a new year, in the thoughtless rush of revelry. Should it please you to join me to spend a brief hour in quiet diversion, then

I can direct you to a special secret place. By my clothes you know me as the watchman of the night. Yet let none take offense at this oft disparaged title, for I am the *spirit* of this trade, calling myself the king of this land's night watchmen. Many an honest member of my nocturnal estate will have told you about me, my deeds and doings. Tonight when the clock strikes twelve it will mark a hundred years that I have been visiting the empire's cities, under bright starry skies and in winter storms. As midnight approaches I shall be in the watchman's belfry in the tower of the St. Alban's Church."

And with that the figure bowed and went its way with all but silent tread.

They were unanimously inclined to accept the strange invitation, whatever its goal and purpose might be; there was no possibility that a malicious joke or base adventure was involved, and they felt sure they could expect a harmless outcome. If it had not been for the guileless look and great curiosity with which Larkens responded to the situation, he might have come under suspicion of having undertaken some kind of hoax, for his sense of humor was well known and had earned him a reputation as a nasty trickster and intriguer — an impression much fostered by his outward appearance, despite the fact that the yellowish taint of his skin and his black sparkling eyes were no more ugly than the wily smile that lurked around his mouth was dangerous. He was one of those people whom one must know well in order not to fear them. As an actor and singer he was highly thought of, and he would have been a favorite of the public had he not harbored the riddlesome and stubborn caprice of wanting to exchange the comic genre, to which he was truly born, for serious roles that, though he did not sense it himself, he played with only moderate success. At times, the suppressed inclination of his nature attempted to take revenge in the form of an irresistible desire to play comedy, and the theater always stood to reap a holiday bounty at the box office whenever the name Larkens adorned the posters for a Holberg or Shakespeare piece of that genre.[8] But then at such times it was as if the spirit of jest itself were upon the man. The applause of the informed and of the common folk alike was assured him all the more that he was better able to keep the pulsing vein of his comic powers within the fine boundaries of beauty that only the genuine artist, guided by the proper tact, can draw between zeal and wisdom. While many in his stead walked as if upon burning ground, Master Larkens seemed infused by a gentle tinge of warmth imbued upon him by the graces, and the sparks of genius he gave off inflamed not only him. Moderation was ever the soul of his acting, and it merited all the more admiration if, as closer friends report, it is true that his every humorous mood was in fact the expression of a passing crisis of a troubled soul stirred by pain. Be that as it may, the directorship of the theater in fact paid him for the sake of these extraordinary performances and otherwise, as he was a difficult man to coerce, let him have his way.

The four friends had arrived at the St. Alban's Tower by just after eleven to find there, besides the keeper, his wife, and his children, some of the local musicians seated about the small parlor's lone lamp, there to carry on the long-standing tradition of playing a song from the tower at midnight. The new guests were accorded a very friendly welcome, especially since they had seen to preserving the stock of wine. After conversing on general matters, the friends learned, by way of their casual questions and to their by no means small amazement, that the legend of a ghostly night watchman had long been part of the superstitious lore of these people, although they did take the assurances that such a visit was expected as a joke that the gentlemen had planned. Meanwhile the conversation turned to similar fairy tales and stories, all true delights for Larkens, and even Nolten would have had the opportunity to enrich his store of fantastic topics with many new traits, had he been less apathetic towards everything that did not feed his current gloom. All the more attentive were his friends, who in such stories felt they had found something akin to an adventurous reflection of the illusions of the masked ball. One such brief tale was the following, as told by a handsome lad among those gathered.

"In Tanners' Lane, as you gentlemen may know, there stands, between two rows of our city's oldest buildings, a small house. Narrow, with a peaked roof, and of late quite in disrepair, it is a locksmith's workshop. Yet on its topmost floor, they say, there once lived a young man, quite alone, more about his life known to no one, and never seen, except every time before a fire broke out. And then they would see him, wearing a scarlet-red knit cap that went strikingly with his deathly pale face, and pacing restlessly back and forth past his little window, the surest sign that misfortune was near. Even before the first alarm bell sounded, even before any one knew that there was a fire or where, he would come charging out of the stall down below on his scrawny nag of a horse and tearing off like Satan, unerringly in the direction of the fire, as if by some premonition he had sensed it all in his spirit. And now it so happened —"

"Hey, stop this boring chatter!" one of the speaker's comrades broke in, "and instead sing the story in the song that you have about it — it sounds a lot better that way and the melody has a haunting beauty. Sing it, Christoph!"

The lad gave his listeners an embarrassed look and, with their eager encouragement, began at once to sing in a strong, melodious voice:

> See you at yon window small,
> There again, the red cap gleaming?
> See it rise, now see it fall,
> Like an omen ill, 'tis seeming.
> 　And the crowd is wildly churning

Through the streets and lanes they're bound.
Hear the firebell shrilly sound!
Beyond yon hill, beyond yon hill!
A mill is burning!

See him dashing, wild his speed,
Through the gate, the fire rider,
On his gaunt and bony steed,
As if it were a fire ladder;
   Through the smoke and mist he's turning
   Racing like the wind's own bride,
   Townsfolk cry from the other side:
   Beyond yon hill, beyond yon hill!
A mill is burning!

Scarce an hour had passed away,
'Til the mill in ruins did lay;
And that wild rider man
No one e'er did see again.
   Quiet, now, the crowds are turning
   Men and horses homeward bound,
   And the bell does fainter sound:
   Beyond yon hill, beyond yon hill!
It's burning! —

Time passed — — and a miller found
The rider's skeleton, cap and all,
Leaning on the cellar wall
Still upon his bony mare.
   Fire rider, oh, how coldly,
   You ride to your grave, so boldly!
   Whoosh, to ashes all does fall —
   Rest in peace, rest in peace,
Below there in the mill!

Even before the song ended, the door opened and the night watchman figure entered quietly. He took his place by the wall and stood motionless. The
startled singer was about to stop but, at a sign from Larkens, continued with
the verse, its impact, owing to the presence of the strange figure, either all
the more intensified — or totally lost.

Now the strange guest solemnly greeted those present, and, despite
some initial embarrassment on the part of the young friends, there nevertheless ensued a conversation that was as natural as it was unusual. There was
talk of the mysterious charm of tower dwelling, of the grandeur and piety of

20

medieval times as evident above all in the forms of its sacred architecture, and of similar matters. The presence of the strange figure, however sparse till now its contribution to the discussion, still exerted considerable influence on the import and growing intensity of the discourse. The voice, resounding hollow from behind the mask, the fiery dark eyes, their gaze calm but penetrating, could even arouse a fleeting sense of fear and give rise to momentary belief in transcendent powers.

Then all of a sudden the strange figure arose, opened a window, and looked out into the clear winter air, saying: "Only a short time remains until the sand has run out; the thread of time, held aloft, hovers on high. Come and feel the fresh breeze that wafts over to us from the near future."

Then the clock struck the last quarter-hour before midnight as the members of the brass and woodwind choir stole away with their instruments to the gallery. From across the way at St. Paul's church, a few soft, almost melancholy tones could be heard that were answered from our side in weak but then ever stronger chords — the former representing the departing year, the latter the new awakening one, and the two meeting in a kind of antiphonic duet that reached its greatest intensity just as the clocks on all sides at last struck the hour. Then the music from the St. Alban's side gradually became more joyful, while that from the other side sounded ever more morose and sad, until, with the tolling of the farthest bell, resonating silver-clear through the night, the sorrowful clarinets gave out their last dying note. There followed a pause, and only then did the present year emerge to its most victorious triumph.

After stillness had descended and the company gathered once again around the cozy table, all present applauded the idealistic watchman's offer to read something from his diary — or, better, "nocturnary" — for the previous year. He produced a notebook with writing in strange figures that appeared to contain, along with its regular entries, the random comments and thoughts that likely occurred to him during his nightly wanderings through the streets of the cities and towns: typical images from the most diverse relationships and situations of people. We shall pass in silence over most of his readings and offer only *one* passage that made all the greater impression on Nolten the more meaningful the glances were with which Larkens attempted to alert him to its significance.

"The night from the 7th to the 8th of January in the village of ***. I approach a neat and well-built house; I know it well; fortunate people reside there. In untrammeled serenity a young girl blossoms to maturity, already the betrothed of a loved one living far away. Allow me, O you domicile of peace, a gaze into your rooms. My eye is sanctified like that of a priest; for a hundred years now it has watched over the nights of this land's kings and the resting places of the poor amongst the folk, and my prayers inform heaven of what it has seen. Behold! What does my magic mirror reveal? It is the girl's bedchamber! How peacefully the sleeping creature breathes, her dear head inclined to the side of her bed. The moon shines through her small window; with a *single ray* it touches only the innocent chin of the sleeping girl. A hyacinth bows down its blue blossoms towards her pillow, mixing their aroma with the maiden's dreams of spring, even as the winter paints frost flowers on her window. Where might her thoughts now be? Woven into her carpet are strange figures, a hundred sailing ships. Perhaps these images caught her thoughtful eye but briefly ere she doused her lamp, and now she dreams her beloved tossed upon the wild sea where her voice cannot reach him. Oh, better he should sink into the depths of the ocean than that you should find him untrue, good child. But suddenly you smile so blissfully, dreaming him in your arms and feeling his kiss. Perhaps in that moment where you play with his dreamt shade he is awake and seeking forbidden pleasures, committing shameful betrayal against your love. But still I see you in friendly happy dreams; you innocent soul, ah well, this is indeed unheard of and unbelievable; what can he be searching for, then, that he would not find with *you*? Beauty and youthful charms? I do not know how mortals call it, but here heaven itself may smile well-pleased upon what it has created. Reason and intellect? Oh, were this eye but to open now! out from its deep blue depths shines with childlike gaze the dawning vision of every highest thought. What, or is it devotion to God? That question sounds as though it were mocking *Him*. O humble walls, bear witness of how often you have seen her kneeling here in fervent prayer when all around lay sleeping! — — Your looks grow serious, dear daughter; how strangely your dream changes its moods! Ah, you will be weeping all too soon. God help you. Good night."

This was the conspicuous passage that Nolten listened to with silent displeasure towards Larkens, for now he no longer doubted that this friend had arranged everything. The rest of the readings from the notebook had no particular bearing on him, and the performance came to an end at the right time, just as Nolten's impatience had reached its limit. He could hardly wait until the company dispersed and he found the chance to whisper to Larkens a few words that were meant at least to give an indication of how inappropriate that signal of his had been. "I thank you," said Nolten in injured tones as they descended the tower steps, "I thank you for your well-meant reprimand in a matter in which I could have every good reason to pass judgment upon myself. I have already given you a general explanation about all this, but you seem not to have understood me. Ask, and I want to give you a more extensive justification of what I have done."

"In the first place," his friend replied, half smiling, "I by no means conceal from you my joy at the fact that you have not taken my veiled attack upon your conscience merely in fun, however strange the comedy was. Yet on the other hand, I would be just as sorry if you took me to be a poltroon or self-righteous moralist. No one would have less right to that role than I do. I have just recently myself escaped the devil at the cost of three-fourths of my mortal soul, but I'll pledge him the whole precious remaining bit of it if I'm proved a liar when I tell you that an unselfish sympathy with that charming creature, indeed with the both of you, is driving me to do all I can do to thwart your calamitous estrangement from that girl."

"Very well, we'll soon discuss this matter further," said Nolten, and reached to take his friend's hand, a gesture that Larkens, who was always embarrassed and irritated by even the least show of sentiment between friends, rebuffed.

After they had accompanied their visiting friends to their quarters and arranged when they would all meet again, the remaining two, who lived in the same house and even on the same floor, went their shared way together in taciturn near silence.

OUR PAINTER FOUND WITHIN his own four walls that the blessed relief of undisrupted solitude, which only minutes before he had sought so urgently, now eluded him completely. The impressions of the last hours were so diverse, so powerful, so conflicted, that he could hardly hope to put them in order and summon the sensibility to master them. The servant who had waited to help undress him he sent to bed and sat awhile in uncertain thought, his head resting on his hand, his eye fixed on the calmly burning flame of the candle before him. Only when his gaze fell upon the unwelcome letter — it still lay before him, unopened, on the table — did his displeasure and melancholy take on a distinctly defined form. "Oh!" he cried out, "must everything force itself upon me today to pain me so? Am I not to find my own inner self? What can she want to achieve with this letter? Must she not sense that we are parted forever? Yes, if only that insight were the content of this letter! If only I could sense that from the handwriting of the address! Yet those letters are true and good, and look as fondly flattering as in our happy days — No, no, I dare not break this seal."

Suddenly he stood up and sought the company of his friend and was consoled to find him still awake, sitting at his hearth, and no less disposed to spend the last scant hours until daybreak in friendly conversation. "It is right and fitting that you come!" was his greeting, "you find me occupied with earnest thoughts — about *you*. It would be quite nice were you now inclined to afford me a closer look at your cards, for from what I could tell from what you were muttering about this evening, one might be inclined to believe that your coolness towards Agnes has been caused by some further specific events, although I was thinking all along that you were merely exhibiting the symptoms of the quite common cooling off of love that rarely has any other explanation than a certain deficit of warmth. In the meantime, then, Countess Constanze may have had some influence, too. What? or could it really be

23

that she arrived in your heart to find the premises already swept as clean as if with a new broom?"

"Let us not talk so lightly of a serious matter!" Nolten responded, "no, believe me, old fellow, my relationship to Agnes did not find the cause of its destruction just where you with your sharp mind are sure you've found it. You probably could have noticed the cause by the change that occurred in me some time ago. But I found a detailed accounting of the whole hateful story too unpleasant, and I may have been held back from it as well by a stupid sense of shame that I could not control. To have to know I was made such a fool of, so hurt, by such a childish creature! To make such a fool of myself, to delude myself in a such a way! Listen then: You know what drew me to the girl, what all I sought in her and found a thousandfold; yet you do not know how much my reckoning deceived me. You see, if the utmost in purity of thought, if childlike modesty and unstinting devotion from the outset struck me as the sum of all that I could ask of a female creature that I was to love forever, then it is possible to comprehend and forgive the willfulness with which my heart closed itself to even the first and slightest signs that belied those qualities. For the more modest my demands were in every other sense, the more adamant I allowed them to be in this one respect, which, as I see it, renders null even the most beautiful and lasting charms of all womanliness." "Ha ha ha!" laughed his friend, "your demands, while modest, are at the same time impertinently grand for the women of today's world!"

"Oh," Nolten went on, "O Larkens! Yes, laugh at me, I deserve it! That I could be such a fool as to believe in the immutability of the original innocence that rendered me infinite recompense for any splendid advantage of upbringing. What happened to the devotedly contented mind that was never assailed by even the most fleeting notion that there could exist anything desirable other than her beloved? What happened to the unadorned truthfulness that would not tolerate even the smallest duplicity, to the humility that is a mystery unto itself? All those qualities once resided in this girl. With what secret rapture did I not, a thousand times, listen to the innocently playing pulsations of her innermost life. As clear as crystal the entire scope of her being seemed open to me, revealing not one single flaw. Tell me then! Did it thus not have to be that the first shadow of feminine deceitfulness would have to frighten me from her forever? My paradise — I confess it to you, Larkens! — was poisoned from this moment on. Can I change it? Can *she* change it? Perhaps she may be forgiven, and I forgive her, too; but the meaning of the whole is lost for me now, gone forever, irretrievable. And even if her love, divinely born anew, were to come weeping to me, I could not reach out, it would no longer find a place in my heart."

Larkens remained silent for some moments, thinking. "But," he then began, "what has the girl done wrong, then? At what weak point did this Satan, who is supposedly now upon her, first set his horn? Where's the evidence?"

"Do you think that it wasn't calamitous enough for me when, a year ago, when I last visited Neuburg, it looked as though the little fool were growing worried about my capacity to care for her satisfactorily? and then when her father, his face full of critical concern, pointed out to me that things weren't moving ahead on any front with my art, my profession, and he himself would be able to provide us little support and that I might give serious thought to whether I felt myself able to provide for a family, and similar nonsense — when that happened, his dear little daughter took me gently aside, kissed the furrows from my brow, gave me a smile, yet was herself only barely able to conceal her worries, her tears. Well, I let that pass and took a lenient view of what they were doing. But then soon after that, damn it! then came this detestable, vile behavior!"

"Well?"

"An elegant dandy started to visit, a surveyor or whatever he is, a distant cousin from the neighboring town. I was alerted by a friendly letter from Neuburg that they wanted the lad on hand as a reserve son-in-law, just in case."

"That's not possible!" cried Larkens, jumping to his feet in alarm.

"Yet certain nonetheless. To be sure, Agnes did not know about the neat little plan herself; they wanted to wait and see if her little mouth would start to water for this fellow of its own accord, so they intentionally threw the two young folks together until the girl really did begin to become dizzy. For after all my rival wore a brilliant scarf pin and knew how to say just the right things about balls and parties and the like and to show really sympathetic surprise about how Fräulein Agnes took no part in such wonderful things, all of which made the dear little lamb start wondering about that herself and become smitten by that magnificent world that she'd never before had the least inkling about out there in her little cabin in the woods. Yet I learned nothing about these visions from her very loving, if somewhat spare letters; those little scraps were dear and simple and loyal-hearted as ever, and they smelled neither of Eau de Portugal nor of mille fleurs but bore instead the good old aroma of mayflowers and strawberries. But I caught the stench of hell from the letters of very honorable personages; they were full of talk about musical and other nocturnal trysts, of rendezvous in the garden nook, and of all manner of things that I first found to be unbelievable and distasteful to the point of despair, but then gradually saw as quite natural and so plausible as to make me want to die laughing."

"Letters. From whom, then?"

"They are from — oh, it makes no difference."

"But it does, that's just it, dear boy!"

"Well, yes, but I do owe those people a certain degree of discretion."

"Well then give me a rough indication; from men? from women? Oho! Now I spot the trouble; these epistles were dictated by envy."

"That's a shameful suspicion! And besides I have other proof that — oh, let me be still, let me forget! just spare me now, surely you see how it torments me!"

"But what did Agnes say in her own defense?"

"Nothing, and I didn't confront her with it."

"By the devil! Are you crazy? You didn't demand an explanation?"

"Not with one word. Her 'Dear Papa,' fearing that I had gotten wind of the game, wrote me first with attempts to justify matters, seized, perhaps, by regret about what's happened. There he resorts to the most pathetic psychological subtleties as if there were some prize at stake for restoring to honor the frivolousness of some silly little maid. He even turns to medicine for help; it is true, the girl was ill not long before, but what, hang it all, did the nerves of my future bride have to do with this surveyor? In short, I now know how I have to see the whole matter. As you know, I ceased writing to her six months ago, and at last I had come to hope that she had resigned herself quietly to the situation, yet now the old man may have heard of the improvement in my situation: yesterday, you see, Ferdinand unexpectedly brings me another scrap of a letter from her — there!"

Larkens reached quickly for the letter — doing so, in fact, with a show of alarm that only in *this* moment could escape his friend's notice. Nolten forced the pages upon him almost imploringly, saying repeatedly: "Keep it, bury it here someplace, O my peerless Larkens! And if possible spare me with the contents, you write back to her, will you? do me this favor. Oh, how it lightens my heart now to be rid of that nonsense. Come, old fellow, let's send for some wine. Let's be of good cheer once again. The day with its troubles is sound asleep. Let this dismal lamp and our morose spirits sparkle in the deep ruby-red of some burgundy!"

In no time there was a cool bottle upon the table, they got onto some of their favorite topics about art and were soon in a heated discussion, and with the dawn they parted to catch up on some of their missed rest.

"And one more thing," exclaimed Theobald at the door, "who was that costumed figure at the St. Alban's Tower?"

"Don't ask me that now, it's not important; you'll hear all about it some other time. Sleep well."

When Nolten arrived back in his bedroom it was lit pale by the breaking light of dawn. He is just about to stretch out on his bed when he notices affixed to the Spanish hat that he had worn to the masked ball a decoration that he'd never seen before: a pomegranate blossom, made to look like a real flower. The blood rushes to his cheeks, a sudden thought flashes through his mind — "it's from her! from her! Oh, surely it's from you, Constanze!" he cried out. "Love makes me understand now that mysterious word that you let fall scant days ago, half serious, half joking. The pomegranate blossom — that was it, wasn't it? Yes, that's what it was! And then just this evening — was my eye not caught more than once by the figure of the gardener girl, with her little servant, as she handed out flowers? And so it was her after all! No doubt, the little fellow fastened it to my hat as I was sitting there in a bad mood by the window. She must have given him a signal. So she recognized me after all. O you angel, angel! And you, my blissful heart! Yes, just hope, and hope boldly. That is a precious, a priceless sign. I am starting a new life. Come then, O sleepy morning! Oh, why does the sun not *at once surge up*, magnificent and enraptured, over the sheltering, shadowing mountain, for a miracle would cheer me so! O you grey day, how strangely you gaze upon the crown of this open blossom! O dear, grey day, prophesy me nothing ill to come with your indifferent mien! And if it is jealous you would be, so know this — and the displeasure it might bring you: *she* loves me. Me! Yes, *she* — me!"

MEANWHILE LARKENS HAD OPENED and read the letter from Agnes that he had been given; it was a simple greeting to offer Theobald hearty thanks for his last letter — which, however, truth to tell, had been written by another hand entirely and, like many another previous message, simply passed off as Nolten's.

"You're asking me," Larkens said to himself after a pensive pause, "you're asking me, poor friend, to bury the letter here with me, to cut the knot, to consign your whole ruined affair in one fell swoop to the forgotten past and make all well again with just *one* stroke. Well, make well I shall, but in a totally different way than you think, and just thank God that this is not the first time that it's occurred to me to take this concern upon myself. How I thank the ingenious inspiration that showed me a way to hide your inconstancy from that good child, to use a harmless deception to spare her all the pain, all the worry, and, at least for as long as there is hope for curing you of your blindness, to leave that fair creature her beautiful dream of your love. Obviously, nothing can come of a relationship with the Countess, a thousand facts of the matter work against it. Constanze herself, as I know her, does not have the remotest notion of such a thing and cannot have. Theobald will have to learn to renounce his passion, I can foresee the outcome, he will take it hard — but no harm done, that will help me to bring him to his senses, help me to make him receptive for Agnes; he will thank heaven if he is able to keep this gem he would cast away. For the present it would be folly to try to force the Countess out of his heart; I hope it is only a passing phase and, unless I am wrong about him, he is hardly likely to take pleasure in a lasting relationship with her.[9] In any case he shares with me all that happens between him and Constanze, and so Larkens is on hand should perchance the roof take fire; as well, I shall keep such a close watch on my people that

27

nothing shall foul my plans. The first thing now is that I find out what this fairy tale with Agnes is all about; surely it is some kind of slanderous deviltry, and my Nolten, most capital fellow that he is, has once again in the blind heat of anger just fired off the mark; I'll be hanged, that's it. — Hm! of course, if only I'd seen this girl just once with these mine own eyes! but as things are, what do I have that vouches for her? Examples do exist that such a little angel can suddenly play a nasty trick — or, one and the same for a woman, a stupid trick. But no, confound it, again I just cannot see it. Are her letters not evidence enough? Truly, she really can't be writing with a poison pen! And suppose that once she had taken a wild notion into her head for a few days and let her eyes stray from the straight and narrow path, that sort of thing might poison things a bit with her lover, but all in all what is the harm? It's damned egotism that we men can forgive just about anything but not such a little fool, as if we alone had the privilege of being allowed to have our hide stroked a bit by the devil himself without having it burned! Heavens! These proper little witches are as much flesh and blood as we are, and the next gaze they cast upon their one and only beloved throws that hundredth part of a thought of being untrue and the most daring castle in the air right out the window; and then there's nothing more piquantly delightful for such a sweet miss than those little tears with which, silently and with a thousand kisses, she immediately atones for the straying of her fantasy, clinging to the bearded, manly neck of her dearest. But then not even these harmless escapades are something that I think Agnes is capable of, either; at any rate it would mean the end of the image of the good-as-gold angel of Christ that I have gradually construed for the girl. Bloody murder! You're not to think one single solitary thing in the world without the old spoiler coming and putting a crimp in it for you. I could tear myself apart with rage! and not on my own account — I have nothing left to lose — but for Nolten, who, in his honest, good, boyish way, thought himself securely set in a village idyll and now seems about to be biting into rotten apples. That's life — aye, and in the end none of us deserves better. But let's see, there's still always the question — damn! How contagious mistrust can be! Wasn't my faith in the girl still solid as rock just a moment ago? And, considered calmly in the light of day, it stands as firm as ever. So let me just keep on playing my machinations! My masquerade correspondence with his little darling can continue as long as it can. Have I not, over these last six months of practice in the style of love, in my tone and individual way of thinking, become so totally a second Nolten that I must fear, should the whole game come to light, that the girl would fall in love with *me*? which really, ceteris paribus, wouldn't be so bad, either. Yet one thing is certain, I believe that for the hundred amorous villainies for which I have previously misused my handwriting skills I have sufficiently atoned by, at long last, using my art of stealing the features of honest people for a good purpose. You dear, deceived child! And did you never, gazing deep in thought at my false handwriting, sense something uncanny when you pressed the page to your lips? Did the angel of your love not whisper to you then: stop! a strange hand is posing as that of your lover! Of course not! Your guardian angel will surely rather conspire with me than dismay you with an untimely truth that would also rob you of your love. So in any case let me go my way. And just as in the past I have had no lack of excuses to console you about the repeatedly postponed reunion and long denied embrace with your Theobald, so I shall, methinks, go on now to succeed in presenting him to you as an entirely new man, and you will not even know that it is a culpable yet converted renegade who weeps at your feet."

That was more or less the gist of Larkens's sometimes silent, sometimes spoken soliloquy. By trying to reproduce it, we have initiated the reader into the secret that was dear above all else to Larkens's heart. It goes without saying that from the start of his remarkable correspondence with Agnes he took every possible precaution, using some pretext to have her send her letters to the Larkens address. This she then dutifully did, though the last note was an exception, since Agnes believed she could conveniently take advantage of the opportunity provided by Nolten's friends, and so that paper had actually come, to the initially by no means small alarm of the secret correspondent, into the hands of him for whom it was least appropriate and to whom its content would have had to betray the whole prettily woven fabric. Some pointedly renewed instructions to the female side of the correspondence were the only immediate results of this happily averted danger; however, a far more important reason to write forthwith to Agnes as well as to the forester Larkens now found in the uncertainty about the aforementioned matter of honor. He sat down to write even in this very hour, yet with the intention of voicing his concerns as mildly as possible and of confining his inquiries to the most general matters, so that no contradiction of previous dealings, unknown to him, might come to light.

IN ORDER, HOWEVER, to give a complete picture of Nolten's relationship to his bride, we must turn to a still earlier time and narrate the following.

The relationship of the two betrothed had blossomed in most desirable fashion when Agnes suffered a nervous disorder that brought her near death. The critical point of the illness then, against all expectations, passed without misfortune, and several weeks went by without the gradual recovery of the girl encountering any noticeable setback. Now, however, it could escape the notice neither of the father nor of those who came to visit that a change had occurred in his daughter, and indeed a significant one. Clearly her entire spirit had been profoundly affected, and physically too, it was noticed, she exhibited a sensitivity that was most unusual. Generally she was quiet and mostly downcast, but then at times unusually cheerful and, in contrast to her usual behavior, given to all manner of jest and foolery. Often she would give vent to her heart in intense weeping and would break out in lamentations about her far-away beloved, for whose company she yearned. Also, she expressed a passionate love of music and desired nothing so much as to be able to play some musical instrument, each time adding that she desired to do so only for Nolten's sake, in order that in future he might find at least one pleasure in her. "I am a much too rustic and simple creature, and such a man! Oh, shall we then ever be suited to each other?" And when others then tried to comfort her, when her father made clear and graspable for her the forthright and loyal mind of her fiancé, then she could only cry out all the more vehemently: "That is just the pity, that he is deluding himself so! You are all deluding yourselves, and I as well in many a brief moment of foolishness. Do you really think that, when he was here last autumn, I didn't notice how he was often bored with me, how something was making him oppressed and reticent? Were you watching when he would sit by me and give me his hand, and I would fall silent and want nothing more in the world but to gaze into his eyes, how then he would smile, yes — oh, and how lovingly, how truly! No, no other can do that as he does! And then did I not often, right in the midst of such pure joy, turn away in dismay and cover my face with both hands, weeping and keeping from him what had come over me? — ah, for you see I feared in his mind he could see I was right, I did not want to help him realize how unlike each other we were, how ill-advised a choice he had made in me." So she would go on for a while and then end in bitter tears; and then it could often happen that she would quickly pull herself together, as if striving to swim against the current of her feelings, and then with the most engaging pride the child would begin to justify herself, to compare herself; her pale cheek would take on some color, her eyes would shine. It was the most touching struggle of suffering humility against her noble self-consciousness.

This strange discontent, this despair about any worth of her own, was all the more striking by the fact that Theobald in fact gave her absolutely no cause for such feelings and that others had previously noted in her scarcely a trace of such anxiety. Now, of course, it became clear from some of her comments that even back in her healthy days she had already been secretly nurturing yet repeatedly suppressing such concerns, and that an unhealthy feeling, left behind in her from her nervous disorder, must have violently seized upon the most vulnerable part of her tender spirit.

In order that we nevertheless shed sufficient light upon the whole matter, we feel obliged to narrate a fact that preceded the outbreak of Agnes's symptoms of melancholy and that may have imparted a far more complex form to something that may have been a mere passing caprice.

Two weeks after Agnes had been released from her sickbed, she received from her doctor permission to partake once again of the fresh air. It was on that same day that a distant relative was visiting, a man with whom the family had actually only now become acquainted; the young fellow had just recently been employed in the neighboring city doing surveying work, and he was an all the more welcome guest of the forester because he possessed, in addition to a pleasing appearance, many a charming social grace. They had a cheery midday meal after which Agnes was then permitted to accompany her cousin Otto for a stretch in the warmest sunshine on his way back to the city. The girl was as if newborn under the open sky and thoroughly enjoyed the solemn and incomparable pleasure of newly restored health; she spoke little, a quiet God-turned joy seeming to seal her lips and lighten her step; she felt as if she were naught but light and sun within; a distinct feeling of physical strength seemed to mix pleasantly within her with the small vestige of weakness. She turned back earlier than planned and took leave of Otto, in order to enjoy the surfeit of rapture and gratitude in complete peace.

Her path led through the small stand of birch by whose last bushes she found a Gypsy woman sitting alone in the grass, a person of imposing and, despite her obvious maturity, still maidenly appearance. They greet, and Agnes walks on; yet she has covered barely fifteen paces when she regrets not having spoken to the unknown woman, whose whole bearing and friendly gaze had nevertheless made a considerable impression on her. She stops and thinks; she turns back, and a conversation begins. After a short while of discussing matters of relative indifference, the brown girl plucks some blades of grass and weaves them into a symmetrical figure; then, shaking her head, she undoes one or the other of the knots and says: "Sit down here by me. — The gentleman whom you were just accompanying is not your sweetheart, yet, mark my words, he will be."

Agnes, although somewhat embarrassed, at first jokes about such an unbelievable prophecy, yet quickly becomes ever more involved in the conversation, and, since the strange woman's utterances and questions seem to be based on a quite incomprehensible intimacy with the young bride's actual situation and relationships, she imperceptibly becomes more open with the Gypsy. At the same time, that woman's good-natured behavior dispels almost all of Agnes's distrust. But then how painfully and unexpectedly her most secret heart is suddenly exposed, when she hears among the words so ominously spoken: "Regarding your current fiancé it would be cruel and unjust to conceal from you that you two truly are not born for each other. See here the slanting line, that's a curse; otherwise the whole arrangement goes very nicely together! But the spirits are at odds with each other and make war with the hearts that for now may well be holding fast to each other. Aye, strange, strange it is! I've rarely encountered such a thing before."

Agnes found sense in these dark words, for they merely explained her own fear to her. "What?" she said quietly and stared long and pensively into her own lap, "so it is — so it is! Yes, you are right."

31

"No, not I, my dear girl, only stars and grass are right. Forgive me for telling you the truth; but sorrow can be medicine, and be assured: time bears roses."

With that the strange woman arose. Agnes, inwardly as if lamed, her limbs as if bound, was barely able to rise to stand up and hadn't the courage to raise her eyes; it hurt her to betray how affected she felt. And yet, looking anew at the face of the unknown woman, she thought she found there something indescribably exalted, trustworthy, even long-known, in the sight of which she felt her spirit freed of the burden of her present sorrows and even her fear of the future vanquished.

"God keep you, my little dove! and be of good cheer, no matter what. When love lets go of you with one hand, it soon catches you up with the other. And just don't cast your new fortune away obstinately; it is dangerous to defy the stars. And now one last thing: before a year has passed you will reveal to no one what I have told you; it could go badly, do you heed me well?"

These last words the Gypsy had spoken with special emphasis. Touched in the extreme, the girl thanked her as they parted and handed the strange woman a fine scarf as a memento.

Left alone, Agnes scarcely even knew herself; she believed she had come under some strange and frightening power; she had learned something that she was not supposed to know, tasting of a fruit that — snatched, not yet ripe, from the tree of fate — could bring nothing but disaster and despair. Her breast was torn among resolves one-hundredfold, and her fantasy was on the verge of running rampant beyond control. She wished she could have died or that God would forgive her curiosity and relieve her of the dreadful awareness of those words that burned like fire ever deeper into her soul and whose truth she could not refute.

Exhausted she arrived back home and immediately took to her bed with severe chills; her father feared a relapse of the illness but recently vanquished, yet of the reason for her state not a syllable passed Agnes's lips. She had recent and earlier letters from Theobald brought to her bed, yet instead of the consolation she had hoped they would bring her she found almost the opposite; the most loving word, the tenderest assurances now, as if tinged by the poisoning breath of the future, she looked upon with melancholy, much as when we look at dried out flowers that we have saved in memory of past pleasant moments: their fragrance is gone and soon too every trace of color will be faded.

Such and similar sorrowful presentiments filled her with all the more urgent distress the more she had to think of a Theobald still laboring under the misapprehension of his love for her — a misconception that she neither could nor would any longer share with him and that struck her now as at once loathsome and enviable.

Meanwhile her attack of fever passed, and, aside from a certain over-excitability, the girl was considered to be well again. The uncertainty of her fate occupied her mind night and day. If she sought even for a moment to counter those threatening utterances with calm reason, berating herself as superstitious, foolish, and weak for believing them, then she would still find twenty reasons to believe weighing against her one, and even if she assumed that the strange woman had perpetrated the most outrageous hoax, the whole strange coincidence nevertheless seemed to verify to her in wondrous wise what she had already felt to be true. For indeed during that conversation in the forest she had not noticed how the Gypsy woman, after the first cunningly chanced word had sparked Agnes's interest, had then been able to feel her out and lead her on so subtly; and much less could she have dreamt that this very same person had come to know of the general state of affairs in the most natural way, that she was no stranger to Theobald and, as will be revealed later, that she even had a strong personal interest in the matter. Yet whatever secret intention was involved, suffice it to say that the poor child was already inclined to see in that whole episode a sign from on high.

In any case, there occur at times in our souls changes of which we can give no clear account and that we cannot resist; we make the transition from waking to sleeping unaware and are afterward not able to describe it: thus did Agnes by and by come to be convinced that her fate and Nolten's were incommensurable, without knowing exactly when this thought had gained irresistible power over her. Her basic feeling was one of sympathy with a man whom she loved and revered and to whom, in terms of intellect, she felt herself to be inferior and whom she feared she would make unhappy by giving him her hand, because with time it could no longer remain concealed from him what an inadequate spouse she was for him. Yet while this feeling, which indisputably had sprung from the purest foundation of unselfish love, urged the good creature gradually towards a devout and, of itself, consoling resignation, her resolve that they should agree to part was countered by an idea that came to her quite naturally, namely: that a future misalliance between them could be conceivable only if Nolten were to disavow totally his original feelings towards her, if he were to turn untrue to the first pure impulse of his heart. Thinking thus, Agnes came to see herself, even prior to any decisions, as having been most deeply hurt by her betrothed and to feel tempted to ascribe to him the guilt for something about which he himself as yet had not the slightest inkling but that nevertheless must unavoidably come about. As strange as it may sound, it is certain nonetheless that Agnes experienced moments in which her feelings towards Theobald approached aversion, even disgust, although of course such stirrings of animosity were so counter to her inmost nature, making her feel like such a loathsome and twisted creature that she would then resolve to emphasize each and every feature that, even in the worst case, could speak for her bridegroom. She felt a morbid anxiety whenever it would strike her as possible to think less of or even feel indifferent towards him, who but the shortest time ago had been the dearest thing in the world to her; she felt that if things were to reach such a state she would be destroying her own self, as if the innermost root of her life were being set upon, as if she would have to renounce every beautiful belief, everything that she held to be worthy, grand, and sacred. In these direst moments she would seek refuge in prayer and plead fervently that God would keep the love for Nolten ever alive and vital in her, that He might only help to ban from her heart all that was passionate in these feelings.

Remarkably this fine girl, guided by a sense of proper tact, took all the while great pains to think and act independently of that suspicious prophet's voice, just as she was also wont to convince herself that the idea of renouncing her betrothed had, when traced back to its original cause, all begun with her. Perhaps on this point she was not being discerning enough, and that dark voice retained the mightiest influence on all that she did — except that she dispelled all recollection of that woman's hateful prophecy, which had pointed so decisively to a new liaison. And not without feeling a secret dread could she think in such moments of her cousin, and in fact for some time she assiduously avoided seeing him, simply in order to rid herself of this unbearable thought.

How greatly the girl suffered under these circumstances, from how many sides her feelings were silently torn and tormented can probably be better felt than described. Unbelievable amidst all this seem the shifts in her moods; for while she banished any hope of keeping Theobald and in her most rational hours even discovered within herself the capacity to release him to a better fate, there was, for all that, no lack of moments when all those gloomy visions fled like ghosts before the rising sun, when all at once her love stood before her again in light most cheerful, and a union with Nolten struck her, in defiance of all the oracles of the world, as more compelling, more natural, more benign than ever. Delighted, she would then hurry to take pen in hand to send her dear friend a loving word and as if to assure herself as well in her overjoyed awareness that she and Nolten were forever inseparable.

At such moments she was also inclined to suffer Otto's presence quite gladly, still treating him with a certain reserve that she had already overcome by half. Only when her father chanced to suggest to Otto, himself accomplished on the mandolin, that he tutor his cousin on that instrument, did she become somewhat embarrassed and tentative, even though she herself had previously expressed the wish to learn to play and even now still felt a certain desire to do so. Encouraged most warmly by Otto, she actually did decide to give it a try, and there immediately ensued a trial lesson that went splendidly. Agnes exhibited the greatest enthusiasm, for she was planning later to surprise her love with this new talent, and her little secret filled her with blissful happiness.

Yet happy intervals of this sort were fleeting; the melancholy doubts of before would return to make her all the more anxious, and such changes, taxing as they did all the strength of her soul, served only to bring about a phase in which the poor thing's spiritual nature succumbed to the weight of a frightening illusion and an ill-fated secret. Agnes still continued to observe the deepest silence concerning the meeting in the forest; only in general terms did her grief express itself in open lament, an example of which we offered at the start of this account.

The music lessons were suspended, but then they were begun again at the insistence of Agnes's father, who felt that such contacts and activities were a good diversion for his daughter. From this time on she exhibited a strange, silent indifference, doing whatever people wanted her to do; or from her listless, dreamy attitude she would shift suddenly into that ambiguous cheerfulness that we described earlier. Her old father was happy to see her having fun with Otto, only he would often be taken aback by the boisterous exuberance, by the audacity even, that his daughter would show when, the music lesson ended, the two young people would take to joking, laughing, and teasing, and the young pupil would suddenly seize her teacher by his locks and even plant a resounding kiss on his forehead, causing even friend Otto himself to be a bit embarrassed and made to look, for all his social graces, a bit awkward before his charming cousin. "But you're my dear cousin, after all," she would laugh then, "why are you acting so coy and foolish? No, but really, I wish we were engaged! You I could live with, you're made just right so that a person can't love you too much — or too little!"

These and similar statements, however casually Agnes seemed to toss them off, struck the old man as disturbing, and we find that he was quite right in being astonished when, on one occasion, when Otto was taking his leave and, as usual, shaking hands with Agnes at the doorway, he noticed a tear in his daughter's clear eye. "But what is it, my child?" the father asked in concern when they were alone. "Nothing," she responded, as she blushed slightly and turned away, "I am often touched to see him, I just like him, that's all." And then carefree, so it seemed, she would go about the room, singing.

Passing incidents of this kind gave the forester all kinds of ideas, and it is easy to understand that eventually he thought it to be more than likely that this unnatural behavior concealed a budding passion for Otto that he could blame only on his daughter's chronic sensitivity. Judging from the time in which the cousin's visits and Agnes's first capricious utterances occurred, there was little to counter this assumption. Readers, however, can scarcely harbor any doubts about the truth behind this wondrous web.

35

The dear creature had lost the balance of her reason, and the sorry rift had no sooner come about than the shades of superstition came raging with renewed force from their dark corners to ambush and vanquish her defenseless soul. That notion about Otto became as if artificially fixed in the poor girl's mind, and the imagined necessity of a tie to him began to weigh against the aversion she felt towards him.

Yet the way Agnes behaved outwardly in fact gave no reason to conclude that she was inwardly so profoundly disturbed, and her father did not believe that she was actually insane. Her strange inclination to merriment disappeared completely, making way for a steady calmness and amiable equanimity that was well-suited to conversation and to the orderly course of domestic activity alike, imparting to what she did and said no sign of anything mentally wrong with her, nothing fanatical about her looks or gestures; but she didn't want to be reminded of Theobald, and even Otto's name she scarcely mentioned as long as he was absent; only when he came to visit was she seen to lavish all her attention, all her charm and friendliness upon him.

When at this point her old father, brought to the brink of despair by such alarming behavior, would confront her about it, admonishing her — now gently, now with warning reproaches — about her duty, about her conscience, she would either remain quietly composed or retreat in tears and lock herself in her room.

Her father had in the meantime come upon the idea of keeping young Otto away from Agnes, and he had given the young man a few subtle signals along that line, which, however, had until now remained without effect; he was experiencing the most embarrassing distress, inasmuch as he now also had reason to fear that the young girl's charms might not have remained without effect on Otto. And indeed, how astounded the old man was when, one day, after he had taken the young man aside and posed his request to him in the most tactful way possible, the latter then quite candidly confessed to him that he was completely convinced of Agnes's affection for him and that nothing would keep him from returning that affection openly if he were to receive from her father the approval to do so, which, in these recent days, he had in any case resolved to request. This, he went on, would then leave it up to the father to decide whether he would hearken to the dearest most wish of his daughter or whether he was resolved, at the cost of her peace and health, to force upon her a union that one would simply have to consider at this point, with all due respect to Nolten's advantageous qualities, to be a blunder of the grossest proportions.

The forester — understandably outraged by such talk — nevertheless suppressed his displeasure and with moderation set the presumptuous young suitor to rights by exhorting him to be patient and by requesting that, for the next while, he avoid visiting them, whereupon the young man, after willingly agreeing to do so and not without some secret hope, left the house.

Now the old man pondered what was to be done and soon made up his mind that in such an unfortunate situation a change of scene and a refreshing distraction might be most advisable. He did indeed wonder at first whether perhaps a trip to visit the bridegroom would not be the most expedient way to set the whole matter right, yet even the slightest mention of such a plan to Agnes caused her the greatest distress, in which she begged her father on bended knee to abandon an undertaking that would surely be the death of her. Yet since Agnes now appeared more pleased than averse to talk of travel of any kind — no matter where it might lead — the forester gladly consented on this occasion to visit a friend residing some distance away, whom he had not seen in many years.

In a short time father and daughter found themselves underway in a well-packed carriage. The weather was most pleasant and after only a few stations they found themselves gazing upon landscapes completely new. The girl was happy, albeit without exactly being any more lively.

With the sojourn in the small city of Wiedecke, where the forester's long-time acquaintance, a jovial and affable man in his sixties who, as the steward of a noble estate, lived as prosperously as a petty prince, Agnes began to spend her days quite differently than she had previously been accustomed to do. That light-hearted man made it his duty to please his guests in the most manifold ways and, in the truest sense of the word, let no hour pass in total peace. She had to inspect the properties under the Count's dominion, the garden, the forests, parks, and fishing ponds, finding occasion to praise the steward's order and wise insights; nor were the guests allowed to fail to make the acquaintance of any and all of the steward's friends in the town and its environs, one outing thus giving way to the next, such that the forester, whose main concern was to ensure his daughter's amusement and diversion, soon saw his wish fulfilled beyond all measure that she could well endure — for, in fact, she put up with all the noisy good cheer more simply out of good-natured compliance than out of wholehearted desire to be involved.

Great and pleasant was the impression that she took away from her one evening's first visit to a theater, to which a troupe of strolling players had invited the people of Wiedecke. They offered a piece of the light and cheery genre and played it right ably, too. Agnes laughed heartily again for the first time and went to bed in good spirits. Yet during the night she came stealing into her father's bedroom and woke him up and, at first, when asked what was troubling her, took some time forming the words. Finally, she confessed that she had dreamt so vividly and clearly of Theobald, dreaming that he was disconsolate and had begged her for God's sake not to leave him; finally, then, she had awakened, smothered by his kisses. "Now, you see, father," she went on, weeping bitterly, "to you I may well confess how indescribably sorry I am for him, even though I really don't love him any more; he is sure to find love with another, but he does not realize it now, and there would be no use in trying to convince him; we must simply wait until he comes to that realization of his own accord. But" (and here she began to sob out loud) "if he were to despair during that time! If he were to do himself harm — no! no! He shan't do that, he can't do that! Is it not so, father, it cannot possibly come to that, can it? Oh, if only I could help him quickly through this phase, comfort him somehow, send him some consolation!"

The old man was secretly pleased to hear these words, for to him they could be nothing but a sign of her reawakening love for her betrothed. "If you could bring yourself to send him your total love, that would surely be the best help. Don't you see, basically nothing has been lost, nothing ruined; yes, look into your heart, my child! be my sensible girl again! Accept once again my blessings upon you and Theobald; write him even tomorrow a carefree happy letter like the one you wrote him three weeks ago, that will make him happy."

Agnes thought awhile and answered: "You know not, father, how the future looks, and that's why you can talk like that. But you see, I now think Theobald doesn't necessarily have to be my husband for me to keep on loving him. In any event it's not yet time for us to announce our engagement formally, and why should I destroy his pleasant illusion before I must, since now he wouldn't be able to understand the truth; why not keep on writing to him as he's used to having me do? Oh, quite clearly, that would be no sin on my part, my heart tells me so; he shall not, he must not learn what is in store for him, and, father, if you hold him dear, if his peace of mind means anything to you at all, then don't you tell him anything either! In return for that, I can promise you that I shall have nothing more to do with Otto. Time will tell what else is to be done."

The forester wasn't so sure what he was supposed to make of such talk; he shook his head, but resolved to hope for the best, and sent Agnes back to her room, where she went peacefully back to bed.

How great was his joy when early next morning he found her busy with a letter to Theobald, and later she even let him have it to check over, reluctantly to be sure, and without wanting to be present while he was reading. But what precious, captivating, and still well-considered words she had written! Only a girl who lives and breathes wholeheartedly for her beloved can write like that. Yet the calculated ease with which the letter passed completely over those deep and serious feelings in Agnes's inner life gave the father pause about his child's honesty. He himself had been uncertain as to whether duty required that he bring these things to Theobald's attention or whether he was not better advised to spare that young man the worry about his fiancée and the embarrassment about the whole matter, which ultimately was really only the involuntary and passing result of a strange illness. And now that there was clearly hope that the whole affair would right itself, he regretted all the less the fact that, in his previous letter, he had spoken merely in general terms of a recurrence of Agnes's infirmities. He already foresaw a happy time when he would be able, in some intimate evening hour, to give his son-in-law a calm and even-tempered account of these past strange events as of an adventure successfully withstood.

The return journey to Neuburg finally got underway. The travelers greeted their home after long absence with doubled love. Agnes struck those left behind in general as more robust, attractive, and sociable than when she had left four weeks ago; yet what her father was especially pleased to note was that she seemed to give no thought at all to the past proximity of her cousin. He, in turn, was taken up with business affairs that kept him completely out of the area, the forester thus not compelled to fear so soon the onslaught that he had already been steeling himself to face.

It also had to strike him as somewhat strange that Nolten had not been heard from for a full month and more. The old man found this inexplicable; for clearly a misunderstanding that might have come about as a result of the miserable story with Agnes was unthinkable since no one else could have known about it, which made it seem more likely that Nolten was ill or that his letters had gone lost. Agnes had her own particular thoughts on that matter and always simply fell silent, seeming, as she did so, to brace herself for something decisive.

In fact, events of no small import had come about in those far off quarters.

There had come to Nolten, soon after Cousin Otto had made the acquaintance of the forester's household, letters from two different parties and in each case very well-meaning persons, through which he was made aware of the very duplicitous behavior of the old man and his daughter in relationship to a certain young person. One of these warnings came from the good Baron at the castle at Neuburg, who had long been on friendly terms with the forester and whose rectitude and judicious judgment ruled out any possibility of precipitous conclusions or partiality. Even these first intimations of suspicion our painter, though far from convinced, still found so profoundly alarming, so laming — yes even demoralizing — that he was long unable to decide even to write so much as a line to Neuburg — this with the exception of his fatherly friend, the Baron, whom he ardently urged to probe once more into the matter. Yet several weeks later he found his suspicions corroborated in a highly unexpected way, namely by a detailed letter from Otto Lienhart — a name that he immediately recalled having heard occasionally from Agnes, and a man who, as we scarcely need mention, is one and the same person as the oft mentioned cousin.

The letter begins by appealing to Theobald's trust in a modest and reasonable manner; the unknown writer asks that he be heard out with manly calm, and assures his reader that what he has to say is by no means as strange and hostile as it could appear at first glance. Then he goes on to deal with the essential disparity between the two betrothed and how it is rooted in the nature of their two characters, without either party being in the least bit at fault. Then he outlines and defends the girl's affection for him, her cousin, and ultimately explains, without becoming presumptuous, in what sense he might hope to replace Agnes's first friend, whose special worth she still holds in esteem, in her heart and at her side. If now — he goes on to propose — these cited reasons were to suffice to move Nolten to renounce voluntarily his claims to Agnes, then all would then depend on her father's decision. He notes as well that it appears to him that the father silently approves of such a change and is only afraid of Nolten's reaction, with the result that he is delaying a decision with his wavering and in fact seeing to no party's advantage when he continues to let Nolten go on harboring a hope on which he himself has privately given up; the father is wrong, so Otto believes, in seeking to confuse his daughter and compelling her to be untruthful to Theobald in her letters. Her heart, he claims, has decided forever, and some of the letters that she has written to him will suffice to prove how she feels in the matter. (The pages mentioned are enclosed, meaning letters that the poor girl had sent to her cousin without the forester knowing about it). He felt it his duty to make these revelations, he said, and Nolten should take appropriate steps to deal with them. Should the forester, as unlikely as Cousin Otto felt it now seemed, nevertheless decide obstinately and cruelly to assert has rights as the father — or Theobald his as the fiancé — then total misfortune for all would be the only possible result, whereas in the alternative case Nolten would at least be left with the consolation that men have always found in consciously fulfilling a duty with uncommon magnanimity.

A resounding roar of despair-filled laughter was the first sign of life to emanate from our painter after he had stood in stunned silence for a few seconds. We shall spare readers the description of what shifting cycles of remorse, rage, disdain, and sorrow this now put him through. What remained for him now to think, what to do? Hate, love, jealousy all tore his breast; he seized upon and then rejected decision after decision. Then, once he had run himself ragged through his swirling range of thoughts to the brink of the impossible and monstrous, he would, suddenly disheartened, drop every resolve and simply sit gazing into a boundless void.

After some days had passed, he had progressed to the point where he was so clear in his own mind that he was resolved to remain silent and let all things take their course while he observed, among other things, how those in Neuburg would comport themselves. To his dear Larkens, who in the meantime had returned from a brief journey and who soon noticed his sadness, he revealed nothing of all this. For one thing, he simply wanted to make sure that his behavior in the matter was not confused by the advice of others, fearing as he did the great fuss that his vivacious and enterprising friend would in such a case not be able to forego. In addition, he was held back by a strange feeling of shame, as indeed it had always been one of his characteristic traits to disdain the sympathy of others, even if it were to come from his dearest friend.

Certain casual asides by the painter, as well as a number of other small details, left the actor nevertheless no doubt as to who was the cause of the ill humor. Yet far from inclined to seek the guilt in Agnes's camp, he made quiet note of what he took in his friend to be no more than the lover's insipid ennui and ungrateful caprice, and the chagrined embarrassment that Nolten exhibited when they spoke of the matter could not but strengthen Larkens's conviction that his friend sensed himself to be in the wrong. The painter was to a degree not inclined to correct Larkens's error, preferring to let it appear that he was being untrue rather than having to read his misery reflected back at him every day in the actor's eyes.

The latter could not fail to notice that the flow of letters to Neuburg had some time ago come to a halt, although from that quarter some were still arriving, and this called forth in the strange man the decision to take over his friend's duties in that matter. Of course he immediately took into account that uncertainty and chance might play a role, yet in fact there was nothing to fear, even if his daring game were, sooner or later, to come to light.

Meanwhile, however — that is, prior to Larkens's secret arrangements, as a result of which all letters to the bridegroom from the forester's household came into the hands of the false correspondent — several letters had come to Nolten, some from the old man, some from Agnes herself, and their nature was such that Theobald's judgment, inasmuch as it had previously been one of unconditional condemnation, was made to undergo a certain degree of modification. There the old man, in a tone as heartfelt as it is honest, begs his son-in-law to take no notice of certain rumors that had spread in Neuburg as a result of the importunity of a conceited young person and that perhaps also could have reached him, so as likely to be the cause of his long silence. The old man then sets forth the girl's confusions as *he* saw them and arrives, without getting it quite right, at a not exactly improbable explanation of them, in which in the end he reduces the whole thing to a strange lack of moral maturity, a melancholy over-sensitivity, and all manner of childish behavior. Nolten might accordingly forgive the girl's youthfulness and inexperience; he then gives his word as her father that the whole episode will bring no disturbing consequences in its wake, Agnes having now pulled herself together, her heart now pure and devoted to Nolten with doubled ardor. At the same time, the father goes on to speak for himself, stating that he is not so unjust as to take it amiss of the bridegroom, it being the case that the whole matter has alarmed him, if he were to wish to let time be the test to see that his bride has not become unworthy of him, it being his only request that Nolten convince himself in person, to which purpose then he is most cordially invited to Neuburg. Moreover, he might, when he writes to Agnes, seek to spare her deeply humbled soul as much as possible; she knows nothing about these messages and seems bent on reserving for herself the right to give him the most accurate account of the situation, soon and in person. Finally, he might be well advised to stop and think before he spurns a creature whose entire happiness depends on him — at least without giving her another chance, in light of the fact that the case at hand was puzzling and hard to judge.

This news put the painter in the strangest state of unrest. He had in the course of his life become sensitive, he was compelled against his will to lay aside his resolute hatred in favor of deep dismay and begrudging sympathy, and that made him feel almost more unhappy than before.

To be sure, when he compared Agnes's otherwise so pure nature with this most recent behavior, the deviation struck him as so hideously absurd that he now marveled at how for a while he had been able to believe in the possibility of unfaithfulness in the conventional sense of the word; this case so defied all experience that the very extraordinariness of the offense sufficed to excuse it. "But whatever may have been the reason" — cried Theobald, despairing anew — "however deep the cause might lie, the fact remains — I have been robbed of the first sacred concept of purity, humility, and untainted affection! What is a twisted, childish creature to mean to me? Shall I now, gnashing my teeth one moment and weeping the next, gather up my most cherished hopes as they lie shattered on the ground as miserable shards and imagine that what I cobble back together will be once again my precious gem of before? Oh, if only I could seize hold of that villainous upstart who has laid his hand on my sweet lily flower! If only I could tear out the eyes that lured my most faithful heart away! If only I might crush under my heel the heinous chatterer who let fall into my flower's twilight quiet the shameless sunshine of the day's coarse vanity. Dependent, inexperienced, still a child, aye, truly, that indeed she was, that could excuse her in one man's eyes or another's, perhaps in mine, too — but does that leave me any less betrayed, does that help me restore her desecrated image, does that help breathe life back into my blood-drained love? I feel it: here there can be no thought of recompense. To forget what I once possessed, that is all I can try to do."

Thus the painter's thoughts, and they remained the same, while life in the forester's house in Neuburg had long since resumed the even tenor of its ways as a result of Larkens's intercession. The old man did, of course, find it surprising that his frank and candid revelations were passed over in total silence, yet he ultimately concluded that his son-in-law's silence was an intentional effort to ensure that the hateful topic was left untouched for now. As to Agnes's inner state, the hopeless delusion that still dominated the unfortunate girl remained hidden from the father and to a degree even from herself amidst the zeal and ardor with which she carried on in the belief that, for a while, Nolten's love still had to be nurtured by writing; and while her sole concern seemed to be his peace, she in no way wanted to see how hungrily her own heart partook for itself of this sweet labor, how gladly her heart, as if to defy the will of fate, listened to the charming tones with which Larkens, deceptively enough, was able to imitate her true beloved. Cousin Otto, while all this was happening, remained the fearsome bugbear of Agnes's deranged imagination; he himself, after the forester had in private emphatically turned him down, had withdrawn in shame and anger.

Meanwhile the Gypsy woman had turned up again: Agnes had encountered her in secret and revealed her plan to renounce Nolten — which seemed much to please the deceiver — and even promised to see that such a letter went to Nolten.

In this way then did the individuals involved come to relate to each other in the most amazing situation, with each struggling — with some degree of deception, with some degree of passion — to delude the other.

Nolten was all the less tempted to reveal to his actor friend the true reason for his estrangement from his affianced, since Larkens ceased pressing him for more information, it being his inclination, perhaps as the result of his own experiences in love, to ascribe it all to a loathsome indifference that only time could cure. From this, with utmost confidence, he hoped the best, if only his friend, once grown wise through minor sorrows suffered elsewhere, would have learned to share his view that the most sophisticated charms of the feminine world afford no substitute for so rare a find as was, according to Larkens's conviction, that simple girl.

Thus even though between the two friends the matter was touched upon only rarely, there was still no lack of scenes like the one readers might still recall from that New Year's Eve, where our painter was held back from an open explanation of the situation by his fear that the actor might try to appeal to his conscience — and that happening at the worst possible of times, when he saw Constanze as a splendid new star rising in his sky.

FOR LONGER THAN USUAL Theobald denied himself the pleasure of a visit to the Zarlins. The Count and Constanze had made a long-planned visit to one of their relatives. For twelve days Nolten whiled away his time with empty distraction, experiencing the most tormenting restlessness, for soon enough he had begun to be plagued by a variety of doubts about the great good fortune that, out of the strange events during the night of the masquerade ball, he may well have interpreted somewhat too precipitously in his own favor. True enough, not long ago, in his presence and that of some friends, Constanze had taken note of a blooming pomegranate tree and declared its fiery red blossoms to be a symbol of ardent affection[10] — deferring as she did so, in mischievously conspiratorial tones, to Nolten's judgment as "an especially passionate connoisseur." True enough, as well, a week later such a blossom had been pinned to his hat by some unknown hand. Yet these facts were likely a teasing coincidence of fate or — as we ourselves believe — probably even the prank of a merry individual who had not only heard those statements by the Countess but also, long since, noted the painter's soft spot. And for that reason Nolten found himself in a state of the greatest uncertainty. He held only one thing to be certain, namely that the Countess had been at the ball that night, and only now did it occur to him to inquire further that matter. Yet even when he expressly talked himself out of attributing any great promising significance to that sign, even when he rejected everything that he had interpreted to his advantage, he could still discern with every inward gaze an inexplicable faith, a silent trust that remained in him, and he would then take that wondrous hope as though it were a new oracle that he could trust implicitly. In such strange ways is a mind wont to play tricks on itself when we are thrall to that dreamy passion.

Finally the evening came when the select circle was once again invited to the Count's. With anxious anticipation Nolten, well wrapped in his coat against the winter air, walked at the side of his friend Larkens towards that cherished street. But they saw that the curtained front windows, whose soft light shining through used to promise the arriving guests, even from afar, a well-warmed and gaily animated room, were not lit up, and they even began to fear an unpleasant disappointment, when then the servant, who in the downstairs entryway was relieving the gentlemen of their coats, swords, and walking sticks, directed them through the garden to the pavilion, through whose illuminated glass doors they could see even from a distance the splendid company.

They entered a pleasantly roomy, semicircular salon on whose walls all around were mounted mirror lamps. The painter Tillsen and the eccentric old Hofrat are the first to draw our friend into a conversation.[11] The lovely hostess, amidst a host of ladies, seemed at first not to notice his arrival. Yet while Theobald cast the occasional sidelong glance over towards those lips so lively engaged in friendly conversation, towards that delicate head ever nodding in pleased agreement, her gaze glided past the gathered groups, and a kindly nod towards Nolten suddenly set his spirits in motion, happy and reconciled with all the world. Meanwhile the Count came by with a roll of paper and whispered: "Here, gentlemen — we couldn't find it so easy to get to this later — it's a new drawing in watercolors by our headstrong artist herself, who would so like to hide her work and put off showing it to us — but this time I myself have a share of the praise that you will be according her: the idea is, so to speak, half mine." He was just about to unfurl the sheet when from behind him a gentle hand intervened. "Allow me, gentlemen," said his sister, who had just come hurrying over, blushing noticeably, "it is fitting that I exhibit this work myself — and at the right time, I think!" she added with a laugh and hurried with the sheet to a cabinet where she locked it away despite the protests of those present. Then she disappeared into a side room to look after the tea.

When she was for moments thus occupied elsewhere, Theobald was inclined to contemplate most peacefully his inner picture of her as he fixed his eyes on some inanimate object with which her person had just been in contact. On a delicate mahogany stand by the wall, for example, there stood a blooming calla in a brightly painted vase that bore the initial "C" on its blue crest. This plant, Nolten thought to himself, does it not in my imagination take on a portion of Constanze's being? Yes, this splendid calyx with the gentlest spirits emanating from its snow-white depths, these dark leaves that, sheltering and sheltered, spread out beneath the sacred flower, how beautifully all that captures my beloved and everything around her! how with its portentous presence the plant stands for the heavenly form of my love!

All at once Constanze was back, now to tend to the entire company by herself. At last, she handed Theobald his cup, and while Larkens was offering up another anecdote to the general merriment of those present, Nolten took the opportunity to complain jokingly to Constanze about the withheld watercolor.

"Oh," she answered, "you don't deserve that I show it to you. You recently gave me a nasty scare that could have cost me my life, albeit only in a dream."

"How so, my lady? I would have been so unfortunate? And yet so happy that my image might, in the briefest of your dreams —?"

"Well not actually you — but yes, your picture, a picture from your fantasy."

"How so, if I may ask?"

"So listen, and laugh at me! Yesterday your ghostly organist took the liberty of stepping, in quite uncalled-for fashion, right out of frame of that ghastly painting and approaching me in person."

Nolten was stunned, without actually knowing why.

"Yes, yes indeed, my good sir! With right curiously malicious eyes she stared me right in the face and said — no! you're not to hear that now!"

"But I insist!"

"Watch out —"

"She said that?"

"Of course not, that's what I'm saying; you're about to drop your cup!"

"And so I am — almost — But what did this ghost say?" Nolten asked, urging her on anew, and after a few moments the lovely woman, her confusion barely concealed, brought forth the words: "Constanze Josephine Armond will soon be playing the organ amongst us as well" —

45

"But, my God," Nolten responded, "surely that dream couldn't frighten you, could it?"

"Well, until I woke up it did; and in any case I am grateful that this dream gave me cause to ponder awhile my calling to that branch of music as well as my entry into such serious company."

Theobald, left alone again, didn't know what he was to make of these last words; by their tone they could have been meant in jest, but the whole thing made a disturbing impression upon him. Why had Constanze dreamed of precisely this figure? He knew too well that in her in particular he had created an accurate portrait of a Gypsy girl, a person who had once intruded fatefully enough into his life. Yet on the other hand anything and everything could be explained by the strong impression that the painting must have made upon a very receptive imagination.

What also served to lower our friend's spirits still further was the certainty, as he had deduced it from the general conversation that evening, that Constanze had in fact not taken part in the New Year's Eve masquerade, having already departed on her journey.

The unexpected late arrival of the Duke caused a sudden stir. But Nolten, instead of letting the presence of his rival make him sink ever more dismally and helplessly into himself, felt compelled by this turn of events to an expenditure of energy that, although at first merely feigned, ultimately, with the support of Larkens's stalwart good cheer, came to have a beneficial effect on the whole affair. Especially welcome for Theobald were the arrangements, upon the Duke's wish, to undertake a certain game that united the three various arts in an ingenious way — dance, painting or drawing, and, in a more supportive role, music. Yet to tell of this requires the following information: Constanze, known to be able and clever in drawing, was also a great lover of the beauty and art of the dance, and was known to display a high degree of gracefulness in solo performances. Nolten, then, had on one occasion uttered the idea that it would have to be a charming diversion if a few people, in the space of a brief hour, were to draw a tableau of some scene by passing the chalk from hand to hand and dancing to some slow melody so as to pass in turn past an easel, each adding a few strokes to the scene they were depicting, until finally a harmonic composition would emerge, about the general nature of which they had agreed in advance, yet whose details were left up to the momentary inspiration of each individual involved. This idea found approval, and after some discussion the possibility of carrying it out had taken shape, although at first they were at a loss to find the appropriate number of dancers who were also good drawers and vice versa. Yet here they had a solution. Nolten himself, although a confirmed enemy of the whole routine that was usually involved in our balls and parties, nevertheless possessed a lightness of limb and a pure enough sense for noble rhythmic movement. The third role had of necessity to be assigned to Herr Tillsen,

46

for, although even the most unpracticed dancer would have been better than he, the other talent still remained more important. "And," he said courteously to the Countess, "next to you a Vestris would go unseen, and so, too, fortunately, will Tillsen, who in this play renounces from the outset all envy and any fame."[12]

Since then they had already tried this entertainment several evenings with some success, and so now too they set up the drawing sheet they had arranged for just this purpose, its pleasingly grey lacquered surface poised to await quite invitingly the application of black pencil. A beautiful carpet lay spread before the easel, and care was taken to heighten the illumination. The three virtuosi had secretly agreed upon an appealing subject. Larkens took violin in hand and began to play with a certain solemnity that served to heighten the anticipation still more. Now entered Constanze, in atlas dress, with measured stride, and stood some moments thinking before the waiting canvas; soon then she began to move with the music, now to either side, now towards the easel. She seemed as she did so to be still pondering the decisive first stroke she was to make; now she stopped in front of the sheet as, leaning slightly forward, she stood firmly on her right foot, the toe of her left balanced behind her. The accompanying adagio of the violin seemed to be gently guiding her hand across the smooth surface, and soon all could see the outline of a lovely boy's face looking up at something with urgent imploring gaze. This expression of emotion was such that even now it could not but call forth in the anticipating fantasy of the audience the vision of arms and hands extended, pleading. Yet here the artist stopped and, stepping back as the music played an allegro, her charming form swaying to and fro, she paused to observe the work she had begun. With a bow, Tillsen took the chalk from her hand, and with little ado that master then added, with a few deft strokes, the powerful upper body of a man, his threatening gesture confronting the small face as it gazed up, inviting sympathy. The anticipation of the audience grew with every line, and even now approving voices could be heard; it's the young Prince Arthur, they said, as he faces his murderer.[13] But then the loudest applause ensued when Constanze, after Tillsen had stepped back to make way for Theobald, caught up in the enthusiasm of her idea, blocked the latter's way so that those two grand figures then, with a splendidly realistic enactment of violent struggle, fought for possession of the chalk, which then in the end broke into two pieces, whereupon the embracing pair danced a duet to lively music, and ultimately approached the drawing arm in arm. The main part of the drawing was completed in no time, the company gathered round, while Tillsen helped finish it off with a few quick strokes. There was praise and faultfinding, laughter and admiration — and, as also could not but be the case with such impromptu productions, there emerged, in addition to the most fortunate traces of a unifying harmonious spirit, signs of something incorrect and half-finished. In all, the scene had turned out so well that Tillsen gladly consented to the company's call to do a copy of it some time.

In the heat of the discussion hardly a soul had noticed how Constanze was growing pale and ever paler by the moment. She withdraws to a side room, there is whispering, the ladies hurry after her, everyone takes notice, the Duke insists on seeing her, blaming himself for requesting such a vigorous dance, Nolten is most disturbed. It could not escape his notice that, at the door, Constanze's last glance had rested upon him with a strange, wan smile. Finally, the company disperses after the Count, re-emerging from the side room, assures all present that there was no fear of any ill effects of the attack.

In the days that followed Theobald received an invitation from the Count to accompany him on a visit to Westerwyl, the summer residence of the King, located not far from the city, where arrangements were underway to exhibit several statues that had arrived from abroad. The Italian artist had to be present for that, and his personality as well as the works themselves were attracting many a cultured and curious visitor. Our friend found the opportunity no less welcome, yet he preferred to take the pleasant and, even in winter, refreshingly diverting ride there alone on horseback while the Count traveled by sleigh. The cheeriest of January mornings graced the outing; the sun had barely risen when Theobald, warming to a lively trot, struck off from the highway towards the beautiful, secluded dales that, beset mostly with growths of spruce trees and brushwood, led up to the royal parks on the heights above. All around the landscape, covered with a thick blanket of snow broken only by dark stretches of forest, afforded a complete portrait of winter, to whose silent impressions Nolten's present frame of mind was quite receptive. A vague mix of love of life and melancholy pervaded all his observations, whereby at first he felt quite clearly that his feelings for Constanze were not at all involved or at best only very remotely so, until amidst his reveries he recalled again a long-forgotten song of Larkens's that now seized his soul and seemed wondrously to explain his present state. He repeated his friend's verses to himself and finally could not resist singing them out loud:

> On this bright winter morning,
> Oh! what is this strange mood?
> O dawn, I am a-glowing,
> Your youth stirs in my blood!
>
> The old cliff in sunshine glowing,
> The forest ablaze so bright,
> The swirling mists withdrawing,
> Down the valley they flee the light.

How down upon us so bright
The purest heaven gleams,
Enveloping in rosy light
Enraptured angels' limbs.

Wondrous powers are playing
Happily through my soul.
My feelings whirling and spinning
To mock my reckoning's control.

With enterprising haste,
My mind and spirit rise,
Their golden arrows chased,
Through all the distant skies.

Whither shall I wander?
Do magic hordes draw me on?
To seize the world's great wonder,
With this my youthful arm?

To the battlements then I'd spring,
From ancient kings to be freed!
Hymnal songs would I sing,
And hasten to mount my steed.

And victory's proud chariots
Before my storm would fall!
Oh, shatter that poor harp to bits,
That only to love did call.

What, heart, such boastful raving?
Thou surely dost not know,
Dear fool, thou'rt sheer forgetting,
What intoxicates you so!

Ah, what in me sings
Is but the joy of love,
The wild tones it brings
Consumed again by love.

What help, what help my longing!
Beloved, were you only but nigh!
In a thousand tears of joy
I'd let the world pass me by.

Upon arriving at the castle he found the Italian, a lively man in his middle years, caught up in comically impassioned command of the servants and workmen, whose task it was to set up the marble art works in the main hall. Half in anger, half in fun, the hotheaded fellow would scream and laugh most shrilly and at times even take his walking stick to one of the workers, none of whom could understand his language. Theobald, after a careful study of the sculptures, which he found to be unique in their own way, spoke to the foreigner in Italian and would have found himself tolerably interested in the conversation, had not the visitor, by always striving to appear paradoxical and to make light of serious matters, made such an unfavorable impression. Yes, ultimately, when Theobald began to give voice to his own artistic character, the man could not resist indulging in some rather malicious teasing. Half offended and resentful, our friend withdrew to await the later arrival of the Count and to order himself a frugal midday meal in the dairy of the estate. Left with time to himself, he took a look at the grounds and at the household appointments of the princely residence. Several rooms offered a rich and instructive array of select paintings. It was easy to forget oneself for some time in these tasteful rooms, and so he was just standing by himself, pondering and observing, when he saw, reflected in a mirror off in a third room, approaching from the opposite direction, two individuals in whom, upon closer observation, he finally recognized the Count and, against his every expectation, Constanze herself. Totally bereft of his composure, Nolten, his gaze fixed and his heart pounding, kept watching in the mirror as the two figures hovered ever nearer, until, with their footsteps rustling behind him, a mutual greeting and welcoming ensued, with Nolten as confused as the other two were easy and cheerful. Never had the Countess struck him as so charming and attractive, dressed in her light grey frock with red fasteners, sash, and ribbons, their color and folds combining to remind him fleetingly once again of the pomegranate blossom. At her delicate cheek, which was rosy tinged from the fresh air, she wore a muff of white fur and, by having put up her veil, afforded to all a full view of her lovely face. First, they all turned, back to the new sights that the raving sculptor had brought to show them, and that visitor's personality the Count found so edifying that his sister, somewhat impatiently gazing about for something else to do, was not disinclined to accept Nolten's suggestion that they stroll about the castle's maze of rooms and halls. Soon enough their conversation turned to their own affairs and personalities, for Nolten's intensely reserved and constrained mood had given Constanze cause to issue him a gentle admonition, which he immediately took up as meant to address his personality in general.

"You are right!" he said, "and not merely today, not merely in certain moments am I assailed by this burdensome ill humor that even I myself detest; it is not a mood that comes and goes; it is a constant uneasy feeling that my life could and should be other than it is."

50

"How do you mean that? Am I to understand that you are not satisfied with your lot in life? I would find that barely thinkable."

"Say it in all directness, dear lady: to think so would be unreasonable. But yes, it is true, I could be happy, but I cannot rightly say why I am not. I would be ungrateful if I did not readily admit that throughout my whole life events have combined to bring me to the point at which I now stand, into a position towards which many another and more worthy man has striven in vain. A benevolent fate, as capricious and ill-intentioned as it might often have seemed, merely contributed to the fostering in me of a talent, the free wielding of which I had always envisioned as the sole goal of all my desires. Many a work I have completed with success; I have, if I may believe what my friends say, done much to comply with the highest demands of art, and, which ought to please me just as much, people expect great things of me in the future, without my harboring the least fear that they will not be fulfilled. An infinite field extends before me, and while previously I despaired of the possibility that I would ever be able to bring to light in radiant form the world that surged within me, so I see that this world is now, as soon as I really will it so, emerging to freedom, easily and unforced, beneath my brush. But how does it come about that just at this moment my resolve and desire begin to flag? Why do I start so many works without finishing them? Whence this impatient drive to be so active out in the world, busy and astir everywhere, instead of finding contentment within the four walls where I belong, in front of my easel? What otherwise must surely lure and drive and encourage the artist is his hope of earning the praise-filled recognition of those who know, the enthusiastic interest of his friends; I too was no stranger to this feeling, yet now it has lost its effect on me. Ignored, empty, and ill-humored I see the weeks pass by, and I truly believe I have lived only in those hours that I am granted to spend in your home. But now, tell me, is such a life not unbearable for a man who senses his duty as well as any other? And do you see any means of changing it? Could you find for me that one sore spot whence all this misfortune comes to rend me from myself and leave me so cut off?"

"With amazement, Nolten, I listen to your words," the Countess replied, "and your laments, I must admit, displease me more than they could stir my sympathy. I don't understand you completely, but I almost think I see the fault to be mostly yours. I was inclined to picture you this whole time being active, vigorous, and full of hope. Did not your conversations show the warmest enthusiasm for your calling and all that it entailed? Was your behavior not far more cheerful than it was distracted and displeased? How pleasant it was for our small circle when you would come amongst us of an evening as an increasingly indispensable guest, taking part in all our activities with such agreeable good nature, inventive when it came to any kind of entertainment, but always humble and without a lot of talk. And then: how can

51

I conceal from you that, just as in numerous ways we owe you many a debt, so too we would like to be convinced that our house especially might be found to be a haven for Nolten where the artist would be able, in a harmless and peaceful way, to share his richly active inner life with the company, so that again and again, his brow free and clear of its cares, he could then return once again to the serious world of his workshop and master there with calm equanimity all that before had surged in upon him, confusing and overwhelming, to numb his senses and depress his heart. Yes, my friend, you might silently mock me, but I do not deny that my hopes went so far."

"God forbid, dear, noble lady, that I should fail to recognize how you have favored me with a kindness I have not earned! More, far more than you have just now indicated, could be afforded me by this magnificent circle, if I were to understand how to make use of the blessing it has offered me. But, madam, what if precisely the new allure of this beautiful sphere were to call forth a rift in me; what if the intimate sympathy that the *heart* must feel here were to stand in the way of the far more general interest of the *mind;* what if, instead of returning to myself becalmed and strengthened, I were constantly to feel a passionate desire to concentrate all the rays of my human and artistic being on the focal point of such a lovely society, to keep them fixed there always, and in that way ensure my striving an all the warmer enthusiasm, a more direct reward than the scattered applause of the world can offer?"

"It is," the Countess answered cheerfully after pondering a few moments, "in the nature of men of your sort to take everything in a one-sided manner only, to expect everything from that one side, and in fact to be all the more demanding in that impossible hope the more harmful it would be. In any case, my dear painter, I am at this moment neither prepared nor inclined to offer you help and counsel regarding your present state, your wishes and desires. The sublime caprices of this artist species are hard to grasp, and, when there are such subtle discussions going on, we clever women, able only to listen and grope our way and respond with half answers, are hard put not to betray our own nonsense, our simplicity. When we talk to a person for whom we harbor heartfelt good wishes, we ultimately would like to make everything better with one stroke and defy all that is unnatural by trying to intervene with the most natural advice. But then quite often we are at a loss for any such magic formula and, indeed, when we think we've found one, it often strikes us as dangerous to make use of it, and so in the end we can do no better than — to maintain a meaningful silence and commend the gentlemen to their own genius."

Theobald found in these words much to ponder: the understanding of the intention that before he had been intimating to Constanze in partially concealed manner these words seemed to conceal in a similarly ambiguous way, and although even now positive conclusions about the good woman's disposition were possible, he nevertheless found the tone of cheerful rejection somewhat disturbing, even insulting.

The Countess looked to the other two gentlemen as she and Nolten passed by; yet, since the Italian was at that moment telling a long and amusing story that might not have been of the most delicate sort for feminine ears, Constanze withdrew once again, and Theobald was quick to keep her company.

They descended the broad stairway to the gardens, and the Countess declared in a droll and teasing manner her joy at the ease with which she was able to slide along on the frozen surface of the snow while her escort at times would unexpectedly find his foot sinking through it. But all the cheery lightness of her attitude weighed but little against the painter's pensive gravity. They came to a dark group of tall Scots pines that marked the entry to the so-called Beautiful Grotto. It stretched some length below a heavily wooded cliff and led directly into the great hall of the orangery. Quite cleverly the whole arrangement was laid out so as to provide strollers with the most surprising experience, when, especially at this particular time of year, having moved from the dead winter gardens into ghastly darkness, they then, after some hundred paces, through broad glass doors, suddenly saw a bright green, warm spring shining magically before them.

Theobald insisted they take a tour of the grotto, and the Countess, as yet unacquainted with the place, hesitated briefly and then took her escort's arm. They walked along an iron railing that guided them safely along the walls, and they had gone a stretch, treading cautiously, when Constanze, still hoping in vain to see the end of the corridor, anxiously insisted that they should turn back right away. Nolten insisted that they continue all the way, and finally he convinced her. But, in persistent fear of making a misstep or colliding with a protruding part of the rock wall, she held close and ever closer to her guide, and, as the two walked along softly and silently beside each other, how strange an experience it was for our friend, with so much youthful beauty so closely yet silently present at his side, breathing gently. His heartbeat quickened, and, with even the wonder and grandeur of such a place having an intensifying effect on his senses, his fantasy rose to a certain sense of solemnity, with everything seeming to portend for him that something extraordinary, something decisive was about to occur.

And this happened only too soon and in a completely different way than he could have imagined; for in that very moment when ahead of him a dimly shining light is promising that they are approaching the exit, he believes that he hears a voice coming from that same direction, the well-known tone of which makes him suddenly stand still as if rooted to the spot. Constanze feels him give a start, senses his breathing quicken impetuously, sees him clutch his fist to his breast. "What is it? For God's sake, Nolten, what is the matter with you?" He is silent. "Aren't you feeling well? I implore you, do speak!"

"No fear, noble lady! Don't worry — but I am going no further — not one step — think what you will, but just don't ask me!"

"Nolten!" the Countess responded urgently, "what is this senseless behavior? Come! Am I to freeze here until I am ill? What do you mean to do? I am leaving this place at once — will you follow me, or shall I go alone? Let go of me! I command you." — He tightens his grip on her. "Nolten, I shall call out if you persist!"

"Yes, call out, call him to us — he is not far away from us — I heard his voice, the voice of my worst and deadliest enemy — Duke Adolph is near!"

Only now did Constanze seem to understand; she stood speechless, not moving.

"The moment has come!" Theobald cried out, "I feel it, now or never, the secret must out that for months now has been gnawing and tearing at my life, that will ruin me if I cannot, at last, cast it out of by breast — Constanze! Don't you sense it? Oh, that I could look into your eyes, that I could read on your brow that you have long since guessed!"

"Quiet, Nolten! Be silent — for the sake of my peace, not another word! Move forward, that way, towards the light —"

"That way? no, nevermore! have mercy — Not that I fear him, the arrogant one — only that the sight of him is unbearable to me — now, just now, as if Hell had sent him, he comes to poison my every brief happiness! I hate him, hate him, because he is on the prowl for your love, Constanze! Is that not so? can you deny it? And might he have a hope? This man? Give me some sign! Let me know! You know everything, you know what I suffer; my heart, my desire cannot be unknown to you; angel! O heavenly angel, give me a sign! Let a whisper tell me, let a gentle handclasp show me what you secretly intend for me, what your kindness might demurely accord me! Believe me, a God has led us here, has started by stirring up the bitterness within me, has then brought together all, yes all — the hate, the despair, the anxiety, the boundless rapture of being near you here in this hidden corner — in order at last to call forth my heart, to tear this confession from me, and also to unlock your lips — so speak then, O speak! every minute counts!" He drew the trembling, silent woman to him. Her head sinks involuntarily upon his breast, while her tears flow and his kiss burns upon her neck. Pressing his lips to her dense locks he would have liked to have smothered to death in the sweetly dizzying fragrance of her tresses — the ground seemed to open under Constanze's feet — heaven and earth seemed to swim before her closed eyes — her thoughts plunge down into a night of blissful torment — enticing images in a burning rosy glow, alternating with threatening, green-eyed masks, press in upon her — yet still her knees hold her upright, still she makes no sound, not a sigh, her body seized but briefly by a fleeting shudder. More powerfully and ardently the magnificent woman feels herself embraced; then suddenly the step of another person rustles near them; sudden terror seizes Theobald, and before he can turn to the side out of the way they feel the clothing of the person passing by brush against them. Fortunately the crisis is then passed. It cannot have been anyone but the Duke. Theobald can breathe again. Constanze, motionless in his arms, seems to have noticed nothing of it all. After a few moments she comes to herself again, as if waking from a dream — "Away, away!" she cries with penetrating voice — "where am I? What am I doing here? We must get out, get out!" With a forceful gesture she tears herself away and hurries ahead, leaving Theobald behind, barely able to follow. A blinding sea of sunlight greets them as they hurry towards the doorway of the conservatory hall in full bloom. Nolten is just about to catch up to the Countess, but the large glass door slams shut behind her with a clatter, and Nolten, unable to open it, watches her adored form disappear among the leaves and oranges. His senses all as if intoxicated, embarrassed, confused, tormented by fear, he stands alone. A second time he tries the accursed lock on the conservatory door, but in vain, and he finds himself forced to go back the way they had come. Furious, he runs on a ways until he is near the fateful spot, where he stops and asks himself whether what happened here was an illusion or reality. It seemed impossible to him that Constanze had just now been standing here between the rock walls, that he had held her, her and no other, in his arms, heard her bosom beating against his. How cold and indifferent the darkness now lay about him, how the raw masses of rock seemed to know nothing at all of the gracious presence whose divinity had just now made the night all around glow crimson. Here resounded the cries of his beloved, here the tear had fallen from her beautiful eye. Oh, that no gentle spirit voice can be heard to assure me that, yes, it was here that it happened! Know thy happiness, O doubting heart! Embrace and seize fast the full meaning, if you can, for boundless is your fortune, and even if you were never to see her again, if you were to be banished forever by her anger, her pride! Was she not yours, devoted to you for a full, eternal moment? Oh, this moment should enrich a destitute, empty eternity.

Aglow with excitement our friend left the grotto and, in order as best he could to collect himself, he intentionally took a circuitous route back to the hall where the company was gathered.

"You were gone some time!" the Count called out to him, "and that's made you miss the Duke, who was here for an hour this morning, but has gone again."

The casualness of this greeting, to which he replied by briefly begging pardon for his lateness, and the calm evident in Constanze's behavior were enough to convince Theobald that their absence together had gone unnoticed. Yet he was inclined to be put off by the way the lovely woman carried on: she struck him almost as a different person, serious without being dejected, reserved and courteous without being distant; an insignificant question that he asked her she answered more naturally and with more presence of mind than he, the questioner, possessed at that same moment. All the while her bearing and expression seemed more to forgive silently than to condone what had happened — indeed, it appeared as though she were totally denying any recollection of the events at all.

It was not long before lunch was announced, to which the Count had gone ahead and invited the Italian, this to the by no means small displeasure of Nolten, who then also had to endure the fact that the Italian requested the pleasure of offering Her Excellency the Madame Countess his arm on the way to the dairy house.

The small meal turned out to be more plentiful even than expected, for in addition to the foreign wine that had accompanied the Count in the sleigh, they enjoyed a rare and tasty bit of fowl, upon the serving of which the Count did not fail to note that the company had the gallantry of His Highness to thank for the exceptional shore bird, the Duke having shot it by the large pond.

The Italian was especially partial to the fine Roussillon and chattered a jumbled mix of all manner of things, which at any other time Theobald would have found more irritating than it was now, when he was content to hide his distraction behind much noise. Since their guest understood no German, they spoke in his language, while Constanze, who had no command of Italian, spoke French, and our friend found in the foreign language a welcome kind of barrier between himself and his present feelings; but strangely he also found that this made the vivid scene of that morning shift all the more into the realm of the unbelievable, with even Constanze receding for him into an uncertain distance, no matter how near him her external form was at the moment. He looked upon the hours just gone by — if indeed he really was supposed to have lived them at all — as a long distant past, yet the present seemed to him to be in no way more real and actual, and the future a total absurdity.

As tolerably as Theobald's mood progressed in this manner, it was soon to be as bitterly disturbed. The foreign artist soon took the opportunity to practice his high spirits upon the man, whom he surely in no way could have taken to be a rival. It started with gently mocking remarks, but then came highly indiscreet questions to which Nolten at first responded in good-natured fun but that he then began to answer quite sharply, yet without wanting to spur his adversary to the level of anger that nevertheless soon enough emerged in the most improper way, causing Nolten to rise quickly to his feet and suggest to the screaming man that they settle the matter outside so that at least the ears of the others would not be offended. Constanze had already left the table.

"You are my witness!" the hot-tempered man called to the Count. "You must admit that the Signor has intentionally taken my joke the wrong way so that he could insult me. But he shall not succeed, as sure as I live, the Signor will afford me satisfaction!"

"With pleasure!" Theobald responded, "yet I am inclined to think it would be I who could be the first to make this demand; and in any case I would have renounced my right to do so because your words cannot insult my honor, neither in my own eyes nor in the eyes of those present. However, should you be inclined to try to salvage your honor in some way, I am resolved to do everything that I can to those ends, however ridiculous I would feel in doing so."

"Ridiculous, Signor?" the Italian crowed triumphantly, misinterpreting the word and laughing hideously as he did so, "ridiculous? Yes, yes, well yes, you are right on that point. I can almost pronounce myself satisfied with this confession, hee, hee, hee!"

Nolten was about to explain the bitter truth to the impertinent fellow when the Count signaled him to hold off, and he heeded him all the more willingly the more he thought of Constanze and her decided aversion to such discussions of honor. But the Italian wanted to take further pleasure in his victory and turned to his man saying: "Congratulate yourself for getting off so easily, my dear painter. A bit more respectful in the future, would be my advice. Otherwise you may measure your German blade against an Italian one, or to put it better, I might one day gladly enjoy the pleasure of raising my scarpello against — a simple German paintbrush — do you understand?[14]

"Very well, sir," Nolten replied calmly, "I believe you would face that test the sooner the better; in this matter I shall, even today, express myself to you in greater detail and in best form. In the meantime, with regard to the 'German paintbrush,' you may well disdain the artist in me without even having come to know him, yet I do justice to the sculptor whose works I have just observed; they are excellent, and in fact to such a degree that it strikes me as a shameless lie when you, Sir, call yourself their creator."

This last attack clearly took the foreigner somewhat aback, although he acted as though he had heard nothing; but he became still more embarrassed when Nolten took a closer look at his face, shook his head, and, with a skeptical smile, motioned to the Count — then another probing gaze at the strange physiognomy of the Italian, then another, and yet another — "Easy, now, my friend!" cried Theobald, seizing the fellow by his mustache since he was just about to slip out the door, "I believe we are acquainted!" — and, surprise, the false mustache came off in Nolten's hands; the poor devil himself fell trembling to his knees, looking like a totally different person as — the barber Wispel, Nolten's runaway servant.

The Count could hardly believe his eyes when he saw this, and our friend, unsure whether he should laugh or be angry, exclaimed: "So you dare, you miserable fellow, after stealing from me so shamefully, to try such deception, such foolishness with me anew — and in this part of the country, where the prison awaits you? Just how did you come by these clothes and even come to play this apocryphal role?"

Indeed, for all his indignation, both affected and genuine, Nolten could barely suppress a hearty laugh. He was no longer even surprised that he could have been deceived about who this person was. For this fellow was clearly no longer the lean, splinter-thin Wispel of old; he must have done especially well on his recent journeys, and he had concealed many of his old mannerisms or suppressed them for a few hours, and then his artificially darkened skin color, altered voice, changed hairstyle, beard, and the rest of his ensemble — all that aided his foolish quiproquo of a deception. From his confessions it gradually came to light that he had come into the service of the Italian sculptor in much the same way as he had once come to work for Theobald; this was all the easier to achieve since he had still retained from his earlier vagabond days some knowledge of his master's language and was thus able to be of service to that gentleman as an interpreter on his travels in Germany, at whose border Wispel had made his acquaintance. The fine clothes he wore were in part a gift from his new master, while in part he had also made secret use of the artist's wardrobe in order to pull off this most recent tour de force of a performance. The Italian, who had arrived only yesterday, was staying in the city and was not to come out to the castle until this evening to arrange his pieces. Yet since as the result of a misunderstanding the workmen had, to otherwise no avail, hurried out early in the morning, Wispel had found himself irrepressibly tempted to act the part of the famous man for them and for any other strangers who might by chance be present, able, as he was, to imitate the bizarre personality of that gentleman in an albeit exaggerated yet still not totally unsuccessful way. He himself, he now confessed, had felt very sorry when Nolten, his former employer, had so unexpectedly become involved in the game, and even now he did not really know what had tempted him for the moment to adopt such an offensive attitude towards him.

"But my dear fellow, how could you be so unbelievably rude, so impertinent towards me? Have you forgotten the score between us that I have yet to settle?"

"Ah, my most charming, my divine sir, how could I not but remember that? but that's in good hands — it's likely about a half a Carolin of my wages that you still owe me — a bagatelle — if it's convenient, but I insist, any time when you have a chance, a brief note will suffice —"

At this point, Wispel received an unexpected slap in the face from Theobald, making his skin sting. "You shameless rascal, a trip to jail for fraud is what I owe you! But account for what I am asking you about: how could you forget yourself that way towards your former benefactor?"

"Ah," he answered, now completely reverting to his customary affectations, clearing his throat and batting his eyes, "heaven knows how that happened, I behaved that way so as to make myself unrecognizable and not let my feelings show, and that's why I was so hot-tempered, so malicious; nor do I deny that I might also have felt a tempting desire to revel in my own hot southern blood, and so — and then — but surely you'll admit, Monsieur, I did rather well at affecting that imperious tone in harassing you and in capturing the properly refined tact for dealing with the point of honor. Wouldn't you say? I beg you, tell me what you think?"

As he went on this way, his vanity was clearly so in earnest, and he was so intent on hearing a flattering opinion from Nolten, that all the painter and the Count could do was stare in amazement at the most absurd form of pride with which this individual was plagued as if by a disease. If they recalled in detail the single moments in which this fellow, step-by-step that day, had made his presence felt, first when Theobald arrived, then with the Count, and finally when he played the man of the world for Constanze, they almost would have had to feel ashamed if the whole affair had not been so funny and novel. Even Constanze, who was called back to the dining room by her brother, could barely suppress a smile after she had learned of the unbelievable deception, although she looked upon the unmasked man, whose humiliation she imagined to be more painful than was fair, almost with a feeling of embarrassment, as one would a deranged person. The questions that she directed at him were of such a truly naive delicacy as to cause an almost comically touching contrast between the noble woman and that despicable creature. It actually made Theobald almost feel a certain degree of sympathy with the poor sinner, and when Wispel approached him most eloquently about taking him back into his service, Nolten, while of course not able to agree to such an arrangement, nevertheless did promise him that, aside from the warning that he felt he owed the Italian sculptor, he would cause him no harm. With that Wispel took his leave with all appropriate decency, although he was denied his wish to kiss Constanze's hand.

The company made no attempt to conceal the conciliatory impression with which this last episode had left them. The Countess herself found the recollection of the morning easier because its effect had, at least outwardly, to a certain degree been supplanted by so many other things; except that as soon as Nolten attempted to approach her she showed a shy and uneasy evasiveness. In general, he might quite rightly have told himself, her behavior could not be interpreted as unfavorable for him, and indeed he was no longer able to overlook in her the deeply rooted seed of genuine love, hoping that its further development would be steady, if slow. Except that any rashness, any urgent impetuosity, however much they were part of his temperament, he had to resolve to avoid, and we ourselves are of the opinion that with such resolve he had a fine enough idea of how to reckon his own advantage and the disposition of women of Constanze's worth.

They all would have liked to have met the real Italian sculptor, yet evening was fast approaching, and it was unlikely that the artist would still come; in addition, Constanze insisted on returning home, and so they prepared to depart.

Nolten rode rapidly after the Count's sleigh for a while, but soon lingered behind on his horse. He had time to immerse himself in thoughts about the day's events and his worries and hopes, and all the while the moon shone down ever more brightly on the twilit snowscape. What all had actually changed in the few hours since he last rode this way! How much closer had he come, despite all rational thoughts and assumptions, to his most desired goal — indeed even attaining that goal and making it his for all the future. And as he pondered this turn of events with ever greater astonishment, all the more was he assailed by his old belief that there are moments when an inner god drives a person forward recklessly and inexorably towards some momentous decision with the result that he, that his fate and fortune succeed virtually beyond his wildest dreams. He felt thrilled to his very core; he probed with wide-open eye the deep blue of the nocturnal sky and called upon the stars to feel his bliss with him. What might be going on now in Constanze's mind! — he would have given the world to know that one thing, and still once again he gave thanks for his uncertainty, since it allowed him to believe whatever he wished. Ought not in her breast too the rapturous tumult of joy, fear, and hope be raging? And is not the fundament of her soul, like the depths of a calm sea, now ruled by that infinite peace that resides in the awareness of an exalted love? — Those were his thoughts, and in such manner did he reflect on still many a matter that he found greatly uplifting; impetuously he spurred on his horse, as if he were intent upon crowning all his desires before the day was out.

T HE SAME WEEK BROUGHT LETTERS for Theobald from Neuburg, as usual to Larkens's address. Full of desire to know their content and devoutly hoping that it would dispel his every doubt about Agnes, he tore open the envelope. He was seized with the most peculiar compassion every time he saw those true-hearted phrases that the girl thought her beloved was to read, and that our actor once again could only claim for himself, since they were all written in response to what he had written, admittedly along the lines of what Nolten once would have said, yet nevertheless felt as if transposed through every fiber of his own deepest feelings. Indeed, in such moments he felt like he was a double being, and not infrequently he found it difficult to exclude himself, his own ego, from involvement in this tender relationship.

As for Agnes's letter, its words struck him at first as somewhat puzzling, until he laid hands on a longer message from her father, which he read quickly page after page with ever growing astonishment. The old man refers to his earlier letter to Theobald in which, as far as was possible at the time, he had explained the girl's strange confusion. Yet now, since some recently discovered facts have altered the situation considerably, he wants to tell the whole story again from the beginning, and so he explains at length what we have already imparted to the reader. Several striking events had eventually left the forester with no further doubts that a form of insanity was silently in play. A doctor was called in to consult, and with that man's insightful help it was soon possible to coax from the girl the actual cause of the trouble. Here the alert observer of such abnormal conditions is bound to note with utmost interest that simply admitting the secret was in and for itself decisive for the cure. For from the very moment when word of the encounter with the Gypsy girl passed Agnes's lips, the demon that had held ensnared the poor creature's soul seemed to release its prey, and a heart-rending stream of the most intense tears appeared to announce the return of her reason. But the revelation of that secret cause was all the less difficult because Agnes herself, since the second meeting with the Gypsy, had begun to harbor a certain mistrust towards her, which she was now not exactly loath to have encouraged. And truly touching it was to see with what desire she took in every word that the others brought forth to prove the obvious deception. With its expression of anxiety giving way to grateful joy, her face vividly expressed the death throes of her superstitious conscience, to which the sweet reason of her father's eloquence now gave the coup de grace. And nevertheless she still felt a kind of inner dichotomy, finding it hard to adjust, and, much as someone who was blind grows accustomed only slowly to the light that cheers the rest of the world, so it took some time before Agnes was able to affirm her fortune and dare to see herself the equal of others. Often it still seemed to her as if some dark witness of her fate were lying in wait behind her back, listening and plotting revenge because she had escaped its bonds. But the transgressor who, by a solemn absolution spoken by the Heavenly Father, suddenly feels himself released from the bonds of an all-embracing Hell cannot breathe easier than Agnes after her gloomy phantom had departed for good. How differently she could now think of Nolten! How boldly her love now tested again the freedom of its wings! How special she found everything that was said or done about him. If someone said his name, she would repeat the name to herself as if blissfully in awe of something strange and wonderful and then rapturously call it out aloud, leaving others struggling to comprehend her. If her eye chanced to light on something he had written, she would think the letters were speaking to her and look at them in a completely new light — in short, it seemed as though he had been bestowed upon her just that very day, as though she were now for the first time Nolten's bride.

This innocent intoxication breathed from the letter from her that Larkens now held in his hand. She avoided as much as possible any mention of those disturbing events, and her words did not betray the least unease about how Theobald would take the history of her illness that her father — with her knowledge but without her being allowed to read the letter — had honestly conveyed to him.

Astonished and touched, Larkens laid the pages on the table after he had read them through two or three times with the greatest care. He had trouble making sense of the alarming confusion, in gathering his thoughts and getting a calm picture of the whole affair in order then to resolve what to do. About the honesty with which the events had been presented he harbored not a moment's doubt; everything bore too clearly the stamp of inner truth. But what especially gave him pause about the whole matter was the intrusion of the Gypsy woman. For immediately it had stuck him like a lightning bolt that he knew this person and that her unusual tie to Nolten was not unknown to him. Going by the specific image that he had of her character, he was somewhat taken aback by the false game she had played with Agnes, yet he had good reason not to confuse her in any way with the deceptive women common to her race. Indeed he was seized by the most profound feeling of sympathy when he thought of how this inscrutable creature, who was guilty of Agnes's derangement, was herself a sorry victim of insanity. And indeed so it was, with her condition involving a passion for Theobald, of the wondrous origins of which we shall give the reader an account in what is to follow. The unfortunate woman believed that in Agnes she had a rival from whose threat she had to free herself, and unfortunately, as we have seen, chance came all too readily to the aid of this intention. Moreover, her cunning was all too likely to have been of the kind that in the deranged is often paired with an extreme of good nature, and Larkens was all the more inclined to excuse her as a result of the fact that he had come to know Elisabeth — the girl's name — from her most innocent, even childlike side. How much actual lie and how much self-deception were involved in that fateful prophecy would thus not be easy to decide, only that it now becomes all the more understandable that the appearance and the whole bearing of the prophetess were able to have such a powerful and captivating effect on Agnes's pathologically sensitive feelings.

For a few moments the actor was resolved to hurry to his friend with the whole pack of letters. But, with the whole affair more closely considered, wisdom ruled out such a step. Nolten would not at the present time be able to view matters in an unprejudiced way, and it was to be feared that he would not just now have welcomed being convinced of the girl's faultlessness and that, pushed to the limit from two sides, dragged to the brink of contradictory passions, he would have been left with no alternative but to despair of everything. Larkens saw all this clearly and for a while was truly at a loss what to do. "I must come up with a master stroke," he cried, "I find hesitation dangerous, it is time to beat the devil!"

Above all he wanted to attempt, come what may, to bring about a break with the Countess. Various signs had recently given him rather serious indications of Nolten's feelings for her, and he began to have increasing doubts about his friend's openness on this point — as indeed the incident in the park had at that time been kept a total secret from Larkens. For now, he was thinking only of calming the girl quickly with yet another letter, which he now, immediately and with unaccustomed warmth and cheerfulness of expression, set to paper.

THERE PASSED, UNTIL NOLTEN WAS once again invited to the Zarlins, two full weeks, and although this long interval seemed to our friend all the more unbearable the more portentous his present status with Constanze was, he still found himself confused and uncertain as to whether fear or joy held greater sway in him. But then on the appointed evening when he found himself with Larkens once again within those beloved walls in those noble surroundings, and when the Countess now welcomed the gathering and even greeted him with a cheerfulness that he had rarely encountered in her before, then he felt himself and his whole being as if bathed in the glow of a light that transformed all the past and future of his life as if with a magical power; and still it was only her lighthearted bearing and the noble freedom of her behavior that he found so profoundly rejuvenating and that, apart from any other apprehension he might have felt, called forth in him the most selfless compassion by assuring him that the beautiful equanimity of her soul had been restored, the disruption of which he counted as his own transgression.

Similar happy feelings enlivened the rest of the company as well, and Nolten felt his last remaining oppressive concern fall away when he heard the news that Duke Adolph would not be present.

The gentlemen and ladies sat paired off together when the Countess turned to Larkens, saying: "You spoke of something special with which you would favor us this evening; tell the company now about what you have in mind; I have no doubt that we may look forward to something quite lovely or at least something unusual."

"Your compliment," Larkens answered good-naturedly, "harbors something so dauntingly challenging that I am just now growing a bit shy about offering up my treasure. Really, it is always risky when one or two members of a cultivated circle attempt to take it totally upon themselves to entertain the others, and on top of that my offering is such that it is unlikely to attract general interest, at least in so far as I am involved in it. But what alone gives me some consolation is the support of my friend Nolten, who will on this occasion present you with an entirely new genre of his art."

"I for my part," responded the painter, "must most humbly beg the company not, on this condition, to yield a nail width in the demands they place upon Larkens, since my contribution merely embellishes and elucidates the main presentation and cannot, by itself, lay any claim to importance." —

"In short, O gracious ladies and gentlemen," the actor broke in on Nolten, "what we are about to present to you on this occasion is nothing other than a shadow play."

"A shadow play!" the ladies cried out, clapping their hands, "ah, that is incomparable! Really? Are we going to see a real Chinese shadow play?"

"Of course," said the Count, "and a completely original one at that, for which Nolten has painted the scenes on glass, and this gentleman, of whom we hear all too little as a poet, has produced the text. As far as I know, it consists entirely of a dramatic fable that is completely of Herr Larkens's invention."

"This fable," the actor noted, "and the place where it takes place, are, I must admit, peculiar enough, and a brief explanatory introduction is required to ensure that the poet is not to be run out of town.

"I had, when I was still in school, a friend whose way of thinking and aesthetic aspirations went hand in hand with my own; we spent our idle hours together and soon created our own sphere of poetry, and even today I cannot but be touched when I think back to those days. Whatever may be said of what came later in my life, I readily confess having enjoyed at that time my happiest days ever. Alive, serious, and genuine, I see them all in my mind's eye, those figures born of our imaginations; and if I could capture in my soul but *one* ray of the poetic sun that warmed us then, so truly golden as it was, it at least would not deny me a cheering pleasure; in fact it would forgive the mature man for taking an idle stroll in the misty landscape of that poetry and even bringing back a small piece of the ancient stone of that beloved ruin. But let me come to the point. We invented for our poetic work a realm lying beyond the known world, a secluded island, where supposedly once lived a race of mighty heroes, though divided into various tribes, boundaries, and nuances of character, yet with a basically uniform religion. This island we called Orplid, and we imagined it to be located in the Pacific Ocean between New Zealand and South America. Orplid was also the chosen name of the city of the most important kingdom; it was said to have been founded by the gods, and the Goddess Weyla, from whom the main river of the island took its name, was its special patron. Piece by piece and following the order of the main epochs we told each other the history of these peoples. Of remarkable wars and adventures there was no lack. Our mythology had a few points in common with that of the Greeks, but for the most part it was all original; it included as well a subworld of elves, fairies, and goblins.

"Orplid, while once the apple of the eye of heavenly beings, ultimately had to suffer their wrath when the old simplicity gradually began to give way to a pernicious refinement of its thought and culture. A horrible fate decimated the human inhabitants; even their dwellings sank into oblivion, with only Weyla's favorite creation, the castle and city of Orplid, allowed to remain, although deserted of all life, as a sorrowfully beautiful monument to past greatness. The gods turned from this scene, with that exalted queen rarely ever granting it even a glance and doing that only for the sake of a single mortal soul who, by decree of a higher will, was long to survive the general destruction.

"In more recent times, after an interval of nearly a thousand years, it nonetheless came to pass that a number of European people, mostly from the lower social classes, discovered the island by chance and established a colony there. We two friends joined them in rummaging through the magnificent remains of an ancient culture. As luck would have it, a university-trained archaeologist, an Englishman named Harry, had come along on the ship; his small library and other materials of a variety of uses had been saved; all manner of sustenance nature herself rendered in great abundance; the new colony took better shape with each day, and a second generation was flourishing at the time when today's play opens.

"As to this dramatic, or rather very undramatic trifle, my wishes would be fulfilled if the esteemed audience were to be able with some empathy to find their way into the spiritual climate of my island, if they were to measure the willful arrangement of my piece in a sympathetic way, and focus more on the character, on the pathological aspect of the piece. The whole thing took shape, I know not how, only a short time ago, after I felt the old memories resonating once again in my ears one evening. A long-harbored favorite tragic idea I believed would find especially compelling expression in the character of the Last King of Orplid. On the other hand I felt compelled to weave in, in a comical way, two modern characters taken from real life, of whom the one has made a name for himself in the career of my friend Nolten in such a way that this person — who is said to have been once again of late lurking about our city — will strike some of those present as a not totally unknown face."

At this point, some of the curious put their heads together, and when it emerged that Nolten's thieving servant would make an appearance in the shadow play there was a general expression of hearty pleasure; they all made ready for an entertaining diversion, with only Tillsen feeling somewhat hurt about that comic reference, although no one else thought there was anything insulting about it.

"On another matter," the actor went on, "as the comrade of that fellow I present my own former Sancho Panza; I enjoyed copying these two wretches so faithfully, Nolten did not miss a single detail, and the company must forgive us for forcing them to look into the mentalities of these low-life types."

In the meantime, Larkens had had the required apparatus brought from his house; the servant brought in a small brown box in which the implements of his magic were locked away; at once, the actor took out a manuscript, leafed through it, and said: "Regarding the way in which the tableaux accompany the text, it is self-evident that the stage must at times, albeit seldom, remain empty, that not every scene could offer the painter something to work with, and that from any one scene he was usually able to portray only one moment, only the one major constellation — and still there is as much variety as possible in the images. And now I have but one request regarding the way the dialogue is presented. I shall, of course, speak the parts of all male figures by altering my voice as they speak with each other; yet for the feminine voices and the children one or another of the ladies should really stand by and read from the script along with me. Which of the ladies would be so kind? You two, Fräulein von R. and Fräulein von G. — you two gave us such great pleasure at the amateur theater; to you I direct my request in the name of all present."

The two lovely ladies had to consent, and they stepped aside with the copies of the script they had been given to read through it in advance, while Larkens asked the Countess for a heated salon with white walls and went to set up his apparatus.

After a short time, a small bell was rung to invite the company to the darkened salon. Behind a Spanish screen that was open on one side, Larkens and his two assistants had taken their places beside the magic lantern that for the moment was casting a bright round circle of light on the ceiling. The audience formed a half circle, and Nolten took a seat that would allow him to keep his eye on Constanze.

After all had grown quiet, an introductory sinfonia began, played on the piano by a member of the group behind a curtain and accompanied by Larkens on the cello. With the last chords there appeared on the widest completely empty wall of the salon an impressively sized depiction of a foreign city and castle, in the moonlight, the lake rippling all around, in the left foreground three seated figures, and the dialogue began.

We do not hesitate to invite the reader to follow along with the shadow play, since it later plays a role in our story with the most portentous results. In addition, it might give a vivid impression of the inner life of the actor, who has already attracted our attention and who will, in what follows, invite our sympathy still more.

The Last King of Orplid
A Phantasmagorical Intermezzo
First Scene

A view of the city Orplid and its castle; in the foreground, a portion of the lake is visible. Night is falling. Three inhabitants are seated on a bench before a house in the lower city; they are conversing. SUNTRARD, *the fisherman, with* HIS SON, *and* LÖWENER, *the blacksmith.*

SUNTRARD   Let us sit here, and then after a while we shall see the moon rise, there, between those two roofs.

HIS SON   Father, in the old days did people live in all those houses up there?

SUNTRARD   Indeed they did. Sixty years ago, when our fathers, driven by storm, chanced to reach the shore of this island that we call The Unicorn and made their way further inland, searching the whole area, all they encountered was an empty city of stone; the people and race that had built themselves these dwellings and cellars had probably died out a good thousand years before; we think this happened by special decree of the gods, for neither famine nor all too severe disease exist on this island.

LÖWENER   A thousand years ago, you say, Suntrard? When I think of those old inhabitants, then, by my soul, I feel just like when I get a ringing in my left ear.

SUNTRARD   My father tells of how he, when still a boy, with only a few people, seventy-five in all, landed in their broken ship and how he and his comrades were so in awe of such a beauty of mountains, valleys, rivers, and growth, and about how they wandered around for five or six days, until from afar they saw something dark on a calm, crystal-clear lake, something resembling a wondrous stone formation or also like the crown of a grey jagged-petalled flower. But then, when they approached it with two boats, it was a craggy city of strange and massive construction.

HIS SON   A city, father?

SUNTRARD   Why do you ask, my child? This very city that you live in. — They were not a little afraid, thinking they might meet with a bad reception; they camped quietly the whole night, in a constant downpour, outside the walls, for they dared not approach or enter. But then, when morning dawned, they were seized by what was almost a still more awful dread; no cocks crowed, no wagons could be heard, no baker opened his shop, no smoke rose from the chimneys. Someone suggested the image that the sky lay over the city like a grey eyebrow over a staring dead eye. Finally, they all entered through the archway of the open gate; they heard not a mortal sound other than their own footsteps and the rain that rolled down off the roofs, even though the sun was already shining bright and golden in the streets. Nor did anything stir within the houses.

HIS SON   Not even a mouse?

SUNTRARD   Well, maybe there were mice, my child. *He kisses the boy.*

LÖWENER   Yes, but neighbor, I was born and grew up here, like you, and I still feel peculiar every time at night I walk through one of the empty streets, and the sound is like someone tapping on empty barrels.

HIS SON   But why do we new people almost all live in this little group here at the one end of the city and not up there in those expansive, beautiful dwellings?

SUNTRARD   I'm not so sure about that myself; that's just the tradition from our parents. Also, up there we wouldn't be nestled together so close and secure, as we are down here.

LÖWENER   Where we live, down here in the lower city, that's probably where the shops of the tradesmen and craftsmen were in olden times. But the whole outer ring of the city is a six-hour walk.

SUNTRARD   When the moon has risen, let's walk a ways up that way, to where the sun clock is.[15] Neighbor, when I was a little boy, and we lads would go wandering through these eerie places late of an evening as far as the sun clock, then I was always tormented by this impulse to touch the stone

68

with my finger, because I harbored the belief that the stone had sucked up the warm rays of the sun, as though it were a sponge, and would give off sparks that would have to look wondrous in the moonlight.

LÖWENER   Listen, what have they heard recently about the ghost of the king that wanders the north coast?

SUNTRARD   That's not a ghost! as I have often assured you. It's the thousand-year-old king who once ruled this island. Death passed him by; they say the gods wanted him to go through this long trial period and loneliness to make him ready so that afterwards he would become one of them, as a result of his great virtue and bravery. I don't know if that is so; but he is flesh and bones, as we are.

LÖWENER   I don't believe that, Fisherman.

SUNTRARD   I have it for sure and certain, that Kollmer, who is a judge in Elnedorf, now visits him secretly; otherwise, no mortal sees him.

HIS SON   Is it not so, Father, he wears a cloak and in his hair a small iron crown with points?

SUNTRARD   Quite right, and his locks are still brown; they do not fade.

LÖWENER   That's enough! it's already late. The light there on the farthest corner of the castle has already gone out. That's where Mr. Harry lives; he stays up the latest. I still want to stop awhile at the tavern. Good night!

SUNTRARD   Sleep well, Löwener, my friend. Come, son, let's go home to your mother.

Second Scene

A desolate beach. In the North.

KOLLMER *alone*   Here he is wont to walk, this is the beach.
The one he paces off with his measured stride.
I wonder where he might be. Perhaps
His errant mind took him on other paths,

For oft I could discern, that his mind
And body wandered differing trails.

O wondrous! I lament his fate,
When I think — what hardly seems believable —
That nature in a mortal being
Outlives itself by centuries —
What? A thousand years? — a thousand — yes, now I feel
For the first time a sudden fear and anxiety,
As if I had to count it out on the spot, live it through
In one breath — Away! That brings madness!

Hm, a thousand years; once a king — oh, a time
So slow that stones, as they say, stones can grow.
Past and present and future —
If there existed for reason yet a third term
Then he would have to linger there in thought.

Yet if it is once a thousand, then possibly
Countless more can come; don't they say
That even a ball, thrown past the boundary
Of the sky to where the breath of the earth no longer
    reaches,
Cannot fall back again, no,
It must orbit, eternally, like a star.
And so, I fear, it is here.

They also say of the island Goddess Weyla,
That she fell in love with a flower of rare
Beauty, never seen, a unique miracle.
This the Goddess sealed in the clear fluid
Of the hardest diamond, that it might last
With color and form; verily no,
I would not like to be loved so by Weyla,
Yet that's what she did to this king.

Often I imagined he himself was a god,
So full of charm is his dark countenance;
That is his greatest misfortune, which caused,
As I well and clearly note, a fairy
To be inflamed by burning love for him,
And he cannot escape her service,

70

She has such power over him that,
When oft her thoughts yearn for him,
Day or night, and from the farthest regions,
He must at once hasten to her residence.
When this call goes out to him, then
The thread of his current thoughts
Is at once torn asunder, quite changed
His being then appears, a bright light shimmers through
The dark night of his mind, the long buried spring
Of his hoarse and deadened speech sounds
Suddenly light and gentle, even his expression
Seems more youthful, yet also more in pain:
For grey in hue is hated love's torment.
     Thus surely he ponders in deep sorrow
How he might rid himself of this pain;
That's how I understand the words
That he once let fall to me: "If thou wouldst serve me, so
    go hence
To the city, where lies in some unknown corner
A long lost book in strange writing;
That book is written upon the broad leaves
Of the thranus, our island's sacred plant.
Search for it without rest and bring it."
Then he gave a sympathetic smile, as if he had
Demanded the impossible, and he spoke
No more about it since then. But now
I chanced to hear something recently
About a pair of filthy, ignorant rascals.
They are rumored to have such an old treasure,
Dust-bedecked and unused, lying in their house.
Perhaps, it might be so; so then I wish
To hear from the king a closer description;
And yet I doubt, doubt very much — Hark! Yes, there he
    comes
From the hill. Oh, sorrowful sight!
His stride is weary. Hark, he is talking to himself.

KING   O sea! You

	Green palace of the sun with your golden battlements!
	Which way leads down to your cool stairway?
KOLLMER	(Might I dare call out to him?)
	My dear King!
KING	Who cast my key into the sea?
KOLLMER	My exalted Lord, grant me —
KING	*catching sight of him*
	What do you want here? Who are you? Be gone! Away!
	Be gone! Will you not go? Curse you!
KOLLMER	You no longer know me? To whom you oft
	Have turned your gracious countenance?
KING	It's you; I know you. So tell me then
	Of what we spoke together
	The last time. My head is ill and aged.
KOLLMER	For that book you bade me search.
KING	Right, right, my man. Yet they seek in vain
	What Weyla has hidden, that clever virgin,
	Is it not so?
KOLLMER	Truly, if her own finger itself
	Does not guide me on the way; but we hope for that,
	my King.
	For now, though, tell me more of the sacred book.
KING	More still, my man? That may well be, may be,
	Let me think; wait, I know very well —
	— If only my mind weren't beclouded! Do you see?
	Misery! Misery! Here, here, do you see it? Time
	Has covered my brain with a tough hide.
	But often I can think clearly . . . .
KOLLMER	Oh, poor creature!
	Leave it, let it be, be calm! Lord, what do I see?
	Why do you raise your arms so to heaven,

Shaking your fist in its face? I am frightened.

KING   Ha! My prayer! My morning devotion! Is that it?
          You would teach a king that he must kneel?
          For a hundred years now his knees have been raw —
          What, a hundred —? Oh, I am just a child! Come here,
          And teach me to count — old fingers! Bah!
          Rise, slave, rise! Call upon your brothers all!
          Tell them how to storm the bastion of the gods!
          Be of some service to me, you cowardly villain, you!
          Let us storm hell, and death,
          That lazy monster who sleeps the day away,
          Drag him up here to earth to do his work!
          Many mortals still live; O fool, you,
          To me you too are important! Surely you don't wish
          To suck forever from the vapid light?

KOLLMER   Oh, woe! He's raving.

KING   Quiet, quiet! I have an idea. It is not good
          To affront the gods. Tell me, my fellow,
          Do you know what wise men believe
          Is most hateful to the blessed gods?

KOLLMER   Teach me, O King.

KING   Weyla forbid
          That I should utter what simply thinking
          Can bring her curse. — You do have a sword, yes?

KOLLMER   I have one.

KING   Then spare your life,
          And let us always fear the gods!
          — And what would it help to defy them? Our fate
          Is bound fast to their prophecy,
          Yours as well as mine. Well — so be it, how runs
          The old oracle of the gods? A priest sang
          It to me in my infancy, and then again
          On the day of my coronation.

73

KOLLMER	At once you shall hear it;
	You yourself recently confided it to me.

"A man lives out his natural time,
Yet Ulmon alone will know
The summer to come and go
Ten times one hundred times.

Once a black willow does grow
A child must fell it to earth
Then shall rush the waves of death
In which Ulmon's heart shall glow.

On the rays of Weyla's moon
Ulmon shall ascend
His divine body then to end
Within their azure room."

KING	You speak it right, my man; a sweet oracle!
	I feel those few words fill all round
	The earthly air with Weyla's violet aura.
KOLLMER	Do you fathom the sense of its words, my Lord?
KING	A king, is he not a priest as well?
	Be still! my sacred soul moils
	As does the sea before the storm strikes,
	And like a seer I would proclaim wonders,
	So vital is the spirit within me.
	— Of course, too dim, too dim my eye remains —
	Ha, slave, bring me the book! My dear slave!
KOLLMER	Tell me more about it.
KING	Be patient.
	I've never seen it, nor has any common man.
	By priest's hand written there
	Is what the gods once revealed to those initiated;
	Of things to come, how they grow and evolve,
	As well, how the mysteries of my poor life
	One day are to be explained, that it tells, too.

74

(But let me finish while my words are flowing —)
In Nidru-Haddin's temple once stood guard
The white snake o'er that holy place,
Until the day of doom came
And all mankind died out; see, then
The goddess took that book and bore it away
To another place, and who might divine it?
My key they took as well,
Those heavenly ones, and cast it into the sea.

KOLLMER My Lord, what key is that?

KING The one to the grave
Of the kings.

KOLLMER Why do you tremble? Why grow pale?

KING The magician, she beckons — Thereile draws me to her —
Farewell! I must go —

The two exit on opposite sides.

Third Scene

Night.

An open green by a gentle forest slope near Schmetten Mountain,[16] *not far from the river Weyla.*

THEREILE, *a young fairy princess.* LITTLE FAIRIES *are gathered around her.*

THE KING *to one side, towards the foreground.*

THEREILE Is everyone here?

MORRY Just count us, sister, we are!

THEREILE One, two, three, four, five, six, seven.
Silpelitt, alas, is late again.
She always has her special hiding places!
Well, now go seek her, lazy things,
With lights on your fingers, worn as rings!

The children hurry away

MORRY   *She stays behind secretly, quietly*
                Weithe!

WEITHE   What?

MORRY   Don't you see there
                Your sweetheart by sister Thereile?
                That is why she has sent us away,
                This must be a special day.

WEITHE   Oh, I don't care so much for him.

MORRY   But stay, and let us hear
                The two exchange their kisses here.
                Look, the coy show she puts on
                As haughtily her braids she plies!
                Oh, she alone's the pretty one,
                For us, no one has eyes.

WEITHE   But we are all still young

MORRY   Well, so tell me now, is not this pair
                As silly as any e'er?
                May one of a sweet fairy's brood
                With a mortal long abide?
                True, both are flesh and blood,
                Yet no shadow casts the bride.

WEITHE   Yes, morally it is wrong.

MORRY   But she was always so headstrong.

WEITHE   Morry, we had better flee.
                Staying here, it frightens me.

MORRY   Look at how they end this play,
                Both are standing, turned away;
                Verily, as if in deep slumber
                The King stands motionless.

WEITHE	Oh, how sad the man seems!
	Dear sister, can it truly be
	That a man must know such misery?
MORRY	His brow is furrowed with worry
	His arms he lets sink!
WEITHE	And what does our dear sister think?
MORRY	Were he to me so nice
	I'd let him kiss me in a trice.
WEITHE	But come now, let us go
	To the forest we shall searching go,
	To see if the nightingales so grand
	In our snares perhaps might land. *Both exit.*

Fourth Scene

THE KING *and* THEREILE *alone.*

KING   *to himself*   Be still, but soft, my mind; calm yourself!
So long you lay in untrammeled gloom,
Fleeing all the while into dreams of the void,
What awakens you again out of such slumber?
Lie still awhile yet!
In vain! In vain! The old wheel
Of burning thoughts swings on inexorably
In my poor head!
Will it not end? Must you marvel ever anew
And see your true self? And ask yourself:
"What, I am still alive? I'm still here?" — Once a king,
Ulmon, by name; Orplid was the island;
Well done, my mind, you remember that so cleverly;
And still I distrust you; Ulmon — Orplid —
I barely know these words, I marvel
At their sound — unfathomable
The abyss opens before me — Oh, woe, be not dizzy!

I was a prince? So take heart and believe it on faith.
The noble powers of recollection
Sink wearily in the deep sand
On the long way traversed;
Seldom's the time through a rare parting of the clouds
A fleeting flash lights up the old scene
Of bygone days, wondrous to behold.
Then upon the throne I see a man
Of my appearance, and yet to me a stranger,
A splendid woman at his side, and she's my wife.
Stop, O memory mine, stop awhile!
It does me good, that lovely image accompanies
The king through the city and to the ships.
Yes, so it was; yet now night falls again. —
Strange! Through these shimmering images
I glimpse the tower of an ancient castle,
Just like the one that really rises up there
To the heavens. — Perhaps all is illusion
Of my imagination, and I myself a dream.

He falls silent, thinking, then looks up again.

Hark! upon the earth's moist belly drawn,
The night labors on towards dawn,
While there, drawn into the blue ether,
The traces scant their near silent way flow,
And now and then with steely bow
The merry stars shoot their golden arrows.

THEREILE *still some distance away*
How sweet the night wind caresses the meadow,
And singing now through the vale does blow!
Since now audacious day falls still,
We hear the whisper of earth's teeming throngs
Spin upwards in the tender songs
Of the harmonious airs a'trill.

KING And yet I hear the wondrous voices
Of the tender wind caressing gently

While, lined in uncertain light,
Heaven itself seems to float away.

THEREILE   Like a web the air oft pulses,
Rising up clearer and brighter,
And all the while gentle tones are heard
As blessed elves in the azure hall
To music of the spheres
Amidst their ardent song
Wend their spindles back and forth.

KING   O glorious night, you walk with gentle tread
On black velvet that grows green only in day,
And ethereal humming music aids
Your foot's light tread,
With which you mark off hour by hour,
Lovingly self-forgotten in yourself —
You dream, and creation's soul dreams with you!

Thereile lies down on the lawn, her eyes longingly upon the king. He continues talking to himself.

In the earth's womb, in grove and meadow,
How now all round nature teems
With the ferment of unsated powers!
And yet what peace, what well-being!
That all awakens in our breast
A resonant echo of plenitude and abstinence.
It struggles and rests within my breast
Such an ebb and flow!

Pause.

Almissa— —! Who whispers me this name,
So long forgotten? Was not my wife
Almissa? Why do I think of it now?
The sacred night, bent low over her harp,
Struck the stings while dreaming,
They gave this tone. Perhaps I enjoyed
In such an hour once love's joy— —

A long silence. Looking up he sees Thereile, who has approached him lovingly.

Ha! Am I still here, and you still standing there?
So deep I had sunk into the silent valleys
That memory has furrowed in my mind,
That I now feel I am seeing for the first time
You, the hated witness of my torment.
Did a god cast me out of all human measure
So that your accursed favor
Holds me fast in blissful suffering,
Sating me with sultry magic haze
And showing me the wiles of all love's charms,
While you are consumed in silent grief
About the pleasure you deny yourself?
For this body, despite all best efforts,
Is still thrall to the blood of which it was born;
No hope that I clasp you to me,
In vain this longing lovely breast,
Our kisses, our gazes remain
Fruitless messengers of unbound desire!

To himself

Alas! Must I feign love's lamentation
To win myself pity and salvation? —
So hear, immortal woman, my humble plea,
Cease to deny the truth of you and me!
Banish me from your sight
To end this miserable wondering,
Release my unworthy likeness
From the golden net of your love's pondering.

THEREILE Quite right! Who can pair two things unlike?
When might a cat wed a dog?
And yet they are alike down to the paws.
How, though it have fins, might an arrow,
Like a fish go and swim the seas?
Every thing has its place and role;
And yet I know nothing like the mouth of man

80

That so many services render can:
Oh, it can divide and combine all things,
It eats, kisses, laughs, cries, and sings,
Not rarely it talks when it might better kiss;
And if something must then be spoke,
Then it's the truth I'd welcome most,
But then, it's full of naught but lies.

    For see your brow as you persist declaiming
We are but half alike and that but seeming!
Can he tell the bitter from the sweet
Whose lips have yet cup's rim to meet?
Still, still! not a word I'll hear!
Disputing with you I have as much hope
As I would of teaching a bear the tightrope.
Do as you wish. Go! Follow your path from here!
I am weary of this banter.

KING   Do you mean that?

THEREILE   Mean it? O heaven forbid!
Only now I feel a genuine urge
To spite you by truly loving you.
Come, let us dance! Come, my friend, you must!

She begins to dance.

KING   *to himself*   How I hate her, yet I still find her so beautiful!
Away! I suddenly feel a fear
To abide with this gold-green snakelet here.
Her red lips, so sweetly smiling,
Beckon with poison beguiling
That would half kill with one kiss.
Ha! How she weaves her magic, adding charm to charm!
And yet something holds me back, I know not what.

From afar someone calls: "Thereile! O Thereile!"

KING   Hark!

THEREILE   The children are coming: such shouting!

Fifth Scene

THE ABOVE *and the* CHILDREN *with* SILPELITT

THEREILE   What is wrong, then? What has happened? speak,
Malwy! Or you, Talpe!

MALWY   O sister!

THEREILE   Well! You stand with bated breath. Where is Silpelitt?

SILPELITT   *coming forward*   Here I am!

MALWY   When we were looking for Silpelitt, we couldn't find her at all. We ran a good eleven elf-miles, that you can be-lieve, and searched around in the reeds where she is wont to sit when she has gone astray. Then suddenly, by the hill where the grass grows out of the mole holes, Talpe stops and says: "Don't you hear Silpelitt's voice, she's talking with someone and laughing." With that we turned off our lantern lights and ran to look. And then, O my goodness, Thereile, there sat a big, horrible strong man, and Silpelitt was sitting on his boot, letting him rock her up and down. He was laughing all the while, but with such a malicious face —

TALPE   Sister, I know very well that is the giant, he is called the trusty man.

THEREILE   Why, of all the audacious waywardness, child! Just you wait, you naughty, cowardly thing! Don't you know that this monster kills little children?

TALPE   Heaven forbid, he's only playing with them, he rolls them around on the ground under his boot's sole, laughing and grunting so nicely the whole time and smil-ing so kindly.

THEREILE   *to the king.* He once killed one of my nicest elves play-ing that damnable game. The fellow is a veritable morass of idle boredom.

TALPE   *to one of the other children*   You remember, don't you? You and I overheard him once when he was standing up over his chest in the Brulla swamp with all his clothes on. He was singing so loud and mumbling in between: I'm a water organ, I'm the prettiest water nightingale of all!

THEREILE   Have you been visiting this monster, too, Silpelitt? I surely hope not.

SILPELITT   He does me no harm.

KING   *to himself*   Who is this child? She is not like the others.
Of strange dignity her bearing,
And grave her gaze. No, this is
No fairy child, perhaps the princess
Stole her cruelly from her cradle.

A powerful voice is heard in the distance:

Trallirra — a — ah — oy — ieu
Pfuldararaddada!— —! —!

Those present take fright. The children scream and cling to THEREILE.

THEREILE   Be still! Do be calm! He won't come this way, he's not coming to us. *To the king* That's the voice of the giant we were just talking about.

KING   Hark!

THEREILE   Hark! . . .

KING   That's the echo of his call as it winds and reverberates around the bends of the mountain.

THEREILE   Be calm, children. By now he must already
Have gone round the bend of the mountains.
But now up and away you foolish things all!
And gather up a thousand roses;
Each with the green twilight glow
Of a glowworm closed within,
For me to adorn, ere breaks the light of morn,
My sleeping chamber down below
In the cool mountain crystal!

The children hop away. Thereile turns once again to the king.

Today you're in no mood to dance,
The defiant one again, perchance.
Oh, what all might I do,
To give the smallest joy to you!
Let us rest in gentle rapport,
Like two boats gliding soft to port.
    See how the willow hangs its green locks
Deep into the moist night of the waters,
While there the first morning breeze
Dares e'en now to bend and sway
And steal its first chaste buds away.

KING   And see you not this noble fairy child
Cheered by the breath of night so mild,
Not sensing what danger alluring
Her virtue is ever closer nearing?

THEREILE You're a rogue! That is not true!

KING   Allow at least that we now part,
And, might it be, forever now;
Otherwise I see no salvation for us two,
Lest that your heart, filled with forbidden love,
Like mine must totally despair.

THEREILE O silly one! I must laugh at you.
Farewell for now. Tomorrow we'll meet anew.
She pushes him off on his way.

Sixth Scene

THEREILE *alone; after a pause, passionately*
O liar, liar! Look into my eyes!
Say free and open, your love is not Thereile's!
Just to think this set my heart a trembling
And shrugging it off as mere dissembling.
Now stand by me, vengeance . . .! Yet this is sure:
Thereile's joy can never more endure.
Had I only a tiger's rapacity,

To devour your blood at once!

Ha, just triumph, you, nature's monstrosity,

It was clear to see — and yet my eyes were blind.

But have I not still the power to hold him fast?

Is he not bound by a secret word?

I can charm him any minute,

If I wish, to call him back to me.

So flee then, yes steal away all you want,

I'll torment you in a thousand ghostly forms!

She ponders again.

Oft in the look upon his countenance

I sensed even then my coming ruin;

I had wounds, yet they pained me not:

Yet seeing them now, I must die of them! *Exits.*

Seventh Scene

A tavern in the city of Orplid. KOLLMER *of Elne and some* CITIZENS *are sitting at tables, drinking and chatting.*

A WEAVER   Listen, Kollmer! You were just asking again about those two scoundrels who I said were eager to sell you the old chronicle they had that no one can read. If you still want it, you can do something about it, they want to bring it to the last lord's castle, to Harry; he's your real fanatic about such worthless junk.

KOLLMER   Don't worry, I've already taken possession of that treasure and we are halfway to agreeing on a price. This evening we'll seal the deal.

GLASSBLOWER   If you want my advice, don't get in too deep with those fine comrades; otherwise you'll never get them off your back.

MILLER   I don't believe I've even seen them.

WEAVER   Oh, they lie about the market place in the bright sun all afternoon, gaping in astonishment, batting at flies and dreaming up all manner of schemes to earn their bread by theft and trickery. They're the only ne'er-do-wells we've got on the island; shame enough that we even tolerate them. If it didn't look as though the gods themselves had by some proper miracle cast them on our shore out of some jocular caprice, we'd have long since drowned them. Consider this: our colony has been here sixty years without a single living creature — with the exception of the storks and quails — having come straying here from strange parts of the world. All the rest of humanity is, so to speak, a fable to us; if we hadn't heard it from our fathers, we would scarcely believe that there are any other creatures like us. But then from nowhere a crazy north wind has to come along and drop these two wretches, the scum of foreign countries, on our coast. Isn't that unheard of?

BLACKSMITH   True, true! I remember as if it were yesterday how one morning everyone came running and yelling that countrymen had arrived from Germany. All the questions and astonishment could hardly have been any worse if someone had fallen from the moon. The poor devils stood there gasping and sweating before the gaping crowd, they thought we were cannibals who by chance happened to speak German. With much trouble we finally got it out of them how they had almost been wrecked with an expedition from what's-it, from — what's that big country? right, from America, and how they'd been driven farther and farther in their life boats and finally become separated from the others, and then at last how they'd found their way to safety here on their few remaining pieces of plank.

GLASSBLOWER   If only a whale had swallowed them up! The one of them's a herring anyway, that lanky scrawny flibbertygibet who's always claiming he was once an expert scientist or, as he says, professor. — Devil take all the foreign words that those fellows have brought with them. A barber is what he must have been. His face is like soap, and he's always blinking and winking through his running eyes.

BLACKSMITH   Yes, and year in, year out, he wears the same tight-fitting little coat made of Nanking, as he calls it, and grass-green trousers that don't reach all the way down to his ankles, yet he's always acting so elegant and dainty, likes he's made out of sugar, and he's always blowing every little fleck of dust off his sleeve.

WEAVER   I've never seen him that he wasn't making anxious, half-friendly faces, as though he were worried with every breath that his friend, the printer, would strike him across the side of his head. I was there when that fellow emptied a pipe full of tobacco juice on his head, just to start something with him.

GLASSBLOWER   Right, the one with the bloated red face, he's really a piece of work; I've never seen such a drinker in my life. His mind is totally choked up, his speech is slow and halting, and he stinks of brandywine from ten feet away.

WEAVER   Well hold your nose, for I see those two noble gentle-men coming to the door.

KOLLMER   They'll be looking for me about buying the book. Good-bye, gentlemen. *Exit.*

BLACKSMITH   What does Kollmer want with that useless thing, the book or whatever it is?

WEAVER   He says he might be starting a collection of that kind of old artifact.

BLACKSMITH   A strange bird. They say he also consorts with ghosts.

WEAVER   We don't care to talk about it. What's it to me!

Eighth Scene

A small, badly furnished room.

BOOK PRINTER   *alone; he stands leaning against the wall, his eyes closed*
I discovered it, not you! That's the way it is. You have no part in the deal, you miserable creature. I discovered

this rarity, in the cellar in the castle, I, the iron chest —
for heaven's sake didn't I open it? Do you want my
crowbar across your temple, you damned hogshead? *He
looks up and comes to his senses.* Sleeping again. Ah! —
Monsieur Kollmer will soon be here. Does the devil
have to fetch him here just when I'm drunk? Pull yourself together, Printer, keep your eyes open, dear
Printer. — And that wretch Wispel has to go, I'm expecting a visitor, he'll be a problem; the stupid ape
will act as if the profit and the honor were all his.

WISPEL   *enters quickly. His affectations fully in evidence*   Brother,
hurry! We have to tidy up, we have to get dressed. The
gentleman will be here soon, at exactly one o'clock and
it's already twelve.

PRINTER   Yes, we must tidy up a bit. I'll clean up a bit. If I wash in
tepid water, he'll be satisfied; that will make a good impression.

WISPEL   *busily rushing about*   It's imperative that I make greatest
haste with arranging and embellishing my toilette.

PRINTER   Where will you be while I'm speaking with our visitor
stranger?

WISPEL   *speaking rapidly*   I'll stay here, my friend, I'll stay. Where's
the toothbrush, the too- — the shoe brush, I meant to
say. — But my teeth are ugly, too, and partly fallen
out. — Eh, what difference does it make? That gives me
a very delicate pronunciation, a diction that is especially
appealing to the ladies, you see, because the letter R
cannot be pronounced in its robust fullness without the
teeth, I am quite right in saying that my missing teeth
are elided R's. But those kinds of elisions contribute infinitely to the sweet Italian character of one's speech.
But, my God, this shirt is far too dirty — Well!

PRINTER   *blocks his way*   And where will you go while the gentleman is finishing with me and paying me?

WISPEL   — and my spats are also somewhat worn. What's that?
I'll stay, I'll stay, good fellow.

88

PRINTER	Maybe while that's happening you should take a walk in the city, brother? Go, get out of here!
WISPEL	Of course, we ought to meet him at on neutral ground, you're right. It really is too untidy in this little room of ours, in our little apartment. An uncleanly mansard doesn't make a good impression. — *malpropre.*
PRINTER	*to himself* I've got to get rid of him — I've got to get rid of him. The way he dresses up! I'd look like a pig next to him; compared to his glib tongue I'd come off like a simple ignorant tosspot. I can't bear the thought of him watching while I'm raking in my profit, he'd get his bony paw into it right away, upon my soul, and he'd be able to do it and say his thanks for the payment with all sorts of expressions. *Aloud.* What's that you've got in that big pot there?
WISPEL	It's just a little bowl of lard, brother. I — ah, ah — borrowed this little bowl along the way in order to grease my hair a bit because we don't have any pomade for our two tonsorial adornments. It's just — eh — you see, that we shouldn't appear before this man totally bereft of elegance; my God!
PRINTER	But that's really disgusting!
WISPEL	You see — eh — no, it's —
PRINTER	*to himself* But he'll get himself so nicely done up with that, next to me he'll be taken for a prince. Good lord! look at what this little weasel is rubbing onto himself! what this nothing of a white runt is combing into his hair.

The printer dips his own hand into the pot and smears some on his hair. The two of them stand at the table, the pot between them.

WISPEL	Listen, brother, they say this is a truly curious man, word of honor; quite a peculiar type, who takes a special interest in talk of things adventurous, strange, and dark. I aim to take full measure of him, confabulate with him good and proper. I'm quite looking forward to it, really.

PRINTER   No, no, no! Just the opposite! The less we talk, the more
             silent and taciturn we are, the more we'll gain in respect
             with this peculiar, albeit unusual man.

WISPEL   God be praised that my dear departed father didn't ne-
             glect my upbringing. For example, I shall expound to
             him about the actual sentient beings of the subterranean
             springs or fountains, about the crystals.

PRINTER   *to himself*   As I live and breathe, he actually does have
             crystal buttons on his coat. I'll tell him all kinds of things
             about corals and stone.

WISPEL   *while dressing*   Since my renowned sea journey I have
             without doubt every claim to distinction; I shall offer to
             hold forth with a practical colloquy on navigation and on
             the fine art of swimming; I shall communicate to the
             good Kollmer the one phantom and the other. And as to
             the rare book, just leave the bargaining to me. We shall
             have to take an opening position something like this:
             Dear sir! It is a volume that, in its present state, as I be-
             lieve I can say without show of self-conceit, does indeed
             assume an antiquarian interest, does indeed take on an
             antiquarian shape. If you were to — eh — add to the
             fixed price — namely to the three tubs of flour, the firkin
             of honey, and the golden chain — let us say some trifle,
             a ruffled shirt collar, a cravat pin, or such like, then we
             might do business. Then he'll either say we're done, or
             he won't; in any case I'll be delicate enough to break it
             off quickly; it would be beneath us, I'll say, to haggle
             about something trivial; let's change to another subject.
             I often have unusual thoughts and ideas, sir, and I know
             you're no less an afficionado in such matters. Thus, for
             example, it occurs to me now that it would be in order,
             if — eh — wait, now I have it — Yes, now it occurs to
             me, I've got it: — you see, in nature, as it lies here be-
             fore us, all about it seems to me to be animated, simply
             all of it, although it may seem to be sleeping at peace in
             silent fantasy; how would it be, for example, if the cob-
             blestones were to conspire to rise up against the proud
             houses, form a mob, and topple the houses so they could
             build their own houses? Eh? Isn't that a fantasy of pure
             genius? *Comment?*

90

PRINTER   You jackass! So what? What if the fingers on my hand
           form a mob and make a fist and split your stupid block-
           head? *Comment?*

WISPEL   *smiling*   Eh he-he-he-heh! That would be taking my idea
           too far, dear friend. — But what are you doing —? *Ciel!*
           Your hairs are as stiff as ropes! Your hair is like a steel
           helmet! You've used up half the pot!

PRINTER   Well blast it to bloody hell! Why didn't you say some-
           thing, you envious little son of a bitch!   *Treats him
           roughly.*

WISPEL   Heavens! How could I have said anything if I don't no-
           tice it until now? Honest, brother — God! Your making
           a total mess of my coat — hit me on the cheek, if you
           must, better on the cheek! For the sake of our friend-
           ship —!

PRINTER   To hell with you! you little frog! you skunk! damn you!
           the brew is running down my neck! Give me a comb, a
           comb!

WISPEL   *drying him with a towel*   So. So. Everything's nice and
           pretty again — I've never seen you look more splendid,
           upon my honor. So. Now we're all right and ready. *Looks in
           a small mirror and jumps for joy.* By all the angels! I'm as
           pretty as a picture. *Sings*
                     My pretty wee bride to greet
                     I cast myself at her feet —
           Look here, you really could have twirled these kinds of
           ringlets too — look — I have several dozen across my
           forehead; yet, as I said, you don't look so bad at all —
           Listen! That wasn't a knock was it?

PRINTER   Let it knock!

WISPEL   Well said! That quite fittingly recalls Don Giovanni,
           where the ghost must enter — an outstanding opera.

PRINTER   *slaps his face*   There's a G. O. Vanni for you and your
           opry. And now you can go wait on the landing because
           someone wants to speak with me, because I intend to

91

take a payment of three Louisdor — Take a walk! *There is a knock at the door.*

WISPEL That's him — brother — It just occurred to me — we haven't shaved yet!

PRINTER Let the devil lather you, you Chinaman!

WISPEL Should I whisper through the crack and tell him to come back in half an hour; that we have shaved already, of course, but that we had to — eh, still write a letter?

PRINTER You stupid dog! — Come in!

A GIRL, *the landlord's daughter, comes in* Downstairs a servant from Elne has brought some things, and greetings from Herr Kollmer.

WISPEL My goodness! And the gentleman does not want to come himself?

GIRL It appears he doesn't.

WISPEL Oh, I could die! I've gotten ready for absolutely nothing — two hours of preparation — Oh, what a calamity! Just think, dear child, I had the most important revelations to make to him!

GIRL My father, the landlord, wants me to beg the gentlemen to kindly consider at this point their half year's account.

WISPEL Yes, dear girl, I even wanted to inform Herr Kollmer about the founding of a learned society. Something like the Académie française.

GIRL My father wants me to ask whether he should take what you owe out of the things that the servant brought and left with us.

WISPEL There were so many things invented by the scientists of Europe that I wanted to introduce to our poor island! for example the art of book publishing, what a wonderful field just for you, my brother! — and then the manufacture of gun powder — coining and printing money — a

	national theater — an hôtel d'amour — I wanted to create a new Paris.
GIRL	What answer shall I bring my father?
WISPEL	And this Monsieur Kollmer was clearly the only man with whom I could associate.
GIRL	Adieu, gentlemen!
PRINTER	Stay awhile with us, dear girl. Help us pass the time a bit!
WISPEL	Yes, grant us a sign of affection!

The girl leaves quickly.

PRINTER	*after a pause* Now we've got to resort to some special measures, and you'll have to go along with it willingly.
WISPEL	What's that rope for, brother?
PRINTER	By my soul, and God keep me, I'll wring your neck if you don't let me do what I have planned for you with this rope.
WISPEL	Grand Dieu! O heavens! Just spare my bare existence, just don't strangle me! think what fratricide means.
PRINTER	Be quiet, I tell you! *He ties both his feet to a post and gags his mouth.* So. I just don't want you getting your nose into everything first while I'm unpacking my profits, you rogue! Adios for now.

Exit. Wispel whimpers and sighs. Then, bored, he starts using his saliva to form bubbles and blow them like soap bubbles. The book-printer watches him through the keyhole for a while. Finally Wispel falls asleep.

Ninth Scene

Night. Moonlight.

A wooded valley. Water Lily Lake.[17] *In the background, moving down the mountain towards the lake is a funeral procession of wraith figures. In*

the foreground the KING, *his gaze fixed on the procession,* To *the other side,
below, not noticing the king, two* FAIRY CHILDREN.

THE FAIRY CHILDREN *alternating verses*

> Look there, what comes now, at midnight's hour,
> From on high, with splendid torchlight?
> To a dance or a gala could lead this strange tour?
> Their songs sound so happy and bright.
>> Ah, but no!
> So tell me, why is it so?
>
> That which you see is a funeral cortege,
> And laments are what you hear;
> For a king, for sure, is meant this dirge,
> Yet spirits are they that bear.
>> Ah well!
> Their song is a sad death knell.
>
> Down the lake valley they come floating
> And walking out onto the water,
> They touch not the water, but stay hov'ring,
> Above it in quiet prayer.
>> Oh, see!
> At the coffin, the woman's fair beauty!
>
> The lake its green shimmering gate now parts,
> Watch, as they dive down now!
> A living stairway upward now starts
> And — e'en now the songs sound from below.
>> Do you hear?
> As they sing him to rest.
>
> The waters, how lovely they burn and glow,
> They play in the green-tinged fires;
> The mists down the shoreline do flow,
> And seaward the pond retires.
>> But still,
> Is there nothing astir?
>
> Something moved in the center! O heavens, O help!
> I believe they're approaching, they come from the lake.

94

Hear the jingle of music in rushes and reeds;
But quick now, our flight we must take!
     Away!
Oh, they've caught me, I'm doomed.

The children run away. The procession moves back up the mountain. As it disappears, the King, arms outstretched, calls after them.

KING   Hold! Stop! Stay! Here stands King Ulmon!
You have buried an empty coffin, O come back!
I, the one who should be in it, am still here.
Almissa, Queen! Here I am, your husband!
Do you not hear me? Know you not my voice?
No, never do you know it. Woe, ah woe is me, woe!
Could I but be a corpse, they would accord
Me, too, such a cool grave. Do I still live?
Am I ever wakeful?
I thought I lay in a crystal coffin,
My wife, that divine creature, she bowed
Over me smiling; well did I know
Her again by her dear countenance.
Curses if they buried another,
If she was so kindly to a stranger!
What? Did love and loyalty die before me?
Surely, too long I have whiled amongst the living —
O Weyla, help! Let death take me quickly!
For but a brief time take me down
Into the realm of the departed, that I might quickly
Ask my wife if she her loyalty
To me does keep until I follow her.
     And if it be not so, if I were totally
Forgotten amongst the dear departed?
O Weyla, help, let me not behold this most
Distressing thing! Anything but that! For rather I pray,
If you in your divinity know no other way,
Then leave me here in the earthly sun
To spin away my dismal days through eternity,
Living, in exile far from those

Whom my regal soul has so
Aggrieved! Oh, for shame, for unspeakable shame!
Almissa, you my dear? Am I to believe that?

Gentle music is heard. Pause.

That nocturnal vision I just now beheld,
I venture now to grasp its meaning — Yes, I know it
Deep in my spirit.
The gods were showing me the imminent end
Of all my sorrows. It was the grand foreshadowing
Of the death foreseen for me.
My heart exults in joy!
And rushes even to the lakeshore
Where at last the dark flower blooms fragrantly for me.
O hasten, gods, with my fate. Let me soon
Feel your kiss! Be it
In the lightning bolt's consuming embrace,
Be it in the breath of wind that, passing o'er,
Bends in silence leaves of grass and sweeps the soul
Of Ulmon away. *Exit.*

Tenth Scene

Midday.

Near the lake.

KOLLMER   *alone*
What a miracle this book will work!
Yes, what a miracle has already occurred
In my presence! For when I gave him,
The King, those pages,
He threw back his head with such a gaze
As if should come to pass that from the heavens a star
Would come shooting down and crashing from behind
Before the orb of that victorious eye.
Then, at once forgetting my presence,
He hurried away apace. Surely

That dark book is a prophecy
And his life's salvation, it reveals
The riddle of his liberation — Hark!
I hear thunder! Hark! The island trembles all round,
Like a newborn stirring
In the swaddling arms of the sea!
Curious dolphins swim rushing
To the shore, in droves they come!
Ha! What a precious summer storm,
So rosy bright, flares up in the cooling air
And colors the green island all morning fresh!
O gods, what does this mean? 'T would be no surprise
If now in light of day from out their graves
The ghosts would rise, if at all shores
In grey clouds the primal times lay waiting!

A loud clap of thunder. Kollmer flees.

Eleventh Scene

Moonlight.

A forest.

KING *enters.* SILPELITT *leaps out of hiding.*

SILPELITT Here stands the tree, O King, the one you mean,
     Which my sister visits so many a night and,
     Leaning her head against it, is wont to slumber.

KING   Of yellow hue is its smooth trunk,
     Slender it rises and, strange,
     The black bows sink earthwards
     To feel it like heavy silk. Child,
     We've reached our goal. My thanks to you, you have
     Struggled to lead me to the hidden path,
     Your tender feet cut by the thorns,
     And still our work's not done. Tell me —

SILPELITT   I will tell you all, keep nothing silent —

KING   What is it? Why do you now tremble?
            I came not here to frighten you.

SILPELITT   No, you must know all, only
            Tell my sister nothing —

KING   Surely not.

SILPELITT   Ever since before I can remember
            I was thrall to Thereile, the princess,
            Though only by night (the fairies' time)
            Did I obey her, like the other children;
            Yet come morning when they went to sleep,
            I again would tie on my sandals
            To wander to Elnedorf, and in the mist
            I stole thither, seen by no one.
            There dwells a man, Kollmer by name; he calls
            Me his daughter, why? I know not.
            He says I am no fairy child.
            He's very kind to me. By day
            I sit at his table, go and come
            With others in the household, then play
            With neighbor children in the yard, or,
            If I don't want to, they drag me away
            And scold me for being such a proud thing; oh, but
            At times they're really quite simple.
            When night comes, I go away again and act
            As if I were running upstairs to the topmost chamber,
            And that's what father thinks, for up there is
            My little bed, where I am to sleep. Yet
            I hurry back over the garden fence
            Through forest and meadow hurrying to Schmetten
                Mountain
            So that Thereile does not note my absence;
            Nor has she ever noticed, except almost once.

KING   Have no fear; trust me, you'll soon hear more.

As the King goes on, Silpelitt disappears into the forest.

> This is the fruit of a strange bond
> That twelve years ago a beautiful fairy
> Joined with a mortal;
> Afterwards she left him, and even took
> From him the memory of what happened,
> By means of a long illness;
> Only this child was to be for him like his own
> To love and trust. Yes, without doubt,
> It is the man who, if my mind does not delude me,
> Often visits me and has found me the book.
> And thus was the father of Silpelitt
> Wisely chosen by the gods to be
> The first means to my salvation; yet his child
> Has still to complete the task, but both
> Shall be equally rewarded. This lovely creature
> Will enact with me a solemn ritual
> As ordained by this book,
> And in that moment when the magic
> Of Thereile releases me through this child's
> Innocent hand, then she too shall be freed,
> A sweet forgetfulness taking her senses,
> And the beloved father will joyfully embrace
> In her his own daughter.
> Tomorrow for the first time, Silpelitt,
> You shall lie down in the little bed
> That till now has not known the touch
> Of your innocent body; and yet you shall believe
> You were accustomed to it, while Thereile
> Will be to you a name of wondrous fable.
> — But where are you, girl?

SILPELITT   *coming*   Look, here I am.
> I had clambered up the cliff face there,
> My sister Morry once lost there
> One of her red shoes.

KING

Be prepared
To climb down the chasm to the right here.
There you will find a grotto —

SILPELITT

Right.
I know it. Just yesterday the giant,
The trusty man, pushed the cliff aside.
Now the entry is free. I watched him
As he worked. Lord, the earth resounded
As he cast aside the block, I saw the sweat
Upon his brow, yet he sang tra-illi-ra!
And said it was but child's play.
Then he took me up and set me on the peak;
I begged and wept, but he left me stranded,
Till I sang for him up there a pretty song.
Then away he trundles and growls to me:
I should greet you for him,
If you need him again, you need only say so.
Forgive me for forgetting.

KING

Very well, now hear me!
Through that small opening you pass through
To a cave whose innermost chamber
Holds a weapon with an arrow.
Fetch both to me.

She goes.

This do I know
From the book of fate, a god bids me do so.
Reposing there is an ancient bow, never yet
Touched by human hand, and only today
To see the light of day,
To shoot the arrow into the poisoned outgrowth
Of seductive love that after brief torment
Will recover and heal. O Thereile,
Bitter is my leave, for the cowardly cut
That is to sever us will soon from behind
Pierce your loyal heart; here stands

100

The dreaming tree with whose life's blood
You but moons ago did mix
Our blood.
Now in sweet ferment still
Within this trunk round and round.
However still this night, my ear
Still strives in vain to hear
The gentle rhythm in this loom
Of love that oft with splendid dreams
Has charmed your resting head.
Yet soon shall run from the arrow of gold
The crimson blood of love from the tree's veins,
And then from afar your heart shall sense
The torment of frightening change,
Yet when madness has raged its fill, sleep
Calm shall descend upon your brow.
      O heaven! How I long for salvation!
To draw back the bowstring of that
Divine weapon takes the strength of a thousand years,
And I have it; yet verily, to be truthful,
Even without it I feel the strength in me
As in that god who shot the diamond arrow
Into the highest heavens, so that with a crash
It pierced the center of the sun and flew on
To where light's last ray dies out.

The child returns with a kind of crossbow. He cocks it with little effort, takes aim, and hands it to the girl, pointed towards the tree. Silpelitt shoots and in that instant all goes dark. A sigh can be heard from where the arrow strikes. Both exit quickly.

Twelfth Scene

Before daybreak.

Valley.

THE FAIRY CHILDREN *enter.*

101

MORRY	Hurry! But quickly!
	Jump out and hide now
	Right here in the bushes!
	Let no one be seen!
	The storm is soon breaking.
TALPE	What's wrong? What's this nonsense?
MORRY	Sister's spitting poison!
	She's raging and howling,
	Her gestures deranged,
	There past the cliff,
	That way through the woods.
WEITHE	What has befallen her?
	O do let us help her!
	Is it a thorn wound?
	Or lizard bite?
MORRY	Stupid rats,
	Hold your tongues and hide!
	I hear her voice —
	And my own knees are trembling.

All duck off to the side into the bush.

THEREILE	*enters*
	See here! See here! O heaven!
	Behold, behold, you trees,
	Thereile, the princess,
	A figure of lament!
	Betrayed, my loyalty!
	And woe! There's no reaching,
	And woe! There's no punishing
	The traitor,
	He's fled!
	O my poor anger!
	And still poorer my love!
	Rage of anger and love

Desperately fighting each other,
Both with tear-filled eyes,
And sympathy in between,
A pleading child.
Away, no mercy!
I must ruin him!
Ha! That I might see his blood,
See him die,
A martyr's death
At these my hands,
That once did caress him
And soothe his brow —
How my fist would lash out!
My vain lust for revenge!
So I tear at myself,
With my own nails,
At my own cheeks,
My silken hair —
You kissed them,
O despicable liar!
Woe! Beauty and charm —
Oh, what are they to me!
If joy is gone forever
And broken is my love,
Then what help is beauty,
What do I care!
And have I no hope?
Ah sadly, ah never!
My world is asunder,
He struck from afar
Attacking my life,
And my magic is done.

WEITHE *running forward* I can't hold back — O dear, sweet sister!

THEREILE You here? And all of you? What is it, you damned rascals?

| WEITHE | We really didn't want to eavesdrop; they merely feared your angry visage so, |
| | So we hid over there in the bush. |

THEREILE	Why do you gape so, do you like my face?
	You can have it that way, if you like.
	Where have you hidden Silpelitt? Answer me! I want to know!

| WEITHE | Be kind, sister, it's not our fault; |
| | She's been missing since yesterday. |

THEREILE	Really? So?
	You lying scamps! Vermin! What?
	I'll teach you to use your eyes.

Shakes her roughly.

| | May the plague take you all! Yes, just whimper! |
| | I'll break your arms and legs, you'll pay for this! |

All exit.

Thirteenth Scene

Night. Forest. An enchanted spot.

THE FAIRY CHILDREN.

| TALPE | This is the place; there stands the black willow. |
| | What now, what were the Princess's orders? |

| WINDIGAL | What do I care? I'll not lift a finger. |

| TALPE | Have you already forgotten yesterday's cuffing? |

WINDIGAL	Ouch! Bumps and bruises all over my whole body!
	I'm going to lie down in the soft moss; just come,
	We'll rest awhile and chat;
	For work there's time enough; the others are
	Not here yet. — See, what a lovely night!

| MALWY | The moon is almost full. |

WINDIGAL   Let's sing a song! Listen!

They sing.

> At night the watchman calls out in the street:
>> Eleven!
> In the forest a small little elf lies asleep;
>> And hears "Elves!"
> And thinks the call comes to him in the vale
> By his very own name from the nightingale,
> Or that Silpellit had called him.
>
> Then he steals away to a nearby wall
> Covered over with glowworms all:
> "What can these little windows be!
> It's a wedding feast for me to see,
> The little ones sitting down to dine,
> And celebrate in the hall so fine;
> So I'll just peek inside here a bit —"
>> Ouch, his head against the hard stone he has hit!
>> Elf, was that enough for you?
>> Cuckoo, cuckoo!

MORRY   *comes with the others*
> Oh, good. So? Well, that's what I call working hard;
> Wouldn't I rather be snoring, too? Thereile
> Will shake you awake all right. Obstinate bunch,
> Still with bloody nose and lip, and yet
> None the better for it.

TALPE   *quietly*   Look how she struts and poses!
> Aping our sister, as if she weren't
> Covered with bruises like the rest of us.

MORRY   You're to dig around the tree, a ring all round,
> Deep as its roots, then we can fell it.
> All this must be done, before
> The first lark heralds the new day.
> Quick, hurry, take up hoe and shovel!

WINDIGAL	Don't you hear the thunder over there?
TALPE	By heaven, yes.
	And blue flashes of lightning from Rocky Peak,
	The moon is disappearing quickly; soon it will rain.
MORRY	Then you've some digging to do. Get to it!
THEREILE	*enters, in mourning attire, to herself*
	For the last time now my hesitant foot I set
	In that place of love that I must hate.
	My heart abhors this parting
	And in tormented pain is orphaned, pining!
	You've shed blood, O much loved tree,
	From the arrow gold, and run out is your dream.
	As grimly you've suffered along with me,
	So now you should at last adorned be!
	Oh, with the finest in Thereile's trove,
	She shall decorate this burial place of her love:
	You sweet tresses, so richly glowing,
	I loose this sash and set you flowing;
	Bind the wound there on the tree!
	Yet bridegroom, how I yearn for thee.
	With you love's joy and sorrow perish!
	After those joys known, no more I'll cherish!
	And you, accursed murderous blow
	For which so many tears do flow,
	My beloved, I know, was the last to touch you,
	So take this kiss that was not your due!

And now, sisters small, a grave you'll dig
And bury it all, from trunk to twig.
And be not afraid, though in times past
Too harsh I was, and angry too fast —
From this day, darling children see,
Your Thereile will ever so friendly be. *Exit.*

Fourteenth Scene

Morning.

Water Lily Lake. THE KING *stands above on a cliff.*

KING   "A man lives out his natural time,
      Yet Ulmon alone will know
      The summer to come and go
      Ten times one hundred times.

      Once a black willow does grow
      A child must fell it to earth
      Then shall rush the waves of death
      In which Ulmon's heart shall glow.

      On the rays of Weyla's moon
      Ulmon shall ascend
      His divine body then to end
      Within their azure room."

      So it was and so it shall be. Quickly now
      The will of the gods is done.
        One more time breathing the air
      That so long has nourished me, I call out one last time
      To the earth, the sun, and you waters
      That embrace and infuse this land.
      Yet you, secluded lake, shall receive my mortal coil,
      And, unfathomable as you are and bound
      In subterranean depths to the sea, your
      Flood shall sweep me into eternity,
      My spirit will be with the gods; I may soon
      With Weyla share the rosy light.
        Fare thee well, you wondrous island!
      From this day on I love you; so let
      Me like a child kiss your ground; true
      I know you less well than my fatherland,
      So dull, so blinded by the years,
      I scarcely know my own cradle; no matter,
      You were at least my stepmother,

I am your truest child — Farewell, Orplid!

    How light and free I feel! How I sense
The old burden of years slip from my shoulders!
O time, you blood-sucking ghost!
Have you had enough of me? As sated full
Of me as I am of you? Can it be?
Is the end at hand? A chill of joy
Thrills my breast! And how am I to grasp it?
And grows my mind's eye not dizzy
As it gazes down into time's .
Deep vortex? — Time, what bodes that word?
A hollow word that I hated in vain;
Time is innocent; it harmed me not.
It casts aside its mask and stands now
As eternity before me, the astonished one.

    As if newborn the weary wanderer
Sees his goal achieved.
He still looks back on the sorrowful
Path he's traveled; he sees the high mountains
Far behind him, and, heart all melancholy, parts from them,
The silent witnesses of his bitter trail:
And so my soul now feels pain
And cheer at once. Ha! Don't I feel
Suddenly the power to run the course
Of turgid life once more — What?
What did I just say? No! No! O kindly gods,
Hear not what I spoke only in delusion!
Let me die! Oh, to die, to die! Take me,
Tear me away! You god of night, are you approaching?
What does the lake whisper to me? What lures me in its
      waves —
What image is that? Ulmon, do you recognize yourself?
Go, go! You are a god! . . .

*With these last words Silpelitt had risen up in the middle of the lake with a
large mirror that she holds out to Ulmon. As the King sees himself in the
reflection as a boy and then as a crowned prince, he plunges lifeless from
the cliff and sinks in the water.*

The play had ended. The piano, after a series of uplifting triumphant phrases, finished with a finale of melancholy calm that was supposed to let the lingering impression of Thereile's grief die out gently. The audience rose to their feet expressing quite diverse opinions. Some, especially the men, offered a hearty round of applause, three or four faces bore looks of doubt and curiosity about what others would say. Even occasionally during the performance there had been some offended whispered attempts to construe the meaning, and now some ladies, their noses ominously high in the air, appeared anxious to read Constanze's reaction in her face and words, but they were quick to alter those expressions when that charming woman, full of innocent good cheer, accorded first the actor, then Theobald, the most forthright praise, in which she was happily joined by the majority of the men and ladies. In the end, the doubtful ones present nevertheless could not hold back from posing the modest question of whether there was not something essentially political, satirical, and personal about the play? some hidden meaning? since it really couldn't be taken alone and simply for the poetry that it purported to be.

"And why ever not, then, dear Madam?" Larkens asked the one lady of the court, showing as he did so that cutting, sharp face that could pierce a person's soul.

"Because — because — I only thought —"

"But how can you think that, when I lift you above all interpreting and speculating, when I assure you it is purely a child's fairy tale with which I sought to entertain you? Yet you're missing the point when you think that — yes, then you've simply rendered the poet a ruined man!"

"He might take care that he does not in fact become one, if people should really find out the point," Baron von Vesten whispered in a Privy Councillor's ear as he pulled him aside, "didn't you notice how the whole thing satirizes our immortal King and his story with Princess Victoria?"

"You don't say? Well, yes, indeed, now I see it! I do believe the figure in the play did bear a resemblance to the features of His Highness —"

"Of course! Of course! well? Is that not a rather unseemly joke? is it not impertinent of this Larkens? though I've always thought he was a malicious person."

"Fine and noble it wouldn't be in any case, I must say, if that were really how it was. For, whatever one might claim, His Late Highness was still a fine, genial man. It is not his fault that time made him ill and miserable, that to the consternation of certain patriots he reached an inordinately old age, and that the Princess — well, but can we not be deluding ourselves when we draw these comparisons?—"

"Delusion? Delusion? Good God! Are you blind then, Your Excellency? Didn't I give my wife a nudge even in the second scene, and didn't she suddenly notice it too? Don't most of the conditions fit? That this bird

109

then took cover by altering other, unimportant features, that was clever enough of him, but he had best take care; there are people who have a nose for trouble, and I am flattering myself a bit when I say I was the first to comment on it."

"But one thing, Baron! I do think that the old fool in the piece behaves the whole time, as far as the poet's intentions go, in quite properly noble fashion, especially towards the witch or whatever she is; and in the end he is accorded, as I see it, something of a divine honor."

"Mockery! mockery! Nothing but infamous irony! They can burn me alive if it's anything else." "And how low-class, as well," lisped Vestin's anemic daughter, joining them, "how vulgar!"

The others had in the meantime returned to the front room. They conversed for a while yet about the strange piece, but soon that discussion died out. A cautious reserve, a certain embarrassment soon befell even the most impartial of the group, and ultimately several believed that someone among the company had been insulted, and they looked at one another expectantly. One person who remained unperturbed was the lovely hostess of the household, as well as Larkens himself, who proved all the more inclined to chat, laugh, and partake of the wine the more coolly the others acted, as in silent equanimity he interpreted their behavior more as a forgivable indifference to the peculiar work than as a sign of animosity.

As it was quite late anyway, the company dispersed. Constanze honored the misunderstood actor at the door with the request that she be allowed to keep his manuscript for repeated edification, and friend Nolten received in parting what he took to be an unusually friendly "Good Night."[18]

O N THE WAY HOME, Theobald drew his comrade's attention to the disturbance. "God knows," Larkens answered, "what those scoundrels had in mind! In the end they were at a loss to say something about the exotic thing; we would have been better to have left it at home, or we should have given them a proper bourgeois comedy — Oh, but it would really have to be a stroke of damnable luck if they were to see if they could find a satire on the old king in it!"

"That's what I fear," said Nolten, "and didn't I advise you, when you first showed it to me, that you had better keep it to yourself, since it would be impossible to answer for any misinterpretation? It was to be expected. After all, you yourself admitted that old Nikolaus and his mistress were on your mind when you composed the piece, and now that's been verified all too clearly —"

"Especially," the other interrupted him laughing, "especially if it were to be true that the devil even guided your brush a few times, because, as you said, you gazed longer than you should have at the magnificent portrait of the old man mounted over my desk!"

"I should be sorry enough in any case," Nolten admitted after some thought, "we don't know how something like this spreads and becomes distorted by peoples' gossip."

"What's that!" exclaimed his companion, "who would be so tasteless as to want to cobble together something malicious out of it? Can you tell me anything crazier? I would find it all too petty if these creatures who call themselves cultured even gave a moment's thought to some strange notion and were able to go beyond the poetry of the simple fable. But that's the nature of these aesthetic clubs, we've always known that. Let's just let it be; they won't make a case out of it."

And so the two arrived home. Theobald, quite exultant in his secretly delighted memory of his beloved's show of kindness, didn't let himself be bothered by the troublesome aspect of the event; he was looking forward to the quietness of his room where he could continue undisturbed the dialogue with his heart. Larkens, as he usually did when he arrived home and unlocked the door, whistled his cheery aria, and in such manner did they leave each other to their own devices.

The reader, however, might find the following helpful in understanding what was happening.

King Nikolaus, the father and predecessor of the reigning king, who about two years before had departed the throne in death, was esteemed well into his old age as an exceptionally fine and even gifted man. He had taken up a tender affair with a considerably younger lady from a related royal family, a relationship which she — with some importunity and, as people believed, selfish political intentions — had been able to prolong, even though the monarch had already outlived the desires and pleasures of youth or had even in fact renounced them. But weakness of character or a sense of commitment that he could not evade made him more susceptible to the enchantress's wiles than likely was wise for his reputation. Throughout his life he was embittered by a serious nervous disorder and, more still, by the concern that he had always failed his people as a regent; with an impatience whose outbursts were said to be horrific he yearned for death, and some claimed that he had made an unsuccessful suicide attempt. Well enough known was an anecdote in which once, in a fit of despair, he had called out in bitter jest: "Heaven would have me be a new Methuselah, and Victoria is dragging me by force back into my boyhood years." These words had an all the more comical ring the more one was inclined to accept the malicious opinion of some mock-makers that His Majesty was not impartial to having his snow-white locks adorned by the young princess's roses. Be that as it may, among those who held the memory of that remarkable — and, early on, benevolent — regent in high esteem, indeed as something sacred, was our Larkens, and in fact, quite aside from the favor in which the King held him as an actor, Nikolaus was in his eyes a grand and tragic enigma of human nature, a mighty grey ruin on the royal palace. Spurned by the tastes of a frivolous age, held in admiration even by less noble spirits, this magnificent pillar, already half sunk into the earth, would have bitterly preferred to be lying completely under the ground together with its inscriptions now illegible for today's race. But it was ordained to be otherwise, and so he was neither able nor inclined to fend off the consolation of being lovingly adorned by a youthful clinging ivy.

Excusable then is the fact that our friend, with pious intent, transposed a part of that idea onto the image of his fantasy and to a certain extent intended an apotheosis of that unfortunate monarch, while neither hoping nor fearing that others to whom he offered his attempt could be even remotely inclined to read any — dignified or undignified — interpretation into it.

I T WAS A PERFECTLY clear and beautiful winter night. The clock was just striking eleven. In the Zarlin household all had grown still, only in the bedroom of the Countess do we still find the lights burning. Constanze, in her white nightclothes, sitting alone at a small table near her bed, is busy letting down her beautiful hair, taking off her earrings and her delicate string of pearls, which always adorned her neck with such simple charm. Lost in thought, she held the necklace on her little finger up to the light, and if we rightly read her brow it is Theobald of whom she is thinking. For indeed it does seem as though she had him to thank for this gift, that such a present had only by an artful detour made its way from his hand, by way of a third hand, to her hand! — but in fact she did not know this. Yet not for the first time did she repeat to herself those words that Theobald, while lost in thought contemplating their form, had once let fall to her. "Pearls," he said, "have for me always had something about them especially profound in the way of sense and meaning, and indeed *these* pearls hang about this neck like a sequence of embodied thoughts born of a melancholy soul. I wish *I* might have been the one who had the good fortune to adorn you with this memento. There is a natural and innocent pleasure in knowing that a person whom we revere and would like always to be near carries with them some small thing of ours that makes our image ever-present for them. Why then may not friends, why may not acquaintances not always give each other gifts of this kind? must our more noble feelings always defer to convenience?"

Constanze well remembered how she had blushed then and answered in jest. Ah, she now sighed to herself, if he knew how deep in my heart I keep his image, he would not envy who had given her this poor trinket.

Restlessly she arose; restlessly she stepped to the window and let the magnificently bright heavens with all their portent, with all their splendor act upon her. Her love for that man, from its first imperceptible stirrings to the astonishing state of her full awareness of it, from that moment in which her feelings had already become yearning and even desire to the pinnacle of the most powerful passion — that whole range she now traversed in her mind and found it all beyond comprehension. She gazed, gently shaking her head and with a smile of awe, down into the seductive abyss of fate. Her eyes filled with tears as they had then in the grotto, where the still disparate elements of her love, incited by Nolten's irresistible ardor, had welled up in full sweet ferment and enveloped all her senses. She had no reason to weep, nothing to regret; these were the tears that so readily come when one ponders one's life and resignedly lays one's head on the maternal bosom of an all-knowing fate that holds our lives in its balance; one observes oneself in such moments with something of a gentle self-esteem — rendered in one's own eyes, by the higher meaning of a life's epochal moment, something akin to a special foster child of the divinity, feeling as though one had been raised up to stand at the side of one's own guiding genius.

Long, long did Constanze, sunk in silent thought, leaning like a pillar on the window post, keep staring out into the beautiful night. Overpowered by the force of her feelings, she sank, unthinking, to her knees, and as she folded her hands she scarcely knew what all was surging in confusion within her; and yet her lips moved to form words of the most ardent gratitude, the most heartfelt pleas.

After she had once more risen to her feet, she sensed that the heavens, by way of the calm serenity that now seemed to lift her soul, were proclaiming to her that her prayer had been heard. Indeed she was now heartened enough at last to evade no longer the question of what ultimately was to be hoped or feared from this love, what was to become of Theobald, what of her? She took frank account of all the relationships, she suppressed no misgivings, ignored no difficulties; she weighed each element off against the rest, and more and more she trusted the possibility of an honorable and happy union; and indeed, when she pondered more closely, she found this hope had long lain ready in the depths of her soul. But not all too boldly did she dare give herself over to this hope, for even the coming moment harbored many an obstacle — not the least of which was her family's noble pride — and revealed those obstacles to have an urgency of which she had previously been scarcely aware. She was seized by an anxiety she had never felt before; she wanted to put the whole matter aside for today, she reached for a book to read: but in vain, she could fix her mind on no other thought; it was past midnight; should she lie down? sleep? It would have been to no avail, as hot and discomfited as she was.

I will waken Emilie, she thought at last, the girl shall chat with me. She was all the less hesitant to seek the girl's company, since to her surprise she actually saw the glow of a light coming from the alcove where the girl slept. She crossed the hall quietly, opened the door, and found the girl fast asleep in her bed and beside it the light, burning out as it sank into the candleholder. The sleeping girl's hands rested on an open portfolio and a number of scattered pages. One call sufficed to wake the girl, who, much startled, moved first to hide the folio and papers, with the result that Constanze, alerted by her sudden move, calmly asked what she had been reading.

"Oh!" came the tremulous answer, "don't be angry, ma'am! They are old letters that I had taken up after some time again, and sleep must have overtaken me — what time is it now?"

"What time!?" said Constanze, looking at her sharply, "I think it must be half — *a lie* that you're telling me. Let me see!"

"O please, dearest, sweetest lady! I've surely done nothing wrong — just leave it to me!"

"No more do I demand, my child, than a look to convince myself."

And with that a trembling Emilie handed over everything as she broke down crying loudly. But Constanze, how startled she must have been when she looked at the portfolio to see the gold embossed letters "T. N." on the dark-blue Morocco-leather cover giving clear enough indication of its owner.

"Where did you find this?" she asked as she struggled to conceal her embarrassment.

"Over there," the girl sobbed, "where the gentlemen were putting on their show today; the portfolio was lying behind the box for the shadow play; I only wanted to take a bit of a look at the colored glass, and then — well, then I took —"

"Behind the box, you say?"

"Yes, yes, ma'am! I am telling the absolute truth, it would do me no good to lie about it now, and it was lying there open, just carelessly, as though someone had simply brought it and then forgotten about it — that's right! the pencil had also been taken out, it must still be lying there on the table. Honestly, if everything hadn't been lying there open like that, I never would have presumed."

"That's not an excuse in any case. But for now — is there anything else left, go check your bed!"

"You have every last scrap."

"I shall take it with me until morning. Put out your light. Good night!" — Uncertain and anxious she hurried to her room. She had no doubt whatever that what she was holding belonged to Nolten; in addition, the fact that it had gotten in with Larkens's apparatus she explained easily by the fact that Theobald on one occasion had stepped behind the curtain to help out with something and that perhaps he needed the portfolio to do so. But the possibility that, aside from the girl, no one else could have been curious about the portfolio's contents, made her all the more uneasy, the more she had cause to suppose that her name too, and with it a dangerous secret, could be mentioned therein. Considering this, and perhaps also harboring a forgivable interest of her own heart, she pondered, breathing uneasily to be sure, to cast half a glance, then a whole glance, and in the end several increasingly curious glances upon the contents of those pages. But then in the heat of excitement the feeling of something forbidden and despicable tore the portfolio from her hand. In pure desperate haste she had to that point been able to read nothing coherent, and she said that to soothe her conscience as, albeit with considerable struggle, she laid the find aside. But then suddenly a worry assailed her that made the blood rush to her cheeks. She had just now caught a superficial glimpse of some letters in a delicate, unknown handwriting, and, without knowing why, she had thought of a sister of Theobald; but now she was struck by a different thought. With resolve she turned once again to the object of her suspicion and took out some written pages; she read and read, blushing, then growing pale; her bosom heaved with heartbeats so loud she could hear them; now the paper slips from her fingers, she sinks back upon her bed, like a corpse, unable to make a sound, unable to shed a tear.

A knock at the door finally brings her to her senses; she starts up and, as she looks about in confusion, the poor woman smiles, as if asking whether all that horror had assailed her only in her sleep. Then she smiles again, but now like a woman in despair, as the letter on the floor testifies to the sad truth.

There is another knock and then the pitiable sound of a girl's voice: "No! I cannot rest, I shall freeze to death here if I cannot speak to her, if she does not forgive me! — my dear, beloved good mistress!"

When no answer came, she asked once again in most plaintive tones: "For the love of God, let Emilie come in, for only two minutes, for only two words! Forgive me!"

"Yes, yes, I do! Do go now, my child!" Constanze answered, her voice barely audible. And the girl stole away consoled, with no idea what pain she had caused her mistress. We dare not depict this pain. But just as all that has been heightened to an unnatural extreme cannot long stay at that peak of intensity, so soon enough did an irresistible slumber descend upon the exhausted woman and plunge her into a benevolent obliviousness to her pitiable state.

Just as calmly and peacefully as, an hour ago, the gaze of the stars seemed to bless her happy prayer, they now shone down on the bed of the unfortunate woman. So quickly can the greatest mortal bliss be followed by the presence of incomprehensible grief.

Even before day had come, Constanze was awake, coming all too soon to ponder the stunning blow she had been dealt. She asked God for strength and composure, arose drained of energy, and with dry eye put the portfolio in order, when out of it fell — as if to compound her sorrow —

a lock of hair, doubtless from the unknown woman who had written the letters.

She appeared to herself in the mirror like a changed being who, after having experienced something monstrous, no longer seems to fit into her old surroundings, within these walls and among these appointments; everything seemed to look upon her as a long departed guest, as someone deceased, and she struck even herself, with her unsteady tread, with her silent feelings transformed by pain, like something just released from the grave that had not yet regained a firm foothold and was able only gradually to rid itself of the impression of the last death struggle.

As she slowly dressed, she was surprised by her own calm, which, to be sure, might better have been called indifference. She hurried from her sorrowful chamber and into the front room, where as yet no one else had arrived. Soon the morning sun appeared in the window, inviting cheer and life. Not thinking, Constanze looked through the panes and, just to have something to do, went over the furniture with the dust cloth, often pausing, distracted. — Emilie came in, full of astonishment at finding her mistress here already. "I have taken over your job!" said the Countess in a friendly manner, "you see, as a sign that I am myself again. But do me the favor of not talking about it anymore." A warm kiss of the hand was her reward of thanks.

Very welcome to the woman in her strange mood was her brother's visit. "Good day, my dear little sister! Up so early with the birds? Worry about the conservatory drove me from my bed; it was a grimly cold night, my thermometer falling almost to twenty-five; I simply must check that nothing down there has been damaged." "I want to accompany you!" said the Countess and threw on her shawl. Her bearing, with its forced cheerfulness and distracted air, took her brother aback for a moment, but he was almost blind out of concern for what he might find in the garden.

The brisk fresh air did Constanze good. In sensitive moments like the one she was going through, a person can for a few seconds be highly receptive to nature in whatever form one encounters it; one might then with a single leap seize totally and solely upon its friendship, its divinely silent life, so as suddenly to cast off and forget a whole burden of old worries and cares. But this quickly flickering feeling is only the brief glimpse of sunshine upon which then follow the dismal clouds of before. Constanze persevered as well as she could. Yet as the Count to his utmost joy found his plants mostly unharmed and strove with each plant to convince his sister of his happiness, she was unable to suppress her melancholy thought: how was I feeling in that hour when these plants, these noble little growths, were threatened by the ruinous frost? They are all growing and blooming, just as I too am walking upright, a wonder unto myself; but perhaps the innermost life's seed of this delicate shrub is already afflicted, and it is still to be seen whether it is deluding us with the mere appearance of healthiness, if perhaps even this evening this bud is not hanging, dead, and — —

Constanze had lost her illusory composure; she hurried with rapid steps, covering her face, back to the house. Upon seeing her room again, whose door she immediately bolted shut behind her, she felt all the pent up pain break forth with double and treble force, and she gave herself over to it unchecked. Only now did she consider what had happened; only now did she dare to plunge completely into the abyss of her misery. However much her reason groped for some information, for some consolation that might offer a satisfying solution or even an explanation for the double relationship in which Nolten bound himself to her and to an unknown woman, she still found no way out, no glimmer of light. When she compared all those ways in which he had shown her the most unambiguous signs of passion with the strange letters whose overall impression revealed a long-standing and still very vital state of betrothal, there was nothing to do but see Theobald as the most despicable dissembler deceiving two creatures at the same time, or else to take him as a deranged man, a man without character living in a scandalous state of conflict with himself. Yet neither of those two can she make rhyme at all with the entire way and manner of Nolten's comportment. For even the signs of eccentric behavior took far more moderate form in him than they were usually wont to manifest themselves even in respected men of like talents and aspirations. Least of all was Constanze able to give up her conviction of the kindness of his heart. Every single moment she recalled in which she believed she had gained a glimpse into the intricacies of his most special thoughts and feelings; she recalled too many an occasion when, in a few strikingly spoken words about life, about art, the intense light of his mind had shone forth and inspired an entire gathering of people; finally, she thought of the whole all-embracing conception of him that she had developed after such long association. All these memories countered the dark and strangely distorted image that perhaps some blind chance was forcing upon her to frighten her and make her anxious — an image that her beloved, her true and unfalsified lover would find cause to smile about in wonderment. She feels a faint glimmer of hope and looks again at the dates on the letters and rapidly takes account of the months, weeks, and days, but the result is still no consolation, for each time a part of the tender correspondence coincides with the time when Theobald was giving Constanze unmistakable signs of his intentions. And even assuming that the affection to which those letters bore witness were only one-sided — which in any case seemed not to be so — and assuming that Nolten had been keeping up the girl's faith and while doing so had secretly made himself guilty of an unbelievable transformation, how would that help Constanze? what should she have to expect of such a man? how could she rob another creature of her dearest hopes? and a creature that she really could not hate, who by all indications is the most touching picture of innocence, of devoted love? — indeed how could even Theobald's most ardent love even remotely flatter her if it committed such a sinful act of theft against this other good person?

Still unresolved was the question of just how Nolten could be capable of such an outrageous betrayal?

Constanze gazed, eyes wide open and lost in thought, into one corner of the room, as her mind gradually formulated the distressing thought: there could very well be a person who, comprised of weakness, wanton selfishness, and by chance a vestige of original good-naturedness, was able to maintain for others and in part also for himself the appearance of unsurpassed character and who was able to justify any misdeed to his own conscience; there could be a degree of dissimulation surpassing all usual conceptions of the term. The exact nature of Theobald's association with Larkens, as little as she had until now mistrusted the latter, could now, as she recalled the opinions of others, only strengthen her conviction that in him she had found the seductive tempter.[19]

Sympathetically she looked anew at Agnes's letters and could not help but wonder at the pure and harmonious sense that spoke in the girl's every word. "Poor Agnes!" she said, "poor deceived child! Is it possible? ought he not have feared the sin of betraying this soul if he had come to know her only as well as I have come to know her through these letters? Gracious God! such a lamb and such a snake, how did *they* ever become betrothed? I had a sign from God to warn *me* in time, but she — am I right in leaving her to this fate? does it not fall to *me* to warn her? Yes, truly, it is my duty — — and yet that could be o'er-hasty; who knows that I would not be making the bad worse, or is this deceiver, should it be heaven's will to save him, to be saved only by this angel's love?"

Her last doubts about Nolten's attitude were completely dispelled when she spied a document written in his hand — the draft of a letter to his bride that he had outlined only yesterday. With a deep feeling of distaste, sorrow, and scorn, indeed revulsion, she perceived here the language of the most eloquent love and a tone resonant with honest manliness. Yet one passage was especially remarkable: "I have been caught up here," it went, "in a less than admirable rush of diversions of all kinds, in the midst of which the mental vision of my Agnes has shimmered through all the more clearly. Indeed, I might well confess to you that, with that suspicious scruple now happily laid aside, I live in thoughts of you with doubled ardor."

That statement looked almost like a hidden confession of his heart's confusion, wrung from him perhaps by his troubled conscience. This confusion itself could now offer, in Constanze's eyes, if not an excuse, then nevertheless an explanation for Nolten's behavior, when she assumed that the misunderstanding, of which she had also found a trace in one of Agnes's letters, had caused Theobald's strong and lasting displeasure and that he, in keeping with his extreme character, had made a desperate plunge towards change of which she, Constanze, had to be the victim. His change had occurred some time between yesterday and the winter outing to the Duke's castle, and all indications were that he had undergone that change quite willingly.

As plausible as these conclusions were, and as well suited as they were at least to casting a bearable light on Nolten's behavior, they still afforded the lovely woman little consolation. For from the moment that she recovered to some degree her respect for Nolten, she also experienced her love for him stirring to life, and that made her feel almost worse than when she had been sure of her disdain for him. Accordingly, Nolten's happiness was restored, the girl blissful in her possession of him, and — she, Constanze, having but briefly filled the gap, was then left standing alone, deserted, forgotten, and with a bitter thorn in her heart. A feeling of anger flared up in her, she felt injured in her womanly dignity, kicked aside; she felt all the torment of spurned love. And while before she had felt a pure impulse of sisterly affection for Agnes, she could not now resist a touch of pained resentment, no matter how vigorously she reproached herself for feeling so. But even when she succeeded in shifting all her resentment from the innocent girl to the beloved turncoat — she was still left with her awareness of her powerlessness, of the insult done her. Every memory of the past, the smallest sign with which she might have revealed her favor, now dealt blow upon blow to her pride, her feeling of honor. Even yesterday when parting at the door she had sent him away with such emphatic friendliness, and — as she now saw it — he deigned to respond with no more than a cool thank-you. Most of all she was humiliated and ashamed of the scene in the grotto, the thought of it causing her to cover her glowing face, weeping and sobbing.

No wonder that she now recalled the lament of Thereile from yesterday's play, which seemed as if to speak prophetically of her; no wonder she gave a moment's thought to the repugnant notion that Larkens at a few points had intended an unkind reference to her. And yet her present state of mind is perfectly described by the passionate lines:

> O my poor anger!
> And still poorer my love!
> Rage of anger and love
> Desperately fighting each other,
> Both with tear-filled eyes,
> And sympathy in between,
> A pleading child.

O N THAT SAME MORNING towards ten o'clock, when Larkens was just returning home from an outing, his servant gave him the small brown box containing the magic lantern, stating that it had been delivered a quarter of an hour before from the Zarlins', accompanied by the gracious lady's thanks. Our actor opened the lid, eagerly pulled out the portfolio that was lying on top, and inspected it from every angle, his mouth drawing to a pleased and still somehow distasteful smile as he exclaimed: "By heaven, the trap has lured its prey! the bait's been taken, and well-seized indeed! Not a single note's been left untouched! I'm worried only that the game has fallen into rougher hands than I had intended. Whatever the cause, Madam's fingers have been all over the portfolio, and I'd have to be a bad judge of Eve's lineage if her fingers had been more discreet than I would have wished for my case. Enough; we'll see that there'll have to be some reaction. This time you've truly worked things out masterfully, Brother Larkens, may the Lord give his blessings on it."

Actually, it was the friend's intention that Constanze might find the portfolio and not resist its secrets. He could count on the fact that she would take it for Nolten's property, although in fact it was a gift that Nolten had given to him at the time when he had wanted to rid himself forever of everything that could remind him of Agnes, the letters, the lock of hair, and the hundred other little things.

Larkens hoped in part that his carefully planned and well-meant trick would hinder any affection for Theobald on the part of the Countess; in part too he thought that from now on, knowing of the relationship to Agnes, she would have to behave so as to become inaccessible to Nolten. But now Larkens, unaware, as a result of his friend's distrustful taciturnity, of the true state of affairs, had erred a bit in his planning; he might, had he been better informed, have taken other steps; yet with the steps taken he did, as we have seen, completely achieve his goals, albeit it in a more cruel way than he had imagined. Precipitous and reprehensible in the extreme is how we would have to term his arbitrary way of actions if he had had any idea of how far Theobald's new love had already progressed, because Larkens could reveal the rights of Nolten's fiancée only at great cost to the painter's honesty. Rash and insecure is how we would have to condemn his one-sided approach inasmuch as he could not have known whether Nolten, even though he had until now maintained a reserve towards Constanze, might nevertheless soon offer her his heart, since then he would have to appear in a dubious light to her. Yet regarding the first point, Larkens did not have the least inkling of how the understanding between the two had grown; and regarding the second point, as far as the future was concerned, he had of late been thinking seriously of presenting Theobald with the evidence of Agnes's innocence, enabling him to consider the matter more closely, and to threaten him if need be with calling in the Countess herself to act as a friendly arbiter in the matter.

Above all he was giving thorough consideration to the question of whether it was advisable to urge Theobald to consider his duties to his fiancée. — We shall leave him to his thoughts for now and return to the Zarlin household.

There on the next day towards evening a distinguished visitor was announced. Duke Adolph appeared, and, in her brother's absence, Constanze received him alone. The woman's unusually pale and distracted demeanor likely struck him at once. He took the earliest opportunity to inquire about how she felt and then deftly turned the conversation to his own concern and, visibly disturbed, related to her what yesterday he had learned about a most unfortunate matter, whereby he regretted that it had had to occur precisely in this house, which he held in such high esteem. The King, his brother, whose honor was also involved, had been informed about it in the greatest detail, and it was from him that he, the Duke, had heard about it.

Constanze was startled and explained how on that evening she had indeed perceived the general turn in the company's attitude as well as how she had later learned the reason for it, but also how she had not immediately been able to believe that men of this sort could have perpetrated such a travesty. She asked that at least *she* be exempt from giving any opinion, since people of better insight and of more reliable judgment had been present. But the Duke admitted that the King had assigned to him the preliminary investigation of the matter, that he had already confiscated the manuscript and other pertinent materials, but that after several readings and careful examination of all the details he could not make up his own mind. He had ultimately come upon the idea of relying on the judgment of a "lady who was as perceptive as she was impartial," and so in this case he would hold to his request, he would trust her judgment implicitly. "Of course," he added with an arched brow, "of course, if I should after all be somehow wrong in my trusted assumption about the total impartiality of my dear friend, if one or the other of the two accused is more dear to her heart than would be appropriate, then, my dear lady, it would be highly indelicate to insist, despite your refusal, that you utter a just verdict."

Calmly the Countess looked at him and responded: "I held both men in very high esteem; you yourself have shown this Nolten your favor, and simply for your sake, Adolph, it should hurt me if an innocent friend of yours were wronged. But as to that misstep or — as I would appropriately say — crime of which people accuse the two, I have no intention of standing in the way of justice, only I am not able to further its cause. You yourself, I should think, are best able to know of what your friend is capable, and from your assessment of him you can draw reliable conclusions about the attitude of the actor, for the two are indeed of one mind and one thought. So you judge, then. You were, of course, not there to witness that evening's events, but you have the documents in hand; what advantage would I have then over you that would make me more adept to judge?"

The Duke arose and briefly paced the room, then said in a friendly tone: "I was unfair to you, my dear! forgive me. I see that we two share a dilemma and would thus be rather similarly inclined to excuse the whole affair or at least turn it for the better. I realize only now how unfair it was of my brother to put me in this difficult situation and how foolish I was to accept the task. Of course, my honor, too, was concerned in this case, but the more passionately I took up the matter, the less could I hope to see things clearly, and my displeasure was scarcely balanced on the other side by my partiality to Nolten, since my favor towards him had been rendered more or less dormant by his failure to tend to it; all the worse then for justice for Nolten if I had any cause to be angry with him. In you, my dear, pure human feeling speaks in favor of this otherwise so proper pair of artists, and I confess to you that in your company I am inclined once again to my old affection for this painter without your even having uttered one word in his defense — but perhaps it is precisely *because* you do not defend him that I could forgive him. If I were able, what with all the noise, with all the bitterness that this crazy incident has caused at court, to stay perfectly calm and protect myself from any suspicion on my brother's part of partisanship, then I would well prefer to let the two gentlemen off and try to cover up the whole affair; but that still does not end my worries, and in any case my relationship to the painter has been irreparably damaged by the whole stupid affair. But why am I burdening you with these hardships? — Let us talk no more of the matter. It would be best," he went on, joking, "if they would establish a tribunal consisting of an archaeologist, a professor of aesthetics, and a lawyer, who would go over the manuscript and pictures. Don't you think so, my dearest?"

Meanwhile, the true attitude of the Duke and the difficult position he was in are evident from the following comments.

Far from the folly of finding in the fabulous figure of the thousand-year-old king any dishonoring link, the Duke found that association instead to be beautiful and well-meant. On the other hand, however, he found the similarity of the fairy princess to Victoria all the more problematic. For even though the true relationship of this person to the late Regent might not have been portrayed so accurately, still the most obvious side of it was still so characteristically worked out that it was impossible to deny that a striking likeness to Victoria was involved. The portrayal of that selfish, roguish, yet ardent creature in fact imitated even the subtlest nuances. That all might have passed unnoticed. But that lady was still a star at court; the trust that Nikolaus placed in her was still honored by his son. In that respect we must consider the play to have been ill-considered in the extreme. Nevertheless it would not have had to be difficult for the Duke to avert the possible damage

122

if in an idle moment the King had not been seized by a curiosity about the infamous manuscript. For in it he could not but notice many a tie; he expressed his great displeasure about such an inappropriate allusion; namely the inclusion, be it frivolously or seriously meant, of the aforementioned esteemed woman enraged him as an unforgivable impertinence. The Duke calmed him for a while by presenting the problematic side of various aspects, and promised to go through the whole thing again and to make further inquiries; yet because he really could not arbitrarily circumvent the righteous feelings of his brother and because he did not want to misuse the trust with which the latter had left it to him to reach a decision on this by no means unimportant matter, he truly faced a dilemma with his two obligations: he would just as gladly have spared the painter as he would have liked to satisfy his brother. For that reason then his request to Constanze was nothing less than mere pantomime; he wanted on this occasion merely to tease her, but found such a feminine oracle quite comforting in his undecided state, and he was simply thinking that, in the event that the story could become a topic of rumor and gossip, he would, out of discretion towards Victoria, have to conceal the actual reason for the trouble and emphasize more the general aspects.

Constanze gazed ahead, eyes downcast and serious, her expression unchanged. The Duke found the sight of her touching and from now on believed to read in her looks only the most noble and genuine sympathy for the fates of two friends of her family. Her entire bearing, so slightly shadowed by this concern, he found as charming and vulnerable as it had ever been. He sat down at her side and turned the conversation to other matters; she commented on these topics as best she could, and the self-control that she showed in doing so made her all the more charming, childlike, and irresistible. That was all aided by the inviting calm of the hour, made more intimate by the two candles aglow on the table. The Duke, as they conversed, took the hand of his taciturn companion, assailed her playfully with the most flattering rebukes for the hesitant reserve with which she always responded to his displays of affection, which this time too met with some resistance, albeit — as the clever man believed — a resistance born more of propriety than of a resolve to reject.

Yet as she became ever less able to conceal her suppressed pain, her restlessness and unease, and as her more warmly enthused lover, about to become mistrustful anew, coaxed her — now with urgent words, now with eager caresses — to reveal her affection, it was alarming and pitiable to behold how the poor woman lost her composure in that moment when, so greatly agitated by her unhappy secret, she had to be reminded of her lost love in doubly painful way, while another, previously despised love was pressing itself upon her in a rush of benevolence. In one moment she vigorously pushes the Duke away, in the next she gives in to his audacity with

123

surprising willingness; the most anxious sigh and warmest torrent of tears are followed suddenly by laughter whose childish charm and heartening ring would, under other circumstances, have had an enchanting effect. The Duke saw in all this only the indescribably touching expression of her previously concealed passion for himself, revealing itself now at last and struggling, in the ecstatic moment of their first embrace, with gracious modesty and sweet regret, even though it made him, despite all that, the most delighted of men. How different things looked in Constanze's breast! She often felt as though she were sitting in the embrace of a demon, a creature of Hell, under the spell of a horrible powerlessness; desire and revulsion alternately rose up within her, she surrendered to his kiss with a cutting feeling of repugnance, even of loathing; she found it unbearable how miserably she had gone astray, her imagination in a foolish rage, as if in this way she could take secret revenge on him who had betrayed her! He — (so her soul cried out in lament) yes he alone is to blame that Constanze betrays herself so, that I do what otherwise I would have detested, and yet — how will things turn out? how is it to end? very well, very well — let come what may! — she broke away and buried her face in the crimson cushions of the sofa, her sobs rending the Duke's heart. He touched her hesitantly, he begged, he pleaded with her to compose herself, urging her to consider why in fact she was in such despair, asking whether the involuntary admission of the affection that was destined to make him for all time into a good man happily reconciled with heaven and earth so tormented her, or whether it was the fear that this lovely accord could ever be exposed to society's crude judgment, or whether it was doubts about his discretion, his loyalty, or his respect for her virtue? "Constanze! Dearest! Beloved! look at me! Tell me that I must leave for today, for now, insist that for my whole life I must in no way, with not one syllable, with not one look, with not the slightest wish, remind you of this evening! But for me let it remain unforgettable. As it is now, so shall this room, so shall the light of this candle and all it has witnessed remain in my memory — O God! and in this way, in this sadly dejected state I must behold the form of this most noble woman and see it dispel again the heavenly charm of these last moments! I am lost, I shall despair, if you do not sit up, if I must leave you in this state."

He took her gently by the shoulders, and leaning back gently she rested her head on him so that her open, tear-filled eyes gazed upward under his chin. She looks up, unthinking, friendly; in friendship he lowers his lips to her serene brow.

Silence, only their breathing to be heard, went long unbroken. Finally he said lightly: "Isn't it a nice expression, when there's a pause after a long, friendly conversation, people are wont to say: an angel just passed by?"

Constanze shook her head, as if wanting to say that the preceding scene we've just been through could not possibly have summoned up such a benevolent spirit.

Once more he is at a loss for words; he ponders the state of the Countess, again finding much about it that gives him pause. Not unintentionally he guides the discussion lightly back to Nolten and Larkens. "No," he says at last, "I would be very pleased if you, my dear, were inclined to reveal your views on this unpleasant matter. I am quite sure you have long since made up your mind, or at least that you have an opinion. Speak to me, I ask in all seriousness — Do you think the two are guilty?"

Posed this question, she thinks awhile and then says with a strange convulsive movement: "Guilty? — he is!"

"But who?"

"Well, Nolten —"

"I'm astonished! — and Larkens?"

"Likely just as well. Yes, my dear sir, rely on it."

"And both culpable, then?"

"As I see it."

"Well, upon my word, then they shall regret it."

The Duke stood up; Constanze remained seated as if chained. Having least expected this harsh judgment from Constanze, he took it for having been all the more well founded. He posed some questions meant to clarify her view; she assured him that she knew no more, urging him to content himself with that and in no case to betray her confidence. Only now that he thought he could be certain, since even this tolerantly disposed woman was so affected by this impropriety as to appear outraged, did anger and displeasure awaken in him; he spared no tender phrase, repeatedly thanking the beloved woman for her forthright sincerity, which he interpreted to be the natural result of a mood of tender openness. He had no inkling of how the Countess was torn by a storm of contradictory feelings since she had made her decisive statement. Her gaze fixed, statue-like, before her, she remained rooted to one spot, was more than once tempted to ameliorate, even to recant completely what she had just said, but something inexplicably held her tongue. Suddenly they hear the Count's carriage roll up in front of the house, and a hasty kiss, a flattering word, seal, for the Duke, this hour's secret.

B EFORE WE COME TO SPEAK of the consequences that soon enough followed upon these events, we cannot refrain from casting a general glance upon the various individual minds and feelings between which, as a result both of the most fatal interplay of relationships and of double and treble misunderstandings, such an immense chasm had grown.

While our painter gives himself over to visions of an unimpeded happiness, looking forward to that good fortune with each day, and is even now occupied with a letter to the Countess meant to offer her a free and noble declaration of his wishes and the prospects he has to offer, that very love for Constanze is even now spinning for him a treacherous net. The well-meant intentions of a friend tenaciously in pursuit of his own hidden agenda had turned into the game of a fate that might be inclined now to good, now to ill: the carefully but capriciously laid mine with which Larkens had meant to dispel with ease a dangerous constellation between the persons involved had backfired and was now about to strike all four of them, Larkens himself included, with bitter misfortune, such that it would be hard to know who of the four was most to be pitied if not that innocent girl whose rightful well-being was at stake from the start. However, while Constanze seems to have forfeited our sympathy since letting herself be driven to exact a harsh revenge while justifying it with a false explanation, and since she now appears intent on casting herself away to a dubious admirer, we shall nevertheless be so fair as to bear in mind the state of a female heart that, most cruelly deceived and plunged from the heights of a wonderful feeling, was forced for a moment to have doubts about herself and about mankind alike. As for Theobald, we already see how his forgivable but still precipitous mistrust of one love was being punished by the very similar mistrust by another, and we shall now wait and see whether this harsh lesson is to work more to his misfortune or to his well-being.

The confiscation of the suspect play cabinet by order of he Duke was already a bad sign for the two friends. Larkens flew into a rage at what he called a distasteful misuse of power. "May they," he called out to the painter, "break their teeth on your poor bedaubed shards of glass! and let the first simpleton who sticks his nose into my harmless work receive a good box on the ears from Old Nikolaus's ghost to sharpen his critical insight!"

Theobald wanted to explain everything to the Duke himself, but the actor would not have it, insisting that they need do that pack no favors, they need only wait until the mouse spring forth from the portentously laboring mountain to reveal how their stupidity had prostituted itself. When nevertheless the well-intentioned Nolten sought out his royal patron, he was, to his greatest shock and dismay, not granted an audience. Totally disconsolate was how he then felt when he found his last resort to the Zarlin household unexpectedly cut off. He had no idea where to turn for help or advice; he would have gladly born the hatred of the entire court if only he could be sure of Constanze.

In the meantime, then, the unpleasant matter was considerably aggravated by an added circumstance — one that put a whole new face on the situation. Just as one misfortune gives rise to the next, and in such cases there is no end of calamity, so there was no lack of voices that in this instance recalled certain criminal cases — concerning seditious intrigues — that some time ago had been brought forward and in part even acted upon; and although such cases were already considered closed, a few people still felt obliged to suspect that some by no means insignificant contribution to such activities was behind the actor's behavior.

The restless spirit that, emanating in part from certain ideas about political freedom, had for a time seized the youth of Germany, especially at its universities, is well known. The government in question here accorded such matters all the more attention when it emerged that, from the start, some men of more mature years, intellectual acumen, and, as well, unassailed character had not been averse to participating, be it in general or in a specific way, in such secret societies. Thus, as it turns out, two close acquaintances of our actor harbored a particular penchant for this dangerous tendency, and Larkens, far from having any serious interest in the cause, concealed from those acquaintances his indifference and disdain behind a mask of fiery enthusiasm, since he could not deny himself the pleasure of having the best of his comrades on what in any case was an irresponsible fashion. He wrote them letters filled with fanatical pathos, made the most absurd suggestions, and was able to dispel the suspicion of mere affectatious imitation by way of an artful air of irony, by uttering the occasional sensible idea, and by achieving the utmost consistency in his personal and oral performance, with the result that the society claimed him for an albeit eccentric, yet nevertheless talented member — even though there was no lack of clever types who secretly distrusted him and kept a close eye on him. This he noticed and played the injured party, but withdrew just at the right moment and, on the condition of absolute silence, was returned all the essays he had written. When two years later the state investigated and disbanded the fraternity and his name came up in peripheral contexts, the discretion of the society actually made it possible for him to slither out of the trap like an eel while other men, some already holding public office, were subjected to harsh punishment. Thus for some time he enjoyed a safe sense of security, but his malicious mischief was not to go unavenged. The infamous play awakened old memories; malevolent, pompous gossips immediately exerted all their energies, and the King saw himself moved to make a public issue of the hated matter once again. The Duke, who, for his part, did not believe in the legal actionability of this new suspicion, regretted this highly unpleasant turn of the already twisted story all the more sincerely the less it appeared Nolten would be able to remain out of danger, and the less he concealed from himself the possibility that perhaps a few felicitous signals from him would have sufficed to dispel the first problematic impression of the said poem and thus to avert any further repercussion. He saw only too clearly that in the end it was that one word from Constanze that had misguided his steps and contaminated his conciliatory attitude with a secret exception. Now there could no longer be any thought of a secret cover-up, and everything took its strictly legal course.

The two friends were as if thunderstruck when they were actually arrested. A commission was assigned to go through their papers, and unfortunately this all happened so quickly and unexpectedly — the two of them being totally unaware of the most recent rumors — that Larkens did not have the remotest thought of doing away with those compromising letters. For unfortunately they still existed; he had not been able bring himself to destroy such remarkable documents, and instead, during the first investigation, they were secretly stored in the house of an acquaintance who was not under suspicion; later, their author had retrieved them and consigned the treasonable trove to a sealed portfolio in his writing desk. To what extent that situation must have worried our actor in the moment when, upon being personally taken into custody, he was faced with sufficient proof of the serious intentions at work, can be imagined. For it was to be expected that the letters would be found and that their content, quite comical in nature though it was, could not but testify gravely against him.

The two barely knew what was happening to them when they saw themselves confined to the sorrowful solitude of two separate rooms in the so-called old castle. Leopold and Ferdinand were their sympathetic company on the way to their dreaded incarceration. In parting, Nolten could not utter a word, barely finding an opportunity to commend unto his sculptor friend one more short note to the Count. Larkens's behavior gave expression to his crushing pain; he averted his face when he took Nolten's hand for the last time.

When a person stands, stunned to silence by the unexpected blow of a most unjust fate, and observes himself alone, cut off from all external contributing factors, when the confused clamor of so many voices hums ever more quietly and faintly in his ear, then it might well happen that suddenly an assuring light of happiness rises within us and in good cheer we say to ourselves, it surely cannot be that this is all happening to me, it is an immense illusion and deception. We take physical stock of ourselves and expect that any minute the fog enveloping us will lift. But with haughty mien these walls and this carefully bolted door confronted the poor painter with their inexorable reality. Shaken and with an audible sigh he sank onto the nearest chair without even going to the window, which could have afforded him a free view of open country and to one side a friendly and consoling glimpse of a small part of the city. In fact the room was pleasantly situated in the upper reaches of the truly imposing, partially fortified old building. This one wing, except for the quarters of the commandant and the warden, was unoccupied, and from another side, where the garrison was located, there could occasionally be heard, albeit not too loud, the lively military sound of drums and music. Likewise Theobald's immediate surroundings did not strike as all

128

that dismal, the walls dry and white-washed clean, the iron bars on the window well-spaced enough so as not to darken the room, the heating reliable in so far as the approaching spring did not make it completely dispensable. But of the requisite diversion in the form of books, writing materials, and the like there was a total lack, and in particular any kind of material for artistic activity appeared to be expressly forbidden. In addition, our prisoner was still not thinking about such things at all. Instead, his thoughts, occupied with his beloved and with the riven and still veiled picture of his future, were still caught up in a dizzying vortex as if confronted with an insurmountable wall that they could broach from no side. Yet whenever he imagined the worst, the ultimate, he still found his faith in Constanze's right feelings, her clarity, her loyalty holding up valiantly. She had rejected him previously, likely because her position at court imposed that obligation upon her; she may, caught up in the general confusion, have harbored some animosity, but her heart would exonerate him, would feel for him, and would even know how to foster some alleviation of the present problem. This one hope of his by and by grew so strong that he came to envision the lovely woman as nothing other than a harbinger of peace expressing love and sympathy and ultimately even the charming ardor of an anxious bride demanding the release of her betrothed. Yet dreadfully did the time of uncertainty weigh upon him until he could hear the first benevolent sign from her! That note to the Count — he scarcely recalled its hastily scrawled words — gave expression only to a vigorous assertion of his innocence and a painful lament that might have been intended mainly to appeal to Constanze's feelings. A previously sketched letter to her, which we mentioned above, he had brought with him; he read anew these lines with their calm expression of happy hopes and bold promises; he imagined he saw the dear woman before him and could take her tender hand, hear her express her assent, feel her breath, and oh! how depressing was then the look of his cell in comparison to that most vivid dream.

Larkens for his part was tormenting himself no less with doubts and cares. His fantasy had to do without the lovely background images with which his brother in suffering was still able to adorn his situation. Also, according to a statement that he had heard in private and that, to spare his friend, had kept to himself, he had to reckon with a much later date of release than they had first thought; and this was all the more distressful for him the more he had to trace all the guilt for this double misfortune back to himself. Regarding his friend's affairs with the outside world, he believed that for the meantime he had taken care of matters by using the pretext of a business trip to assure Agnes in case there should be an extended interruption of their correspondence. Some advantage to his secret plan he found in the removal of Nolten from personal contact with Constanze. But this small gain, how dearly bought! And when he gave full consideration to what deprivation he himself suffered by being separated from Theobald, when he thought what the consolation of a conversation would mean to him in such adversity, or when he pondered the impossibility of so much as a letter from time to time to express himself or revive his spirits, he could have broken out in a rage and screamed out loud at a life led in a monotony of which he — uninhibited, impudently spoiled, and labile person that he was — had never conceived. The only hope he held out was for a hearing.

Some days had already passed when the situation of the two promised to become more bearable as a result of their being granted permission to pass their time reading. But Larkens obstinately rejected doing any such thing, and while Nolten, as he experienced every thinkable sorrow, nevertheless enjoyed the advantage of finding the ever renewed stuff of his inner life stimulated partly by his love and partly by the helpful insights of other artists, the actor sank all too soon into the darkness of his own self, becoming the voluntary prey of a malevolent spirit that we have encountered in him but little because until now he himself, to a certain degree, had fought it off well enough. In order, moreover, to make ourselves understood on this point, the following information will suffice.

Born into an affluent family and not accorded an attentive upbringing at home, he entered the academy at an early age and there, with no specific plan in mind, he was still able, amidst the merry doings of comradeship, to perform well in the study of philosophy and aesthetics. A sojourn in England and his encounter there with the best of its dramatic achievements confirmed his resolve to devote himself to that art in utmost earnest. His earliest schooling in the theater involved public performances on one of the most respected stages, and the attention of the public soon gave way to admiration when, albeit unwillingly and following the advice of an experienced actor, he concentrated for some time solely on comic portrayals. In the same measure that, following a strange inner compulsion, he turned more towards serious parts, the public approval waned, and so he wavered, in dissatisfied ill temper, for a full year, not wanting to acknowledge to which of the two fields he should best devote his talent. That was compounded by the drawback that the practical artist is more hindered than helped by his own poetic productivity. He wanted to live in the realm of his own writing and took it amiss when, in the midst of his creative pleasure, he was disturbed by the demands of his craft, a reaction that was all the more unavoidable for the fact that his own works lay far afield from the basic sphere of the stage and could be grasped and appreciated only by his close circle of friends. This divisive conflict between poetic avocation and theatrical vocation called forth the first disruption and disorder in his life; dismayed to find impracticable his dreams of a world of higher spirituality, he cast himself into the maelstrom of a base and common one, and the passions that he had thought, through artful portrayal, to hold in pleasing balance with his better self, he now let rage unchecked in real life.

At about that time there emerged among his friends a peculiar penchant for competing with each other in inventing and executing intrigues. Larkens in his good-natured way gladly played the master in these undertakings, but unfortunately this mischief soon involved him with an actress known equally for her beauty and wit, and that association soon drew him down into a vortex of the most depraved pleasures. He came to find his calling a tiresome secondary concern, and, more than once on the verge of being dismissed, he saved his position only by giving from time to time a performance in which he summoned up all his genius so as to take his employers' favor by storm. Sadly they watched him depart of his own volition the place that had been the witness of his sad depression. He renounced that unworthy life, summoned his strength for a new enterprise, and proved a pleasing asset for the city in which we later encounter him as Nolten's friend. Yet that much-blemished phase of his life still left behind even then an insurmountable restlessness, an emptiness in him, even long after he had, with the best of hopes, salvaged his moral and physical existence from the shipwreck. The cheerful and clever man was seized by a profound hypochondria, he believed himself physically ruined and felt he had forfeited forever the original strength of his intellect, although he disproved that double fallacy with daily achievements. How often he would counter Theobald, whenever his young friend would try to dispel the actor's moody whims, by laughing ruefully and offering up the sorry argument: "That remaining bit of me that still glows and glimmers is only a desperate, teasing trick of light, its size and beauty increased by an optical illusion born of the fact that it flares up amidst the dismal witch's brew of my howling melancholy." With such phrases he could fire up his passions for hours on end against Theobald, and only after he had essentially lacerated and destroyed himself totally did he regain some calm, some natural cheer, in which state he was, by the account of all about him, said to have been unbelievably gentle and amiable. Yet except for Theobald and perhaps one earlier acquaintance, not another soul knew him from this melancholy side; he was adept at hiding it completely, and on this point his behavior gave even to the keenest observer of human nature no clue. There was also no mistaking the positive influence that contact with Nolten and with his good sense had on that dark temperament, for although our painter himself might have suffered from a certain one-sidedness, his basic moral character was still unshakeable, and his striving for complete spiritual health was manifest from early on in the upward inclination of his art more and more towards the universal, in the cleansing away of all those elements that still persisted from the fantastic phase of his development. Larkens was happy to draw from this well a pure water for his barren land; he held passionately to his new-found friend, although of course without stormily revealing this ar-

131

dor in words; rather, he came quite unintentionally to play the more subdued role of a mentor who, made wise by his own unspeakable suffering, believes he can occasionally help guide the younger man onto the right track.
And by partaking in this manner of the rapid stream of a spirit striving forward in the plenitude of youth, he experienced a growth of new trust in
himself; the scales of his aged self fell away to reveal a fresh new form beneath. Ever more seldom were his outbreaks of self-torment, indeed they ultimately disappeared entirely. No wonder, then, that a feeling of gratitude
bound him forever to our friend, that he took it as his duty to work with all
his strength for that loved one's well-being. And while we may in no way
overlook in one striking example of this warm enthusiasm its tendency to
strange behavior, still the intention behind it was most pure and brotherly.
And who would wish to reproach him if, by devoting such tender care to a
broken love relationship, he provided his heart with the feeling of triumph
that he saw evidenced by the fact that, much tempted adventurer that he
was, he could still take an inmost fervent joy in the imagined love of an an-
gelically pure creature — of a girl whom he had never seen with his own eyes
and whom he had never thought of possessing for himself, however desirable
such possession might appear. He was happy to content himself with his capacity to embrace a lovely ideal with his inner self and give it form in the
outer world; he was beginning to be reconciled with himself and with the
world. So far everything was on the right track. But now, cut off from all activity, from the diversity of his convivial life, from the very element of his existence, and tormented as well by the thought of being the cause of a dear
friend's involvement in a dubious misadventure, he could no longer fight off
his general melancholy; his old wounds opened, and frantically he delved
into them. He saw past and present merge in a grimacing image; he saw
himself as the most miserable of men and lost himself in the blissful thought
that the man over-ripe in guilt and misery was given the power to shake off
his life of his own free will. The more surely he could reckon on that last
sanctuary, and the more calmly he learned by and by to master that thought,
the more did his mind gain, on the other side, in freedom and in the courage to wait patiently for what the immediate future would bring; he became
more calm, even serene of mood.

An unexpected interruption of this brooding inactivity, however pleasant
it might appear, still tended to strike him as an almost disturbing surprise,
since he saw the first threads of his slowly growing cocoon torn apart by the
intrusion of a fresh breath of life and himself encouraged to take new hope.
For one morning in the fourth week of their incarceration, the commandant
came to his room with the news that the two gentlemen were to be allowed,
on occasion, to have one or the other friend come to visit, albeit each only in
his own room and without the two prisoners themselves coming together.
Larkens thanked the man as well as he could; he was especially displeased

with the last condition. In addition, the officer had with no lack of clarity dispelled inferences about any further positive prejudices that his concession might have allowed, and Larkens supposed as well that they owed this favor to the Duke's special attention to Nolten.

The first evening Ferdinand and Leopold spent with Theobald; the following one with the actor, when they were joined by a third friend. As lively as such a reunion must have been, as friendly as the dear guests did their best to bring news of all kinds and the best wines to cheer the spirits, it was still a forced joy, and Theobald was all the less able to give himself over to it for having heard right at the start that his note to Zarlin had indeed been received but that, during the visit that Leopold had paid the Zarlins, the Count had merely expressed a general and rather cool regret. Inasmuch as Leopold was not supposed to know anything about the true nature of the connection that bound Nolten's interest to that family, the latter was able to ascertain only through indirect questions that Constanze had been neither seen nor mentioned.

This state of affairs did indeed weigh heavily on the heart of the anxious lover, but how must he have then felt when the sculptor repeated the offer he had made some weeks before to take a letter to Agnes, and then when he cheerfully explained how he had been in doubt the whole time whether he should take this duty upon himself and give the girl's father a considerate report of the unfortunate events, but how a passing word from Larkens on the matter early on had dissuaded him. "Yes indeed," said Nolten, "that's already been taken care of!" and dismissed the matter, while to himself, unable to make sense of the dismissive comment the actor was supposed to have made, he hit upon the most unfortunate connections possible.

The way Larkens received the visitors was basically more appealing, for he always considered it advantageous to be at his best when among others and to respond to a well-meant gesture in a good-natured, kindly, and pleasant manner, even when it occurred at an inopportune time. Yet the news that they hoped would cheer him the most — namely that the theater and those who loved it had loudly and heartily lamented their greatest favorite — he greeted with indifference and wanted to hear nothing of it. As for the views of the city in general, the word was that there were all manner of exaggerated opinions about the transgression of the two prisoners; reasonable people shrugged their shoulders, no one was inclined to believe in the complete innocence of the two. In addition, in the meantime there had been three hearings that had not brought matters any closer to a favorable decision.

While our pair were in a lamentable enough state under these circumstances, the painter was yet to face his greatest ordeal when, with all these severe shocks, he came down with a fever that the doctor at once saw to be serious. The ailing man did not leave his bed for three days, often lying there unconscious, while in his waking hours he only felt his misery all the more intensely; the fantasies of his fever carried their vivid play over even into his waking moments, casting the tormented sufferer mercilessly back and forth between waking and dreaming. At one moment Constanze would approach his bed, and when his heartfelt lament would inspire her sympathy, her love, just when her noble form seemed about to descend towards the poor sufferer, she would flee once again, shocked and angry. In another moment the spurned Agnes would appear at the door, her silent gaze fixed sadly upon him until she could endure it no longer and fell to her knees beside him, covering his hand with a thousand kisses, and he was for his part then compelled to take the poor repentant girl lovingly in his arms.

Such visions, in which what remained of his affection for that misunderstood and loveable child now found resonance in the very depths of his feelings made soft by illness and by his vulnerability, recurred with ever greater frequency and were all the more difficult to avoid since they were first called forth by a strange coincidence. For one morning he awoke before dawn from a state of restless semi-sleep to hear a woman singing, her voice seeming to come from the warden's kitchen right below his window. The content of her song, though it could hardly be meant for him, struck him to the depths of his soul, and its infinitely touching melody resounded through the silence of that dark early hour, its tones even taking on in his imagination a wondrous similarity to Agnes's voice.

> Early when the roosters crow
> And the starlight's ending,
> I then to the hearth must go
> And the fire be tending.
>
> Lovely is the shining blaze,
> And the sparks are flying.
> I amidst them cast my gaze,
> Sunk in sorrow, dying.
>
> Suddenly I think of you,
> O my faithless lover,
> Knowing I dreamt the whole night through
> Of you and of no other.
>
> Tears and tears upon each tear
> Do ceaseless fall and flow,
> And so the bright new day does near;
> But oh, that it would go!

For the first time in ever so long Theobald felt the beneficial effect of unchecked tears. The voice fell silent and no sound broke the peace of the slowly dawning morning. The ailing man buried his face in his pillows, given over totally to enjoying the sweetness of a — still so bitter — sorrow.

THAT SAME MORNING Larkens, barely out of bed, had a visit from Leopold, the sculptor. He had actually meant to visit Theobald, but hearing from the porter that his ailing friend, after a tolerable night, was just now still sleeping peacefully, Leopold did not dare to disturb him, and had them open the actor's door. He found that man in the saddest mood, plunged into it by his concern for Nolten, and Leopold, deeply moved himself, found it hard to console him.

After some time, the sculptor began: "Now I must tell you something that was, of course, originally intended for Nolten. It concerns an occurrence that I have been pondering now for three days without being able to find the opportunity to tell anyone else about it — the colonel, you see, denied my request twice, since the doctor wants to make sure that the sick man will be disturbed as little as possible by any company; yesterday I had trouble getting permission for an hour's visit. My worries about Nolten and, if I may say so, my own news, gave me no peace or rest. What I have to tell is shocking, quite incomprehensible, and in any case it is not suitable for Nolten under the present circumstances."

"Well, for God's sake, just as long as it's not a new misfortune!" said the actor, smiling grimly at the length of Leopold's introduction; "am I to imagine I'll have to hear about a new resolution that we poor wretches have been sentenced to hard labor with bread and water?"

"Nothing of the kind! Sit down and listen! It was on the evening of our recent visit; Ferdinand and I had barely left you, we had left the castle, I was just about to turn into Prinzenstraße, and then, with a chance sidelong glance into an empty row of chestnut trees that we had to pass, I spy a female form leaning quite calmly on one of the trees. The eyes of the unknown woman met mine, and I almost lost my senses at the sight of this physiognomy, for — but first I must ask — do you recall that crazy painting by Nolten?"

"Which one?"

"Of the woman playing the organ."

"Of course."

"And when I now tell you: *it was her,* will you believe me?"

"Not until I've re-counted how many bottles we drank that evening."

"Go ahead, make fun; it was bright moonlight, I saw her face as clear as daylight, and as for my sobriety —"

"Enough!" Larkens cut him off, rising to his feet; he paced back and forth a few times, thinking, while Leopold went on. "I must yet confess to

135

you a weakness, my dear Larkens, and you may rebuke me for it if you like, but who in all the world is totally free of superstition, especially under such circumstances? Scarcely had I heard, the day before yesterday, that Theobald had taken to bed seriously ill, than I immediately took my encounter with the ghostly organist to be an omen, for I recalled what people say about bereavements having been foretold in like manner. And this stupid fear plagues me still today, although I well know that my apparition was no vision, nor ghost, nor anything of the sort, but a proper human being."

"Honestly spoken, dear friend," said Larkens, "I am not in the least in doubt about this apparition, and perhaps I can perhaps even give you the key to the riddle. But keep silent on this matter towards our friend, promise me you'll keep quiet about it."

"Certainly, if you think it's necessary."

"Very well, then — but first I would like to know how your adventure ended. Did you speak to this person?"

"My God, of course not! For (as I am almost ashamed to admit) the encounter gave me such a start that I turned back to look three times, perhaps four, and then, when I looked around for where I'd left my friend, that image of the night had already disappeared and wasn't to be found no matter what. All we found out was the next day when Theobald's servant told us that a beggar woman whose description exactly matched that of the person I saw had called at Nolten's the day before and, when assured that he would be away for a longer time, had stolen away. All my questions and investigations remained fruitless."

"Very well" — Larkens began — "now listen. Two days before last New Year's Eve, which I hope you still remember, I encountered in my entryway a girl whose appearance struck me at once, and in fact in the very same way you mentioned. She was a Gypsy girl, tall and slim, no longer young, really, but still a true beauty, in short just as in the picture, except for the few intervening years. She was carrying a basket of wooden carvings, yet my first impression that she had come for some reason other than making a sale was soon verified by her question about a painter who was said to live here; she took out a letter and it was in the handwriting of Nolten's fiancée, yet it was addressed — I don't know why — to me, though the content itself was meant for Nolten. I learned that the Gypsy girl's wanderings had taken her to Neuburg, and she brought greetings from there. I found this person, according to several of Theobald's stories, to be no less than strange, but the more I knew about her earlier contact with our friend, the more dubious did I think it would be simply to go ahead and help fulfill her wish, which consisted in seeing the 'handsome, wonderful boy,' as she called him, just one more time. At least I thought the wonderful boy would have to be prepared for such an encounter, and on closer consideration it seemed to me that thwarting such an encounter would be the safest and most appropriate thing to do. I used all manner of pretexts to put her off making any attempt to see him; but then, since in the meantime the foolish thing insisted and her demand seemed to be as justified as it was simple and well meant, I tried to think up ways that she could see Nolten without his becoming aware of her. That could be done in a variety of ways. But I liked, as I gladly admit, a somewhat romantically unusual way more than a simple peeping through a crack or keyhole, and so, in short, the New Year's masquerade served my purposes perfectly and —"

"What?" Leopold exclaimed in surprise, "so at last the night watchman from St. Ablan's tower steps out of the story and into real life!"

"That's easy to guess now; but listen briefly to how it went. After I had acquainted the girl with my plan — which at first she could not understand at all — and she had also given me her promise, in the most unforgettably touching way, to do nothing, come what may, that ran counter to my instructions or aroused suspicion, I dictated to her a few pages, which, to my great joy, she wrote down in strange signs, since she knew how to write our letters only very badly. But it still cost me trouble enough until I was able to get her to write my words down properly, and more trouble still until she had learned her role. With that I found for her the right clothing, and a true pleasure it was to see the naive look with which she observed herself in her ideal disguise. She treated the whole thing with a certain solemnity and took pleasure in doing so; her recitation may well have been rough and dry, yet her conception of this poetic figure was basically sound. All our preparations took place in another room outside the house where I occasionally give lessons to actors of both sexes, so that the project attracted no attention. How properly the girl did her part you saw for yourself, and I myself was quietly surprised by the successful production."

Leopold could hardly express his astonishment as he recalled the details of the New Year's party at the tower. Since he now showed all the more desire to learn more about the strange person of the Gypsy and her earlier relationship to Theobald, the actor was not loath to oblige. He was just about to begin his narrative when he paused, thinking, and then finally said: "Do you know what, my friend? You will best come to know this short story from some few pages on which I have attempted to give a true account of what Nolten entrusted to me early in our acquaintance, since I deemed the event worthy of preserving; especially remarkable, bound up with the whole story, is the fate of a certain long-deceased relative of the Nolten family, in whose life I believe I have found the prototypical explanation for our friend's story. Several weeks ago, an acquaintance borrowed the notebook from me, I'll give you a short note to him, and he'll hand the notebook over to you. If one gives thoughtful consideration to this fragment of our Nolten's life and compares it with his subsequent development up to the present day, then one can hardly refrain from pondering more deeply the wondrous ways in which often an unknown higher power seems to guide and plan a person's life. The inner kernel of fate, usually unfathomable and hidden, from which an entire human life evolves, the secret bond that weaves through a sequence of elective affinities,[20] those peculiar cycles in which certain events recur, the striking similarities that emerge here and there from a closer comparison of earlier and later family members in respect to their character, their experiences, their physiognomies (just as when at times we unexpectedly hear one and the same melody in the same piece of music, only with different intonation), and then too the strange fate that often a descendent must play out the uncompleted role of a long-passed predecessor — all these things strike us in a more obvious and surprising way in the example of our young friend than they do in the case of hundreds of other individuals. And nevertheless you will discover in all these relationships nothing incomprehensible or crudely fatalistic, but rather only the most natural unfolding of necessity. The point of the whole matter consists, however, in the way that our friend was guided even as a young boy towards his inmost devotion to an art whose essential character can still be seen today in the majority of his paintings. Enough, you may judge for yourself. But oh! what will you feel while reading all this when you think that the very man whose ominous boyhood figure you encounter in these pages has now, as an adult, been cast out of his own sphere by the unthinking fist of an alien fate, and now, ere it is even half accounted for, his life is to wilt and perish so quickly behind these walls! For, O my friend! I fear all this, and this worry will grind me down, will kill me even before him — and may it be so! Look at me; I believe I feel it, and my mirror says it's so, that the grief of these three days has made me older by twice that number of years. But enough; I must break off if I wish not to lose my senses. Go over to the poor man and take his hand in Larkens's name. Oh, might I one more time at least see him face to face! And yet — I fear doing so!"

Leopold reached for his hat and asked directions about the remarkable notebook; since the keeper was just coming in, he hesitated no longer in order above all to visit the beloved patient. With a longing gaze the actor watched him depart; he was overcome by a boundless yearning for Theobald, but in vain; his door was closed and across the way he heard the lock rattling on the door to his beloved's room.

With that the sculptor stood at Nolten's bedside and, secretly horrified by the extreme misery of the ailing man's appearance, had to summon all his composure so as not to betray his feelings. Nolten's emotional state he could not fully make out; Nolten spoke little, straining to do so, his voice weak. At one point he asked the warden who it was who was always singing so early in the morning under his window. Somewhat chagrined the old man answered: "That is my daughter; but I will forbid her from doing so, it's not right; and oh, singing is her whole life!" Theobald requested urgently that they not put the girl off such amusements; he asked how it came about that she seemed to know only serious, sad songs? "The devil knows," came the answer, "where she gets all that; she's been a silly thing since childhood and not happy and impetuous like other young people, but hard-working and sensible, and she's taken care of the whole household for me since her mother's death." And as the old man immediately broke into the most touching laments about the death of his wife, whose virtue he could not praise enough, and then, as he opened up more and warmed to the subject, started to discuss an unhappy love affair his child was going through, it was easy to notice what an exhausting effect such matters were having on Nolten, for which reason Leopold gave the old narrator a sign. Finally, the sculptor departed with uncertain and heavy heart. He hastened, after first having retrieved the aforementioned manuscript, on his own away from the bustle of the city, following a little-known path. A warm sunny day was melting away the last remnants of snow and ice, a refreshing breeze was already teasing with promises of spring. Thus does our serious stroller arrive, even before he notices, among the most rustic surroundings, a friendly village greeting him with a smile. There he seeks a quiet garden out behind the first inn he encounters and soon finds there as well a pretty clearing high among the vineyards with a table and bench from which he has the most pleasant view. He orders a bottle of wine, sits down, and takes out that piece of writing whose content we cannot withhold from the reader.

A Day in Nolten's Youth

THE TIME HAD COME AGAIN when sixteen-year-old Theobald was allowed to leave the school in the capital city and visit his family for two weeks. The parsonage at Wolfsbühl was thus filled for the time with great joy, for father and sisters hung upon that blossoming young person with all their hearts. An especially close bond prevailed, however, between Adelheid and her brother, younger by but a few years. They had their own topics of amusement in which no one else could be included; they had a hundred little secrets and, yes, at times even their own language. This subtle empathy was based mainly upon a similar fantasy that had first been nourished in their childhood days, influenced by a village and its unusual environs rich in fairy tales and inclined almost to superstition — a fantasy that, in a peculiar and very subtle way, had gradually set them apart from their normal circle. The direction that these two youthful temperaments had taken appeared to leave nothing to fear, and even outwardly the relationship did not exist at all in a one-sided way at the expense of the remaining three, less susceptible, sisters. There prevailed a good-natured, cheerful compatibility; only the older daughter, Ernestine, to whose care matters of the household were usually left, exhibited at times a dark and domineering attitude, and she had already gotten the father on her side more often than was fair.

One grey day towards the end of October, Theobald and his soul mate are strolling in the garden behind the house. He has just been telling her his dream of the previous night, and his sister seems to be listening earnestly, while casting a detached gaze to one side, looking to where she knew the old ruin, called the Rehstock, lay hidden deep in the mist.

"But you're not paying attention Adelheid! Just now, in order to test you, I intentionally brought crazy nonsense into my otherwise sensible dream, and you accepted it as naturally as two times two is four."

The girl was a little startled at being caught out, but still laughed at herself about it right away and said: "Yes, right! I was only half listening while you were going on incessantly about a big underground cellar door that in the end kicked out at the poor man with its two hind legs. And then, what's not possible in a dream? But just be so bold as to give me a slap! I actually did have other things to think about. Listen! and just so you know, we're going to the Rehstock today. I've never seen it on a day like today, and I think that then the old walls, the autumn woods must be quite striking; I feel as if today we could just this once have the pleasure of eavesdropping on and surprising a pair of quiet, secretive clouds if they choose to lie down just right in the hollow windows. What do you think? Let's agree. We'll get permission from Papa to let Johann saddle the horse for me, and of course you yourself are sure-footed enough to walk. We'll go right after breakfast, all alone if possible, and not come back until evening."

Her brother liked the suggestion; they planned that they would do everything possible in the way of favors in order to set the others in the right mood. Adelheid braided her older sister's hair — that was the vain Ernestine — this time with unusual care and without even asking for a return favor, and the kiss she was given for doing so was for the two about the same good sign that others, if they had had a similar plan, would have seen in the first glimpse of sunlight. Before they'd thought about it, Theobald had arranged everything with his father, and soon the horse stood bridled and ready in the courtyard, complete with the comfortable woman's saddle. They let the pair go unhindered. The old man stood under the window and, with a satisfied gaze at his daughter's trim riding posture merely muttered to himself: "Foolishness!" Ernestine called after them shrilly some final little thing about taking care with the fragile containers filled with edibles, which the hired hand was carrying along behind in a leather bag among the umbrellas, and the good people of Wolfsbühl, long accustomed to seeing the woman on horseback, offered up their friendliest greetings all through the village.

The sun kept obligingly to its hiding place behind the clouds, and the day retained, to Adelheid's greatest satisfaction, "its grouchy face."

"Although quite likely," she began after a while, "I would be quite happy to feel really gloomy, like this day itself is; I'm still moved almost against my will by a wondrous feeling of jubilation deep in a small, fine corner of my innermost self, a joy springing from I know not where. In the end it's really just a reverse effect of this melancholy autumn scene, and I've noticed it quite often in myself since I was a child. I've noticed that on such sad-colored days the soul becomes most aware of itself; it is assailed by a homesickness, yearning for it knows not what, and suddenly it swings back to happiness again, yet cannot say why or how. I enjoy the freedom riding on my good horse, I wrap myself with childlike pleasure in my little cloak against the cold air that is blowing in on us, keeping my happy heart warm, and I give myself to my thoughts. But back when we still lived in Rissthal, wasn't it different when we went out riding? The narrow valley, the dense woods whichever way we looked. Here we have the flat field and nothing but fruit trees. We have a good hour-and-a-half to ride before the path begins to wind more. We're lucky we don't have to use the main road."

The two then ran through inexhaustible conversations about the high points of their earlier days in Rissthal, an impoverished settlement where their father had worked twelve years as pastor. They shared with the most heartfelt joy so many a pleasant memory that still lingered faintly in their minds; by and by they ventured words of mutual feeling and emotion, as so rarely happens between young people with their ever watchful false sense of shame.

Finally the brother said: "As we chat now so open-heartedly, I can't keep from confessing to you that I am still keeping *one* secret from you, Adelheid! It's nothing suspicious, nothing that I would have to keep secret; a whim has held me back until now from telling it to you. But today you'll hear it, and indeed beneath the walls of the old Rehstock, so that in the future you may think of it whenever you look up that way."

"Good!" his sister responded, "I look forward to it, and for now not one word more about it!"

As their conversation took a hundred turns, less than two hours had brought the pair, without their noticing, quite close to their desired goal. Clear and ever clearer the outlines of the towering ruin became visible; in no time they stood at the foot of the sparsely wooded mountain, at its back a long stretch of densely forested mountains. Here they rested and, with less indifference than when they had seen it packed that morning, opened the almost forgotten sack of food. Then they proceeded slowly up the winding way, after giving the horse over to Johann so that he could put it up at a nearby dairy farm and then bring it back to meet them as arranged. Arriving at the top, the happy twosome roamed, first hand and hand and then going their separate ways, about the vast reaches, over ramparts and moats, through tumbled-down chambers, dank passageways, wild growth. They

141

willingly lost each other and then met unexpectedly at a variety of points. And so it happened that Adelheid was trying to decode an unintelligible inscription when suddenly she heard the lost tones of what seemed to be a woman's singing. The girl was frightened without knowing why. For a moment she was seized by a worried thought of her brother, of calling for help, of an accident. She perked up her ears and even thought that she had been mistaken, but in that moment she heard the same voice again more clearly and apparently from inside the walls, rising up not unlike the melancholy tones of an aeolian harp. Her feelings a mix of solemn reverence and uncertain fear, as if ghostly voices had awakened round her, the startled girl ventured only a few steps forward and then stood still with each crescendo of the ever more charming song, and, while her lips moved involuntarily to form a smile of pleased wonderment, she felt her whole self seized at the same time by a slight shudder. Now the mysterious voice fell silent; only the rush of the wind in the dry leaves, the quiet fall of a piece of stone breaking off here or there, or the sound of a bird in flight broke the silence of the place. The girl stood some time lost in thought, undecided, ever in anxious expectation that the invisible singer would appear at any moment around a corner; she even prepared herself for something bold and daring to say in case this apparition should show herself. Then suddenly came the sound of firm, hasty, but well-known footsteps. Theobald came, gasping for breath, climbing up a pile of rubble; he was happy to see his sister again and said: "Just listen! I had a strange encounter —"

"So did I; did you hear that amazing song?"

"No, what song? — but at the entrance to the rampart, where that blocked well is, sits a figure in brown women's clothes, with hooded head. It turned its back to me; that's all I could make out, and I ran off to look for you."

His sister told her version of what had happened, and the two soon agreed they had to have a closer look at the person, speak with her, whoever it might be. "Another interest like ours this person's visit here has likely not awakened," Adelheid remarked, "with today's weather there's surely not anyone except you and me willing to go on such an outing; I suspect it's an unfortunate woman, lost, an outcast, whom we are meant to console." — "And even if it's a ghost!" exclaimed Theobald, "we'll go and see who she is!"

And so they hurried back to where Theobald said he had seen the hooded figure and found a young maiden whose strange but by no means unpleasant appearance seemed at first glance to reveal her to be a Gypsy. Her face, expression, and demeanor made a striking impression of beauty and strength, all such as to instill respect, even trust, if one went by a certain sorrowful look upon her countenance. Until Adelheid uttered words of greeting, the unknown woman had not noticed — or wished to notice — the two approaching; yet now she gazed, her black eyes wide and calm, at the two young people and responded only after a pause in sonorous German: "Good evening!" — the calm seriousness of her bearing giving way to a shimmer of friendliness. Encouraged by this greeting, Adelheid was just about to say something more when the Gypsy girl's startled look at Theobald cut her short. She saw how he was trembling and pale and how he had gone weak in the knees. "The young gentleman is not well! Let him sit down!" the strange woman said, and was herself trying to help him into a comfortable position and put her bundle under his head. "He must likely have taken a chill here in these drafty chambers," she added, half-questioning, to Adelheid, who was hovering in silent, uncertain agitation over her passed-out brother and who now began to weep. The strange woman tried to console her: "Child, child, what is it? I hope this isn't a serious mishap; wait a bit, let me help!" and she reached into her pack and brought out a small bottle of a strong-smelling essence, which she said should have a powerful effect on "the fine, handsome boy," as she called him. But when after repeated tries her brother's eyes remained closed and Adelheid was about to walk away, disconsolate, the Gypsy admonished her with a commanding gesture to be calm, with the result that the girl simply looked on, unmoving and as if paralyzed, as the strange daughter of the forest laid her hand flat on the boy's brow and inclined her head, whispering quietly to him, towards his face. This mute gesture lasted several minutes without any of the three making a move. And behold, the boy's eyes opened, wide and bright, and gazed long and hard, yet still not conscious, fixed upon the two dark stars that hovered so close over him. But then when he closed his eyes and opened them again, awakening to clarity, he saw blue eyes instead of black; he saw his sister's tears of joy. The strange woman was standing off to one side; he could not see her right away, but he sat up and smiled with satisfaction when he had found her. There were now some signs of cheer in all three faces, and Theobald felt better with every breath.

While Adelheid hurried to the innermost court of the fortress to fetch for her brother the travel bag she had left there with wine in it, the two left behind began an unusual conversation. Theobald, it seems, after some silence, began, his voice agitated, "Tell me, I beg you, do you know why that happened with me, what you just saw?"

"No!" came the answer.

"What? you did not gaze into my soul?"

"I do not understand you, dear sir!"

"You see," the boy went on, "when I saw you, it was as if I were sinking deep into myself as if into an abyss, as if I were spinning dizzily, tumbling from one depth to the next, on through all the nights when I saw you in a hundred dreams just as you stand before me now; I flew spinning downward through all the phases of my life and saw myself as a boy and as a child standing beside your form just as it is standing upright before me now; yes, I fell into the darkness where my cradle stood and saw you holding the veil that covered me: then I lost consciousness, perhaps I was long asleep, yet when my eyes opened of their own accord they were gazing into your eyes as if into an endless well that held the riddle of my life."

He fell silent and rested his gaze calmly upon her, then, becoming animated, he said: "Let me hold your right hand!" The stranger granted his wish, and he sat, weighing her beautifully formed brown hand in his, lost in blissful thought, as if he were holding a miracle; and only when at last one warm drop after another began to fall on her fingers did she pull her hands back; then the maiden moved away with a striking gesture, going off to one side where she disappeared behind a wall. In this moment Adelheid came bounding briskly down the rampart, yet she suddenly stopped in surprise, for the song rose up, its resonance imposing, sounding different than before, wild, like a black banner rippling in the air. They could not make out the words. A passionate dark spirit was the soul of the melodies, however gentle and lovely at times their tones, as they rose and fell in irregular cadence. Astonished, Theobald rose to his feet; frightened, his sister came to his side. "We have found an insane woman," she said, "we must get away." "For God's sake, stay!" exclaimed Theobald, his strength greatly enhanced by the unusual events: "Dear sister, you were never one of those so quick to give a bad name to something strange that you didn't understand. Yes, and even if she were an insane woman, she'll not harm us. I know her, and she knows me. You shall soon hear more." With that he went to where the song — which had just stopped — had come from. His sister, barely believing her ears as she watched him go, was a confusion of misgivings, her concern intense. She waited some moments, and then, her anxiety unbearable, she called out her brother's name several times.

And come he did, hand in hand with the strange girl, the two approaching slowly, in intimate friendship. It seemed that time must have brought a definite understanding between the two. While Theobald's countenance expressed only a deeply contented, blissful devotion, there still radiated from the young maid, like lightning flashes, faint reminders of the preceding turmoil of her senses, yet all the more charming and touching then was how, as if constrained by her own will, her gaze took on a gentle, pleasant calm. Adelheid saw none of this; yet the look of the strange girl now eased her fear greatly, awakened her understanding, her sympathy. "She's coming home with us, sister, just so you know!" Theobald began, "I have already thought out a plan. You are coming, Elisabeth, aren't you?" Shaking her head to this question she seemed to be shyly denying something she had already silently agreed to do. "But we had better set out right away, evening is about to fall!" the boy went on; and so they made ready, packed up their things, and departed. "I cannot see," whispered Adelheid to her brother in an opportune moment while Elisabeth had run on ahead, "I don't understand what can come of this! Have you even considered how father will take this adventure? If it's your intention that this person stays with us tonight, what good can that do her? or what do you have in mind? For heaven's sake, give me some idea about your puzzling behavior! What feelings! What passions! What does it all mean? I think you're acting like a dreamer!"

"You may well be right," was his answer, "yes, like a dreamer! why, I hardly know myself how this has all come about. I have doubts at times about the reality of what has happened here. But doubly miraculous is the fact that what I wanted to reveal to you today at the Rehstock and what existed nowhere but in my imagination had to appear to us two today incarnate in human form."

By and by he explained that the girl had been able to tell him no more about herself than that four days ago she had secretly separated from her company — which happened to be a publicly accepted band of Gypsies — because she had wanted to seek out the home from which she had been abducted as a child and that she could barely remember. This information did not serve to increase Adelheid's sympathy very much at all; instead, the girl's stated reason for her flight aroused a high degree of suspicion as being improbable. In the meantime, the sensible girl assumed that it would do absolutely no good to reprimand her brother, and she was concerned only with preventing, at the very least, still greater trouble in an already bad situation. Theobald's health, which she feared might be dangerously weakened as a result of the unusual excitement, was the first thing that worried her, and to her suggestion that they should see whether the neighboring cavalry officer would lend them a carriage, her brother objected only on the grounds that Elisabeth for her part insisted on going the whole way on foot. Johann, who had been waiting faithfully this entire time, was nevertheless dispatched with the pertinent requests to the nearby farm of the old captain, a close acquaintance of the pastor. During an awkward half-hour's wait, Adelheid had the opportunity to become acquainted with the object of her displeasure and distrust from what was at least an innocent side. Elisabeth gave the most emphatic expression to her almost childlike regret at having stolen away from her band, where they now quite rightly missed her, where no harm had ever befallen her, and where, whenever she had been ill, she had been well comforted and ably cared for by these completely cheerful and honest people. When she said "ill," she pointed to her forehead with a sad grimace of a smile, in this way voluntarily and openly admitting what Adelheid had feared at the outset. But she went on to assure naively: "Only don't worry, you two good children, that I would harm anyone if my affliction should beset me. Don't worry about that. When that happens, I go off alone and sing the song that Mother Faggatin, my grandmother, taught me, and then I'm all right again. You, poor boy, you should also learn that song, you suffer too

145

much; I noticed that right away, that's why I am going with you until you're home, yet you can't keep me. Nor will I sleep in your house tonight. Even this very night Elisabeth will move on, back whence she came, for her home is no longer to be found. They have hidden it from me; the mountains, the house, the green lake, they have hidden it all from me! How can that be possible! It makes me laugh!"

The farm hand arrived with the borrowed carriage, and not a moment too soon, for it had already grown dark. All the less were Theobald and even Adelheid inclined to let Elisabeth walk alongside. Yet she was not to be persuaded, and so they proceeded quickly enough nonetheless.

While now in this manner brother and sister, although with markedly different feelings yet in agreement about their next steps, are approaching their paternal home and Theobald is at last revealing to his sister the entire wondrous meaning of the past day, those at home await their arrival with great anticipation, and the father has been making the others feel his consternation at the long delay of the young people in his usual way. In order to convey with any accuracy at all the prevailing mood in the parsonage, we are absolutely compelled, however much we are disinclined to do so, to make mention of a certain habit of this pater familias that was at this very moment being brought into play again. This father, it seems, a man of the most contradictory moods — now benevolent, now spiteful, unsociable and hypochondriac, yet also much loved as good company — counted among several highly repugnant habits and to an almost detestable degree the fault of laziness, and it induced him to the most tasteless amusements. When he was able to take the pleasure of staying in bed the live-long day in perfect health and yawning away over one and the same page of newspaper, then that, at least, made no one unhappy. But now he, who had in earlier days been an occasional friend of the hunt, had found a way to pass the time by lying abed and shooting all around the room with his fowling piece. For this purpose he would roll and knead with his own hands little pellets from a lump of clay that he always had to have on his night table. He was positioned so that from his bedchamber he was able to command almost the entire living room with his tube. Yet the goal of this target practice was not always the large vinegar cruet sitting on the oven, nor the little door of the bird cage, nor the old portrait of Friedrich of Prussia; rather, the pastor now and then looked upon it as one of the most pleasant aspects of child rearing to reprimand certain bad behavior that he claimed to observe in his daughters with such shots. Fräulein Nanette, for example, working by the light of the sewing table, required longer than the father thought proper to push the thread through the eye of the needle, and suddenly a pellet stuck to her bare arm; and the shot must have been so sharp as to make the good child gasp in real pain. On this evening a few such instances had occurred, though of course Fräulein Ernestine was spared, a privilege that usually Adelheid, too, and of course Theobald, were permitted to share with her. Yet what kind of reception can we expect those latter two to have under such circumstances? It was eight o'clock by the time they approached the village. They had agreed in the meantime that they would keep Elisabeth, who persisted in her stubborn refusal to stay the night, at least for supper, to which she too ultimately consented.

The ultimate arrival of the absent twosome had, in the meantime, become known in the parsonage through the boy the family had sent out to meet them and to whom the faithful Johann had confidentially whispered the most remarkable things that had occurred. This then gave rise to great wonderment and a mighty outcry back home. The pastor let his toy gun fall from his hand when he heard about the Gypsy girl, the cavalry officer's carriage, and his son's feeling unwell. He arose from bed and put on his robe, saying as he did so: "What? a card reader? a vagabond woman? by the devil! a witch? And as a result my son suddenly doesn't feel well? — and a carriage — a pagan, is she? I mean to convert her, I shall confront her with the nativity! hand me my cane! not that one — the Spanish one! What did Johann say? The horses got shy when the Gypsy ran along beside them?"

The door opened, and there stood Adelheid and Theobald in the room; she with halting voice, choking back her anxiety, he more ashamed and glowing with bitter resentment at the undignified behavior of his father. In vain he blocked the impetuous man's way, pleading, as, lamp in hand, the pastor was about to walk into the vestibule where Elisabeth was standing motionless, staring back at him, wide-eyed and unafraid. Yet now there followed a scene that ran totally counter to the tense expectations of all present. The pastor's harsh words die out upon his tongue when he sets eyes on the facial features of the strange girl, and with an expression of utmost astonishment he takes a few steps back. At the room's threshold he casts one more glance back upon the girl, and in laughable confusion he runs through all the rooms. "How does she find her way to you? What do you two know about this woman?" he asks Adelheid, while Theobald steals out into the hallway. The girl reported what she knew, and then added that her brother had spoken of a picture that even as a child he had often seen up in the attic and that bore the most miraculous resemblance to the girl. The pastor made an impatient gesture with his hand and sighed out loud. He did indeed seem to be more in the know about the strange person's identity than he himself might have liked, and the last doubts disappeared after an interview that, as well as he could, he conducted alone with Elisabeth in his study. He was convinced that he was confronting here the sad fruit of an affair that, long concealed in silence, had once caused immeasurable anger and unspeakable misery in his family. Yet what Elisabeth told him about her fate up to the present was not much more than what the others already knew about her, and the pastor did not think it a good idea to enlighten her about the mystery of her birth and about the close connection in which it placed her to his household. The striking fact that the runaway girl had come to precisely this area was clarified by some of the girl's statements, from which emerged the fact that a discontented member of the band had wanted to take revenge on the leader by causing Elisabeth's disappearance, the opportunity for doing which Elisabeth herself had supplied with her frequent request that he might just once take her to visit her homeland — and of course that person, as later emerged, was totally informed about the girl's true origins as well as about the presence of some relatives of her father. He had intended to bring her to Wolfsbühl, where he expected to be accorded no small degree of gratitude, but a few hours away from that destination he had discovered traces of Gypsies who were without doubt pursuing him. He left the girl on her own and continued his flight alone.

Fräulein Ernestine reminded them for the third time of their already delayed supper; they made ready to dine, and no other mealtime is likely to have offered a stranger sight than this one. This one proceeded in taciturn manner. The strange guest was, of course, constantly the target of curious and uncertain glances that, whenever they were met by a flash out from under those dark eyelashes, would merely dart back shyly to their own plates.

Elisabeth watched after dinner for the best moment to slip out the door and quickly leave the house without the others' being able to find her when they noticed she was gone. The father seemed more relieved by that than worried. Yet she had, as they now noticed, left her bundle behind; thus she would likely have to come back, and Theobald consoled himself with this hope.

A powerful and deep-seated passion, as we can surely see even now, had taken control of his sensitive feelings — a passion likely without equal in its origins and of a dangerous nature not in the least lessened by the fact that it seems to entail a glow of *purity*. The young man found himself, since the mysterious creature had disappeared, in a state of silent, aching pain that caused him, whenever Adelheid gave him a sympathetic look, to have trouble holding back tears. She urged him to go to his bedroom, where soon she bade him goodnight. The pastor was so disturbed in the usual equanimity of his ways by the unexpected events of the evening that he could not think of going to rest. The memory of a momentous past, of the unhappy fate of his very own brother, was called to life in him again for the first time in a long time; he felt a need to confide in his oldest daughter, and Ernestine, always told little about that unusual family affair, now watched with curiosity as her father fetched forth a dust-covered manuscript in which was recorded the story of her uncle, largely in his own hand. All the others of the household had gone to bed, with only Adelheid sitting, lost in thought, in a corner of the room and listening quietly, while her father told from memory, soon after he had once again, with melancholy, even dread, pushed aside the manuscript lying in front of him.

"My younger brother Friedrich," he began, "your late uncle, was a genius, as they were wont to say, and unfortunately, for all the goodness of his heart, an eccentric mind, who even in his most youthful years neither did nor desired anything that would have been right and proper. He exhibited an extraordinary talent for painting, and in time the Prince supported him in the most generous fashion. He had him travel to Italy for six years and after his return showed him the most exceptional signs of his favor. At the start he resided in the capital city, but later he bought himself, five hours from Rissthal and three hours from here, the small estate F., where, still unmarried, he lived only for his work. During this time I saw him quite often. He was a tall, handsome man and quite content with his own life. He could have been happy, but a journey led to his ruination. For he decided in the spring of 17xx, on the advice of his doctors, to recover his health by traveling to Bohemia to visit a friend who had been in Rome with him. Oh, he had no idea what fate awaited him!"

Thus the pastor began, and there followed the narration of a story that the reader can come to know better from the diary of the painter.

In the vicinity of H***, 22 May

For weeks now I have been feeling in better health than ever; but for the last few days my mind has been reaching out with its dormant organs so eagerly and hungry for work that I am astonished at myself. I feel a new life is about to surge forth, a miracle about to grow in me. I would know of no one to whom I could so intimately confide the cause of this mighty revolution, the story of the last four days — but to these silent pages. Yet truly, I do so only out of the capricious concern that my present fortune, or even my memory of this extraordinary time, could be taken from me.

On the 17th of May I undertook from G. a short excursion, going alone, as my friend was kept from accompanying me. I found something enticing about the thought of just setting out here on Bohemian soil, as I had occasionally done in my fatherland, without a specific goal or particular intention, thinking only of the beautiful mountains over towards *** that I had seen from my window as a dark blue band on the distant horizon. So I set off in that general direction and took my ease in following whatever path I came upon, lingering over whatever struck me as new and remarkable. I made my observations on man and nature, took out my sketchbook, sketched or read as the spirit moved me, and now and then took my pleasure as best I could in the most modest village inns. By the second evening of my wanderings I already found myself in an appealing mountain area, and the following midday saw me roving about deep in the most magnificent woods where I tasted the wild breath of nature to my heart's desire, felt the thrill of loneliness, and gave myself over to a hundred diversions. Unnoticed, dusk descended, and only then did it occur to me to find the footpath, which, as I had been told, must lead to a good hostel situated in the midst of the forest. Doing so was not so simple; for a full half-hour I groped about without finding the trail. Now it was almost night. I had little choice. I took a chance and moved on for a while until the ever thickening underbrush and my great weariness brought me to a sullen standstill. My impatience and anger about my lack of caution had reached an extreme, when I was suddenly surprised by the thought that before I had often wished myself in such a situation and that this apparently vexatious chance was quite well in keeping with the character of my journey. And with that I actually accepted what was happening. Uncomfortably enough I made my bed under a tall oak tree, murmured something about the loveliness of the summer night, about the pending rise of the moon, and couldn't keep my thoughts from taking me at times to the inn I had failed to reach, where a proper supper and a more tolerable bed would have awaited me. Occupied with such images, I now noticed, some distance away through the branches, the light of a fire. My whole imagination lit up in this moment with a thousand more or less pleasant conjectures; but soon I decided to make a closer investigation. After struggling through a distance of about fifteen paces I discerned a colorful company of men, women, and children sitting in something of a clearing around a fire and partly covered by a kind of makeshift tent; they were carrying on, as far as I could hear, a contented but lively discussion.

My heart leapt with joy to encounter here a troupe of Gypsies, for my old prejudice in favor of this peculiar folk was not inhibited even by my awareness of my complete vulnerability. I don't know what rash and trusting feeling convinced me that, at least with this gathering, I was taking no risk by approaching them openly. My small spyglass was of no help in any case, for a physiognomical investigation of the faces illuminated by the red light of the flames would have left me undecided in my judgment, despite the striking clarity with which I saw each feature. I stepped forward, offered a candid greeting, and was fully accorded the reception I had hoped for after I had managed not to let the first harsh words of the captain put me off. My uninhibited boldness suddenly seemed to please him, and my clothes too he now assessed with visible respect. They invited me to sit down on a carpet and offered me something to eat. I behaved with an increasing candidness and loquacity, whose positive effect on my hosts soon became evident, as they listened attentively to my descriptions of foreign lands, while at the same time I was able to take my pleasure in the remarkable faces and exquisite groupings gathered round me.

This went on for some time uninterrupted. But now distant thunder could be heard, and they prepared for bad weather, which then did indeed descend with unexpected rapidity. We all took shelter as best we could.

In the general commotion, with the rain pouring down, the thunder and lightning, and one of the horses off to the side beginning to shy, I had dropped my portfolio. I was looking for it on the ground in the dense darkness and had just succeeded in finding it when all at once in a sudden flash of lightning I spied close beside me a woman's face, which of course in the very moment I glimpsed it was then swallowed up again in the darkness. Yet I stood as if blinded in a sea of fire, my mind's eye holding fast to the one image of that face as though it were a mask set against the green-flaming background of the glistening wet branches. Nothing in my life had ever made such an impression upon me like that moment's apparition. Involuntarily I reached out with my arm to convince myself that she really was there, but she had already slipped past me in the dark, and a longer time than — impatient as I was — I would have wished went by before I was to find out who she was. But find out I did.

A girl who at first had likely been hidden in the tent and whom they called Loskine now appeared among the others when, as the rain let up, they started the fire again and, exchanging joking and scolding comments about the disruption, put things back in order. The girl is the captain's niece. — Loskine — how am I to describe her? Since that night four days have passed in which I've been eye to eye with this image of the most exquisite beauty without it occurring to the painter in me to appropriate it to my paltry medium of lines and strokes! Oh, these few days, how rich they have been in discoveries, how immeasurable in their impact on my whole way of life!

Since then I have chosen to accompany this roving band. Yes, I am their fellow traveler and blush not at all at doing such a thing, which should give no professor ordinarius of the fine arts cause to shrug his shoulders, because I shall certainly tell no professor ordinarius about it. Or does a man of reason whose calling bids him discover original forms risk harm by observing for a while a wild folk, if among them he finds an inexhaustible store of ideas, the most surprising traits, and mankind in its most robust state of physical development, and in so doing looks upon the rest of nature as if with eyes renewed and receptiveness doubled? I am learning with every hour, and these people are the soul of kindness towards me. A degree of self-interest is involved, of course; my generosity suits them, but I shall never regret it.

A day later

I have to laugh as I read yesterday's sophistry about the study of painting and the gain of art. That might all be right, but where is this high-minded self-justification coming from if there's not something behind it all that I am trying to cover up with fine phrases? Yet I do confess that Loskine by herself could make it worthwhile to go tagging after the troupe for a week. I cannot look at this creature without finding some new charm — be it intellectual or physical — to admire. I find her irresistibly fascinating, and be it merely out of interest in the unusual mix of her character.

151

Utterances of a fine reason and of childish innocence, dour seriousness and sudden flights of uninhibited gaiety alternate with totally unexpected and highly charming contrast and make for this enchanting play of colors. While at first apparently incomprehensible, this composition and these shifts for me already reveal the compelling order of a beautiful harmony. Astonishing at times is the agility of her physical movements, and magnificent her smile of superiority when at times she seems to take pleasure in flirting with danger. I tremble as I watch how she dashes down a steep slope, catching hold only briefly as she plunges from tree to tree, or when she leaps onto the back of a horse as it lies on the ground and brings it quickly to its feet with a few slaps. Among the others she is a rather isolated figure; they let her have her way because they know how she is, and yet they all feel a certain fondness for her. In particular the leader's son, a clever fellow of manly good looks, seems to be more attentive to her than I would like him to be, and while on the one hand I like her coolness towards him, I feel on the other hand a distinct feeling of secret displeasure. She likes to have me around, yet I am almost afraid of Marwin — that's the young man's name — and I am already accustomed to making the most of especially those opportunities when he is sent to scout the area or take care of some other business, which happens often. I have already bought her many a small gift, and I take care to cover up my intentions by giving the others similar gifts. — But my God! what do I really want? And still I find I have not the trace of a thought of turning back. Yesterday, using a less than probable pretext and not making the least mention of my current life, I wrote to my friend S. that he might send my entire store of funds to the town of G***, where we, as the captain said, were to arrive in four days for market time. This march brings me five miles closer to the place from which I departed. But what a distance that remains nonetheless! Just as well that in these parts I need not fear running into a face I know, provided that I could still be recognized in my present state. I have used some borrowed garments to give myself a freer look and to conform to some extent to my companions. Even just a peaked cap of violet and red on my head and a broad belt around my waist really do much.

26th of May

There has been quite a scene. We were resting in a pine forest after a tiring stretch one afternoon. Marwin was away and almost all the others had given themselves over to sleep. Loskine was looking for her favorite food, the pleasantly thirst-quenching leaves of the wood sorrel that grows here in great abundance. I accompanied her, and eventually we sat down on the far side of a hill in a shady spot on the moss-covered ground thick with fallen pine needles. I don't know how, but we came to speak of all manner of fairy tales and wondrous things, of which she had a by far richer store than I. Among other things she could tell of the spinning forest woman who, at early morning when the autumnal forest was aglow from the dawn, would wander among the trees and, as if from the distaff, would spin the leaves off into green and gold threads as her spindle danced along beside her. She also confided to me about the secret powers of herbs and roots much that cannot be repeated without her own words. All the while she was deftly at work with a carving knife, fashioning a whittled toy like the ones the Gypsies made out of yellow wood to sell. Eventually I had almost stopped listening to her stories, fascinated as I was with the movement of her lips, the play of her features; finally, assailed and excited within by my quietly glowing desires, I turned from her so that, sitting somewhat lower, I had her face at my back and her naked foot — for that's the way she went about most of the time — close before my eyes. As if drunk in all my senses and no longer in control of myself I seized her foot and pressed my lips firmly to her fine brown skin. In this moment Loskine laughed and gave me a good push, we both stood up and I noticed a bright red in her cheeks, a confusion that I quickly understood. Thus made bold, I put my arms around her wonderful form without stopping to think, and she did not resist me. Her lips burning hot, the black fire of her gaze flashed into mine. This but for a moment, and then it turned away, confused, and the next object upon which it lights, at the same time as mine, is — Marwin, who, leaning quietly on a nearby tree, is witness to our scene. Loskine stood as if thunderstruck. I tried, without letting on that I had noticed Marwin, to deceive him as to what had happened by complaining loudly and playfully about her coyness and how she had scratched up my face so horrifically. With this little comedy I got not the least bit of support from the girl. She stared straight ahead and, her tears falling silently, moved slowly away. Only now, with a show of total surprise, did I greet my rival, walking over to him and continuing to play my role; yet he looked at me scornfully for a few seconds, and then he went away and left me standing there.

Sixteen hours have passed since then without the least bit of consequence, except that Loskine avoids me wherever I go.

In a peasant cottage in ***

I am separated from my band, but separated at what cost!

On the same morning that I wrote the preceding entry the captain took me aside and, with a restraint that did not conceal his dark displeasure, explained to me that I had to leave him or behave just as if Loskine were not present. His son wished to have her as his wife; he himself had promised her to him, and Loskine would not continue to withhold her acceptance. He went on to say I might best be on my guard in any case, since Marwin bore me considerable ill will, such that only his fear of him, his father, had kept him from some violent act against me. I responded that if my innocent pleasure in the girl aroused ill feelings it would be easy for me to be more careful in the future, yet if my presence itself made Marwin ill at ease, then I would put an end to it as well. The captain, aware of the considerable advantages that my company brought, became more reasonable, to which I responded again with noncommital comments, and so the matter was left to me to decide. Yet soon I came upon a heart-rending scene in which I myself was immediately to become involved. Loskine, her knitting in her lap, was sitting on the ground, covering her face with both hands, while her lover, in most intense pain and uttering the vilest deprecations, tried to force from her an open confession about the incident. When he saw me, he jumped at me like a man possessed, seized me by the front of my jacket, and demanded of me what the girl was withholding from him. He drew his knife and was still threatening me when we were surrounded by five or six people who had hurried over. His father disarmed him on the spot. But only Loskine, who now rose to her feet with an expression of dignified calm that I shall never forget, put an end to the uproar; without saying a word and with a meaningful gaze, she took Marwin by the hand, and he, who seemed to be as moved by the significance of her solemn gesture as I was, followed her like a lamb as she led him along with her deep into the bush.

After a while she came back alone, stepped resolutely up to *me,* and motioned me away from the center of the gathering.

"I have promised him," she began, when we had stopped sufficiently far away, her tone serious, "I have promised him that I would tell you that I hate you as much as my worst enemy and unto death. So that is what I say to you. Yet you know otherwise. I tell you for myself that I love you much more than I do my dearest friend and do so as long as there is breath in me. But you must leave us, that too I have told him. Be fast, I cannot remain here long. Kiss me!"

"If I must go," I answered, the grandeur of the moment almost lifting me above any emotions, "if I must go and if it is true that you love me more than anything, then let us go together."

She looked at me in astonishment, and then thoughtfully she shook her pretty head.

"Loskine!" I cried, "you have but to will it, and what seems impossible to you shall surely be made possible. But answer me still one thing first: Can't you voluntarily fulfill Marwin's request? Can't you be his?"

She was silent. I asked the same question again, and she answered with an emphatic: No! I felt a mountain lift from my heart, and in the same instant my decision was made. At lightning speed I formulated a plan in my head, yet immediately, I must admit, I sensed how uncertain it was. Its aim was that after immediately departing her people I would travel on alone to G***, the town where, as I well knew, they would next be arriving. There, she was then to steal away from her band and inquire wisely and discreetly about the most respectable hotel, where without fail I would already be and have made all arrangements for a rapid flight. Loskine had barely heard my suggestion when she had to hurry away, for we heard noises. In a confusion

154

of anxiously conflicting thoughts about the uncertainty that threatened my plan in more than one respect, I was left on my own. Did the girl understand me? Shall I have an opportunity to ask her about it again? or, if she did understand me, will she decide to take this step? and is that step at all viable? These doubts caused me no little unease until I hit upon the felicitous idea of leaving all to the will of fate and ultimately to take the success or failure of my intentions as a test of whether they were good or bad. I was really quite pleased with this idea as well as with my strict resolve not to seek out Loskine for now or at least not to discuss the matter with her any further. How much more meaningful — so the thought hovered in the back of my mind — how much more splendid will that then make the fulfillment of your expectations! But also, even in the event of my plan's failure, I envisioned myself undergoing the appealing pain of a beautiful renunciation.

Now I returned to the company, drew the captain aside, and explained to him the necessity of my departure, offering him a last token of my gratitude the better to console him. He accepted my, as usual, fine gift with a look of pride and friendliness, offered to escort me — which I declined — and promised, in accordance with my request, to greet the others in my name, since out of consideration for Marwin I wanted to avoid a general farewell. Basically, however, I dispensed with the farewell to spare myself, out of my own feeling of shame that kept me from facing the one person whom I intended to trick out of his most cherished hope. I tried to take comfort in the fact that I was not robbing him of anything that he had ever possessed or that he ever could possess, for Loskine's heart was far beyond his grasp.

In a short while I found myself alone again and wearing my proper clothes. I proceeded on horseback with a likewise mounted escort from the next village bound for G***, but going by a roundabout way that I supposed the captain would not be taking. I took this precaution for any eventuality, just as I had falsely informed him about the direction of my journey.

In G*** I arrived betimes and took my lodgings according to what I had told Loskine. Whatever could further my plan I undertook immediately. Some new garments, above all a decent coat, were ready for my beloved. I located a comfortable closed carriage, the sight of which filled me with anticipation, by turns happy and anxious; yet I kept my hopes up all the better the further off I set the time in which, according to my calculations, the arrival of the troupe could occur. This was to be on the following morning, on the market day itself. Quite casually I was just looking down from my window onto the street below and pondering, not without a concerned eye to the reduced state of my available funds, the ways and means by which I intended to have the packet from S., which was sure to arrive here by post in the next days, sent on home in the most expedient way. Thinking thus, I was watching calmly as, below my window, a young boy from the house was

155

playing with a new wooden crossbow, and I vaguely sensed in passing that I had encountered a similar instrument somewhere in the last days. Like lightning the thought suddenly struck me that I had seen that kind of carving work just two days ago in Loskine's hands, and that she must already be nearby and could enter the house at any moment. I was beside myself with joy, with expectation and anxiety. But this painful state was not to last. O God! who can describe the moment when that magnificent creature slipped into my room, when I took her in my arms and she cried out, gasping for breath: "Here I am! here I am! Do with me what you will!"

In a short time we were sitting in the carriage; first, I rode alone a ways out of the city and waited for her there. We traveled through the day and night and for the time being have come far enough not to be afraid anymore. But what trouble, what sweet trouble did I have calming the dear creature's distress. She seemed only now to think about the momentous step that she had dared take for my sake; she tormented herself with the bitterest reproaches, and then again she laughed through her tears, clinging to me passionately. So we arrived exhausted at daybreak at the border crossing at B. I am writing this in a miserable hotel, while Loskine is nearby enjoying a brief sleep on a meager bed. Take comfort, dear heart, in a few days I shall show you a homeland. You shall be the queen of my house, and together we shall found the kingdom of heaven, and the opinion of the world shall not keep me from being the most blissful of men.

HERE THE PAINTER'S DIARY broke off. The pastor paused, and Fräulein Ernestine said: "So he brought her back to the fatherland and actually made her his wife?" "Yes, unfortunately, may God have mercy! he made good his wish. He denied the person's despicable origins, but people at once smelled a rat, and who in our family would not have had to cross themselves at the thought of entering upon such an utterly alien relationship? We all advised my brother against it, we all conspired against this union. I myself, may God forgive me, fell out with him, as much as I loved him. But in vain, the Prince was on his side, there was a quiet ceremony, and he lived lonely enough with that woman on his small estate. He supported himself solely with his art, but the union could not be blessed; the two of them, they say, loved each other, idolized each other, and still, word is, she became ill in the first months out of homesickness for her forests and her friends. You can tell me what you will, I say that rabble can never leave off wandering, and my poor brother must have endured a thousandfold miseries. It lasted barely a year until death intervened; the woman died giving birth to their first child. Your uncle, instead of giving thanks to heaven on his knees, as we had hoped he would, reacted to the loss like a man in despair; for a while he lived no better than a hermit; his only remaining consolation was the child, who had survived and in time bore a striking resemblance to her mother. He had the child carefully raised in his household until she was six. Then God punished the sorely afflicted man with yet another loss. One day, the child went missing, no one had any idea where she could have gone. Later, they found reason to believe that the infamous band had found out where my brother lived and, because they couldn't steal back the woman, had avenged themselves on the father by stealing the girl. Half his fortune he spent to get back the apple of his eye; but in vain, he had to give his daughter up as lost, and no one ever heard any more about her. And now today — it's incomprehensible, it's enough to drive one mad, my mind boggles when I think of it — now today I have to go through the experience of having my own children bring the bastard across my threshold. I'm just glad she's out of my house! Just as long as she doesn't hide somewhere! that's her bundle still lying there; I just hope the whole troupe isn't sneaking around here in the area! Dear God! If they put fire to my house, the murderous arsonists — Up children! I feel a chill go up my spine; I sense trouble! Search every corner — let the hired hand wake the mayor — let's raise alarm in the village —"

"For God's sake, father, what are you thinking?" the girls cried out, "just think of what you're doing! the Gypsies are miles away from here, and the girl won't harm us."

"What? not harm us? do you know that? Isn't she out of her mind? What all isn't there to fear from that girl!"

"So Johann can keep watch through the night. We will all keep watch."

"I'll not have a moment's peace until I am convinced that no fire's been set. Come! I've just got the idea in my head; come with me."

So the three of them went groping about the whole house without any light; the hallways, the stalls, the attic; they searched it all carefully. When they came to the attic, where the remarkable picture was, the girls felt a secret but pleasant shudder; it was hanging so that the moon's bright light shone upon it, and even the pastor had, against his will, to pause at the sight of the demonic beauty of the portrait; they really could have thought it was Elisabeth; unique and otherwise indescribable was the expression of the piercing brown eyes. None of the three wanted to utter a word, only Adelheid asked her father whether their uncle had painted it and whether it was of his wife. The pastor nodded, sighing as he took the painting from the wall and hid it in the farthest corner.

As they passed by Theobald's bedroom they looked in and saw him sleeping peacefully, his hands folded over his blanket.

It was past midnight. The old man had little desire to go to bed; his daughters wanted to keep him company, and, to keep them awake, he had to tell he rest of the sad tale. "This all happens very quickly," he said. "The calamity with the child totally destroyed your uncle; he couldn't bear staying in the fatherland; he journeyed to France and England, but is supposed to have stayed in constant contact with his Prince and continued working for him until, for unknown reasons, he had a falling out with the court. Then all at once he disappeared, and all they know is that he lost his life traveling by ship between England and Norway. The greatest portion of his fortune he had with him, but judging from what he had left behind it seemed he had not given up on the idea of returning home. His estates went back to the sovereign, who laid claim to them. Aside from a small store of personal effects that included the painting and the diary, we received nothing. — So ended your father's brother. I say, peace be with him! I shall weep for him sincerely until I die, even though I cannot condone what he did and shall warn everyone upon whom God has bestowed so dangerous a temperament that he might avoid the snare of the tempter and never depart the path of wholesome order. I think as I say this of my son, Theobald. The boy, as innocent and gentle as he is, has already frightened me on many an occasion. Such a contrast to me! So much about him that is extreme, unnatural! Like today again — I almost boil over when I think of it — what is this curiosity about this strange girl? Nothing but that his fantasy has gone mad! And you, Adelheid, you often make common cause with him instead of guiding him. — He doesn't carry on like other lads of his age. There — for hours on end sitting up in the belfry, like a dreamer, feeding and training spiders, burying secrets, notes, and coins in the ground — what am I to make of such bizarre nonsense? And that I'm going to make a painter out of him is an idea he'd best get out of his head. There's his eternal sketching and daubing! and wherever you look you're disturbed to see the grotesque face he's scrawled out, even on a tin plate. If he'd just sit down for an hour some Sunday afternoon and, for a change, do an actual tree, a house, and such like by copying a proper original, then I'd have nothing against it, but all there is are his own caprices, witch-like caricatures, and who knows what. By God! That's just the kind of foolery that Uncle Friedrich was up to in his youth. No, upon my poor soul, my son's not going to become a painter! As long as *I* am alive and in charge he's not going to do it!"

The girls stared in wide eyed wonderment when they heard him talk this way, for it was almost the first time that their father had seemed displeased with his favorite, and still it was all only the anxious expression of his boundless affection for the boy. At last he set off to bed, and while he was undressing he was, as was his passionate habit, still talking loudly to himself about the disturbing events of the evening.

The following morning the hired hand announced that, when he had arisen at daybreak and gone into the yard to fetch water, the Gypsy girl had come running up to him; she had only wanted him to bring her bundle of clothes so that she could move on right away. She had bid him give friendly greetings to Adelheid, but especially to the young gentleman. A medallion that she unfastened from her own neck was to be passed on to him as a present from her. The father immediately took possession of the treasure; it was of fine gold, with blue enamel and an inscrutable oriental inscription.[21] He locked it away and strictly forbade anyone to say anything about this message to his son. The young man had, apart from Adelheid, not a soul to whom he could reveal his inmost thoughts. He wandered about for some time after having seen Elisabeth, as if in a dream.

Since from his early years on, even when he lived in Rissthal, he had spent many a stolen moment looking at that irresistible picture, since this had gradually developed into a raptly religious attachment as to the idol of a patron saint, and since the good faith with which the boy guarded his secret so unbelievably intensified his pleasure in it, the moment in which he encountered that wondrous image in flesh and blood had to have an immense and indelible impact on him. It was as if a magical light had illuminated the most remote reaches of his inner world, as if the underground stream of his life had suddenly burst forth out of the depths at his feet, as if the seal upon the gospel of his fate had burst open.

No one had been witness to the strange bond that the boy, in a state of rapture, had entered into with his revered Gypsy friend there among the ruins, but, according to what he confided in Adelheid about it, it was to be believed that a mutual oath of spiritual love had occurred, whose mysterious bond, bound up with a wondrous physical necessity, was to unite the two souls forever despite all distance between them.

Yet it was a long time before Theobald overcame his deep yearning for that far-away girl. His whole being dissolved in melancholy; with doubled ardor he clung to that precious picture. His drive to create and paint now grew irresistible, and his calling as an artist was confirmed.

Not long after, the father died of a stroke. The children went separate ways. Theobald was sent to board with a reliable man (the forester at Neuburg), from whose house he went to attend the nearby art school at ***. After five-and-a-half years of diligent studies he found a rich patron who was inclined to provide the means for the young man to further his education abroad. Fruitful to a high degree were his sojourns in Rome and Florence, but even the manifold insights of that world of magnificent art were never able to displace completely those early impressions for whose aura of mystery he next found an analogous satisfaction in the basic ideas of Christianity.

Elisabeth he never saw again.

Part Two

LEOPOLD WAS RETURNING to the city deep in thought. He approaches the garden of the eccentric Hofrat. That man's favorite pet, a tame starling, is sitting on the roof peak over the water pump in the shade of a weeping willow. The bird is just starting its little song as Leopold is about to pass by, and it interjects a mocking phrase apparently meant for him: "There go riding three — rascals — out through the town gate"; at the same time the powdered head of the Hofrat emerges; he entreats the sculptor to come in for a while. "I have some news," he says, "the pleasant nature of which will make you forget the impoliteness of that scoundrel up there. Monsieur Larkens was hurriedly called to a hearing this morning. We may expect a desired result; I was given a signal en passant and quite in general, but still from a reliable source. Bring your dear friends this consolation, but tell no one else." Filled with joy, the sculptor thanked him and wanted to hurry away, when the Hofrat, who was in a fine mood this day, seized him by a coat button and said: "But do grant that fellow up there a glance! Note the philosophical clarity, the fine sarcasm, with which he sticks his nose out into the world! If we imagine, shall we say, that the pump shed is a monument, a gravestone, then it would doubtless better suit the elegiac tone for us to think that Philomela was there in the hanging willow branches, that sweet singer of melancholy and love, rather than even the most clever starling whose mere figure already has much too much of the erudite man of the world.[22] And then at the same time I think a harlequin, sitting thoughtfully on a sarcophagus, wouldn't be such a bad idea either, perhaps a subject for a Hogarth.[23] One could give the rogue, say, a sleeping child to hold, and, behind his back, half in anger, half smiling, a white-haired old man with a staff would be eavesdropping on his strange reverie. The fool's face would have to show how he is struggling to be deep in thought and serious; but that doesn't work, and his meaningful head-shaking is accompanied each time by the jingle of his fool's bells. What do you think of that? that winged rascal there, who yesterday had the misfortune — I don't know how — of falling into a pot of yellow paint, and still bears the traces of that accident — doesn't he resemble right to a hair such a motley-dressed mocker of the world? Isn't he an incomparable lad?"

The sculptor had to hold forth in praise of the bird, but he was pleased at last to come away and deliver his happy message to his friends.

And indeed not four days passed before the incarcerated friends learned of their release. In neither of the two had evil intent been detected — certainly, however, a culpable impropriety in the way they had acted, for which the mercy of the King granted them forgiveness.

All their friends found this to be quite in order, with only the actor finding the rapid turn of events quite strange; he shook his head and intimated with no lack of clarity that there had to be something behind it; but beyond that he expressed no further suspicions and joined wholeheartedly in the general jubilation.

The moment in which he greeted Nolten for the first time again, albeit at his sickbed, caught up everyone with emotion and joy. Never had they seen a more passionate friendship, and even though otherwise Larkens's aversion to any signs of sentimentality drove him almost to hardness, he could on this occasion not have enough of embracing and kissing his ailing friend, apologizing most urgently for the calamity for which he blamed himself alone. Fortunately the doctor promised that Nolten soon would be able to make full use of his freedom, and indeed the sick man himself vowed that he lacked but little to make him feel he would like even today to get to his feet; at the very least he wanted to be released from his sorrowful arrest room, even if they would have to carry him away, bed and all. Larkens took the jailer aside, had himself taken to the nearby rooms, and soon returned with the happy news that he had discovered, just a few paces away from Theobald's cell, a location that the whole world could not improve upon: a small wood-paneled knights' hall with a balcony that offered the prettiest view out onto the entire castle. With that he described the archaic charm of the richly decorated oak walls, a row of life-sized wood carvings of counts and dukes with their coats-of-arms and mottos, the beamed ceiling on which, in equal-sized quadrants, half of biblical history was to be seen painted in touchingly tasteless fashion, two gigantic ovens that both could be fired up if need be; off in one corner there was a heap of rusty weapons whose weight the patient would have to use day-by-day to test his recovering strength; available too were a few small water pumps, and Larkens planned, for the day when they were to celebrate their release, to fill them with Tokai wine, for then the wine really had to flow in streams. While all this was spoken in jest, he was still so totally serious about moving Nolten to the hall of which he was speaking that on that very morning he sought permission from the warden and made arrangements to make it all quite clean and orderly. The move occurred the next day, and Nolten had to confess that he felt himself truly relieved and enlivened by such cheery and imposing surroundings. Window upon window lined the long walls, and the former magnificence was evident even in the small round panes, whose leaded joints still bore the traces of fine gilding. The hall was said to have been known in bygone times, owing to its lavish appointments and brightness, as the "golden lantern."

One of the first of the visits that our friend now received in his new quarters in great number was from Tillsen and old Baron von Jassfeld. The two had, during the incarceration and supposedly out of respect for the court, refrained from fulfilling this obligation. The actor for that reason was unable to suppress a sarcastic remark, but for Theobald at least the present proof of their attentiveness was all the more important in that he drew from it favorable inferences regarding the disposition of the Zarlin household. Yet on this point he was wrong, for quite soon he was given to understand that in that house a noticeable ill will still prevailed such that he would do well for the present to keep a distinct distance. To do so he was now quite firmly resolved, especially since in the following days he had received from the Count not even a curt congratulatory wish, not to mention, as would have been expected, a friendly word.

Under different circumstances these prospects might have made him disconsolate, but in this instance his pride was hurt; he saw himself being rejected in unfriendly and disdainful manner, and since he knew how little inclined the Countess had always been to allowing her brother or anyone else to prescribe her feelings and actions, he could by no means ascribe her current behavior towards him to another's account. In his own mind he considered himself decisively disappointed in this woman's extraordinary attitude; for the first time he detected in Constanze the pettiness of her gender, the narrow-hearted preciosity of her social rank, yes, and, even more than all that, he was convinced that she never really could have loved him. He was sad, yet he was surprised that he was not so to a greater extent.

In this way, of course, the actor, who had to be very concerned with extinguishing all signs of this passion in Nolten, had a far easier job of it than he had always feared he would. He was highly surprised to himself about his friend's reasoned calm, and gladly acquiesced in his wish that there should be no more talk of the matter.

Moreover Larkens had all manner of things to ponder and determine. Immediately after his release from custody, one of his main concerns had been to find out whether that strange Elisabeth, whom short days before Leopold had seen on the street, might not still be in the area: yet for several reasons it seemed beyond doubt that she had already left the city. Then, too, he wished to learn more details about the state of feelings in the Zarlin household as well as about the real reason for the rapid dispatching of the legal matter that at first had been treated with such seriousness. He was all the more curious since some voices had intimated in secret that Duke Adolph had vouched with his royal word for the two arrested men and in that way had cut through the problems with one stroke. This the actor did not find to be so unlikely, although the Duke, it appeared, did not want his magnanimity mentioned publicly and as well had declined any contact with the two charged men. Highly embarrassing did Larkens thus feel his uncertainty on this point, as well as the impossibility of expressly thanking his benefactor, if in fact he should secretly be one and the same as the Duke. On the last point he became more convinced the more he thought about it, and soon this speculation was joined by still another, albeit still remote conjecture that he might well have had good reason to conceal most carefully from Nolten. For he began to wonder whether perhaps Countess Constanze herself could not have been, initially in Theobald's favor, the hidden driving force acting upon the Duke. He did not really know what led him to this view, but in general he assumed that Constanze harbored a quiet and very lasting affection for Theobald, and he found it impossible to think of her being other than in a state of sorrow.

One morning he finds his friend out of bed, sitting under the half open window and warming himself in the bright rays of he springtime sun. The actor loudly expressed his joy about the felicitous progress of his friend's convalescence, while Theobald smiled at him and signaled him with his hand to be silent, for the tones of most lovely song were coming up from below in the outer ward of the castle where the warden's daughter was busy with her first garden work of the year. She herself was hidden from view by a protruding ledge of the building, yet all the more audible was her little song, at least one verse of which we would cite here:

> Springtime lets its bright blue band
> Flutter through the air with ease,
> Sweet remembered fragrant breeze
> Caresses, promising, all the land;
> Violets dream alone,
> And will soon be drawing near;
> Hear, from afar, the harp's gentle tone! — —
> > Springtime, 'tis you!
> > Springtime, 'tis you!
> I know 'tis you I hear!

The verses captured just perfectly the tenderly aroused mood that the new season is wont to visit upon people — and far more intensely upon those recovering than upon the healthy. A rare cheerfulness enlivened the conversation between the two men while their gazes roved afar over the budding landscape. Never had Nolten been as eloquent as he was today, never the actor so humane and charming. All at once the painter rose to his feet, looked long and earnestly, as if lost in thought, into his friend's face, and then said, as he laid his hands on the other's shoulders and in the calmest of tones: "Should I confess to you, old friend, that this is the happiest day of my life, indeed that it seems to me that only today I am actually beginning to live? But grasp what I am saying. It is not this refreshing sunshine alone, nor this new breath of the world, nor your enlivening presence. You see, the feeling of which I speak lay nearly ripe in me even during these recent days. I cannot say that it is the result of long deliberation, yet it is based upon the most clear and sober awareness, and it is as true as I myself really am. I have been forced in these last days to see, as if in a mirror, the form of my past, my inner and outer fate, and this was the first time that I beheld so clearly and distinctly the meaning of my life since its first beginnings. And that could not have happened earlier, nor should it have. I had to live through these spans of time as if blind, perhaps it will be no different with the times to come, and perhaps that is how it is with most people; but for that brief moment when the direction of my course changed; the blindfold was taken from my eyes; I can look freely around me as if to make my own choice, and I am happy that, even as a divinity is guiding me, I am still actually aware of *my* will, *my* thought. The power that leads me does not stand invisibly behind me like some independent self-willed driver, it hovers *before* me, it is *in* me, and to me it seems as if since time out of mind I was in accord with that power about where we wanted to go together and as though it were owing only to the finite limitations of my life that this plan had been expelled from my memory and that only at times did I experience with profound awe its dark and wondrous recollection. Man guides his chariot where he wishes, but beneath its wheels the orb he travels is turning imperceptibly. So I find myself attaining a goal for which I had never striven and of which I never would have let myself dream. A few weeks ago I seemed so far from that goal. Many a matter that for so long a time had appeared to me to be the necessary condition of my fortune, of my completed self, that I had nurtured and tended with unbelievable passion, lies now like an empty shell that I have sloughed off; thus is Constanze little more to me now than a mere name; and thus did Agnes even earlier sink away from me.

"Great losses are usually what brings a person inexorably nearer to the higher calling of his existence; through them he learns to know and value what is essential to his peace. I have lost much; I feel that I am inexpressibly impoverished, and precisely in this poverty I feel that I have an infinite wealth. Nothing remains for me but art, yet now too I fully feel its sacred value. After for so long having a strange fire rage within me and purify me totally, I now feel deep stillness within me and slowly all my strength is gathering within me in solemn anticipation of things that are now to come. A new epoch has begun for me, and, God willing, the world will soon know the fruits of it. You see, I could weep tears of joy for you when I think of how I shall soon, for the first time again, take brush in hand. Many hundreds of new unseen forms are evolving within me, a blessed throng of them, and awakening the yearning for good hard work. Freed from the heartache of any anxious passion, I am possessed by but one powerful emotion. I almost believe I am once again the boy who in his father's attic knelt before that wondrous painting as if before the genius of art, so youthful and innocent and undivided is now my ardor for this divine calling. There remains nothing for me to wish for, since I have felt the all-fulfilling power of art and that exalted solitude in which its disciples must forever immerse themselves. I have renounced the world, that is: I may no longer possess it any more than I may possess the cloud, the sight of which awakens in me an old yearning ever anew. I am not saying every artist has to feel that way; I am saying only that no other way can suit me. To this resignation each of my tests has guided me, this was the signal of my entire previous life; there will no longer be anything to confuse me."

The painter fell silent; his pale cheeks were flushed a light red; he was moved in the extreme and noticed with indignation his friend's displeasure as well as his doubting smile, which in any case expressed less mockery than uncertainty as to how he was to respond to Theobald's unexpected declaration.

"If I may," Larkens began, "If I may be honest, I cannot deny that I have the feeling my Nolten has at no time ever before understood himself less than at this very moment, when all of a sudden, as if by inspiration, he thinks he has arrived at the one true conception of his self. And yet I do know from my own experience how readily a person, ever the old conjurer, will sanction a wrong idea — the fair-haired child of his own egoism, the capricious notion of his cowardice or defiance — by developing some willful system of thought, and how easy it becomes for him to use words to make a biased or half true idea complete. For you must admit —"

"Stop, I beg you," Theobald cried out excitedly, "enough of this tone! you are making me regret having revealed my inmost thoughts and exposed to you the most sacred feeling that would have been lured from me by no other person under the sun were it not the friend from whom I might have expected a loving sympathy for my way of thinking, even if it did run counter to his own. Listen, I know you as a rational and clever man, except that where certain matters are concerned, certain foibles of a loyal spirit, I shouldn't have forgotten that we've always argued about them in vain. I would rather we drop this matter now and act as though we hadn't been discussing anything; there's no need to go into it, since I can go my way with no harm to our previous relationship."

"Yet you surely cannot expect," Larkens answered, "that I would let you follow some whim that can only be harmful to you. — For the present I find your error forgivable; misfortune makes a person lonely and inclined to hypochondria; it makes him draw his fence as close as possible around his little house. I myself could probably get into such a state, only that would be a case quite different from yours. The Lord guides his saints in wondrous ways.[24] No doubt your life has much meaning, yet you take its lessons in much too narrow a sense: you attribute to it some kind of demonic character, or I don't know what — you think you're being led by a wondrous spiritus familiaris who was spooking about in your father's attic. I do not want to become involved in these mysteries; what is sensible about it I see clearly as well as you do: only tell me, my dear fellow, you spoke before of solitude, of independence; depending on how you mean the word, I quite agree. In all seriousness, I think that your artistic nature, in order to preserve its nerve unweakened, cannot endure a very intense social life. Precisely the most noble seeds of your originality always demanded a certain constant temperature, the changes of which had to depend as much as possible on you; it required a silent, melancholy circumspection as a dark foil to that inexplicably deep warmth of the heart that so rightly springs forth from the innermost feeling of our self. In all, that is so with every artist of genius, I mean with every artist of your type, with only the one knowing better than the other how best to share his feelings with the world. Yet, you see, as far as contact with the so-called great world is concerned, I thought it was clear from the outset that you would never lose yourself to it. The sudden venture into that world that you made through your acquaintance with the Duke thus struck me as the greatest contradiction of your own true self. Accustomed to looking upon you as a rare lad who, blessed with higher powers, would have to feel awkward and almost helpless as soon as he was drawn into those dazzling circles, I found the agility with which you fit in there almost — how shall I say? — not suspect, but at least quite unusual, and I sensed it would not last in the long run. How easily possible it would be, I thought, that under such influences one or the other of his original colors would be diminished, that his ambition would take a wrong turn, that he would sacrifice something of his loyalty to his genius! In short, something pained me, and even if it was only the foolish sympathy that can assail a person who sees the crystal torn from the maternal darkness that fosters its growth falling into people's unchaste hands. Of course, such thoughts are farcical. But you can just see from them that I am neither so narrow-minded, nor so arrogant, nor so frivolous as to deny your true essence or to disturb the quiet ground in which your being since earliest times has so lovingly taken root. Certainly, I have seen the magnificent fruits spring forth; and — Nolten! don't you see, you were not displeased or dismayed when, for all the time that we've known each other, you've heard me utter not one word of over-extravagant praise or of enthusiastic discourse about the development of your intellect and such like; I am simply the way I am. But in this moment when so many serious observations force themselves upon us, and when you seem to be taking matters to an extreme, then I might well loose my tongue so that I could tell you how, from the start, I have observed your development silently touched and with admiring joy, indeed with more reverence and concern than you seem to think me capable."

Nolten listened with growing astonishment to his friend's confessions, by which he truly felt more highly honored and warmly encouraged than by the grandest praise that any powerful patron might have accorded him. He was just about to say something in response when the actor went on:

"Let me tell you something. You recall the conversation that we had when we rode out to L. together. It was the finest evening in mid-July, the setting sun cast its red glow on our faces, we were chatting on all manner of things about art. With every word, though you didn't intend it, you revealed more completely to me how your nature had formed; for the first time I was allowed to immerse myself in the innermost vessel of your being. We were discussing, you know, the relationship of the devoutly religious — meaning Christian — artist's mind to the spirit of antiquity and to the poetic sensibilities of classical times and pondering the possibility of an almost equally perfect development of both tendencies in one and the same subject. I granted you a high and rare degree of universality, as on this point there can be only one opinion. I convinced myself that for your art there was nothing to fear from your Christian feelings, which still do predominate in you, even if ultimately the displeasure of certain zealots were still to be proved right in their suspicion that you are a secret Catholic and a budding apostate. You have, so I thought, for good and all plucked the flower of classical antiquity clean from its beautiful slim stem; it blooms unwilting at your breast and mixes its enlivening aroma into your fantasy, no matter what you choose to paint; nothing narrow, nothing arcane will ever stem from your brush. You see, that became so clear to me even long ago! and now when I see the whole fortunate harmony of your strengths and how willingly your nature could be found to melt and fuse every harsh contradiction in you, and when I think of the single priceless good fortune that art, so early in your life and almost without your doing anything, was bestowed upon you as the ripe fruit from the hands of benevolent gods who seemed to have resolved to present in you the example of the most fortunate mortal — well, tell me, should I not be hurt, foolish lad, should I not get my blood up, when you, driven by the strangest illusion, mean to create by force a one-sidedness where none exists and where none should be allowed to exist! I am not talking about your relationship to the world in general — there can be, as I have said, no argument about that — but the fact that you wish to let the friendliest side of life die off and to renounce a happiness that would indeed be as natural for you as it would be for any proper good fellow — that is what enrages me. True, I'll readily admit, love has not gone all that well for you, I don't deny that since Agnes —"

"Oh, so?" Nolten suddenly exclaimed, as if falling from the clouds, "that's what you're getting at? that was the intention that you thought you had to prepare for up to this point with so much flattering eloquence?"

"Don't be unfair, good friend! What I may have said before in praise of you was the pure and honest truth, and there should be no need to attest to that between the two of us. And you may nonetheless take me for a match-maker, too, but in the present instance I see that business as a praiseworthy and honorable one. — What actually bothers you, I know very well. Your calamities in love have revolted you a bit on that point; so now you're pull-ing back, hurt and angry, into your shell, consoling yourself as you do so by saying that you're making a sacrifice for your art. You fear the pain of pas-sion, just as you fear the extravagance of its joys. But devil take it! what are we to think of an artist who is too cowardly to take those two upon himself in the fullest measure? What? you, a painter, want to present a world in all its thousandfold rapture and pain, yet you cautiously mark off the boundaries of how far you want to join in the joy and suffering? I tell you, that's like going to sea and not wanting to let the water wet your ship!"

"How you exaggerate!" exclaimed Nolten, "how unjust you are to me! as if I had invented for myself a dialectic of enthusiasm, as if I were cutting the artist and the man into two pieces! The latter, believe me, may turn any which way he wishes, but he will still have to know privation and loss, and without that — who would do art? Is it then anything else but the attempt to replace or to augment what reality withholds, or at least to enjoy in dou-bled and purified form what reality does indeed afford us? So if, accordingly, yearning must be the artist's element, why am I being faulted if I think of preserving this feeling for myself as undiminished and as young as possible by voluntarily renouncing before, for a second and a third time, I allow common experience to pluck the petals of my blossoming ideal and am left standing, fed up and disappointed with the object of my love, with a with-ered heart? You note I am speaking here first of all about the much praised happiness of marriage: for this, after all, is what your whole demonstration is all about."

"And what do you wager I really will set you right once I have toned down your crazy pretensions! Who told you to get ideals in your head where love is concerned? By all the graces and muses! a good natural creature who brings you a heaven full of tenderness, full of selfless loyalty, who can uphold for you your healthy attitude and your fresh perspective on the world, who can offer you release from the gnawing desire of an active imagination and at the right time lure you out into the bright sunshine of everyday life, which is indispensable to wise man and fool alike — what more do you want?"

Nolten looked down in silence and finally said: "There was a time when I thought just the same." He turned aside, shaken; he strode vigorously through the hall and then sank down exhausted some ways away on a chair.

The actor, after he had — with considerable wisdom and vigor — thus far guided the discussion of a topic that was more important to him than anything, was full of desire to seize the moment and speak out more deci-

169

sively now in favor of Agnes; but he had to hold off from this daring step when he noticed how deeply Nolten was affected; for that reason he tried to change the subject, but their discussion went nowhere; they were both out of sorts, and at last they parted on very bad terms.

SINCE HIS RELEASE FROM CUSTODY Larkens had made a decision that until now he had not mentioned to Nolten. He wanted to leave the city and go abroad indefinitely. In more than one respect this seemed desirable and necessary. His acting contract had recently ended, his sojourn in the city had been made unpleasant by the recent public incidents, the court itself seemed not averse to the prospect of his absence, at least for a while. But more urgently than all that he felt his own need to repair and heal himself inwardly by some diversion, indeed by a complete departure from his previous way of life. He revealed his intention to Theobald as far as he felt was advisable for the moment, and Theobald, although quite unpleasantly surprised by it and almost hurt, could, upon closer consideration, say nothing against it.

Yet just as we, before we can think of the future, must above all do proper justice to the present and past, so Larkens had quietly planned an evening intended for celebrating right cheerily their release from so much lethargy and lassitude. He saw to a well-chosen dinner and took special pleasure in decorating the small table, meant for a dozen guests, with all manner of spring flowers and greenhouse plants, as well as with a variety of gifts, of which a rather colorful collection had arrived from sympathetic friends and well-wishers. What figured most prominently among these pretty and in some cases expensive things was a large vase finely styled in alabaster and meant for Nolten, placed in the middle of the table with its luxurious display of growth. It was a present from the painter Tillsen, who proved this day the most hearty and eloquent of all. The eccentric Hofrat had, as was his wont, not accepted the invitation and sent his regrets, yet, as proof of his concern for the well-being of the others, sent a basket of fresh oysters. The rest of the company consisted mainly of artists.

Our painter, surprised and touched from the very start by such honest demonstrations of friendship, had to fight off melancholy feelings, which, out of consideration of the cheerful demands of the moment, he had to dismiss for the present. In all, the conversation tended more to lively and joking uninhibitedness than to seriousness and gravity. Indeed, the amusements of one certain actor and singer predominated to such an extent that for a while everyone forgot to make any further contribution to the general amusement other than joining in the hearty laughter. Larkens was giving only remote support to the high spirits of his theatrical colleague and sat rocking in his chair, smiling, and occasionally tossing out a word to keep things going; but soon he too got into the act and, by posing, as was his habit, a paradoxical statement that incited everyone to attack, he was able by

170

dint of his merry-witted defense of his proposal to effect the most lively participation of all the guests, always coaxing with ease from each individual the best that lay hidden in his nature, be it spirit, experience, or wit, so that the entire conversation subtly developed the highest degree of diverse interests. Finally, after all had done their utmost to ensure the general cheerfulness, Larkens became noticeably more quiet and morose. When the others teased him about it, he was happy to explain that he was adding to the cheerful occasion of the evening another of his own and that the company might now empty a last glass with him in honor of just that special point; he would be departing from the area for a long time or short in order to visit some relatives he had not seen in some years. — This plan, as natural as it was under the given circumstances, nevertheless aroused great, even tumultuous regret, and all the more so since some suspected that with this move the esteemed artist, whom the entire city thought had just been as if restored to them, would on this occasion be lost to them for good and all; but Nolten spoke up for the loyal sensibilities of their departing friend. And so the goblets were filled anew, and amidst all manner of well-wishing toasts they finally, late in the night, brought the merry banquet to an end.

THE URGENCY WITH WHICH from now on Larkens pursued arrangements for his departure did not keep him from pondering his friend's further fate. Rather, as he had made it his most serious task to guide Nolten's affections back to his fiancée; as he had repeatedly convinced himself, by way of the innocent delusion of his correspondence with Agnes, of her charms, of her pure and lovely reason, but above all of the natural desire with which a tender child, quite rightly, wishes soon to be in her loved one's arms again; and as he considered Theobald's entire situation and the lingering threat of Constanze's proximity, then he could think of nothing more urgent than giving Nolten's undecided vacillations a swift and decisive turn. His plan was thus settled, but it was not to take effect until after his departure; indeed the favorable outcome, of which he was absolutely certain, was to some degree dependent on his absence.

Now he wrote to Agnes, and in fact, as he was loath to think, for the last time. "What fools we are!" he exclaimed, as, reflecting on it all, he laid his pen aside. "On occasion I had taken such pleasure in assuming possession, as it were, of this lovely creature's soul, and all the greater was my fortune the more I was able to enjoy it, undetected and like a thief. I imagine to myself, the girl surely wants me, while in fact I mean as good as nothing to her. Using an assumed style I pour the entire fire, the last laboriously fanned embers of my worn-out heart upon the paper and flatter myself royally at the thought that this page will then warm her feelings for *me*. O foolish devil! You could disappear, be dead and buried tomorrow, and would it change that beautiful girl's life by so much as a hair? And for all that, the deception

171

was good for me, helping me in a hundred dismal moments to uphold my faith in myself. I wonder if similar deceptions don't occur especially where our most wonderful feelings are concerned? And yet there seems to be something about all those deceptions that gives them an eternal worth. It may be that I shall never encounter this good child face to face anywhere in the world, and it may be that she would never know of all my warm concern for her — but should that be able to diminish in the least the height of my happy feelings? Does not the joy of pure affection, does not the awareness of having done a good deed become something truly infinite and inalienable only when it is all that remains to you in solitary defeat?"

In his thoughts now he took his heartfelt departure from the girl, and since, as he conjectured, even her next letter was to be delivered directly to Nolten again, he instructed her as necessary, yet in such a way that she couldn't think anything of it. If now in these last days the actor's behavior at all betrayed a certain restlessness and unease, then at his departure from Theobald he was still less able to hide his intense emotions, and this, taken together with some of his statements, seemed to point to some secret plan and for moments really gave our painter a strange feeling — which Larkens, in his usual way of leaving people unable to tell whether he was serious or joking, was quickly able to dispel again.

In addition, Nolten felt now all too soon the immense gap — both without and within — that the actor's absence would necessarily have to cause in his life, and the various inquiries from other people were sufficient evidence for him that he was not the only one so afflicted by this change. His two friends Leopold and Ferdinand also departed at this time, and doubly and trebly did the painter feel sharpened his desire to restore complete balance to his life. The plan for a new work, the idea for which had come to him during his incarceration, was sketched out on paper, and now he went about executing it with zeal, showing a self-confidence the like of which he recalled having known only in the happiest years of his first efforts. Yet by and by he could not help but notice that he was still lacking much to achieve a complete freedom of his soul; he became moody; exasperated, he set the work aside; he could not say what was holding him back.

One morning he is brought the keys to the actor's rooms. Larkens had left them with a third friend when he departed, with the express wish that they be delivered to the painter only after some days had passed and that Nolten should then not delay to open the rooms and, in part, take away, in part, take care of whatever he found there. At that time Nolten was given a list of all the actor's effects, including an indication of what was to be done with them. He was not a little taken aback by this assignment, and he asked the messenger with some anxiety what it all meant. But that young person was not able to give any further information and soon left. Immediately Nolten opened the rooms, where he found furniture, books, etchings,

172

clocks, and the like, as usual in the best order. But soon he found his eye caught by some packages addressed to him that were specially placed on the small table. Quickly he tore open the letter that lay on top. Right with the opening lines Nolten was greatly moved, the letter shaking in his hand; he had to stop; he read again, now from the start, now from the middle, now going back from the end, as though he had to consume the entire bitter content all at once. As he was doing so his glance fell upon the other packages, one of which bore the inscription: "Letters from Agnes. From her father. Drafts of my letters to Agnes." Another bore the title: "Fragments from my diary." Without rightly knowing what he was doing, he reached for the single letter and scanned it without thinking as he moved restlessly from room to room and window to window; he tried to compose himself, wanted to understand after he had already understood everything, guessed everything. He cast himself upon the sofa, his elbows propped on his knees and his face pressed into his hands, sprang to his feet again and dashed about as if out of his senses.

His servant had just led his horse around to go riding and announced it was ready. He ordered the boy to take the horse away, then he ordered him to wait, he contradicted himself ten times in one breath. The boy went away without having understood his master. After half an hour, during which Nolten had neither looked at the other papers nor been able to calm himself to any extent, the servant repeated his question. Quickly, the painter took his hat and his riding crop, pocketed the most important papers, and fled the city like a drunken man. We shall briefly turn away from him and his sorry state and look for the present to that important letter:

Larkens to Nolten

"As you read these lines, he who has written them is many miles from you, and when he confesses to you that it was his intention to steal away and not soon return, that he would leave behind his previous relationships forever and part from you, his only friend, perhaps for years, then the following brief comments will explain this step as well as they can.

"Surely now you no longer take to be hollow and wantonly exaggerated words that you often had to hear me say, namely: that my life is played out, that I have begun to outlive myself. That has become so clear to me in recent times, during which people such as myself truly had ample opportunity to unravel the results of the past thirty years as one would pull out threads with one's fingers. I don't care to sing you the old litany; suffice to say: I have never felt at ease in my own skin. So I want to pretend that I am shedding it by casting from me what until now seemed inseparable from my being, above all the mantle of the actor, and then other things as well that I need not mention. Many a capricious saint went into the wilderness imagin-

173

ing that he could pursue his idle time wasting there in a way pleasing to God. But I still have something better than that in mind. In the end, of course, it's only a new mask to put on, in which I would like to delude myself; and if it doesn't work out, well perhaps then heaven will see fit to render my poor soul the last service, of which then I shall have no fear at all.

"Spare me, dear friend, the act of bidding farewell! Oh, I mustn't think of what I am losing in you, lovely boy! But enough: you know how I have cherished you in my heart, and so I am also well aware of your love for me. That is no small consolation on my way. And, as well, it can indeed very well come to pass that we greet each other once again somewhere on this earth. But we do well in any case to see this possibility as no possibility at all. At any rate, don't try to find me, your efforts would surely be in vain.

And now the main point:

With the packages I give over to you an important and — I may say — a sacred legacy. It concerns your relationship with Agnes, with which I occupied myself almost totally over the last ten months. My dear man! listen to me with calm and reason.

In the surest conviction that the time had to come when your most ardent prayer would be to be united with this girl, I took a daring step to keep open your way to this sacred treasure. Forgive me for deceiving you! only my hand was false, but surely not my heart; I thought I was writing out a faithful rendition of your feelings! don't make me a liar! Let me have acted as the prophet of your love! I was its martyr in any case; for as I was weaving the rose wreaths of your love, do you think it was not driving a thorn into my own flesh? But that is not important here; suffice to say that my epistles have served their purpose. Carry on now with the truth from where I have ended with deception. O Theobald — if ever I had any influence on you, if ever the name Larkens had the ring of pure friendship for you, if ever the judgment of another person could seem better and more right than your own, follow me this time! Had I words of piercing fire, had I the golden speech of a god, I would use them now to touch your inner feelings, friend and favorite of my soul. But as I am now, I cannot; my blade is blunt, my words flat. As you know, all beauty has passed me by, leaving me with but the frank, naked truth, it and — regret. From this latter I would like to spare you. I am your guardian spirit, and, as I part from you, let me recommend another, a better one. By that I mean Agnes. Return the girl to her rightful place in your heart. You'll not find in all the world anything more heavenly than the soul of this child. Believe me on that, Nolten, as sure as if I were swearing upon my deathbed. — In your anger you have made a hurtful mistake. Read these letters — especially the father's — and the scales will fall from your eyes. But then tarry no longer; be resolved! Hasten to her; come before her with no fear, she shall mark nothing strange about you, she knows nothing of a time when Theobald was less hers than he has ever been; the field is free and pure between you.

It is up to you whether the good little thing is to learn about your interlude or not; until a few years have gone by I would advise against it. Then the two of you will think of it as though you had once played parts in a summer night's dream and that Puck, the deceptive elf, were still laughing up his sleeve about his successful magic trick.[25] Then think of me with love the way you would quietly think of a departed one whom you well might miss at times, yet whose fate you mustn't lament."

O N A SEPARATE SHEET there was the following:

Postscript

"My letter was already sealed when I immediately had serious scruples about having said nothing to you about a situation that might displease you but was able — ad inclinandam rem — to render me no small service. A skirmish against the Countess. So listen then, curse me all to hell and call me a knave if you've a heart to do so — but I know what I had to do. Constanze was informed by me, or rather by an arranged coincidence (at the bottom of which she can suspect neither me nor anyone else), that a certain friend's name already stood somewhere on the list of happy bridegrooms. I hope that I didn't compromise you too much with my coup, and some small risk had to be taken. If she didn't care for the news, that's quite in order; and not because she was in love with you but because she is a woman. We ascribed the disfavor into which she let us fall right after that farcical play to a miserable impropriety against those kindred to the court, and in part I am still of that opinion; but if I now admit to you as well that at the same time she was given the entire Agnesiana to swallow, then I can readily predict in my mind's eye what manner of desperate new hypotheses you'll be breaking your head over. What if Madam were to have had completely different reasons for anger, but hidden them behind the general fuss of her sycophants? Ho-ho, that's enough to make hot and cold tingles run up your back, isn't it, my boy! And I'll be a rhinoceros of a prophet if you are not this very minute envisioning the touching figure from afar, her head of black curls bowed in sadness, weeping for your love. A seductive picture, truly, that so stirs your heart! But stop, I can show you another one. — In the sunny little garden behind her father's house behold for me the simple child as she hums a happy song and waters her violets, her myrtles. From looking at her it is clear that she is thinking of the bouquet that she shall soon give her homecoming fiancé in welcome, along with a thousand thousand kisses; every day, ever hour, she waits for him — —

"What now? Away to her, then, comrade? Is it not a bitter crossroads? Here I have you where I wanted you! that is how far I must go. The path back to Constanze — perhaps it is still open, I am showing it to you after you already believe it closed forever. You should have a free choice; that much I owed to you. In the meantime you have learned that it is also possible to live without a — Constanze, and with that, I believe, much is gained.

Theobald, once again: think of that garden. Recently she put the arbor in order, the bench where her dearest is to sit with her. Will you soon be coming? Or won't you? — Just dare to deceive her! to plunge, with one desperate stroke, the sweet, bright summer day of this innocent soul into a dismal night; oh, woe! the whimpering creature! Do it, and you shall find out how, in a few moons, I, a lonely pilgrim, would weep upon the girl's grave for the ineffectual farce, the nothingness of our friendship, and the dashed hope that my miserable life, shortly before I end it, at least would have been useful enough to make two good people happy."

WHO WAS MORE UNHAPPY than the painter? and who could have been happier, if only he had at once been able to encourage his spirits as sufficiently as necessary to raise himself above the circumstances — whose demands now seemed beyond his control — and clearly survey his situation. Yet he had far to go before he would be able to do that. In a state of dreamlike indifference that even he found peculiar, he was riding, now slowly, now in haste, along a lonely path; and instead of being able to think through in order at least the most important points — as he tried to do a few times — he found himself — so peculiarly! — persistently pursued by a silly melody that some goblin, just at the wrong time, had teasingly put in his ear. No matter how much and in what manner he tried to force it out of his mind, the same old tune kept coming back and buzzing away unmercifully in his head, aided by the rhythm of his riding. Neither coherent thought nor cogent feeling were possible for him; he was in an unbearable state. "For the love of God, what is this?" he exclaimed, gnashing his teeth, and digging his spurs into his horse so that it lunged forward in pain and charged ahead unchecked. "Am I still myself? can I not shake off the grip of this thing that has taken such a hold of me? and what is it then? what? am I to let this revelation destroy me? what have I lost by learning everything? all things considered — nothing! And gained? — nothing! — oh, but yes, a girl, who, someone writes me, is a true lamb of God, without equal, an angel!" He laughed heartily at himself, he cried out with joy and laughed at the sound of his own voice, which seemed to burst forth from him with a totally new self.

As he goes on reveling and raving so, his mind is obsessed not by that musical phantom but by another obsession that at least does not plague him so. His excited imagination was providing him, at astonishing speed, with a whole horde of ideas for paintings that he had to picture to himself in fragmented dramatic form and to the lively accompaniment of poetic words and sketch out hastily in broad strokes. Most remarkable about it was the fact that these images had not the slightest connection to his own situation. Instead they were, so to speak, purely preliminary sketches for the painter as such. He thought he had never had more ingenious conceptions, and afterwards he recalled with pleasure this strangely inspired hour. We ourselves quite rightly extol it as a sign of heavenly preference that the muse favors the artist above all others by catching him up, at times when fate brings him to a transition of immense consequences, in a lovely and vibrant illusion, thus concealing reality from him behind a magical tapestry until the first dangerous moment is past.

Lost in such thoughts and visions, our friend has ridden a considerable way from the city, and before returning to it by another path he sees, lying not far away in a pleasant dell, the so-called Camp Mill, a well-known locale that he had come to appreciate on many an outing. He was always a guest much welcomed by the miller, who was one of that strain of Pietists with whom everyone gets along well. In a certain sense the man could be considered well-educated, except that he had good cause to conceal some peculiarities that at times he found embarrassing. Thus because in his younger days he was meant for a career in scriptural work and had some knowledge of ancient languages, he had in later years come upon the idea of reading the Holy Scriptures of the Old and New Testaments in the original texts, likely with chiliastic purposes in mind. After very tedious and ill-ordered studies for several years he was unhappy to find himself convinced that his undertaking was naught but idle piece work and that his whole grand undertaking was leading nowhere. Dismayed by the time he had lost, he plunged into daring economic speculations from which, to be sure, he suffered no loss, yet also reaped less than his full benefit. His wife, an intelligent and quiet housekeeper, knew how to guide and steer him with a gentle touch, never explicitly pointing out his error, even though she made him aware of it. And since he could encounter nothing more unpleasant than being reminded in some way of the pointlessness of his academic activity — and indeed, since, in order not to admit any wrong in the matter he would make as if someday he would still reap the richest of benefits from that research — his wife was happy to be considerate of this weakness and secretly pleased when she could make him forget a new bad idea. So for the most part he was known as cheerful, affable company, as the best husband and father of his, for the most part, well-cared-for family.

Nolten yearned for the harmless presence of another human being just as much as he felt inept at taking part in any company; thus he was just pondering whether he should take the path on to the mill or turn back to the city, when he encountered the miller's hand who told him that his master and mistress had gone to the fields and would not be back before evening.

How well that news suited the painter! actually he wanted only to seek out an intimate spot in the miller's parlor: it seemed to him the only place in the world that suited his present state of mind. And he was right, for who has not already learned from experience that one can come to terms with complex feelings, certain pains, surprises, and embarrassments far more easily in strange and undisturbed surroundings than within one's own walls? Nolten left his horse at the stable where he was already known and entered the clean, brown-paneled parlor where he met no one, while in the room next to it there a ten-year-old girl was sitting on a stool holding her little brother on her lap. An older daughter, Justine, a wonderful lass, slim and red-cheeked with coal-black eyes, came in offering her usual good-hearted greeting and expressing regret that her parents were away; she hurried at once to fetch the keys to the cellar and was happy when Nolten allowed her, since those at home had already eaten, at least to bring him a piece of cake. He immediately occupied his old bench and window, from which he had a direct view down onto the water-dam and also out to the most refreshing green meadow and rounded hill. How much more lovely and special did he find the experience of spring and sunshine in this enclosed spot than when it surrounded him out in the free expanse of nature! Long did he gaze then at the surface of the water. He felt strangely oppressed and anxious about the future and at the same time secure in this sheltered environment. All at once he took the papers out of his pocket, intending to open the first thing that his hand lit upon without choosing: it was his fiancée's letters that she had thought she was writing to him, Theobald. Taking a look he finds his attention instantly caught by a passage that makes him inwardly begin to swell with a feeling that had long since become foreign to him; he is about to continue reading when he hears Justine coming with glasses; quite unnecessarily he quickly hides his treasure, but he feels like a thief who has a booty of the greatest value that he himself does not yet know and, frightened by every sound, hurries to conceal it. The girl came and began to chat in a lively and cheerful manner, and Nolten responded as best he could. She likely sensed that she was superfluous, but for whatever reason she withdrew, leaving the guest to himself. He has approached, by chance, a small, poorly done etching hanging under the mirror and portraying a kneeling figure; below it are inscribed a few pious verses that he immediately recalls often having heard quoted in his earliest youth by his late mother. And as now tends to happen that often the most minor object, the slightest shock, is all it takes to cause a sudden and powerful release of a whole mass of feelings that were lying pent up deep in one's mind, Nolten's inmost self all at once was thrown open to melt and stream away in an indescribably sweet flood of pain. He sat, his arms on the table, his head resting on them. He felt as though knives were boring into his breast with thousandfold pleasure and pain. He wept intensely, not knowing for whom the tears were meant. He sees the past before him, Agnes hovering near; with a thrill he feels her being touch him; he feels that the impossible is possible, that the old can become new again.

These are the moments when a person willingly renounces understanding himself or comparing himself with the known laws of his previous existence; he calmly gives himself over to the divine element that bears us all and is certain he will arrive safely at a specific goal.

Nolten no longer found peace here; he quickly took his leave and rode homewards at a walking pace, deep in thought.

How he spent the rest of the day, what all moved about within him, what he thought, feared, hoped, how he felt in general — to describe all this would likely have been as impossible for him as for us, especially since he was the entire time as if cut off from himself by an unavoidable visit. This he was, to be sure, ultimately successful in shifting to a public location where they encountered still other company, although he was not able to extricate himself completely.

Of course now he had decided at least that he had to seek out Agnes and that he wished to do so. He had still not even looked at all at the written presentation of the facts that served so well to exonerate the dear child; a silent faith that assumed the most wonderful and allowed no more doubt had grown within him in these last hours, he himself knew not how. Yet in the night as he read the remarkable report of the forester and as Larkens's diary gave him so many explanatory clues, how astonished he was! how he shuddered to encounter the terrible Elisabeth at every turn! How touched he was, what pain he felt, to read through the story of Agnes's illness, of that most pitiable of girls, whose love for him had earned her such a bitter cup of misery! And then her letters themselves, in which that lovely soul emerged to view as though reborn! — Theobald felt, pulsing through his every nerve, the inexpressible thought of being able to clasp this singular creature to his breast, when and as soon as he wished, as his own possession. Then all at once an unknown something overshadowed his heart's bliss. These tender words of Agnes, for whom else were they meant than him? and yet for moments he would think it was not for him: a phantom has come between him and the girl writing, a phantom has appropriated the spirit of these words and left him only the dead letters. Indeed as occurs not rarely in dreams that we know people yet don't know them, that they appear simultaneously far away and near, so he saw the form of the dear girl as though she were always only a few paces ahead of him but always with her back to him; the view of her eyes, which should have been the truest evidence, was denied him; from all sides he tries to overtake her, but in vain, she eludes him: he cannot grasp her real self.

To these feelings of anxious half measures — from which, as he foresaw, only the direct proximity of Agnes could release him — there were added now worries of another kind. The inscrutable fate that the enigmatic person of the Gypsy woman had to cross the path of his life anew and in such an intentionally threatening way, the thought of how close he had recently come to her again without even knowing it (for the actor's diary had revealed to him the two occasions of her presence), all this gave him much to ponder and awakened his concern that this deranged woman might sooner or later confront him or act behind his back, perhaps at this very moment, in Neuburg, to cause renewed confusion. A further cause of his unease was Larkens; he was able to see the fine intentions of his friend — even though he could not condone the individual steps taken and was, in part, inclined to condemn them bitterly — from the positive side and appreciate them with gratitude; he recognized in them also his friend's wise caution in using his own departure to put a complete end to all further negotiations between himself and Nolten about Nolten's own duty, about his inclination or disinclination in this difficult case, and to force the painter, by putting him completely on his own, to acquire a fresh grasp of what was good and necessary. — But what was one really to think of the actor's hasty departure? What was to be that inscrutable man's fate? Of nearly a half of his domestic goods he had divested himself, a good portion had doubtless been converted to cash, another portion, which remained behind here, was either designated as gifts or was to be sold off by Nolten and the proceeds used to satisfy his creditors. Deprivation for Larkens was not to be feared. But if everything made it clear that a profound weariness, a deep-seated pain was driving him away, and if even some passages of his letter could be taken to indicate that he might voluntarily force the fulfillment of his fate — then one might well ask how that made Nolten feel! A third, but not the least, worry was the negative and even scornful opinion that the Countess, since she learned a one-sided and false version of the relationship to Agnes through Larkens, must necessarily have of him. Not that he feared such a discovery would have made her unhappy, for in fact his idea of the Countess's passion had been significantly reduced, and at most he wanted to believe that to some extent she could have been flattered by his love. But since he had in fact so urgently and so decisively confessed his intentions to her then, how miserable, how vile he must have appeared to her as an engaged man, how malicious and calculated his silence about that bond. Would she not have had to feel, aside from any passionate interest of her own, that she had been insulted, inasmuch as even his attempt to make her too the object of such a duplicitous game demonstrated a lack of the respect that she should have had a right to count on from Nolten? In that sense did not the anger and coldness with which, since that evening, she had not accorded him a single glance not seem quite forgivable and justified? Our painter felt the shame, the full pain of this suspicion: not another hour could he rest, the ground burned under his feet, he wanted to hurry, he wanted to cleanse himself, cost what it might. But that was not so easy to do. How was he to contact Constanze? how was it possible to justify himself and yet at the same time observe the greatest delicacy? For the Countess could quite easily understand him to be saying that he was assuming injured love for himself on her part, a mistake that, he thought, would have to make him the most ridiculous person in the eyes of that lovely lady. He pondered the matter studiously and resolved to wait until a felicitous way presented itself.

O N THE FOLLOWING DAY he had the idea of seeking the advice of the Hofrat, whom in any case he owed a visit, about the mood of the Zarlins, and he set out immediately.

Arriving at the Hofrat's house he chanced to find the main door left ajar, which greatly surprised him, since it was one of the first principles of the man's household rules to keep the entrances locked at all times. Aside from the letter carrier and an old maid who lived off the premises and appeared at set times to serve the meals, visitors rarely crossed his threshold, and if so, then they had to pull the bell, whereupon a grey old servant, the only living soul around the old Hofrat, would look cautiously out of the window and then open the door. In the downstairs vestibule, where the master's love of art and taste were immediately evident in the form of well-placed plaster figures, Theobald finds an unassumingly dressed boy sitting on the stair and eating candies out of his cap, the lad seeming, as well, to be quite at home here. An unbelievably pleasant form of face, the brightest eyes, greet the painter with a look of mischievous laughter, while he is struck especially by the boy's delicately curled locks. The lad, after calmly taking our friend's measure from head to toe, stood up and gave the door a good kick so that it closed with a crash. "Can you tell me, good boy, whether the Hofrat is at home?" The little fellow did not answer, but as he went up the stairs he signaled Theobald to follow. Upstairs he quietly opens a narrow door and roguishly motions him in. Finding himself in a small antechamber, Nolten was just about to knock on a second entry when, through a small side window, with its curtain not fully closed from the other side, he spies in the side room the most remarkable silent scene. In reduced illumination, almost only twilit, sits a woman dressed in white and bare down to her waist. Her pose is one of reflection; her head slightly tilted to the side, she is holding her hand — or rather only the index finger — under her chin, barely touching it. Her armchair stands on a dark red carpet down onto which the rich folds of her garment and robes fall in a wonderful array. One leg, which is crossed over the other, allows a glimpse of her foot only to just above the ankle where her other hand appears to be holding it gently. But what a magnificent head! Theobald had to cry out involuntarily to himself; the Roman strength in the arch of the back of the head, from the strong neck upwards, was such a touching contrast to the childlike aspect of the countenance, whose expression would reveal only pure modesty if that modesty did not seem just on the verge of giving way to the loveliest surrender to the necessity of the moment. Obviously the woman was not used to acting as a model. And in the Hofrat's house? Was the old fool himself perhaps playing the dilettante? Unfortunately it was impossible to see a second person, who surely had to be in the room; nor did one hear a sound; the beautiful woman kept her same pose like a marble statue, with only the slightest heaving of her breast indicating that she was breathing; it also seemed once as though she were casting a weary glance over towards the window from which the light was coming. Nolten would have sworn the Hofrat was sitting there. Wasn't there a rumor that the old gentleman actually used to paint? and didn't some claim that he had secretly turned to sculpting in his old age? How surprised our young painter was then when, in response to a noise coming from the corner, the young woman arose and a slim, black-bearded man stepped discreetly up to her, kissed her in gratitude on the lips in such hearty and uninhibited manner, as though she were his sister. Theobald at once recognized the curly-headed fellow to be a sculptor, Raymund, whom he had seen often and in particular at Larkens's farewell banquet, but without having come to know him any better. Yet it was at last time to withdraw, as difficult as it was for him to part from this scene, which struck him as just as touching and guiltless as it was charming and uplifting. Scarcely has he pulled the door shut behind him and noted with pleasure that the devious little rascal was not about to be witness to his stilled curiosity — than the Hofrat sticks his head out of the main hall and the two men greet each other with a palpable embarrassment that lingers on even after their conversation was well underway. Theobald was completely distracted by his lovely adventure; his face, his eyes bear an unusual glow, the cause of which the Hofrat deduced cleverly enough. "I notice, I notice something!" he grinned and clapped his friend on the shoulder; "only don't let on about it! he's a wild boar, this Raymund, and not to be joked with." Nolten candidly recounted the strange coincidence. "Between us," said the Hofrat, "you should know what the situation is all about. The young man, as passionate in his art as in his life, insisted that his fiancée, whose pretty figure long seemed to be the only good quality of which he was aware, sit or stand for him as he, as an artist, required. The girl could not bring herself to do it; it came to a falling out that soon became so serious that Raymund didn't even look at the stubborn thing anymore. So it went for half a year, and the girl, otherwise a gentle, reasonable creature who loves him infinitely — and on top of that comes from a poor family — is quietly beginning to despair. In addition, she receives an advantageous offer to be trained for the theater, since she is said to be a very good singer. She declines the theater offer resolutely, and this upright resignation suddenly brings her young hothead of a fiancé to have quite different thoughts about the girl's worth, with the result that he visits her again for the first time a few days ago. On both sides the joy at the reunion is said to have been boundless, and even in the first quarter-hour, so he tells me, she had agreed to grant him his artistic whim. Since now Raymund, as he lives with another artist, was at a loss for a location, he found at my house — since I otherwise try to be of use to him from time to time — the required space. Today was the second sitting. The crazy thing about it is that he cannot make up his mind what he should actually do. He claims that if he just improvises for a while and lets chance take its course, then he often comes up with the best ideas."

"He's right!" said Theobald.

"He's not wrong," responded the old man, "as long as I don't see such an approach becoming all too dilettantic! For example, he recently started to work on an Amour in clay, for which he came up with a model from the beggar boys on the street; really a delectable young colt, dirty, but with a figure fit to kiss. But since Raymund's beloved has turned up, the God of Love is free to go; now Raymund has the importunate little urchin, who stood to gain by the deal, on his back day in and day out, and it's all we can do to keep him from showing up in the house already wearing his little chemise; recently he got really spiteful and was lying in wait for Raymund's fiancée with a stick; quite the Cupido dirus!"

"An Anteros!" exclaimed Theobald laughing.[26]

"But do seek contact with Raymund," the Hofrat went on, "that will be easy for you to do: he has great respect for you, and from that proud man that itself means something. You find in him a man of the most honest blood and an eminent, although still wild, talent. There is much about him that can be annoying, small things, perhaps, that for now do betray a lack of education, but still I find them offensive; just *one* example and you'll agree. You'll readily grant that I am not a pedant about all manner of detailed archaeological facts that do not help the artist. If I'm presented with a well-done Ariadne, then I don't give a hang whether the artist knows that the wife of Bacchus is also called Libera.[27] For doesn't it make a man laughable when he talks about gods and demi-gods but sounds just like a dragoon when he does so? Will he ever be forgiven for doing so by those who cannot possibly know at a glance that this person understands as well as anyone else the basics of the myths and has enough sense of feeling in his eyes and fingers? Now imagine this: recently one evening in the Spanish Court, no one there but knowledgeable people; soon the talk turns to a couple of art works, Raymund gets into the enthusiastic spirit and says some excellent things, but instead of talking about Pans and Satyrs, he just goes right ahead and in total seriousness talking only of forest devils![28] Have you ever heard of such a thing? I was sitting on pins and needles, ashamed to the depths of my heart, almost stomped his toes off and tried to help him; but no reaction! One forest devil after the other! And he didn't even notice the smile that went creeping across people's faces from time to time. Afterwards I reproached him for being so out of place, and what is his answer? He laughs: 'Well, old Papa,' he exclaims, 'I have to be allowed to speak on occasion as the Netherlanders were allowed to paint!'" The Hofrat himself had a hearty laugh at this, and it was clear how fond he was of the very man he was just criticizing. "What a stupendous ego! I'm only sorry for his fiancée."

"Who is she, then, actually?"

"She's the daughter of the castle warden, F."

"What! Do I hear you right?" Nolten exclaimed full of surprise. "O good Henriette! How often did your melancholy song from beneath my prison bars console me!"

"Yes, yes," replied the Hofrat, "that was still in the period of the love-sick nightingale!"

The painter paused for a few moments in sweet thoughts. The happy union of these lovers he took as a good omen for himself; for had not that abandoned girl on occasion in his feverish dreams borrowed Agnes's voice? and was he not on his way to restore to that latter girl her fiancé?

But now he found time to question the Hofrat in the matter that had actually brought him there. The old gentleman thought for a moment and shrugged his shoulders. "I don't know, in your place I would go there straightaway myself — the Countess is said to be unwell, but you can always speak with the Count. My God, what are these people actually supposed to have against you then?" As far as Theobald could tell from the rest of the conversation it was more advisable not to compromise himself personally. But he thought of the best way. A Frau von Niethelm, the most intimate friend of Constanze's, a fine and highly gifted lady whose time and talent were devoted mainly to the education of two princesses, had always seemed well-disposed towards him; he now hoped to enlist her as a mediary, and that happy thought momentarily so filled him that he wanted to hasten away from the Hofrat just as Raymund entered the room. That fiery man embraced him immediately with enthusiasm and sought to demonstrate his respect for him in every way. In order not to appear unfriendly, Nolten remained another quarter-hour, whereupon he politely paid his respects.

Towards evening he set out on his way to the governess, having been extended a polite invitation after he had announced himself. Only on the way did it occur to him how little prepared he was for what he was to say and how he was to say it; he quickly gathered his thoughts; before he knew it, he was standing in the governess's room.

That fine lady received him, all in all, in friendly enough manner, and even though there was still something of a reserve to be felt, it seemed as though she were unwillingly imposing some restraint upon herself out of consideration of Constanze.

"I am," Nolten began when he had taken a seat opposite the charming lady, "I am obliged in a short time to bid farewell to this city and its environs; duty and desire lead me elsewhere; but how much I must wish to be able to depart with my mind fully at ease! It is such a lovely consolation to know oneself secured in the memory of one's friends. The love, the affection, that we leave behind in one place give us a silent assurance that a good star also awaits us elsewhere. Oh, that I might be allowed to take this consolation away with me! Oh, that you, dear lady, might be able to strengthen me in this certainty. — While in these last days I have envisioned in my mind's eye in doubly living form that body of outstanding persons whose acquaintance has so often afforded me such joy during my three years here, and while I now go about saying a heartfelt word to each of them individually, I must think above all of that esteemed house whose hospitality I shall never forget and that brought me into contact with the most noble people of the city and — how pleased I am to say it! — with you as well, my dear lady! Unfortunately, that lovely relationship was recently disturbed in a way that can only dispel for me for all time any pleasure of grateful recollection, and this is all the more painful for me since the reasons for my misfortune, as far as I am supposed to have caused it myself, have been kept secret. Should it now not be possible for you, revered lady, to resolve my doubts, so allow nevertheless that I submit to you my assurance that I am not aware of such a transgression with respect either to your dear friend or to the Count; grant me that to the friends who no longer wish to see me I protest the rectitude of my sentiments through you.

The governess, who, the whole while the painter was talking, had attentively been trying to read his face, seemed by no means unmoved; true, she responded in only the most general way, yet it was clear to see that she would have very much liked to say more. Nolten felt encouraged to continue as follows: "How could I reproach you, dear lady, if you, as we now feel towards each other and after all that in the meantime may have been said, were to feel in your heart an insurmountable distrust of me. I feel very distinctly — and you yourself do not conceal it — how in so short a time you have come to see as so strange a man whom you had previously found to be not totally without worth. In times past, we found it a welcome pleasure to exchange experiences and feelings in cheerful conversations, in a lively mix of matters of both remote and immediate interest; always you lent me an attentive ear whenever — as surely often tends to happen to a younger man who has just entered a completely new world and finds much cause to be displeased with himself — I too felt stirring an inner need to confide humbly in a sensitive and intelligent woman, to express to you, at the first moment of my happy astonishment, my respect for that noble house. Now again today how gladly I would like to reveal to you openly and in good faith my inner state, yet your silence intimidates the words on my lips! how gladly you would like to come to my aid in my unrest, yet it becomes difficult to take up again the thread of trust so quickly. Very well, my dear, my esteemed

185

friend, let me at least live a few moments of pleasing illusion, as though we were sitting across from each other as we once did! Allow me to tell you what since those times has become of me, what has changed in me. Let me state no intention that this confession is to serve. Let it be as if I were speaking to a lady whom I know to have a basic well-meaning sympathy with my fate and who would greatly cheer me by uttering a favorable prediction regarding my future fortunes."

With a gentle smile she encouraged the painter to speak by saying: "You will find in me an eager listener, and what she lacks in the gift for prophecy will be compensated in the most sincere wishes for your well-being." With that Theobald was about to present in detail his relationship with Agnes and how it had been recently transformed by Larkens's actions and, in so doing, justifying himself to Constanze. But in the moment he is about to begin he is surprised by the whole difficulty of his task and is truly in need of his good sense coming up quickly enough with a suitable means of saving him from his embarrassment, whereupon he then said: "As presumptuous as it would be to want to talk to you in riddles, it can do little harm if, at the start, to fill in the gap that has occurred between us only step by step and approximately, I disguise my presentation of the general situation with changed names; in that way I can speak more uninhibitedly without becoming less understandable or disloyal to the truth." Forthwith then he related in all its detail the engagement of an Antonio to Clementine, from its origins to its threatened dissolution, along with the enormous confusion to which Elisabeth had given rise. A Cornelia was added, Antonio's feelings for her not denied, yet admitted to have been only one-sided. A mime named Hippolyt secretly unties the fatal knot, yet the fact and the manner in which he does it by way of Cornelia Nolten is careful not to mention, as though he himself did not know about it. He took his time with his narrative, and all the more so when he became aware of his hostess's intense interest; and he was, as he could clearly note, being understood perfectly well. The whole story, by itself adventurous and incredible, gained the greatest verity through his deft and lively presentation. At last he finished, and after some silence the governess (looking at him with a gaze in which he was meant to read her gratitude for the kind consideration that he had observed towards her friend and to a certain degree towards herself with his fable) said: "One would truly think it's all a fairy tale the way things are so wildly interwoven!"

"Proof of its veracity is available," responded Theobald. "Indeed I emphatically request permission to present you in these days with some papers that, in any case, you will study with interest."

"Perhaps," answered the governess, "I can make use of them elsewhere in a way that you might find desirable."

"For whatever you will do, gracious lady, you have my sincerest thanks in advance!" Nolten responded with some haste as he respectfully kissed her hand. She, in the meantime, had become pensive. Unobtrusively, she turned the conversation towards the Countess, and tears came to her eyes. "Unfortunately I must tell you, dear Nolten," she went on, "for some time now things are quite changed at the Zarlins'; and our gatherings have stopped. Constanze is no longer the woman she was. A strange sorrow depresses her. For some time no one knew the cause, not even I, and wrongly we blamed it all on physical causes, for indeed her health is suffering more than ever. But God knows how all these factors are connected. The night before last, as I was sitting alone at her bedside, she uttered — half in the heat of fever, half in a state consciousness — that which I must believe is, if not the sole cause, then in any case at least one reason for her anxious state."

Nolten, in whom these words awakened a rash and precipitous presentiment, did well to hold his silence, for at once the matter went differently than he might have expected.

"I am convinced," the governess went on, "that it is merely a remarkable coincidence, a trivial matter that would make some people smile; all the same it is very important now, and you will be able to enlighten me about it completely. — You have a painting in which a woman is supposed to be shown playing the organ?"

"Quite so."

"Tell me, what is it about this picture? Do you know such a person? Does she really exist?"

Naturally, Nolten was stunned by the question. He had, as the reader knows, in the sketch that was the basis for the painting, accurately enough drawn that insane woman; indeed, in the tableau that Tillsen executed, he had added a few strokes to give that remarkable head the utmost similarity. For Constanze the picture had always been very important, and Nolten now suddenly remembered the dream that she had revealed to him with such great agitation. He now said to the governess: that, when before in his story he had spoken of a Gypsy, this very girl was the original for the picture of the female ghost.

"Strange!" said the governess, "very strange! — Do you know whether this person has recently been seen in this city?"

"My friends claim to have seen her here about a month ago."

"Well, thank God!" exclaimed the governess, "so it is indeed as we suspected; and so the poor woman can no longer challenge my words of consolation and reason!"

"Who?" asked Theobald, "who saw —? Surely not the Countess?"

"Well, yes!"

"Heavens, and where?"

"In church."

Now all at once the painter recalled a situation that people in the city had been telling each other about several weeks ago, and of which at that time he had not been able to make much sense. Constanze, it turns out, when she was in perfectly good health, had gone to church early one Sunday morning and during the service by a strange chance suddenly fallen unconscious, after making what those sitting nearby took to be an audible sound of the most intense fright. She had to be carried home, where she soon appeared to recover. The true cause of the unfortunate incident remained a complete mystery. In the church itself some people claimed to have noticed that, right before she fainted, the Countess had fixed her gaze upon the open main entrance where several of the common street people had gathered in the doorway. Yet no one noticed among that motley group the object of such extraordinary apprehension, nor was anyone tempted to seek that object in the, for all that, striking enough form of a Gypsy woman.

Theobald no longer entertained the slightest doubt that the same monstrous creature who had been intentionally pursuing him when she approached Agnes was unintentionally doing the same here with the Countess. This willfulness of fate was now beginning to make him downright anxious. He had trouble putting it out of his mind and thinking instead of the present time and of Constanze. He was very worried about her condition; for from all that the governess had repeated of Constanze's own utterances he saw clearly that her horror at the appearance at the church was directly linked with that dream and that since this occurrence the Countess was harboring secret thoughts of an early death. The painter sank into silent thought, and his breast rendered up a deep sigh. How many factors, he thought, must have combined to becloud the bright and stable mind of this woman. How can it not be believed that she must have been at odds with herself before such dreams could captivate her mind! He did not refrain from stating these thoughts to the governess, who agreed, nodding sadly. She looked at him and said: "Let us not forget, our friend is ill, and — ill in more than *one* sense."

A visit announced in that moment necessitated Theobald's departure. He took his leave with the request that he be allowed to come by again in the next days. The papers he had promised he sent on that very evening, yet only selections from them — namely, by being so carefully considerate as to withhold the postscript to Larkens's letter.

Although in certain respects he could not have wished the interview with the governess to have gone any better — for it had been the surest way to initiate an amelioration of the most abhorrent misunderstanding — he still continued to be driven by an incomprehensible unrest. He could not wait for the day when he would finally be able to leave the city. Without delay, therefore, he began to make arrangements for his departure; he looked after the affairs of his friend and arranged only the most necessary visits, since he found all too depressing the inappropriate though honestly meant sympathy that people constantly thought they had to show their departing friend. To the Duke he sent a basically obligatory note that he could not fold without a smile at having this time succeeded in using several words to say as good as nothing. The most heartfelt send-off he was accorded by Tillsen and by the Hofrat. The latter, with the most remarkable statements, seemed all at once to want to reveal to him a never adequately enough expressed affection, this by alluding to a special relationship that had long existed between the two of them and that he had right up to that moment not been able to decide to reveal; and now too the departure of the painter took him so by surprise that he would necessarily have to await another occasion. Theobald, who had always suspected the old man of taking mischievous pleasure in playing the mysterious type, paid little heed to these ominous signals, even though the good man's emotions were plainly evident in his eyes.

Nolten's last visit at the end of his very busy week was to the governess. Unfortunately, she was just entertaining company, and the charming lady could afford him only a few minutes alone in her room. She produced a sealed letter and said: "Your recent communications have given the Countess an unexpected light, of whose first profound effect I shall now say nothing. I thank God that this struggle is passed. Take with you here these last words from our friend. Since she resolved to confide in you, there is at least a shimmer of peace, the sustaining of which I shall make my concern to the best of my powers. But as to this letter, I must not keep from you the fact that it was written in the first moment of pain when it seemed as though she would be able to find release and a welcome measure against total despair only in the unchecked expression of her guilt. Thus draw from this letter no conclusions about her state in general, which surely time too will heal. Perhaps you will recognize even in these lines, whose content I can well imagine, the lovely heart that feels its transgression only all too clearly. Surely I may say that without intending it as an excuse — oh, sad, that I cannot excuse it. But how gladly we would forget all for the poor woman, if only she would first regain her peace. Oh, if you knew, Nolten, what sad worries I felt about the direction that her mind was obstinately threatening to take. And yet I am not over all my concerns. Too often I still see her gaze turned towards that dark side where she sees her early grave proclaimed. For even your friendly revelations, as welcome as they were to us, could not completely destroy this notion. Of course now, to a certain degree, she looks at everything naturally; yet because there's just no denying that there does seem to be something extraordinary about the coincidence of events, and because that early impression cannot be erased, she cannot let go of her thoughts about such a premonition. But let me stop there before I grow soft and fall to complaining. How greatly do I regret that you must just now leave us in such haste — and yet things will go well for both sides again. And

189

now" (she went to a cabinet and took out a case that she then pressed into his hands) "two friends ask that you add this to the wedding jewels of your dear bride and say to her how well she is known from here afar, how she is loved like a sister. Farewell, and think kindly of me."

Before Theobald could think to thank her properly, she had already withdrawn quietly, trying to hide her rising feelings. Hastily he returned to his rooms, astonished in the extreme about the puzzling matters of which he had just heard. Was it not as if a crime of Constanze's were to be revealed to him? Did not the governess speak as though he already knew about it? — Arriving in his room, he locked the door behind him and read the following:

"No last look of affection, no eye of sympathy are you to grant this page that comes to you from the most miserable, oh, and at the same time, most unworthy woman, for (and until this moment you had no inkling of this) like my unhappiness so too my guilt is without bounds. Never can I hope to console you, and even if that were possible I can receive no forgiveness, forever no forgiveness, from myself. But the punishment that, horrible enough, I bear in my conscience, I am about to intensify to the utmost by revealing my transgression to you, by voluntarily calling down upon me all your scorn, all your rightful hate. What holds me back from making this most debasing confession? Is one still vain, is one still clever, does one still anxiously seek to maintain an illusion for oneself once one has made a desperate start at despising oneself? Uncaring I renounce those bits of artfulness with which otherwise we poor women in such moments of affliction attempt to beautify ourselves in our own eyes and in those of your gender. Away with them! To the best, the most noble man I shall now show, just as she is, the miserable creature that has deceived him so outrageously. — Hear it then: it was Constanze through whose malice you came to regret your harmless participation in that last evening's entertainment in our house, and — such was the wish of a woman whose confirmed love believed itself deceived in such unequaled manner — perhaps I would have, no! I *surely* would have taken the maliciousness to an extreme had it then been in my power to do so. Yet heaven at the right time found a miraculous means to cow and chasten me. Now all at once transformed into a foolish child, tormented by gods and spirits, I hastened in my great distress to free you. I succeeded, and in fact by turning to the same hand to which I at first betrayed you. Oh, shame, shame! My short measure of life does not give me time enough to weep for it as it deserves to be wept for, and — no, I must fall silent; in order that you do not think it my intent to use exaggerated self-reproach to gain by stealth a spark of heart-felt sympathy, I shall renounce the pleasure of crawling in the dust before you. But hate me, damn me outright; indeed let me call my entire gender up to speak against me, and let the best of them spurn me from their midst! I would endure the harshest judgment just to enjoy the lone consola-

190

tion of seeing my penance completed ere my blemished life reaches its end. God, so just, knows whether I could ever think myself capable of such a misdeed before he tested me with this temptation. Yet the way I faced that test so badly, that opened my eyes in awe to see myself, to see my whole being. To see, too, those lovely hours when love deluded me with hopes of a happy future and seemed to cast a solemn blessing harmoniously upon my coming life — in tears I tell myself that even the worth of such pure moments, of such heavenly resolutions, recedes, worthless, into that vast abyss that this heart, not knowing itself, had previously hidden from me. Yet now that I know myself, now, God be praised, I know where all my striving must lead. Yet about that I'll not talk to you, all that is between me and a higher power.

"Accept my gratitude for the information you passed on to Frau von Niethelm; it was faithfully delivered to me. I would have been lost without it; and for that a thousand, thousand thanks for your mercy!

"But with what feelings have I also had to look at the paths upon which your fate is guiding you! Only a saint like Agnes will, with her child's hands, lift the wondrous veil that covers your fate. In this magnificent creature truly lies preserved the fulfillment of your highest striving. — Farewell to you! farewell! Oh, from the deepest fundament of my soul I wish, I pray all might go well for you. What consolation I seek in that for myself you can scarcely know. And might I but once in my life embrace Agnes, the angel whom I praise. She is the most fortunate on earth, yet I am the first who does not begrudge her this fortune. Live well the both of you, you dears, and let me, the poorest one, pray for you."

WE SHALL NOW LET FALL THE CURTAIN upon the previous scenes of Nolten's life, and, when it rises again, we meet the painter already two days into his journey. Whither he is going we need not ask. We are certain as well that it is surely not the lover's passionate rapture — as so often portrayed with such journeys — nor either merely the cool sense of duty that draws him to Neuburg; it is instead more a silent need that bids him quietly hope for a happiness that unfortunately now is very uncertain for him. For in fact he himself does not know how everything is to unfold. His heart endures in silence, expressing no longing; and only in brief moments, when he envisions his journey's goal, can a sweet thrill of tense anticipation befall him.

On his lively horse he has reached, even by the fourth day of his travels, the end of the mountains that mark the boundary and from whose heights he can see the broad flat expanse spread out before him. It was a warm afternoon. He took an easy ride down the long descent and stopped at its foot. He led his horse to the side of the road and tethered it to one of the last beech trees of the forest where fresh water came bubbling up from a rock spring. He himself sat down upon a rock outcropping covered with new moss and looked out upon the abundant plain with its various villages near and far and the shining bends of a stately river. From down below he could hear a shepherd crossing the meadow playing his pipes and larks chirping everywhere, while nearby he smelled the sweet fragrance of primroses.

The painter was assailed by a mighty yearning that he thought had nothing to do with either Neuburg or any person he knew, but instead was a sweet urge to reach an unnamed place that seemed to beckon so gently through the touching forms of nature all around him and yet retreat before his grasp into the infinite distance. And thus did he give himself over to his dreams, which, as they would dissolve of their own accord in melodies, we shall help to convey with a lovely tune:

> Here I lie on the hill in spring,
> A cloud serves as my wing,
> A bird flies on alone.
> — Oh, dearest love, do tell me
> Where you are, that with you I'd be!
> Yet you and the winds have no home.
>
> Like a sunflower my heart is opening,
> Yearning,
> And searching
> For loving and hoping.
> Springtime, what is your will?
> When will my longing be still?
>
> The cloud I see wandering, the river run,
> I feel the golden kiss of the sun
> Burn in my blood so deep;
> My eyes, enchanted wondrously,
> Seem to have gone to sleep,
> Yet my ear still hears the hum of the bee.
>
> I think now of this and then of that,
> I yearn and cannot say for what;
> Half is desire, half is lament.
> My heart, O do say
> What it is that your memory weaves
> Midst the twilight's golden green leaves?
> Ancient, unnameable days!

But not for long could our friend's feelings hold to such a general strain. He took out a lock of Agnes's hair, and, shining in the grass beside him, lay the precious necklace from the Countess (for this was the contents of the elegant case), and the actor's letter rested upon his breast. Tenderly he pressed each of these objects to his lips as if they all laid equal claim to him.

A light rain began to fall, and Theobald arose. We shall leave him to travel his road in peace and not see him again until with the fourth sundown of his travels he arrives in the last village, where he is assured that he has only three short hours to go to Neuburg. At this last station he wished to stay for the night to gather his strength and composure. This he did in his usual way, writing, and then, calmed and settled, took to his bed. Morning was barely dawning, and the moon still shone as bright as at midnight when Theobald left the village. Just as day inexorably approached, so did our friend feel the tightening grip of excited anticipation seizing his breast; yet the first glint of sun flickers in the reddening eastern sky, and with resolve he casts off his faint-heartedness. With an unexpected turn his path opens upon a quiet valley that seems to go on without end; it gives way to a second and a third valley, so that the painter is not sure if he has chosen the right one; yet he rides on, and the mountains finally seem to part somewhat. "Heart, hold fast!" he calls out aloud, as all at once he believes he spies smoke from nearby houses. He was not wrong; already he could see the forester's cheery cottage with its green shutters as it lay nestled alone at the side of a mountain not far from the church. "Heart, hold fast!" echoes for a second time within him as he rides into the narrow streets. He left his horse at the inn; he hurried to the forester's house.

"Come in!" called a man's voice when Nolten knocked on the door. The old man was sitting, his feet wrapped in cushions, in his easy chair and, in the shock of joy, could not stand up, even if his gout had let him. We shall say nothing of the jubilant tears of this first reception and, with Nolten, ask at once about the daughter.

"Most likely," came the answer, "she's taken a small piece of cloth over to the churchyard to bleach it in the sun; it's a beautiful sunny day; follow her there and give her a capital surprise! I can't wait to see the two of you together! Oh, my son, my dear, fine young son! are you the same old fellow, then? How fine and imposing you look to me! Agnes will be astonished! Go, go sir! The child has no idea. This morning at breakfast we were talking about how a letter would probably come today, and now!" — Theobald embraced the good man again and again, and with that the old fellow let him go. As he passed, he chanced to glance into his beloved's room, where his gaze fell upon a simple dress of hers draped over a chair; he recognized it at once, and at the sight of it he felt a stab of melancholy shoot through him as, with a thrill of awe, his mind had to breach the gap of time.

The way to the churchyard behind the parsonage between the hazel hedges, how well known yet how strange it all was to him! The small gate in the wall stood open; he stepped into the quiet green space, its rustic graves and crosses surrounding the modest church. Eager and shy he looks for Agnes; behind each tree and bush he thinks he sees her, but in vain; his impatience grows with every breath; wearied he sits down on a wooden bench under the spreading walnut tree and surveys the peaceful scene. He can hear the steady beat of the tower clock's pendulum; bees hum about the young herbs, the turtle dove coos here and there, and — as it always makes a not unpleasant impression when, bound up with the gloomy images of death and destruction, there are cheering images of actively vital life — so it was pleasing for the observer to encounter, in the midst of this field of decay, single traces of everyday, living existence. There the joiner from next door had leaned a few freshly painted boards against a weathered gravestone to dry; further along a few strips of linen laid out on the grass billowed in the cheery spring air, and Theobald had to feel strangely touched when he thought which hands had spun this fabric and carefully carried it here, when he pondered how many hours of the long day and the long night that truest girl, her thoughts ever turning to her far-off beloved, her diligence rich in hopes, had spent on this work while he, o'er hasty and deluded, in sinful passion, had pursued a new affection.

He could no longer stay where he was; yet he could not find the courage simply to go and look for Agnes; uncertain, he stepped into the entryway of the church to encounter a pleasant coolness and, despite the meager decor, a spirit of solemnity. Bound up after all with these worn brown pews, with these columns and paintings, was an endless array of pious impressions of his youth; and this small organ with its simple tones had once filled the whole expanse of his feelings and raised it to the highest; and there too, opposite the pulpit, stood the pew where Agnes had sat when she was a child; and that small gold strip of sun that was just now shining on its back he well remembered having seen on many a Sunday morning just as it was now; from each corner a wondrous ghost of the past seemed to harken to the half-strange visitor and whisper to him: See, here, in the end, everything has remained as it was; how have you lived these years?

Now he climbed up to the choir loft; he saw an old pencil sketch that he had once scribbled at a portentous moment, superstitiously, as if posing a question to the future — but how quickly startled he turns his attention when through the dusty windowpane he catches sight of a female figure that leaves him not a moment's doubt — for Agnes it truly is. His breast gives a breathless start, he cannot move from the spot, and all the less so the more striking, the more touching the pose in which the girl appears just now. He cautiously opens the window casement slightly and stands watching, as if rooted there.

At half its height, the wall enclosing the churchyard forms a broad, continuous ledge, upon which a free-standing cross of old stonework has been erected; at its foot on the ledge, still at some height above the ground, the lovely creature is sitting with her knitting and wearing her housedress, positioned so that her friend is afforded a full view of her face's profile; from one arm of the cross above her head hangs a fresh wreath of evergreen, while she herself is holding her needle softly to her lips just as she leans attentively forward towards a shrub on which a butterfly is busily fluttering its shining wings; now, as it flies away, her gaze glides briefly up past Theobald's window, almost causing him to cry out in the shock of pleasure; but her dear head was already hovering quietly again over the busy play of her fingers. At occasional intervals the sweetest aroma of flowers would waft up to the eavesdropper, only to give the mental string of his memory an all the more exciting and captivating turn tighter, for this special scent, he thought, the violet had never given off anywhere else but right here, where its perfume mixed with the early feelings of a pure love.

He now pondered seriously how he would most easily emerge from his hiding place and present himself to the unwitting girl; but while until now he had, in lovely anticipation, been allowed to observe unnoticed the figure and all the action and movement of his beloved, so a favorable coincidence now let him hear the sound of her voice so long denied him. The stork that since times long past had made its nest on the church roof was just now striding by with much gravity, first down in the grass and then up on the battlement, as if to pay a visit to Agnes. "Have you already had your breakfast, old fellow? come, get along!" she called and snapped her fingers; the long-legged bird took little notice of the hearty greeting and marched calmly on past behind her. But now, suddenly, the old forester put his head roguishly through the gate: "Just had to take a bit of a look at the pair of lovers who wish to keep their pleasure so to themselves — well, my dear? your visitor? so he's run off again?" Agnes, who takes these words as meant for the stork, points with a laugh off to one side where the bird is continuing on his pompous way; yet before the forester can explain to her what he meant and before the girl has climbed down off the wall, Nolten appears in the church door: Agnes, catching sight of him, turns to her father beside her and, with a short cry, throws her arms around his neck, where she buries her glowing face, while our friend, who with lightning speed lets his guilty conscience find an explanation for this shocked turn away, hovers near, slightly embarrassed, until he can tell from a stolen, half-raised glance from the girl over her father's shoulder that it is joy and not disdain or pain that leaves her sobbing at her father's breast. But when the wonderful child now turns suddenly to him and, embracing him with all the force of passionate love, utters only the words: "Mine! Mine!" then he too would likely have wept openly if the power of such moments did not benumb the pleasure of even the happiest tears.

AS THEY WALKED BACK HOME they expressed great regret that Theobald would not be able to greet the good Baron for some days, since he had been away traveling for a week.

"I am still quite confused and befuddled with joy," Agnes said as they entered the parlor, "just let me come to my senses!" And so they stood about together in happy amazement, looking at each other and then taking each other anew in their arms.

"And Papa, how beautiful she's become, my child!" exclaimed Theobald, giving her whole figure a good looking over; "how she's grown! Forgive me, and just let me gaze in wonder."

Really, her entire figure had become more defined, more robust, yes, as Theobald thought, and taller too. But as well, all the charms that her fiancé had always valued so highly in her he recognized again. That deep, dark blue of her eyes, that special shape of her eyebrows that differed from all others by curving off towards her temples at an angle that was indeed quite endearing. Then there were still, especially when she laughed, the perfect rows of teeth that gave her face an uncommon degree of striking charm.

"Yet the most wondrous thing, and one that I myself take some pride in, it seems this gentleman does not want to notice!" said Agnes, as a delightful red colored her cheek. Well did he know what she was talking about. Her hair, which when he was last present he had still seen as almost blond, had changed completely to a beautiful, dark chestnut brown. Theobald had noticed it at once, but at the same time he had also had the strange feeling that illness and dark grief had played a role in this lovely miracle. Agnes herself seemed not to think such a thing in the least, but instead went on quite cheerily: "And do you suppose that took an especially long time to happen? Not at all! almost noticeably, in less than twenty weeks, I had changed color. The pastor's daughters and I, we still joke about it today."

That evening Nolten was to tell about himself. Yet he could not give a very orderly account of things; for even though he had seen clearly from the drafts of Larkens's letters how conscientiously his friend had prepared the way for him with respect to certain embarrassing points so as not to disturb the dear good folk — this especially on account of the imprisonment episode — he still found that remembering that dangerous period in the presence of this incomparable girl made him feel ill at ease and embarrassed at heart. For that reason he proceeded with his narratives in a very fragmentary and willful manner. And in any case — as often tends to happen with lovers who reunite again after a long period full of change — the pure pleasure of the present with all its seriousness, fun, and laughter, so too the silent delight when they looked at each other, consumed all other interests and all inclination to consistent thought. Yet while now the young pair wanted for nothing, for nothing at all in the world, and indeed at times gave to understand with a hearty sigh that they were all at once having too much of a good fortune and that, given the wealth and abundance of these first hours, they would be quite unable to manage the bliss of the coming days, the old man for his part was not quite so pleased. He sat after dinner — table cloth and glasses had to remain — in his easy chair, calmly smoking a pipeful, and he expected to hear many a new thing about Theobald's journey and about distant places; he wanted to sit back in comfort and hear this and that pleasant or illustrious bit of news about Theobald's acquaintances. This caused Agnes, who noticed what was wrong, to give her fiancé a sly nudge a few times, who then, chatting away for all he was worth, was soon enough able to put her father in the best of moods and even move him to hearty laughter a few times. Revived to youthful good spirits, the old gentleman even came upon the idea of having a bottle of genuine capuchin wine, much admired by the Baron, brought from the cellar, and the evening grew ever more cheery.

Regarding the father, whom we already know in general terms, we shall say at this point only the following: He was a man of good, sound reason, of the best quality through and through, and while his obstinate rigidity of character seemed quite charmingly mellowed by his extreme tenderness towards his daughter, still on the other hand his son-in-law was almost the only person for whom he felt an unbounded respect. For in fact the old man tended to think something of himself, and since as a forester, especially in earlier days, he had had extensive dealings with a large staff of hunters and gamesmen and was valued as an experienced and well-versed man, he might well have felt himself quite justified in such an opinion.

When after eleven o'clock they finally got up to go to bed, all three insisted that none of them would be able to sleep for joyful excitement. "I can't sleep even without all the excitement!" sighed the forester, "for with all the work I did in my early years, day and night in the cold and wet, I robbed myself of the well-earned sleep of my later years! it's my feet that give me trouble. But so be it! There's much to think and learn about from midnight through to the dear bright day. And if I can lie in my good bed and tell myself that all my house and goods are safe on all sides and well closed-up, with no secret fire burning anywhere and all's well so far, and then the moonlight hits my window, then I can imagine to myself thousands of things, imagine the creatures afoot out there at dawning on the forest meadow in peace and joy in their maker's eyes; I think of the old days, of bygone years — so goes the Psalm — I think in the night of my harp (for that's what the huntsman calls his gun) and commune with mine own heart: and my spirit made diligent search.[29] Yes, yes, my son, go ahead and smile, I can be sentimental too, as you call it, you young people. Well, sleep well!" He gave a friendly tip of his nightcap and let Agnes light her fiancé to his room.

ONCE AGAIN THE MOST MAGNIFICENT sunshine came breaking through the windows of the forester's house to bring its inhabitants together in good time.

Agnes, long accustomed to acting as lady of the house, was the first one up. And what she offered her dearest's gaze to behold anew! In a different dress than yesterday, a rather more simple one; — but how it all fit her so well, too, clinging to her truest self, indeed completely one with her! Just like this new day, so she was completely new for Nolten; surely, we do not go too far to say: she was the golden morn itself. She had just watered the potted plants, and there was a bright droplet on her brow; with what pleasure he kissed it away and kissed her hair parted so smooth and neat on either side!

He made a comment that the girl had to accept after some objection. Brides whose fathers work in forestry are always, in the eyes of their lovers, one charm ahead of the other girls, either through the contrast of their delicate femininity to their involvement in an adventurous and often dangerous life, or because even the daughters still seem to have about them the fresh free breath of the forest; the shared color of green also serves to convey such an idea quite well. Only that last point met with an exception in the case of Agnes, who had the idiosyncrasy of not liking to wear that cheery color as a rule and then only sparingly.

She went to look after breakfast, leaving Nolten to talk with her father. The conversation turned to Agnes's illness and then soon, as neither party wanted to dwell on that matter, to a topic of which the old man spoke with enthusiasm and the son with a quiet, almost timid pleasure — his wedding. They mustn't hesitate much longer with it, was the father's opinion, and Nolten's too, and even Agnes had become somewhat more comfortable with that serious idea. One major question was not yet decided, namely: where the young master would settle down. The gentlemen were just discussing that matter when all at once Nolten asked, raising his head and listening, "Who's making music out there in the kitchen? who's that whistling, then?" "*She* is, Agnes," the old man answered nonchalantly, opening the door slightly and then calmly going on with what he was saying. They heard the girl talking with the maid, moving the cutlery around, and in between trilling and whistling as if in thought. Unintentionally, Nolten had to laugh out loud: the most trivial thing in the world had surprised him. There are innocent trifles that simply seem to conflict with or even offend the image that we have of a person even if it is only in some measure an idealistic one. Immediately Nolten had this feeling — an unpleasant one, if you will — and immediately he sensed that feeling turn into quite a different one or at least into a mixed one that had about it an irresistibly exciting attraction. He would have liked to leap to his feet and kiss and bite those pursed lips, yet he kept his seat until the child, unwitting and innocent, came back into the room, whereupon he could not but give her mouth a good sound pressing, albeit without — and he could not tell what forbade him to do so — betraying the silly reason for his lover's mood. "Say," called out the father at that moment, "until we have our coffee just go fetch the mandolin, I don't think you've thought of doing that yet." As red as fire the girl went at these words. There is a degree of embarrassment that is truly terrible and elicits the greatest sympathy; this rarely happened with Agnes, but when it did, her eyes, without actually weeping, would suddenly overflow with tears and open extremely wide as often happens with sleepwalkers; it was impossible to look at her then, for she gave a person the distinct feeling that she was about to dissolve in some miraculous way, that she was on the verge of breaking up completely like a wisp of cloud. She stepped anxiously behind Theobald's chair, her fingers playing fretfully with his hair. No one dared say anything more, and there was a tense pause. "Some other time," she said meekly and hurried back into the kitchen.

"It's plain to see that it troubles her to think of her cousin, her mandolin teacher, with you around. But, to tell the truth, I wouldn't have expected *that*."

"We won't trouble her!" said Theobald, "let's just be cautious. I can well imagine how she feels. But the look of the girl astonished me, almost frightened me. Didn't you see how, when she left, her color changed a second time, turning snow white?"

"Strange!" said the father, more annoyed than worried, "back in those sad days you could often see her become that way, but never again since then, until this moment." Both men had begun to ponder the matter when Agnes brought the cups.

At breakfast they discussed what they were to do that day. "Before I can think of anything else, before we let Papa get a word in about visits to be made and obligations to keep, allow us the pleasure that Agnes first shows me the whole house from gable to cellar, from the shed to the garden, and then all in order again, everything that cheered me as a boy. What lovely times those were! You had your four boys in the house, dear father, the two Z. brothers, that wild pair, then me and Amandus, who's now the pastor over there in Halmedorf. How I look forward to seeing him again! we must get over there right in these next days, do you hear, my dear? do you hear, Papa? For that, each must bring his little pack of memories along, and together we'll have a good portion of past times." "Unfortunately," said Agnes, "there's not much to be said about me from those days; I was only seven when you came to us." "What? not much to say? do you think that day, that fateful, black, catastrophic Sunday afternoon, won't be written up in our school annals, the day you got a hold of my exercise book, took it to your chair behind the oven, and, starting right after where the rector had entered his red failing mark, drew in your awkward hand and with all the best intentions a whole row of angular Ps and Vs? What a calamity when I discovered the scandal. I seized you, God forgive me, by the ears, and the others were after you too like a swarm of angry bees when the enemy tries to break in! — Oh, and what a dreary walk that was every morning, on my way with my bundle of books to the city to go to the Lycee! For the good rector had an especially sharp eye on me. But, then came Saturday, the long awaited end of the week! we said: in heaven it must be Saturday every day, for even Sunday was not so wonderful any more. Oh, I must see the loft again where we would tumble in the hay, the sheaf-hauling rope we used to swing on, the pond in the yard where we raised fish!" "The church and the churchyard," laughed the old man, "these treasures you've already set eyes on; we'll likely be able to find the stairs up to the bells." "Say," interjected Agnes at this point, "and your old favorite, your Geschaggien, you've already heard him!" Theobald didn't understand right away what she meant by that, but suddenly he recalled with a happy laugh that she was talking about an old night watchman that they used to make fun of because he would distort the last syllables of his hourly call in a manner that was supposed to sound especially pretty.

Just then the messenger from the city brought the most recent newspapers, which the father seemed to have been expecting for some time already, for he'd kept his coffee, and his second pipeful was just lying there, ready to light. Courteous as he always was, he gave his son half of the bundle, but Theobald left them lying there next to him. "No," he said, turning to address Agnes while the father engrossed himself in political matters, "I didn't hear little old Casper in the night." "Well I did!" she responded, "at three o'clock, it was still dark, and he called out the morning; and" she added quietly, "I thought of you! but in such a way! Just as I had awakened it came to me all at once that you were here, here with me under one roof! I had to fold my hands, I was seized by a joy that made me press them together; with such happy, thankful ease I have never prayed in all my days." "Listen to this, children," the father began: "here's an idea of the Russian Tsar's! Superb! Excellent! Just listen." And with that he read aloud a long article, all the while puffing out his clouds of pipe smoke. Nolten barely caught the first words of the edict, still so captivated by Agnes's last words, in which he sees shimmering all the gold of her soul; he rests his penetrating gaze upon her and at the same time he is seized by the most vivid memories of Larkens. "Oh," he would have liked to cry out, "why must I miss him now? Him, whom I have to thank for this blissful happiness, why does he disdain witnessing for himself how wonderfully has grown the seed that his true hand sowed! And I am to enjoy myself here while a cheerless fate, oh, his own insatiable heart, bids him wander afar, alone, and yearning by himself, without a helpful sympathetic soul who could discuss his secret sorrows, who could shed some modest light of consolation down into the dark depths of his misery! To think of him that way! and no trace, no idea which corner of the world hides him from me. And if I were never to find him? God! if in this very moment he had already carried out in despair what he had threatened he would do — —!" A worry that at first had occurred to us only as a weak point that we were always lucky to dispel tends in its malicious way to assail us most tenaciously in just those moments when everything else unites around us in friendly harmony. Driven by the vigorous wind of a stirred-up imagination, cloud upon cloud crowd in until all is night around us. Thus in the midst of the most lovely surroundings did the immense ghost of an absent fate shake its threatening fist in Theobald's face, and suddenly he felt dawning upon him the strange certainty that Larkens was lost to him forever, that he had ended in some horrible way. He could bear it no longer and arose from his chair to pace the room. The sweet presence of Agnes makes him strangely tense, an inexplicable anxiety befalls him; he feels as if this present so pure were, with a silent reproach, casting him out as an unworthy stranger. This room, the old man with his daughter, the whole scene that the flash of a thought was unveiling and revealing to him in its full arresting contrast with his past he now thought to be no more than mist and dream; and indeed, if all that he now saw about him with his own eyes suddenly, by some powerful magic, were to have sunk away and disappeared before him, he would have seen it as only the natural dissolution of an immense illusion.

Fortunately, Agnes's attention during Theobald's intense feelings was devoted totally to her father, who loved to discuss political events with her and test and train her judgment in such matters.

Our friend felt totally cast out and alone, and when his gaze fell upon that dear girl she seemed no longer to belong to him at all and to have never meant anything to him.

But now just as our heart possesses the beneficent capacity to let the intervention of some small circumstance change our mind quickly from one extreme back to our natural feelings, so our friend, as soon as the door opened and the good old Baron walked in, was restored to his old self, and the appearance of a deity could not have done him more good. With outstretched arms he runs to him and clings to that venerable man, sobbing like a child and covering his white locks with kisses. The others, too, showed great joy and surprise; they had thought the old gentleman still far away over hill and dale, and now he told how chance had led him homewards earlier, how they had told him last night when he arrived that the painter had arrived, and how then he had not been able to wait to greet him.

There is on such occasions an especially pleasant feeling in noticing how friends, particularly older people whom one has not seen in some time, retain unchanged certain outward mannerisms and customary habits. This constancy affords us a kind of assurance about our own lives, for while the old people make us doubly fond of the life to which they cling so tenaciously, we younger folk find ourselves at the same time strengthened in our own claims to the right to live life and enjoy it heartily. Thus with this visit the Baron had in mind the customary morning walk that for years he had taken at the same hour; thus he placed his walking stick in the corner just as he usually did between the oven and the gun rack; as usual he had not taken off the unfashionably stiff collar that recalled his earlier military bearing. But our happy affection gives way to pained sympathy when we must note that all such features convey only the illusion of his former state, when we see how age and frailty contradict these remaining signs of better times. And so too did Nolten quietly grow glum as he took more careful stock of the old man. He walked considerably more stooped forward, his lined face was markedly paler and thinner, and only the good-natured friendliness of his mouth and the alert glint of his eyes could dispel these impressions.

While now the conversation among the four unfolds with cheerful pleasantness, it cannot but happen, even with all this apparent openness and candor, that Nolten and the Baron, by their looks and expressions and still more through certain chance, indefinable features of their thinking, unintentionally reveal to each other what each of the two might in particular be thinking and feeling during this encounter; and our friend believed he understood the Baron perfectly when that man, with special pleasure and a kind of solemnity, laid his hand upon Agnes's head while letting his gaze turn to rest upon Nolten. Nolten found special consolation in the fact that he was allowed to share with a man whom he so revered the silent reproach for having so deeply misunderstood the dear creature. Indeed it had been this thought, however darkly he may have sensed it, that had lifted the greatest burden from his heart right when the Baron had entered the room. That fine old gentleman might, moreover, have been right in immediately terminating their veiled dialogue of thoughts by presenting the general happy outlines of Theobald's good fortune as it evolved from early years on, which brought them to speak of Theobald's youth. Agnes, in the meantime, had gone to look after household matters.

"They tell me to my face even today," the painter began, "and even my worthy Papa occasionally gives to understand that I have remained a boy longer than is right. There's no denying my pranks as a lad of sixteen years were not a hair's breadth better than those of an eleven-year-old, indeed my pastimes and hobbies may have seemed more narrow-minded, or at any rate they lacked that practical significance that makes it possible to forgive boys that age many a game, no matter how passionate and time-wasting such pursuits might be. My way of having fun rarely involved anything physical; climbing, jumping, tumbling, and riding scarcely interested me; I was more inclined to the quieter pursuits, frequently to curiosities and oddities. I used to like to retreat to some quiet corner where I could be sure that no one would find me, at the churchyard wall or on the top floor of the house between piles of seed crops, or outside under an autumn tree and give myself over to a contemplation that you could have called innocent if an inner turn of the soul towards nature and the immanent outer world in its most minute phenomena deserved such a term; for whether expressly religious feelings played a role I wouldn't know, in any case they weren't excluded. I would occasionally nurture a vague feeling of melancholy that was akin to joy and whose circle — whose atmosphere, I might say — I was able at will to go in and out of as easily as I moved in and out of the place associated with it. With what inexpressible pleasure I could, when the others were playing in the yard, sit up in a dormer window, taking my afternoon tea and working on a new drawing or design. Up there in the attic, you see, there's a boarded-in space, narrow and low, where the sun always seemed to me to have a special gleam, a whole different quality in general, and also I could make it completely night and (this was the greatest pleasure), while outside it was bright daylight, light a candle that I had secretly gotten hold of and knew well enough to hide." "Dear God, my goodness gracious!" exclaimed the forester, "if I and my late wife had known what kind of dangerous fireworks —" "And so would pass an hour," Nolten went on, not liking to be interrupted, "until I too wanted company, and then I would take part, as lively as the rest, in a catch-the-robbers game that I liked best of all. The younger children, Agnes among them, liked to listen to the fairy tales I would tell in the evening, all about the friendly ghosts that were at my service to help me or to scare someone. Then I would let them look at the two knotholes in the wooden wall on the staircase where I kept those kindly fellows locked up; in the one knothole, over which I'd nailed a dark cloth, I kept the evil spirits, in the other (or rather it wasn't a hole at all, since naturally the round knot was still stuck fast in the wood) the friendly spirits; then, when at certain times of day the sun would happen to shine back there, the plug was lit up a glowing red by the prettiest crimson ray; through this portal, as long as the round part appeared so glowingly translucent, the spirits could still easily fly in and out; right behind it one imagined that one could see in very miniature proportions a rather extensive sea with a lovely mist-shrouded island. Then it was a joy to take the children, who were gathered attentively around me, and lift them up, one after the other so they could see that magnificent sight from as close up as possible, and each of them thought he or she saw the most wonderful things in that lovely glow; naturally! after all, I almost believed it myself. — Yet isn't it terrible to go on talking about oneself for so long; but Papa, only if I'm able to amuse you with these confessions I'll gladly admit that the old Theobald occasionally catches himself dwelling on some trace of these childish pursuits."

The forester shook his head and, as was his habit whenever something would surprise him, emitted a long "sss-t" through his teeth. The Baron, on the other hand, had listened the whole time with a smile of delight and now said: "Similar things I have heard or read about others, and everything you said agrees with the view of your individuality that I had from very early on. And in general I consider to be lucky that young person who, without being slow or stupid, remains, as they say, far behind his years; he usually carries an unusual seed within himself that need only be felicitously developed by the circumstances. In such a case every absurdity is the start and statement of a noble strength, and this brooding that appears to produce nothing, that produces no piece of work, is the proper gathering time for the truly inner person who of course simply does not get out into the world very much. I cannot picture it charming and attractive enough: the silent dampered light in which the boy sees the world hovering, where one is inclined to put upon the most everyday objects the stamp of the strange, often even of the mysterious, and to link them to some secret just to make them have some special significance for the fantasy, where behind every visible thing, whatever it may be — a piece of wood, a stone, or the cock and newel atop the tower — something invisible lies waiting, behind every dead issue something spiritual that his own hidden life devoutly harbors closed off within itself where all things take on meaning and physiognomy."

"Yet you will admit," rejoined Nolten, "that those kinds of habits can also become dangerous, after I have told you about the, to be sure, slight beginnings of an obsession in a child's mind, a case that you wouldn't have expected to come across — at least not in someone of such a young age. I am speaking of my fiancée, of Agnes. Since the good child isn't here now to listen, we can speak openly of it; for it is also proof of how an uncanny tendency was present from early on in her otherwise so pure and lovely nature, and it is also proof, since the events of the previous year, of how much we might have reason to take care where she is concerned. Tell the Herr Baron about it, father, since I too learned about it only from you; you know, the whim the girl used to have on occasions when anyone talked of places abroad and foreign cities."

"Well, my daughter was about ten years old, when your brother, Herr Baron, the District Chief Forester, returned from his travels and was on occasion so gracious as to come to my house and tell of his travels. This gentleman, thoughtful and serious, but friendly and kind to children, made a special and lasting impression on this girl. Now one time — the company had just left — she comes from her seat behind the oven, where she had sat awhile quite quietly, doing her knitting; she comes right up to me, looks me straight in the face, and laughs at me as if at something that I would already have had to know about; as she does so, she runs the point of her knitting needle playfully across my brow. When I ask what that all means, she gives no clear answer and goes back to her place. That's what she did a few times on different occasions. Finally I became impatient and spoke to her quite sharply; then she broke into tears, saying: 'Just admit it, father, that those countries and cities don't exist that you're always talking about with that gentleman; I see it clearly, you just do that when I'm around so that I'm supposed to believe all sorts of wonders about what's happening out there in the world and about what really doesn't exist; that's why you never let me go farther than to Weil, Grebenheim, and Neitze. No doubt our King's land is very large, and the world goes far far beyond it, and there are other peoples, all that I know well; but *Paris,* that's surely not a word, and *London,* there's no such city; you just thought it up, and you speak as though you knew all about it so that I'm supposed to imagine it all to myself.' — That's about the nonsense the simple thing chattered; partly I was annoyed, partly I had to laugh. I took the trouble to explain everything to her clearly, showed her the maps that she had seen quite often anyway; while I was doing it she was looking carefully at my expression, and the slightest sign of laughing brought her almost to despair. Well, that caprice soon passed, and when I reminded her of it a few years ago, she had a good hearty laugh at herself about it, explained more clearly how she had felt then, and said — I don't know what." "In short," Theobald took up the story, "it all comes down to her seeing herself as the center and objective of a great educational project that with all the talk about countries and cities meant to put all kinds of vivid ideas into the child's head and broaden her perspective by way of a deception, the use of which she thought she sensed but could not understand. She suspected that they knew people, everywhere she went, who would encounter her here and there, and all the words were written down and everything planned with utmost care so that she wouldn't encounter any contradictions. In addition, this whim had not taken such total possession of her that she wasn't free of it for longer periods in between; she didn't seem quite to trust herself about it. I never cared to ask her about it."

"In the meantime," said the Baron after some thought, "if we consider more closely, we see that this skeptical case, as highly remarkable as it surely is, does not belong in the category we were just discussing. Let us turn back for a moment to that happy mysticism of a boy's early years, for in fact it is actually boys and not girls in whom we find it. That's what I was going to say: do you think that subjects of this pleasantly fantastic complexion — to which I add a considerable quantity of intellect, which does not necessarily have to be there and occurs most infrequently — do you think, I say, that such individuals are always born to be poets and artists? I should think not."

"Not at all!" said Nolten. "I have noticed in a man who appears not to belong to this category, in Napoleon, some secret qualities that can be linked up to certain features of Lichtenberg's own most special nature; of course, they don't relate to precisely what we're discussing, but they are related to a type of superstition that is a close neighbor of all idiosyncrasies."[30]

205

"Napoleon!" exclaimed the Baron, "as if his superstitiousness weren't also just an assumed mask!"

"Don't make him completely into a common criminal!" responded Nolten. "He was always rational and calculating, only not in the deepest reaches of his heart. Don't take from him the only religion he had — the worship of himself or of the fate that seemed to hold up to him in its divine hand the mirror in which he saw himself and the necessity of his deeds."

"We won't go into that," said the Baron, "but as far as I understand you, you're completely right. Fate uses the powers that can lie entwined within one person in truly manifold ways, and from a mixture of poetry now with political understanding, now with philosophical talent, now with a sense for mathematics, and so on, there can spring forth from one and the same subject the greatest and most wonderful results that leave learned scholars gaping and shaking their heads and through which the tired old wheel of the world is given a good and lasting turn. In such cases nature seems, when viewed from our limited perspective, all at once to contradict or even outdo itself, but it is actually doing neither. Two apparently heterogeneous powers can mutually strengthen each other and bring forth the most excellent results. Yet I digress. — I wanted only to proceed from your childish confessions to the point where the philistine and the artist differ. While the artist as a child saw the world as a lovely fable, so as a grown man he will still see it as such in his happiest hours, and that's why he always finds the world so new from all angles and such a delightfully strange surprise.

"Most of all Novalis — though I don't feel quite right about the way he does it — is an enthusiast who has expressed this point as far as it applies to the poet."[31]

"Quite right!" Nolten interjected, "but while the true poet, when viewing the external world in this special way, must absolutely possess this delightful estrangement, even in the case where it might not be revealed in his works, the graphic artist's way of imagining things can be quite far removed from such a perspective, and indeed must necessarily be so. So too the spirit in which the Greeks personified all things seems to me to be completely different from what we are discussing here. For me, their fantasy is much too free, too beautiful for that, and has, I might say, too little hypochondria. Something dead, extinct, fragmentary could in its natural essence no longer have any heartfelt appeal for them. I would have to be mistaken if we weren't dealing here again with the difference between the classical and the romantic."

Now the conversation turned to Theobald's most recent works, and since, with that, things were again about to take a certain general turn, the Baron said, as he looked at the clock: "In order that we don't inadvertently become involved in the most unfruitful of all disputes — for we are on the way to debating whether it is more invigorating to breath Ionian air or the

206

sweetest heaven where it caresses the cheek of a Madonna — let me be on my way, so that I might continue my usual march. This evening I hope you will come to visit me and tell me more about the Narcissus you have begun." Since Nolten knew that the old gentleman liked to walk about his estates alone each morning, he did not insist on accompanying him. He asked Agnes to take a walk in the garden; she assigned the maid a few tasks, went to her room to fetch a scarf, and Theobald followed her there.

"Here, look at all this girl's stuff!" she said as she pulled out a drawer where several cases and little boxes and all manner of modest jewelry lay in lovely colorful array. She took up a red jewel case, clasped it to her breast, lay her cheek upon it, and gazed tenderly at Theobald: "It's your letters! My finest possession! You once made me go so long without their consolation, and then again when you were arrested; but surely I cannot complain." Our friend felt a pang in his heart and made no response. "Your most recent gift" (it was a small clock), "you see," she went on as she opened a second drawer, "shall find its place here, it merits distinguished company. But, my dear soul! what were you thinking when you sent me that? That is finery for a countess, not for the likes of us!" (she was showing him a spencer of dark green velvet rich with gold buttons and delicate chains instead of brocade; Larkens had found a sly way to learn her measurements and thus sent the garment ready-made to size). Theobald stood dazzled, undone by his friend's generosity. While thinking, he was playing with a bouquet of Italian flowers without noticing how miserably he was crushing them with his fingers;[32] Agnes gently took the bouquet from his hands; he smiled, but he was closer to tears. He remembered the necklace the Countess had given him for Agnes; yet he still didn't dare give it to her. How everything, everything hurt, tormented, and enchanted him! yes, even the charming aroma that tends to be so peculiar to girls' wardrobes suddenly seemed to stifle his breath; he had to excuse himself and go to his room, where he cast himself miserably to the floor and willingly gave himself over fully to all his suppressed pain.

Soon Agnes knocked outside on his door: he can't open the door to her, he must not let her see him in this state. "I am getting dressed, my child!" he calls, and quietly she goes back down the hall.

After a while, when he had composed himself, her father came. "A word with you!" he said, when they were alone, "the crazy thing, the girl, now she's got it in her head she should have played for you before; she's afraid of doing it and will keep on being afraid until she's just gotten over being afraid; now she's got the idea she wants to decide quickly." "Only not now!" exclaimed Nolten, "I beg you for God's sake, just not this morning!" "Well, why then?" said the old man, thinking that Nolten merely wanted to spare the girl, "we must seize the moment, otherwise we'll make her uncertain; she's got her courage up: I told her she should appear in her new dress and surprise you, that seemed to make it easier for her, for she can imagine that the new clothes are the main thing. Let her do it this time! She'll be ready soon and then you can come over." So Nolten had to give in; the old man left and called him after a short time.

And there she stood! Dazzling, beautiful, like a young princess. Nolten felt a genuine surprise and joy at the sight of her. He found it so strange to see her dressed up like that, and yet the dress seemed worthy of her alone. Her white gown went very well with the magnificent spencer and some flowers adorned her hair. With what warmth he receives the blushing girl into his arms! with what bliss she gazes into his eyes!

"But now don't laugh at me!" she said, as she looked around for her mandolin, and they all sat down. "I want to tell you how it came about that I learned to play. I once asked you, do you still remember? on that evening when we collected the glowworms in the glass jar, I happened to ask you whether you were sorry that I didn't understand a thing about the fine arts in which you find so much worth and importance, not even a bit of music or being able to paint a nice flower or such like, as other girls can. You said that you didn't miss that in your fiancée at all. I believed it, too, just as I believe everything you say, and thanked you from my heart for your love. And you also said that the couple of hunting songs that I sang every now and then, they were dearer to you than anything. Two days after that we went to the pastor's after dinner to visit. The oldest daughter played the piano, and so beautifully that we could hardly hear enough of it, you especially. But one thing irked me then, about the younger daughter, about Auguste. I had to remind you. Lisette had barely gotten up from the piano than her sister calls upon me to let my voice be heard as well. I didn't suspect anything unkind from the girl, and so I began singing the first song I thought of. But suddenly I become embarrassed and red, for Auguste is holding a sheet of music in front of her face to hide her laughter: the notes tremble in my throat, and as I am at least trying to pluck up enough courage for the last verse, Auguste peers mockingly at me through the rolled up page as if it were a telescope, making me totally confused, and I barely wavered my way to the end in a small voice. While the rest of you went on playing and singing, I had enough to do at the window drying my tears. Later — you had already gone away — the whole thing started to nag at me; I would have liked some respect too; I felt genuine grief for your sake; on top of that came my illness; I still believe even now that I would have recovered more quickly if I had on occasion been able to pass my time with music; in the meantime, thank God, it passed. At this time our cousin would come from the city to visit us, and" (she stopped and, embarrassed, ran her hand over the instrument) "well, so he taught me how to play."

"One of the happy ones first," chimed in her father, hurrying to her aid. Quick and hearty she started out, in a voice strong yet gentle, yet more inclined to move in the lower than in the higher register. Her singing gradually became more provocative, more bold. "The gentleman may look at me if he likes!" she called over once between songs to Theobald who had been avoiding looking at her. He pointed, when the song was over, to another one in her folio entitled "The Huntsman," whose text he liked, and Agnes, although she did not feel the same, nevertheless began at once:

> For three days now the rain I've heard,
> And still the sun's not shining;
> For three days now for one sweet word
> From my sweet love I'm pining!
>
> We both were cross, both she and I,
> And thus in anger parted;
> Yet all the sorrow and the grief
> Now leave me aching-hearted.
>
> What joy to be a huntsman free
> All weathers to be braving!
> My coat drawn close, I go with glee,
> For storm and wind I'm craving!
>
> She with her sisters sits at home
> In mirth and laughter vying;
> While in the woods by night I roam,
> Where leaves are softly sighing.
>
> And now she bitterly does cry
> And think of me, her lover;
> While in the soft green woods I lie
> And darkness is my cover.
>
> No stag I see, and not a deer!
> A shot perhaps will cheer me!
> Its sound to hear, with echo clear,
> Does make the time less dreary.
>
> The thunder through the vale does steal,
> Away 'tis softly dying,
> My heart a sudden pang does feel,
> And oh, for you I'm sighing!
>
> We both were cross, both she and I,
> And thus in anger parted;
> Yet all the sorrow and the grief
> Now leave me aching-hearted.

> — Well up! and to my love so true,
> For naught us now can sever!
> "Now dry my locks all wet with dew,
> And kiss and love me ever!"

Both men clapped loudly. She was about to stand up. "All good things — as they say?" called out the old man, "one more!" So she leafed through the folio, uncertain, none of them suited her; while she was looking and choosing, her father had stepped out of the parlor; she snapped the book shut and was talking with Theobald as she struck the occasional chord. All at once she began to play an opening verse, a more substantial song than the previous ones; it gave expression to the deepest, most touching lament. Agnes's gaze rested earnestly on Nolten, as if lost in thought, until she began to sing.

We shall also add this short song, and we think the reader might be able to have some remote idea of the music from the simple verses, especially from the second refrain, with which each time the melody took an indescribable turn that seemed to express whatever pain and melancholy can lie hidden in the breast of an unhappy creature:

> Blossom time! How soon you've passed,
>   Soon you've passed,
> Gone away from here!
> If my love had but held fast,
>   But held fast,
> I'd have no need to fear.
>
> In the harvest's happy mood,
>   Happy mood,
> The reaping women sing;
> Oh, but from my ailing blood,
>   Ailing blood,
> Nothing forth shall spring.
>
> Wandering through the meadow vale,
>   Meadow vale,
> Dreaming and forlorn,
> A thousand times upon yon hill,
>   Upon yon hill,
> His true love he had sworn.
>
> Up upon that hill's steep side
>   I abide,
> By the linden, crying;
> On my hat the rose-strewn band
>   From his hand,
> In the wind is flying.

Agnes's voice had almost given out towards the end from emotion; now she cast the instrument aside and threw herself impetuously upon her lover's breast. "Faithful! Faithful!" she stammered as she wept, unceasing, her whole body racked with sobs and trembling, "you've remained so to me, and I to you!" — "I shall remain so!" Theobald could say no more, could allow himself no more.

O N ONE OF THE FOLLOWING beautiful days they had planned to go on their much discussed outing to the young pastor and his family in Halmedorf, whom they had already informed of their plans. The two old gentlemen, the forester and the Baron, arranged to ride in the latter's carriage; for in any case it was a three-hour journey to get there. The young people — namely our pair, and a son and two daughters of the local pastor who, despite some objections from Nolten, by Agnes's unrelenting insistence had to be invited along — intended to go on foot; the one party was to set out in the morning in good time, those going by carriage not until after the midday meal. Unfortunately, however, the Baron had in the meantime become quite unwell and — long an unheard of thing — had to take to his bed; his previous travels had been hard on him, as he himself now admitted. And so the forester resolved to stay behind himself, to keep his esteemed friend company.

So the small group set out and soon passed from their small valley on up to the fertile plain above that then declined downwards again where they could see ahead to the tidy village that clung to the steep slope. Long in advance they saw the hill before them, known as the "Fiddler's Hill" — not too much to look at from its foot, but offering an extraordinary view from its top.

"Lovely! lovely! That's what I call being on time!" exclaimed the pastor, who had seen them approaching and walked out to the next field to meet them. "See there, my little pup will beat me to it with his greeting! The little fool remembers you from four years ago, but his master surely wouldn't have recognized you so quickly — Come embrace me, old comrade! Ad pectus manum, said the rector whenever we had lied: manum ad pectus, I love you and have not lied. Oh, I could call out that the mountains would dance, and I would like to have all the bells peal at once, through the whole village I would trumpet and toot it, did I not just happen to be the shepherd of their souls, obliged to keep up respectable appearances, rather than someone else."

In this tone Amandus went on to greet the others one by one, and even when they had already arrived at the parsonage he was still not done. Then out jumped, as light and lithe as a sixteen-year-old newlywed, the pastor's wife, although with the ebullience of her husband she could barely get a word in. Amidst much jubilation they finally reached the parlor, bright and

211

new, quite truly a mirror of its inhabitants. Barely over the threshold they all notice at once how the pastor is in an embarrassed rush to hide a green uniform tunic that was hanging on the wall; yet once he sees his plan betrayed he stops in the middle of the room: "Dash it!" he exclaims, turning to Nolten — "well, dear friend, I'm truly sorry, but now that you've caught wind of a secret, I'll just tell the whole strange story." (He gave his wife a secret nudge and proceeded with feigned seriousness and much good cheer.) "Since yesterday, we have had staying here in our house a strange officer, a colonel, who is actually waiting just for you; he has just ridden out for now, but will be back by evening. He arrived here late last night, and since we don't have a decent inn in the village, he invited himself most courteously into my house as my guest, which was all the greater an honor for me in that I sensed in him a friend of yours. Yet I soon noticed that things couldn't be in the best order with that friendship; he scarcely mentioned your name and fell into brooding, almost dark silence whenever I started talking about you; also, as we conversed, he showed much experience with the world and all the charm that one finds at times in educated military men. My wife gave me to understand in no uncertain times when he arrived that he had such a *visage de contrebande,* and indeed I don't know — the mysterious aspect of his connection to you — just as long as he has nothing against you —"

"What's his name then?"

"Yes, your obedient servant, that he did not tell me."

"Where's he from then? What regiment is he in?" asked Nolten more urgently and not without some emotion, for momentarily, though he knew not why, he thought of a brother of Constanze's who, in the last days of the painter's sojourn in that capital, was said to be visiting the Countess. He himself had not seen the man and was not able to compare the description that Amandus gave of the strange visitor with anyone else. Nor did the guest's home, which Amandus chanced to mention, contradict his worried suspicion. "I would have liked," Amandus went on, "to keep quiet about the whole adventure, which really does not bode pleasant; there would have been time to mention it this afternoon, and the stranger's delicacy in not wanting to disrupt our first mealtime gathering was in fact quite laudable, he intimated this intention to me quite clearly as he rode off. Now of course it would almost have been better if he were here right now and you were released from this devilish uncertainty. Listen, let's hope in the end it's just not an odious matter of honor! You know those officers — You haven't had some trouble, have you?" "Not that I know of," said Nolten and paced the room a few times in silence.

In the meantime the pastor's wife had quietly taken the uniform coat into the anteroom. All at once the door opened wide, and in came a tall handsome man and with lightning speed embraced Theobald. It was none other than his dear brother-in-law S., the husband of Adelheid, with whom we have already become acquainted. "By thunder!" exclaimed the pastor, while everyone watched this heartiest embrace, "this re-encounter is not as totally hostile, not as much a matter of life and death as I had thought after all, unless of course they're breaking each other's necks out of love. Well! didn't I make a fine job of it then? When worry doth to joy give way, rejoicing fills the live-long day. — Well then" (he grumbled to himself) "that takes care of number one." He was then roundly scolded for his mischief. Doubly and trebly did Nolten have to marvel, for S., since they had last seen each other, had been promoted to colonel, which was why the uniform meant nothing to Nolten. The pastor told in triumph how, upon receiving news of Theobald's arrival in Neuburg, he had hit upon the splendid idea of sending a courier to invite the brother-in-law, whom he knew to be only five hours away on regimental business.

Joyful indeed was the midday meal, an imposing spread, with the son and daughters of the Neuburg pastor sitting, part timidly, part delighted, in what was for them such a happy new circle of fine people. Our painter, seated between Agnes and his brother-in-law, held the hand of each in his own, unwilling to let go of either and feeling once again, after so long a time, total release from the weight and oppression of his life, his eyes time and again welling up in tears.

The pastor became increasingly agitated and occupied as the meal went on; he left the table frequently, giving secret orders at the door, and was pleased at last to see the meal's final course served. Before dessert he rose and said: "Let now the prelude to the second act begin, with some clinking of glasses if you like. Let the worthy company now rise up, take up their hats and parasols, and proceed betimes from out my house, where for now nothing more is being served. First, however, direct, if you please, your gazes here towards the window and take note of yonder sun-shone peak." They caught sight, set up on that hill, this side of the forest known to us already as "Fiddler's Hill," a large linen canopy with a colorful banner that appeared to be sheltering a round, white-covered table. The dense array of garlands hanging down the five sides of the canopy gave the entire arrangement the appearance of a bright arbor. Amandus had some time ago had this portable shelter made for the annual children's festivities as well as for the comfort of visitors, since the nearby linden tree provided the site with more decoration than cooling shade. — The visitors were beside themselves with joy and set off without delay, all longing to give freest rein to their happy feelings in nature's vast expanse. The younger folk had gone on ahead.

On the way, Nolten and his fiancée could not have their fill of hearing tell of Adelheid. We know of the affection, almost more than brotherly, that bound the painter to his sister, whose quiet depth, as is claimed and as we gladly like to believe, had in the meantime blossomed and taken shape as a character of the greatest charm and rarity; at least Agnes, in her modest loving way, at once seized upon this sister-in-law as a model of genuine womanhood, although the two of them had seen each other but once. Now they thought of that far away woman with all the more intense feeling, since they had heard at the outset that she had become a most happy mother for the first time. We add on this occasion the fact that an older sister, Ernestine, had also been married for some time, although, as some claimed, not very happily so, as she did indeed not seem cut out to hold a man forever. The youngest girl, Nanette, was just in the prettiest bloom of youth and lived with an aunt.

They passed a stand of pine trees known as heron woods, renowned for its echo. The pastor called out, with appropriate pauses:

"O Adelheid mine,
At this very time
In your small bed fine,
You must far off pine,
Must far off pine,
Yet not all alone.
Sir Stork's been at her home,
Wherefore her heart laughs,
Though her wee boy might whine.
— Dame Echo, O speak, I pray,
Yet I know not what to say:
What hugs there my dear lady,
A lassie or a laddy?"
"A laddy!"

Soon they found themselves atop the mountain, catching their breath and astonished at the unhindered view. "With women," began Amandus, "when they have taken the last arduous step and then look about them, I differentiate between two types of sigh. The one is of a quite basic material nature, no breeze is able to pluck it from the rosy lips and bear it off blissfully over the splendid landscape, but rather it at once falls heavily to the ground as prosaic as the handkerchief with which one mops one's brow. T'wer better the beauties totally refrained from its like or it least suppressed it, for to a certain degree it must insult the host, the Cicerone of the company, who is showing off this magnificence with such enthusiasm as if it were his own and thus can't understand how in such moments others can still have the least feeling of the meager trouble at which price they purchased such a view. Indeed, I have seen ladies who took the trouble to bring forth this sigh in a quite charmingly consumptive and ethereal fashion, making a piteous face as they did so, as if a swoon were soon upon them. One can barely keep from asking in tones right plaintive: would you not care for a sip of spirits, miss, or some such? In short, then, if that first type of sigh says no more than: Thank God,

214

we made it! then the second" — He hadn't gotten to the end when Agnes finally arrived, who, as in fact no one had noticed, was missing until that point. She was carrying the pastor's child; it hadn't been able to keep toddling along, so she'd picked it up and carried it on her back to clamber up the steep edge at the side. Out of breath she set the child down on the ground and let out a half-audible "Thank God!" Hearing this word the others looked around, and none could resist laughing, yet nothing could be more touching than the dear girl's startled questioning look. Amandus gave her a warm hug and kiss as he exclaimed: "This time, truly, Martha's trouble is even more beautiful than the one thing so needful up here."[33]

But what a pleasure it was now to plunge with thirsty eye into this shining sea of landscape, to let it drink in the violet of the most distant mountains and then let it glide again over the nearest villages, forests and fields, highways and waters, in their inexhaustible play of lines and colors!

Here one's gaze met, not all too far away, a long chain of mountains trailing off the alps, grave and vast, closing off almost the entire eastern horizon, with mountain arrayed behind mountain, layer upon layer, but so that at times it was possible, with or without a telescope, to spy a remote valley partly lit by the sun and to point it out excitedly to the others.[34] Especially long did Agnes's eye dwell on the folds of the nearest chain of mountains where the sultry mist of midday lay so enchantingly, the ghostly play of light ever changing as evening approached, appearing now dark, now steel-blue, now light, now inclined to black, as if misty spirits were harboring some golden secret in those moist warm depths. A sizeable ruin crowned the furthest chain of mountains, and even through a weaker telescope it seemed near enough to touch, while far off behind they could see only the declining slope of the forest ridge on which the Rehstock had to be situated. In the meantime, eager hands had built a fire between some stones, the coffee was beginning to boil, cups were clattering, and the pastor bade all be seated. But still no one wanted to make use of the lovely tent, which until then had been serving as a kind of kitchen; they sat about on the ground in random groups, each eating as preferences dictated, but they all moved closer together when Amandus arose and spoke as follows:

"This lovely spot, whereon we now repose, my dears, must not lightly be visited without our recalling the memory of that hero whom it owes its name. Surely, not one of you is totally unacquainted with the remarkable saga, but likely only the fewest have had the opportunity to compile, from the various and in part mutually contradictory folk stories, a complete picture of the character of the wondrous entity of whom I now speak; it can thus displease no one to hear now a more exact account, whereby I allow myself to be concerned less with bringing in every single story and anecdote than with making clear instead the main features. Perhaps with that I can bring my friend Nolten to make the strange fiddler the subject of an artistic

215

composition, a long-cherished wish of mine, which he once solemnly promised me to undertake but which until today he has not fulfilled. You, dear
Colonel, will surely support me vigorously in my request, as you yourself
have such a lively interest in the figure of the poetic fiddler and still show
even today an active interest in a complete rendition of his story. Aye, and
quite right it is that I chance to recall that now. You shall be first to have the
honor and present to us the results of your musty research in the form of a
gay and lively portrait, yet I shall come to your aid should you leave any
gaps." The Colonel did not have to be asked twice, and the company gave
careful heed.

"In these parts ages ago a robber, Marmetin, is said quite often to have
gone his way, a man known to all by the name Young Volker. A robber, did
I say? God forbid that I should give him this despicable name, this child of
fortune, this most merry of all the daredevils, adventurers, and rogues who
have ever earned their bread from the possessions of strangers. True it is that
he led a band of seventeen to twenty fellows who were the terror of all rich
misers. But, by heaven, the pedantic goddess of justice herself had to look
on, I would say, with a pleased smile as the most infamous of all trades took
on in this Volker's hands a look of charm. The glutton, the arrogant noble-
man, and dishonorable vassal were not safe from my hero and his daring
band, but he filled the stalls and pantries of the peasants. A man brimming
with physical grace, brave, sensible, amiable, and yet enigmatic he was in all
his parts, considered by his comrades an almost supernatural being, and his
penetrating gaze tamed their behavior down to the point of modesty. Had I
then been duke of the land, who knows but that I might have tolerated and
closed an eye to his doings. It was as if he led his men only into happy battle
games. And see, here, this hill was his favorite place where he came to rest
after he had made a good catch; and as he then harbored a passion for certain areas, he would lead his troupe every year, when spring came, right back
to this territory that he might hear again the cuckoo of the bygone year in
the same place. He was a fiddler like no other, and not on some zither or
such like, a worn-out old violin was his instrument. There he would sit while
the others were off in the forest or in the village tavern, alone on this hill
under God's firmament, playing his music all by himself to the four winds
and turning on his heel like a weather vane, taking in the world and all its
blessings. The hill is thus even today called "Fiddler's Hill" or often, too,
"Fiddler's Hillock." — And then, up on his horse, with the hundred-colored
ribbons on his hat and at his breast, always dressed up like a shepherd's
bride, how attractive he must have looked then! A bird of paradise midst a
flock of wild ravens. Somewhat vain I like to imagine him, too, but on the
girls, at least, he had no designs; he was a stranger to such passions his whole
life long: he looked at those lovely children only in passing, as if they were
fairy-tale beings, the way we look at exotic birds in cages. No worries

plagued him, as though he were playing away the hours of his day just as he often liked to play with colorful balls that he would toss up and down in the air in harmony with the music. His feelings mirrored the world as a cup of golden wine mirrors the sun. Even in danger's midst he was wont to joke, yet he had his eye everywhere; indeed, had he been on a lion hunt, caught up in all the chaos, I believe he would have fought the gnashing beast with his one hand while with his left he shot a sparrow just flying overhead. There are hundreds of stories about his generosity. Once, for example, he encounters a poor little peasant who, as soon as he spies him, takes to his heels. The captain feels sorry for the man and displeased by the bad opinion people seem to have of him; he catches up with the fleeing man on his fast steed and, with friendly words, brings him to a stop. Surprised that the old man is going about bare-headed in such bitter cold, he says: 'Before the Kaiser himself Volker does not take off his hat, but he'll give it to a poor man!' and with that he hands him his brightly beribboned felt hat down from his horse, except he takes a long heron feather off the hat and fixes it to his doublet, not wanting to part with it for the world; they say that feather had magic powers to protect him who wore it against all dangers. — With that I would come to Volker's piety and his wondrous conversion, but since this is a kind of legend it is most fittingly told by the Reverend."

"I only doubt," responded Amandus, "whether I shall acquit my task as deftly as my eloquent predecessor has come off with his. But I call upon the shade of the hero and tell you truly what I know, and also what I don't know. Well then: in the woods that lie before us they once came upon the track of strange game, a stag with milk-white pelt. No huntsman could take him. The captain's ambition was aroused, an irresistible desire to conquer this noble beast drove him to wander the forest all night with his rifle. At last one morning before sunrise the object of his desires appears before him. Only fifty paces away the magnificent creature stands before his eyes. He feels his heart beating; still, sympathy and awe stay his hand, but the hunter's ardor predominates, he fires and hits. Scarcely has he looked at the victim at close range than he becomes disconsolate at having destroyed this vital creature, this most beautiful image of freedom. Now, there stood at one corner of the forest a chapel, and there he gave himself over to the most melancholy thoughts. For the first time he felt great dissatisfaction about his entire footloose life, and as the dawn broke behind the mountains and now the sun rose in all its splendor, it seemed as if the Mother of God were whispering distinct words to his heart. A resolve arose in him, and after a few days people read upon a plaque that had been hung in he chapel the following confession written in decorous script (which I have learned by heart, word for remarkable word):

"This small plaque I dedicate[35]
to our dear lady.
I,
Marmetin, known as Young Volker,

in lasting memory of a vow. and he who reads such might only learn and take to heart in what wondrous wise God the Lord may touch the human heart with quite lowly things. for as I here with no right and authority hunted the whyte hynde and did hit her well with my rifle good, then did the Lord so decree that upon me a strange pity came for so fyne and gentle a creature, and a righteous fear for my great sin. then thought I, now mourns all round the whole forest what I have done and is like a ring out of which a thief hath broken the pearl. a silken bed still so warm from the sweet body of the just now stolen bryde. at my feet sank down the lovely miracle. dying it fell as like unto a flake of snow that melts on the ground and lay there like a maiden fallen so from the bright moon.

But as well as all that I have still had to notice with great fear a strange sign on the poor creature's back. namely a beautiful perfect small cross of black hair. and 'tis thus that I could see I have sinned grievously against the property of the Mother of God herself. now that my heart was so softened God seized that very hour and thought to strike while the iron was hot and showed me in my mind all my brash unchristian doings and footloose actions all these six years and there talked to me the mother of Jesus in most gracious wise that I neither can nor will repeat. clear pleas as when a wee mother in pain admonishes her lost child. then I knelt right here in this small meadow and prayed and vowed that I would begin a pious life. and marvel did I well at a merciful shyne and clearness that shone all round. then in good while I stood up to hide deep in the forest in heavenly thoughts the whole day until it was night and the stars came out. gathered I then my men and spoke to them of all that had happened to their volker saying too that I must part with them. they then raised a lamentation with much outcry and some of them weeping. I had them swear an oath that they would go their ways and lead moral lives. where I then myself shall stay that should worry nor grieve no one nor cause to hope that he might find me. I stand in the hands of one other than man. but may this plaque give a pious and humble witness of volker and thank forever the heavenly gracious virgin Maria that her blessing remain upon me and upon all children of faith. thus dedicated on the third day of the fallow moon in the year of our Lord's birth 1591."

"Unfortunately," the pastor went on to his company, who were listening with obvious interest, "unfortunately the original of this votive plaque was lost; an old copy on parchment is in the Halmedorf City Hall. The chapel too has disappeared; the oldest people tell that their great grandfathers had still seen it. Wherever Volker went afterwards remains unknown. Some assume he made a pilgrimage to the Holy Lands where he is then supposed to have entered a monastery."

"Another saga," the Colonel now took up the thread, "tells of him being kidnapped on his way to Jerusalem by his mother, a sorceress, and here I recall only some old verses that likely comprised the conclusion of a longer lay. They refer to Volker's fabulous birth and make him — and, I would say, in a manner quite characteristic for the free and powerful man — into a son of the wind. He himself is supposed to have sung the song:

> And she who bore me, gave me life
> I never got to see,
> A free brown beauty, but no wife:
> I'll trust no man, quoth she.
>
> And laughing bright and jesting free
> Aye, leave me to live my life.
> I'd rather now the wind's bride be
> Then any other's wife.
>
> Then came the wind, the wind so wild,
> And took her as a lover,
> From it she bore a robust child
> It made of her a mother.

"I do feel in this moment," said the pastor's wife, as she furtively let her glance glide up the linden tree, "I do feel so strange with all this talk of magic that I wouldn't be so shocked at all if now the fable of the singing tree were to come true, or even if Volker were to come among us now incarnate as a merry ghost."

"One more song," said the Colonel, "I still recall, that one must imagine being sung by Volker's band. I want, if the ladies haven't already found the previous song — —"

Suddenly the narrator was interrupted by the tones of a stringed instrument that seemed to come from quite close by in the dense leaves atop the linden tree. Those present were startled and all eyes were fixed on the tree. No one moved; deep silence prevailed as the music in the branches began anew and the invisible fiddler sang the following song in a lively voice:

> Young Volker leads the robbers' band,
> With fiddle and flintlock too,
> So that play or shoot he can,
> Come storm and strong winds, too,
> Yes strong winds too!
> Fiddle or flint,
> Fiddle or flint,
> Volker, play on!

I saw him basking in the sunshine,
Up on the hill he was sitting;
He was playing his fiddle and drinking red wine,
And his bright blue eyes were a-glinting,
    Yes glinting!
Fiddle or flint,
Fiddle or flint,
    Volker, play on!

He tossed his fiddle to the sky,
And onto his horse he did leap,
And we all heard well how loud he did cry:
Attack, like the wolves on the sheep!
    Yes, like sheep!
Fiddle or flint,
Fiddle or flint,
    Volker, play on!

The music died out, and a general silence ensued. Those in the group exchanged smiles, and even during the song some knowing glances foretold a pleasant surprise that was likely to have a purely natural explanation. Now there was a rustling and snapping up in the branches, among which someone appeared to be climbing down carefully. They could already see one foot on the lowest bow; then a daring jump, and, least expected and known but to the fewest, there stood Raymund the sculptor, holding his zither and bowing deeply before the pleasantly surprised gathering. Amandus and the Colonel clapped and called out "bravo." Raymund leaped forward to greet the painter, who was standing there as though he had just tumbled out of the clouds; the others heard from the pastor's wife who the gentleman was. Agnes had suspected it was the actor Larkens, and, yes, Nolten himself, when the music first started, had felt his heart tremble with the same thought, and it took some time for him to compose himself.

They all took their proper places at the round table under the canopy; the glasses were filled afresh with the best wine, and, as the women took out their knitting, the sculptor began: "First of all it is my duty to dispel with a few words the horrible and monstrous appearance of my arrival, especially for the sake of the ladies, who, I am sure, must not yet have shaken the feeling of terror from their bones, as until now not one of them has dared to give me a friendly look. Well then: two days before you, dear Nolten, set out on your return to your fatherland — a journey I could not have expected to be so near at hand — I was required, by not very pleasant matters concerning my brother, to travel to K***, which lies barely six miles from here. I knew at that point nothing of your ties in this area, and neither a Neuburg nor a Halmedorf existed for me in all the world, otherwise I would have inquired whether you had any messages for me to deliver and perhaps not so rudely missed the chance to bid you farewell. Yet against all hope and expectation my good fortune was to increase considerably. I had already been in K*** eight days when an urgent letter to me arrived there — (from whom? that you'll surely not guess!) containing the request that I make a small detour to see you on my way back and to deliver expressly into your own hands an enclosed message." (He gave Theobald the letter and turned to the others.) "A nice coincidence I must give due praise for bringing me together with the Colonel just two hours from here; we kept company as two strangers traveling together and almost would have parted as such, too, if it had not emerged at just the right time that we both had the same intention. Who can tell me of a nicer turn of fate? I was quite happy to ride on at once to Halmedorf. There I was cordially asked to stay, and the good pastor was quite delighted at being able to arrange a double surprise. The plan for all this amusement we worked out this morning, and I was quite pleased to take my midday meal here beneath the open sky, to drink of Volker's red wine and practice my part. And also, should one wish to paint the fiddler, I have in the meantime found a perspective of this hill where it would have to make an incomparable background."

In the meantime, Nolten's countenance had come to reflect with clearly legible joy the message he had received: indeed he was so deeply moved that all he could do was silently offer the letter to Agnes and, his gaze aglow with gratitude, extend his hand across the table to Raymund. "Well," said the latter, "let me be the first to wish you happiness." "And let us not be the last!" exclaimed the Colonel and the pastor, as all raised their glasses. It was explained immediately that Nolten and Raymund had received a very advantageous call to the service of a highly cultured and respected Prince in northern Germany, initially to be employed on a specific private project of the art-loving regent, though the appointment was to be for life. The whole arrangement had occurred by way of the painter Tillsen and the old Hofrat, whose recommendations, so it seemed, they had to thank for the whole turn of events. Something mysterious was always involved, and Nolten had cause to believe that quite other pressures as well had been brought to bear. The letter itself was from the Hofrat. In it he takes pains to present the offer to his friend in as convincing a manner as possible, though as well he had placed Raymund's oral eloquence in reserve should Nolten have harbored any doubts about accepting the position, a concern of which only the Hofrat could have been capable, since he always acted according only to his own strange views. And as to Raymund's mission, things really had occurred as he had previously explained; he himself, when he set out on his journey, still had no idea of what things were in the works.

221

The two artists now, in view of their common goal, at once pledged each other brotherly friendship, and who should not have shared in their happiness? Everyone talked most excitedly about the matter among themselves.

"Yes," asked the pastor's wife, "and the move is likely to take place soon?"

"Sooner or later! as we wish; every day's delay bores me!" said Raymund as he turned impatiently on his heel. "The appointment starts in two months."

"Then first we'll have to make a pair of you two!" said the pastor to Agnes.

"Just as I thought!" exclaimed Raymund, "just keep away from me with your formalities, you gentlemen in black! Whatever you can make of those two they are already." He spoke half in jest, yet the pastor could not have known that Raymund considered clerics to be superfluous and had never really cared for them.

"What!" cried Amandus, "You are, as I hear it, likewise a bridegroom: you're not going to marry at all then?"

"God save me from that!" answered the sculptor. "The union has already taken place."

"So, you're a heathen, then?"

"Yes, and a devout one, too!"

"But what does your bride say to your plan?"

"I haven't asked her yet."

"And," said Amandus, lightly taking another tack, "what does dear Agnes say?" She looked up, not having heard what they were talking about since she happened to be conversing with Nolten. After the strange, almost unpleasant turn that the conversation between the two men had taken, it was natural that the women already, but quietly, felt sorry for the poor girl who had to end up with such a wild and foolish person, and this sympathy at last could no longer be concealed when Theobald eagerly asked about Henriette and Raymund began to tell with all his own true vivacity of what good terms the two were now living together and about the vices of which he had already cured her and about what new talents he had instilled in her. Since, for example, he was a passionate practitioner of bowling and considered it to be the healthiest exercise, he had taken it into his head that his wife must learn it thoroughly. He had begun the lessons at once at an unoccupied alley. Of course, she was a bit sour on the idea, he conceded, but she showed the best intentions and with time would make great progress. Furthermore, as he had noticed that she was afflicted by a foolish fear of all firearms and shooting and as he found such exaggerated aberrations deathly repugnant, he had begun by convincing her theoretically of the ridiculousness of her behavior, had then calmly and properly explained to her the mechanism of a flintlock and the effect of powder, and finally had made a practical start at the target in the castle's dry moat, though it had not yet yielded the success he had hoped for. In the event that it really was, as the clumsy thing had tearfully assured him, a case of weak nerves — though he still doubted it — then, of course, he would have to give up on the project, yet he still hoped to prevail.

The women as well as the men could not refrain from expressing their disapproval, there was a general dispute, and Agnes began to harbor a hearty dislike for the sculptor; she did not know him well enough and considered him malicious; and as now all her feelings had been in a highly excited state since that message arrived, she responded more emotionally to the present issue than she otherwise would have done. She believed that one of her sisters was being mistreated by a barbarian, and her cheeks glowed with resentment and her voice trembled, causing Theobald, who feared such outbursts in her, to take her gently by the hand and lead her aside.

How serious the reproaches — especially those of the ladies — were meant, Raymund had not noticed at all, since he suffered from a total lack of social tact. His restless mind, as it jumped from one thing to another, was already thinking of something else while the others were imagining they had made him think about his shortcomings or even almost hurt him. He looked through the telescope into the distance and occasionally shook his head; all at once he stamped his foot vehemently on the ground. "For heaven's sake, what's wrong?" asked the Colonel. "Nothing!" laughed Raymund, awakening from his dream, "it's just such a cursed thing that I can't have Jetta here now, that I can't seize her by her forelock and give her a good kiss! You see, my dear Colonel, actually it's only the impossibility that torments me, the basic physical impossibility that the mere space separating two people does not suddenly disappear when one of them has the good firm will that it be so, that this law does not fall away when my spirit rebels against it with all its desire. Isn't such a thing enough to make a person tear out his hair and kick at himself with both feet? Look at the way that mountain there, the big fathead, glares and swaggers, so audaciously propping his fists on his belly just because he's so broad!" Here Raymund let out a resounding laugh, took a leap in the air, and went bounding down the slope like a madman.

"Well, yes, God be with us! that sort of thing is unheard of!" spoke the others in *one* voice. But Nolten warmly took the sculptor's side; he portrayed him as an incorrigible child of nature, as a man who was as free of malice as he was of affectations, and in fact he succeeded with a few memorable anecdotes to reconcile the company with the good-heartedness of his boorish friend to the extent that they could only shake their heads and smile. All the sociable good fellowship sprang to life again; they spoke now quite cordially of Nolten's and Agnes's future; the sculptor had returned as well; a few hours passed unnoticed, and at last some voices reminded everyone gently about the way home. The sun was beginning to set. The most splendid sun-

223

set lit up the sky, and the conversation died out gradually as people observed the show of light and color. Agnes rests her head on her beloved's breast, and as both their gazes bask peacefully in the horizon's glow, he feels as if nature were celebrating the ultimate transformation of his fate. He presses Agnes closer to his heart; he sees himself raised up with her to a pinnacle of life beyond which no further happiness seems possible to him. And much as in such moments a slight element of superstition tends to be mixed in, so too it happened here when the bright double ray that emanated from the midst of that red ethereal weave of light and color gradually diffused into four. What could be more natural for our friend's hope, if one were inclined to interpret, than to let one portion of that delightfully split beam of light fall upon two beloved yet far away figures, the melancholy recollection of whom assailed him more than once each evening. Yet how strange, how painful he must now find it to be that to this most faithful child — who was lying here in his arms and gently covering his hand with kisses and who then raised up to him her eye so full of all the heavens — he was for now forbidden from opening his whole heart! The circle of his happiness, of his wishes, he had to close off and bless, quietly and for himself, though in its midst he was allowed to set up Agnes as his guardian angel.

The others had gotten to their feet, they were about to go. Theobald found it hard to leave this happy place; once more he surveyed the landscape's panorama and then departed, his soul completely at peace.

Soon the troupe was moving happily down the hill. At the woods they did not forget to call upon the echo once again. Raymund brought forth all manner of wild animal noises and, with huntsmen's hussahs and barking dogs, did a complete rendition of a hunt in full swing; the women sang many a song, and at an easy pace they reach the parsonage, where those from Neuburg at once are about to turn and depart despite the proposals of the pastor who, in comical enough fashion, was presenting his plan for accommodating the entire company in Halmedorf for the night. Raymund joined Nolten's party in order to travel on from Neuburg the next morning. At least they had to wait for the moon to come up, said Amandus, and he wanted to have his caleche, an ancient but extremely comfortable family heirloom, made ready as they did so. And so they lingered anew; the men seemed only now to find the wine especially tasty, and Nolten himself went past his usual limit. In the meantime the sky had become overcast, night had fallen, and Agnes, seized by a strange unrest, would not desist from asking and urging, until at last the final words had all been said and the heavily laden coach rolled away from the house. Raymund rode on ahead of the horses, and barely had they put the village behind them than he burst into hearty song. In his high good spirits he took from the young farmhand, who was riding along to provide light, the two torches and swung them, left and right, in wide circles, while taking immense pleasure in the wonderful play of shadows that he was able to throw immense distances, forward and backward, by the various motions of the burning lights. As often as he could, he would come back to the carriage door and bring the company to hearty laughter with all manner of fantastic comparisons about his riding style. He was really quite charming in this mood, even Agnes had to do him justice on that point. The painter vied with him in the impromptu telling of fairy tales — some frightening, some charming — an endeavor in which Theobald proved inexhaustible. As they passed through the forest along a stretch of marsh, the story went that here, hundreds of years ago, the heart of a deceased sorcerer had been buried and that it then, transformed into black moss, had kept spreading, an eternal ghost, all around on the ground. Out of it then the giant Floemer had made an endlessly long rope ladder, which he had tossed up at the half-moon; the one end had caught onto the silver horn of the moon by its slipknot, and then the triumphant giant had clambered up to heaven. Agnes recalled, in contrast to such monster stories, a charming little elf tale that she had heard Nolten tell when he was still a boy, and so each had something to contribute; neither did the three young people hold back; rather, the cozy darkness seemed only now to bring them to life. The sculptor found quite delightful Nolten's idea that, in order to make the romantic journey complete, Raymund ought to have Henrietta behind him on his horse, and at once he began to recite with pathos all the ballads that have to do with nocturnal abductions, ghost brides, and the like.[36] Yet now it was for our two lovers a sweeter pleasure to turn for moments, amidst these games of a restlessly capricious imagination, inward to their secret hearts and to direct their thoughts towards the delights of their immediate future, to say to each other with a whispered half word, with a handclasp, how they felt, what each possessed in the other, and what they hoped the future had yet to make of them.

For some time now already, Raymund had thought he heard another carriage; now it approached, with a lantern being carried alongside. It was the Baron's carriage. The forester had sent it out to meet them, the servant said in a tone that made them fear bad news. His Lordship, he reported, had suddenly been struck down — the doctor spoke of a stroke — and for the last two hours they had been keeping the deathwatch; they had best hurry if they wanted to see him alive. What dismay! what a change in the happy mood! Quickly they changed carriages, the one turning back, the other hurrying on to Neuburg.

The Baron no longer recognized the painter; he lay as if asleep, his breathing rapid. Theobald did not leave his bedside; he and the dying man's only sister — a respected matron — and an old servant were present when, towards morning, the esteemed old gentleman passed away.

THUS HAD NOLTEN LOST ANOTHER FATHER, and the forester his dearest friend; indeed this totally devastated man, knowing at this time of loss the consoling growth of a new happiness in his children, was still barely able to master his first feeling of sorrow to a fitting degree so as to give loud and thankful praise to heaven for the kindness of so richly compensating his loss with the one hand no less unexpectedly than with the other it had torn from him a dear possession.

As for Theobald, such a loss had for him a further special meaning. When we unexpectedly lose a person whose warm and understanding sympathy has accompanied us since youth, whose unstinting affection had come to be for us like a silent assurance of our enduring well-being, then we always feel as if our own life had suddenly faltered, as if in the workings of our fate a wheel had broken, which, though it could have seemed almost dispensable right where it was, only now, as the machinery grinds to a standstill, reveals its true significance. Yet should it then be that such an eye closes just when the most important epoch in our life is about to begin and before that happy news could reach our friend, then we claim a total lack of courage to embark upon a course that seems to lack the best blessing and thus appears strange and sorrowful.

Who was least able to help Theobald through this sad mood was Agnes herself, whose behavior was strange to behold indeed. Since yesterday she had fallen silent; she let the others speak, lament, or console, let happen around her what would, just as though it did not concern her in the least, as though she were moved not by this general sorrow, but by something completely different. She was fighting with dignity against a feeling that she seemed unable to share with anyone. Then again her whole being was all at once solemnly exalted; she took on the usual domestic chores with all outward calm, as usual, but only her body, not her mind, seemed to be engaged in them. At the sympathetic urging of her fiancé and father she finally confessed that an inexplicable anxiety had been upon her since yesterday, an unknown oppression that constricted her breast and throat. "I see you all weeping," she exclaimed, "and I cannot weep. O Theobald, O father, what kind of a state am I in? I feel as if every other feeling were being consumed by this one, this fiery pain of anxiety. Oh, and if it were true that I am to save my tears for a greater misfortune that is still to come!" She had no sooner said this than she broke out in a fearful fit of weeping, whereupon she soon felt relieved. She went out into the garden alone, and when after a while Theobald came out to look for her, she came to meet him, her face bearing a look of mild cheerfulness, only unusually pale. The painter was quietly amazed by her beauty, which had never struck him as more complete. She began at once to recant those sorrowful forebodings and called it a sinful weakness to yield to such evil doubts, which one could best be rid of by sincere prayer, and she said that was the last time that Nolten would see her in such a state. With the natural eloquence of a pious mind she urged him to trust in God's power and love, of which after such a trial of faith she had received into her inmost self only an all the more joyful testimony. And no matter how truly all this flowed from her heart, she still responded to Nolten's questions as to the actual cause of that despair with a somewhat uneasy evasiveness. She felt she had to spare him the confession that, when they had read the Hofrat's letter yesterday, her joy about it had immediately been strangely mixed with a dark fear about this good fortune, perhaps for the very reason that she thought it was too great.

The following day was the Baron's funeral. Everyone, Agnes too, who had woven the burial wreath, had seen him lying in his coffin and retained a completely pure and uplifting impression of his beloved image. Raymund, with Theobald's letter of gratitude to the Hofrat, had traveled on in good time. The two artists set a date to meet again at the new site of their vocation and to greet each other more cheerfully than when they had parted.

There then ensued in the forester's house a quiet but comforting week of mourning. In intimate conversations, which often lasted deep into the night, they would recall the special character of the deceased in all manner. Recollections from the earliest and from recent times emerged. A variety of sketches for a monument to decorate the grave of the deceased in a simple and noble way were attempted. Outlines of his kindly facial features were dawn, carefully altered according to everyone's views, and drawn again. At this time Nolten's personal effects arrived. He found among his papers a collection of older letters from the Baron (for in the last years he wrote hardly anything at all, and all contact between him and the painter occurred only occasionally by way of the forester's house).[37] For the most part, this correspondence was from the time when Theobald was living in Rome; they retrieved the responses completely intact from the Baron's posthumous papers, and these now afforded both instructive and edifying reading.

The transition then from such remembrance accorded the dear departed with reverent affection to lively enjoyment of the present came easy at every moment. Long walks and short, returning visits from neighbors, a hundred small chores in house, field, and garden gave way one to the other in turn to make the days go by quickly and untroubled. With all that, Nolten would never fail, when there was talk of the great changes that he and those dear to him were facing, to reveal, only remotely and as if joking, a plan, about which, however, one evening, as all three sat gathered round the cozy light, he spoke seriously, to no small surprise of father and Agnes alike. He was resolved, he said, to arrive at his future residence by way of a small detour that would lead through some German cities that were worth seeing, and he wanted to do so accompanied not only by his beloved, but also, he half hoped, by their father, whom in any case he had for some time in his own mind been looking upon as a permanent guest in his future house and whom

227

now, with Agnes's support, he was sincerely and with childlike devotion ask-ing to consent to such a move. Touched, the father promised to ponder the matter; "but," he added, "as for this next journey, a frail old comrade like me is no longer fit enough for such an escapade. And on top of that" (he had spread the map out on the table) "I just don't find the detour my dear son is talking about to be at all so insignificant. Look here, this triangle, take it as you will, still makes a rather sharp angle here at P***, where you wanted to turn north. No, dear children, for now I shall stay here. To keep putting you off until I have my house and home in order and handed over would be senseless, and still one has to be able to take the time to do that; the idea that I would set out with you now, only to come back and put things in order here later, would be, although possible, still more difficult. Once you two have arrived and gotten settled, then we can see what else can be done and whether it's God's will that I follow you."

Agnes could not go against her father on this point; of course she would have most liked to talk Theobald out of the second part of his plan, which she — and, as she could clearly see, even more so her father — found ques-tionable because of its considerable cost. Nor did she completely hold back with this objection; yet when they saw how much the matter meant to the painter, they did not want to spoil it for him. So they began to calculate, and Theobald explained that, in view of how favorably things were going for him, he could incur a debt with no danger, and in fact he admitted that he had already arranged the loan and had the draft in hand. This gave rise to a bit of a quarrel, but they had to let him have his way.

Yet now they could not avoid talking about the wedding. It was a point that in these recent days had given Agnes much to think about; so she took heart and brought up the subject herself, yet only to request that they not rush into it, that they might wait through this month and the next. "What is that supposed to mean?" exclaimed the father, scarcely believing his ears. "You know we'll be traveling by next week, child!" cried Nolten. That will be no problem, claimed Agnes: they would not necessarily have to marry in their country, which of course, if there were no other plans, she would much prefer, but they could just as well marry in W*** (where they were to live), or even better in H*** (a close relative of the forester lived there, and the travelers had to pass close to H***, which was only a few miles from W***); they could arrange a week to meet the father and conduct the ceremony there. — The old man kept his dismay to himself until he heard his daugh-ter's reasons, yet as these were purely subjective and as the dear girl herself wasn't all that clear about them and they weren't suited to standing up to rational scrutiny, the father lost his temper and there ensued a scene that we prefer to spare the reader. Suffice to say, the forester, after he had bitterly unburdened himself of his opinion of such selfishness, left the room in a fit of pique. The poor girl, filled with pain, cast herself upon her bed, and

Theobald, to whom she only reached back to give her hand, sat in silence beside her. She became more calm, she ceased moving as a gentle sleep benumbed her senses.

Our friend, on the other hand, was beset in this strange, silent situation by a variety of observations that, since that morning when he received his beloved back into his heart again, he never would have thought possible; but now who might blame him for feeling stealthily growing doubts about whether the enigmatic being who lay disconsolate before him could be destined to find happiness with him or to be the foundation of his enduring happiness, about whether he must think it a desirable rather than an extremely risky union with which he would see himself bound for all his life to this wondrous creature. But at least he had no need to ask himself the one question: whether he really loved her, whether his affection was not merely some artfully transferred feeling? for on the contrary he had never felt so radiantly aglow with that feeling as at this very moment. He continued pondering and had to realize that the dark cliff upon which Agnes's otherwise so balanced life had broken for the first time was the same for which his magnet had striven incessantly from early on. He had to see that (if he might be permitted a metaphor) the evil magic flower in which the girl's spirit had first felt the rush of dangerous notions had sprung up only from the very soil of his own fate. Thus inevitably and forever he is bound to her, their measure of evil and good to be weighed out on but one scale.

His thoughts blurred and blended by and by in a bottomless depth, yet without anxiety, but rather with a kind of devout desire for death; with unchecked affirmation he kisses the seam of the deity whose sacred child he feels himself to be. He could have sat like this for an eternity, only this sleeping girl at his side, only this calm candle to look upon. — He leans over Agnes and with gentle lips touches her cheek; she starts up and gazes long into his face until at last she comes to her senses. Silently, the two step to the open window, a balsam breeze greets them; the full moon had just risen and now bathed their surroundings, the little garden, in its light. She points down to ask whether he would still like to take a walk. They did not hesitate. The father had gone to bed, the whole village lay in peace. They wandered the middle path from house to arbor, between new blooming rose bushes, hand in hand, back and forth. Neither could quite find the first words. At last he began by excusing their father and in that way approached the object of the dispute in order to learn how she had come to this timidity, to this resistance to such a natural and pleasing plan, about which just weeks ago she had spoken with all openness, indeed quite in the manner of a regular girl for whom outward requirements of such a day, the pondering and selecting of the finery, are a delightful matter of care and concern. How touched she was recently (as we have omitted mentioning until now), how awed, when from Theobald's hands she received the beautiful necklace from the unknown lady friend and held it against the black party gown! "See," said her fiancé now, with a friendly stroke of her chin and cheek, his tone hovering between melancholy and a reassuring cheerfulness, "there stands the church, looking our way and acting so sad that it is not to see the joy of your day! can't you fulfill its wish, then? — Surely, Agnes, I don't want to besiege you; here you have my hand that in the future you shall suffer not a word, not an unkind look — not even from your father — if you just cannot bring yourself to do what we want, but just think about it one more time. I will set aside what father says to support his view; I will say nothing of the fact that anyone would have had to find it surprising, that it would give cause for suspicions and so on. But don't you owe it to the home in whose bosom you lived your happy youth and from which you now take leave for good, don't you owe it the celebration in which it would like to take such pride? The house, the village, the valley where we're raised we imagine to be watched over by an angel who remains behind when we make our way into the wide world; this at least is the favorite image for a natural feeling in us; ponder now whether this devout guardian of your childhood could ever forgive you if you were not to allow him to set the wreath upon your brow and send you on your way at the threshold of your parents' house with his most beautiful blessing. All your playmates, young and old, hope to see you before the altar, the entire village has its eyes upon you. And may I say something more? Of two people I must think who were not to celebrate this day with us, your dear mother and our recently deceased friend: their greeting we shall dearly miss upon that morning, but still we shall encounter traces of their lives in those places where they once were with us, and from their place of rest shall —"

"For the love of Jesus, Theobald, no more!" cries Agnes, no longer able to restrain herself, and falls to her knees sobbing before him. — "You'll be the death of me — It cannot be — Release me!" Dismayed, he helps her to her feet, caresses, soothes, and consoles her: far be it from them, he says to her, to force her heart; he went on to assure her that he had convinced himself how impossible it was for her and also that it was not that important an issue, he would explain it to her father and everything would be alright. They approached the arbor and she had to sit down; a slim shaft of moonlight fell though the branches onto her face, and Theobald saw her tears falling in bright drops. He should journey alone, she said, then he should return, and by then the time that she so feared would be past, and then she would gladly do all they desired wherever they desired. When asked whether it was not the journey itself that she feared, she replied: no, it was simply that she could not suppress the feeling that there was something extraordinary in store for her in the near future — something was incessantly warning her against this rapid wedding. "What is this extraordinary thing that you cannot tell me, dear heart?" She was silent awhile, and then she re-

230

sponded: "When the time is past, then you will know it." Nolten now avoided speaking of it further; he resolved to spare and guard her in every way. But what especially urged such caution upon him was one of Agnes's own comments. For after their conversation had resumed a calm and — as a result of Theobald's gentle treatment — even cheerful tone, they both went back to the house, it now being near midnight. She lit a candle for him, and they had already said goodnight, when she kept hold of his hand, pressed her face to his neck, and said in a barely audible voice: "It's true, isn't it, that woman won't come back again?" "Which woman?" he asked, taken aback. "You know which one," she answered, as if she didn't dare to say the word. It was the first time that she had touched upon the Gypsy when he was around. He assured her with few, yet decisive, words.

Back in his room he eagerly went through the box in which the fatal painting was buried among others; a momentary worry that the crate might have been opened by mistake had assailed him when he heard Agnes's words; yet he found everything untouched.

The next morning, even before Agnes was up, he recounted the previous day's scene to her father, whom he found, against all expectations, in a conciliatory mood. The father confided that soon after he had left the two of them he had begun to fear something similar, if not worse, and had regretted his outburst. They could do nothing else but relent, he felt, but they must surely act to prevent her from refusing to go on the journey as well. — "Let us make peace!" he said to his daughter at breakfast, and offered her his cheek for a kiss; "I have slept on the matter, and we should do it your way; we have only to think of an excuse to tell people. But I can see one thing already," he added jokingly, turning to his son-in-law, "the apron looks good on you, the one this nasty girl here is making you wear."[38] The nasty girl was a little embarrassed, and the quarrel was forgotten. Regarding the journey she proved agreeable, and preparations were begun that day. For cheery company they planned to stop on the way and pick up Nanette, Theobald's youngest sister, whom he was now resolved to take into his household in any case.

For the present we shall now jump over a time span of a few weeks, by which time the carriage of our two lovers may already have rolled along a good stretch on strange new road. Their number had been increased by a pair of happy eyes, and indeed made all the richer by them. For if the happiness of a couple who are granted the opportunity to see a goodly portion of the world together in an independent and comfortable way is by itself quite rightly held to be the height of blissfulness that is part of the state of betrothal so richly woven through with tender cares and joys, then this happy duality gains considerably in heartfelt charm through the addition of a well befriended younger person whose vivacious, more outwardly directed attentiveness reveals the passing world to those two lovers with intensified reality and shakes off that wordless contemplation in which lovers in such a situation otherwise so gladly like to lull themselves. Of such diversion our pair were all the more in need in view of the fact that, as little as they admitted it to each other, they could at first not at once dispel certain serious concerns deep in their souls. This was an advantage that Nanette's presence fulfilled completely. In the carriage, where she was able to put things on a cheerful footing with the coachman, Konrad, a true-hearted young fellow from Neuburg, as well as in the inns where she would observe carefully the peculiarities of strange people, listen to all conversations, and be the first to find out about the special features of each city — in all this she exhibited a ready and practical agility, and wherever they went she reaped with her appealing looks and with her naive and nimble reason the most charming praise. —

The weather, which, in the first days, had offered up mostly rain, had settled down and promised to remain constant. So they arrived one evening in good cheer in a former imperial city where they had to stay overnight. Our company had found lodgings in the hotel, and while they enjoy themselves in their own way, let the reader not be averse to joining for a short time a far off company of drinkers among a lower class of people. Konrad hopes to find his bill more agreeable there than at the other place; people have awakened his curiosity about a large brewery building, the Capuchin Cellar, and he will show us the way there.

The cellar they had told him about was situated in a rather grim and dirty corner of the old town and formed the end of a cul de sac that was occupied mainly by coopers, tanners, and the like. Konrad is sitting in the general drinking parlor in front, close by the open door to a side room to which he is directing his full attention. For there a circle of five or six regular guests has its table, the narrow end of which is occupied by a broad-shouldered man with a pock-marked face, a quick-witted and, it would appear, somewhat depraved fellow. His small dark eyes sparkle with a light sarcasm, an imagination ready for any flight of farce. In addition, he was delivering his witticisms with a straight face and was the life of the party. They called him the gunsmith, likewise too the peg leg, for his one leg was of wood.[39] Two places down the table from him sat a person of about thirty-six years of age. No fine powers of observation were required to detect in this figure, in this profile, something of greater substance and of more nobility than would be expected in such a circle. A narrow, rather weather-beaten, and deeply furrowed face, the wandering, fiery eye, the passionate eager haste of his refined movements bore clear testimony to the unusual storms that the man had likely faced in life. He spoke little and mostly just looked distractedly down in front of himself, and yet, as his mood dictated, he could even outdo the peg leg with his comments, only that he always did this in a more refined way and without the least bit of concession. All the others looked upon him with noticeable deference, indeed with a certain timidity, although he was known simply as Joseph the Joiner.[40] Across the table from him a younger comrade by the name of Perse, a goldsmith, had set his glass. He was the only one with whom Joseph also cared to have any contact outside the tavern. About the others we would know of no more to say than that they were all clever people and honorable craftsmen.

"There's something amiss with me today," said the gunsmith, "and I don't know what it is. I've trimmed my wick four times in a row now with the intention of finding a new thread of thought in my head, for I am completely sick of your monotone chatter about masters, customers, and clients; I've long since lost interest in such nonsense and would like now to hear no more of it. One more trim of the wick! and now something new, gentlemen! I've got a bee of a whimsical idea in my bonnet. It wouldn't be bad if a person had for his head, when his wick gets a bit too long, a kind of instrument or apparatus at his ear to give him some fresh line of thought again. True, even as a schoolboy I was assured that the invention of the box on the ear left nothing more to be desired in that line; that might be true for young heads, but I am almost forty; and only in this precious oil, by which I mean this drink of malt and hops, do I find a small surrogate for —"

"All joking aside," cried Perse, interrupting him, "I simply can't imagine at all, Lörmer, how you can find an hour's pleasure in the useless life you've been leading for two months now since you left Hamburg. By God, several times already I've wanted to talk to you on this subject, for it weighs upon my soul when you tell about how you were a skilled worker, how you had the grit and gifts to equal the best masters in your field and make your life's fortune — and now! you laze about here, at most taking on a piece of work here and there for day wages to keep from starving, working in someone else's shop, and taking bad pay for good wares, the like of which not even the most practiced can produce. Wouldn't you call that a sin against yourself that screams to high heaven?"

The man addressed looked up in surprise at this unexpected lecture and glowered a bit ashamed in Joseph's direction, as if trying to read his thoughts: but Joseph fixed him with a dark and meaningful look that seemed to make the others ponder all manner of thoughts.

"What?" Perse took up the word again, "won't anyone tell this fellow the truth? doesn't anyone have the heart to read him Leviticus, as is right and fitting?[41] Say something, you fellows!"

"Don't say anything, you fellows!" the gunsmith responded gravely, "that, devil take me, is no text for this evening and for the tavern where a fellow wants some peace. I tell you — and this is my last word on the matter — I know full well what I am doing with my life, and one thing is certain: if I want, this crazy life can end overnight. Old Lörmer will just shed his skin, from head to foot, the way you take off a glove. You'll see. But in the meantime leave me in peace with your preaching, it can't accomplish in two years what the chance gust of wind of a fresh moment can bring out in me. — But if today you must talk of rascals, well then I will" — and here the speaker resumed his easy-going, cheerful manner — "then I will present you with a riddle concerning a rascal who in an incomprehensible way has in twenty-four hours puffed himself up into a stylish man, and it's one of our group, too." "What? How?" some exclaimed. "No doubt about it," answered the gunsmith; "he's not among us at the moment, of course, and hasn't been for several days, but he counts himself among the company; he promised to come today, and it would be uncharitable if you weren't to let him be included, at least as an appendage, a small tail of myself." "Ah!" they all exclaimed, "the figure, that figure! he's talking about the figure!"

"Of course," the other went on, "I'm talking about that anemic broomstick of a creature who, uninvited and without previous close acquaintance, has followed me from Hamburg, in order, as he told me, to weep in my arms over the death of his unforgettable friend and brother, Murschel the printer. Now, as you know, I have been residing for some time with this delicate barber, Sigismund Wispel, in one room; he dines with me, and out of Christian charity I share everything with him except for the bed, which, for understandable reasons, I reserve for myself alone. Yet you have no idea what suffering I go through with such company. Even just the sight of it can change you. A multitude of curious habits, an inexhaustible fastidiousness in rubbing and caressing his mite-ridden skin, bedaubing his reddish hair with all manner of common grease, and clipping and filing his fingernails down to the bloody quick — it gives me the gout just to think of it! and when he purses his lips so sweetly and bats his eyes, because, as he always says, he has something wrong with his eyelashes, or when he comes snuggling up to me with a thousand caresses and gestures, then I feel my stomach turn, and these demonstrations of friendship have caused me more than once to bounce him off the wall as if he were a feather duster. Now, I've been pondering recently how to get the creature off my back in some good fashion. Perhaps you don't know that the fellow's hands and feet, but especially between his toes, have real webbing, and as well I am firmly convinced that they would pull from his limbs, instead of bones, nothing but narrow sticks of fishbone, and find the most wondrous things about him in general. So my advice was to have himself examined by a professor and then commended to the Prince, but above all to get himself out of my lodgings. This suggestion of mine came somewhat unexpected, of course, and I had to give him a few days to pull himself together. But yesterday morning he got out of bed earlier than usual; I was still lying half asleep with my eyes closed, but had to follow in my mind every move the disgusting fellow made while dressing, every expression, no, I might better say, every facial flourish that took shape in him twenty or thirty times while he was washing. Then he took his usual breakfast, a full glass of well water; then I heard him spreading his bony fin-

234

gers on the table and cracking his knuckles until the walls rattled, his usual maneuver when he wants to wake me up or start a conversation, and then: 'Good morning, brother, how did you sleep?' he lisps, but I don't move. He repeats the greeting one more time, but without success; then I feel my nose being delicately held by two ice-cold fingertips, I start up and my friend has just enough time to evade my anger by ducking away quickly. Yet how great was my astonishment when I saw the dog standing in the corner in a new black frock coat with the latest style of high collar and a superb shirt front. He had on the faded Nanking trousers that I knew so well, the worn-down shoes I knew from yesterday and the day before, but the rest of the splendor, how did such a scoundrel come by it? Stolen or borrowed the clothes weren't at any rate, for soon I noticed the canceled bills from the draper and the tailor pinned like skewered butterflies to his well-known shabby little hat, which, perched on the bedpost, was looking saucily at its altered master. In vain I asked about this felicitously begun improvement of my simpleton's situation; I received only a mysterious smile, and even today I have yet to solve the riddle. The scoundrel must have cash, as well; he was talking about compensation, of board wages and the like. In addition, he's now dining regularly, as I hear, at the Golden Swan. Well! Tell me, is there one amongst you who can prove to me that such things happen in natural or even honorable ways? Tell me, shouldn't we give the fellow a friendly talking-to before the authorities become suspicious and put our brother in jail?"

They talked, they speculated, they laughed about this and about that. Finally, the peg leg spoke up again, saying: "Since in any case we've gotten into the chapter about miracles, you should hear another little story. It just happened today, but it's not, I hope, connected with the previous tale. This morning a Jew comes to me, a sack under his arm, and asks if I have anything to barter since he has a good coat to sell. The fellow must have noticed the weak spot in my own coat; that made me angry, and I hated the rascal like poison in any case. So while I am quietly pondering in which way I might most efficiently throw the sinner down the stairs, my eye chances to light on my pocket watch. Now, I don't know whether it was soft-hearted thoughts about my father, who passed that heirloom on to me, or what it was, but suddenly I began to have sympathetic sentiments. I thought, a Jew, too, is pretty well one of God's creatures, and similar observations; in short, deeply moved, I took the watch down from its nail by my bed, looked at it one more time, and asked him how much he would give me for it. The scoundrel came up with a trivial sum for an estimate, and I gave his face a slap, on which he put no price, and finally we made a deal."

Everyone laughed at this strange tale, only Joseph remaining silent, apparently offended by it.

"Just wait," the peg leg went on, "the best is yet to come. The two thalers I stuck furtively into my pocket as if they were the wages of sin and left my house without knowing where I was going. The only sure thing is, I ultimately arrived at the best wine house, there to take a modest breakfast. Yet since, as I said, I had let a Jew steal my timepiece, I had utterly no idea of where I stood as to time of day; in short, evening had come before the waiter brought my last bottle. I finally go home, I go to my room and pace back and forth in the twilight; from time to time I squint over at the empty nail, whistling like someone without a clear conscience. All at once I think I can hear the ticking of one of those very things, the like of which I had lost that morning; quite startled, I prick up my ears. That's probably coming from the woodworm beetle in my peg leg, and I bang the peg against the wall, just as I always do when I'm irritated by that critter. But pinka-pink, pinka-pink, I keep on hearing it, and from just a few feet away, too. Upon my soul, I thought for a moment of the ghost of my good father. At that moment, my hand lights on a small packet; I tear it open and, to make a long story short, there's my old Geneva ticker! I can't tell you how I felt when that happened; I was a veritable fool for joy, speaking French and Kalmukian with my dear old watch,[42] feeling as if we hadn't seen each other in ten years. At that moment a note falls into my hand, and it — but that's not part of the story. Look, here's the dear old beast!" and so saying he laid the watch upon the table.

"But the note?" one of them asked, "what did it say? who sent the package?" — The gunsmith reached in silence for his full glass, gulped down a hearty mouthful, pressed his lips together with soldierly resolve, and said, with a shake of his head: "I don't know, and I don't want to know." "But you've got the watch back again?" "And for good, too," was the reply, "I'll take it to the grave, that I swear you."

During this story, Perse had several times cast a sly glance over towards the joiner, and he and the others could clearly see that Joseph had been the anonymous benefactor.

Now the gunsmith slowly lifted his wooden leg up high and laid it in the middle of the table. As he did so he said with affected seriousness: "Behold, gentlemen, therein houses a deathwatch beetle;[43] so this leg is indeed my death clock, ticking off the hours to my demise; once that rascal has gnawed through the wood and the leg cracks in two, say for instance when I'm just strolling across the town moat on my way to a glass of red wine, then my last hour has struck. There's no other way to do it, my friends. I think quite often of my peg, that is, my death, as befits a good Christian. It is my memento mori, as the Latinist is wont to say. Thus shall one day the worms take their pleasure in your fleshly remains. Good appetite, and I wish you an easy death! But we think until then to make us many a trip to the Capuchin Cellar and stumble on homewards over many a stone,

till the peg leg breaks, hooray,
breaks hooray,
till the peg leg breaks!"

So the gunsmith sang with a crude twist that was otherwise not his way, inspired by a desperate good cheer that caused him and, more so, Joseph, pain. — All at once Lörmer gave the table leaf three such vigorous kicks that it knocked all the glasses together, and in the same moment a loud laugh went up, for at this very moment the door opened and a figure entered that could not but be taken for that of the elegant barber Wispel.

He floated through the front parlor a few times, huffing elegantly, pausing before the mirror to stroke his frizzy Titus curls, and casting a sidelong glance at our party.[44]

"O human folly!" Joseph grumbled into his beard, as Lörmer had at once signaled the others to act as if they took no notice at all of Sigismund. He in the meantime had very gracefully taken a seat at Konrad's table, where he could watch the others from four paces away. He was sipping primly from a goblet of liqueur, casting portentous glances about, clinking his knife on his plate, and trying all manner of things to draw attention to himself.

"Have you," the gunsmith began, addressing the others, "hey, have you too been hearing about Joko, the Brazilian monkey that virtually all the papers have been writing about?"[45]

"Yes," responded Joseph, "but they say he's gotten away; they suspect that he stole some items from a theater wardrobe and shaved his hands and face to make himself totally unrecognizable and taken it into his head to have a bit of a look at the world."

This talk occasioned Wispel to start carrying on like a connoisseur about the ballet to his nearest neighbor, the coachman of our three travelers. Konrad, totally unable to respond to the windbag's high-toned phrases, gathered all of his wits about him to get the better of the fellow, which afforded the gunsmith's party rich amusement. Yet the longer the coachman observes his man, the more it seems to him he had already seen the fellow somewhere before, and indeed at last it actually strikes him: it had been at Neuburg, where three years ago Nolten had had this wretch with him in a serving capacity. Scarcely has Konrad whispered this thought to him and let fall something about the presence of his master than Wispel leaps to his feet as if possessed, seizes his hat and cane, and, scattering chairs and tables, takes flight, with the coachman, just as quick to depart, following on his heels, before the surprised company can even ask what the whole crazy scene means.

Konrad arrives just in time for the astonishing scene in which Wispel reveals himself to the painter. The latter was just having dinner in his room with the two girls, and each of them was heartily enjoying this ridiculous apparition. "But," the barber starts lisping after a while with secretive precios-

237

ity, "if I am not totally mistaken, you were, my most worthy Sir, until now fully unaware what rare acquaintances you would have the opportunity to renew in this city."

"Really?" answered the painter, "I didn't in my wildest dreams imagine that I was to re-encounter your noble countenance here; yet upon peaks, valleys must follow, and the next time I'll see you, God willing, upon the gallows."

"Aye! Je vous rends mille graces! You are joking, dear sir. Yet just now I was speaking not merely of my humble self but rather also of a certain person who, previously very much attached to you, at present resides within our walls, albeit under such precarious circumstances that I doubt whether a man like yourself finds it proper even to remember such a liaison. Also, I must admit, the individual of whom I am speaking more or less made it my duty under no circumstances to betray his incognito —"

"Oh, go to the devil, you wretched, insufferable chatterbox!"

"Aha, so that's how it is, then! You notice where the song is coming from and don't want to hear any of it. O amitié, O fille d'Avril — so goes the old song. You two were, after all, like Castor and Pollux! — But — loin des yeux, loin du cœur!"

Now Nolten suddenly pays attention, and with the strangest sudden feeling of presentiment he seizes the barber and shakes him as if beside himself, and after a hundred unbearable evasions that fellow finally whispers in Theobald's ear a name, which makes him go pale and cry out vehemently: "Is that possible? Are you lying to me, you wretch? Where — where is he? Can I see him, can I talk to him, now, in this instant?"

"Quelle émotion, Monsieur!" Wispel croaks, "tout-beau! Ecoutez moi!" Now he strikes a serious pose, quietly clears his throat, and says: "Are you perhaps acquainted, dear sir, with the so-called Capuchin Cellar? le caveau des capucins, a building that, owing to its monastic origins, does indeed have historical significance; for you see even at the beginning of the ninth century it is supposed to have —"

"Quiet, you devil, and take me to him," cries Nolten, as he pulls the rascal along with him. Agnes, her every limb shaking, understands nothing of all this and pleads in vain with Nanette to explain it to her; Theobald, as if out of his senses, hurls a few incomprehensible words her way and storms down the steps with Wispel.

They arrive at the aforementioned establishment and enter the large front serving room, which in the meantime has become quite full. The smoke, the bustle and buzz of the guests, are so extreme that no one notices the newcomers. Now Wispel taps our painter gently on the shoulder and points along a line between some heads at a man to whom we previously referred as Joseph the Joiner. Nolten, as he looks, as he recognizes the stranger's face, feels as though the ground is sinking beneath him, his breast contracts in a horrendous rush of joy and pain, he dares not look a second time, and yet he does dare and — yes! it is his Larkens! it is he, but, God! how wretchedly transformed! As if with shackled feet, Theobald stands leaning against a pillar, his hands shielding his eyes as he weeps a torrent of glowing tears. So he remains awhile. He feels as if, borne by a giant hand in flight through the raging space of Hell, he had glimpsed his dearest friend's form seated among the depraved and outcast. He still sees the dreadful image hovering before his soul, sees it sink and sink and still not sink away — then someone taps his arm again, and Wispel hastily whispers to him the words: "Sacre-bleu, Sir, he must have seen you; just now he stands up, pale as the wall, and, just when I think he's about to come over to you, he pulls open the side door and — he's gone as if the devil incarnate were after him. Quick, follow him, he cannot have gone far, I know where he is going, get a hold of yourself!"

Nolten, as if deaf, stares at the empty chair while Wispel keeps on chattering, laughing, and urging him on. Now the painter hurries into a private room, orders paper, pen, and ink, and scrawls three lines on a sheet that Wispel is supposed to deliver to the actor at all costs. Like a shot the barber hurries off. Nolten returns to his quarters where he releases the women from their horrible uncertainty and, in however a confusing and fragmentary manner, explains essentials.

It takes an hour before the messenger finally returns and, what is the worst of it, without having accomplished his mission. He had, he said, sought the fugitive everywhere, in every possible spot he could think of; at his rooms they knew nothing, yet they suspected he had locked himself in, for a neighbor claimed to have seen him entering the house.

Since it was already very late, they had to give up any further efforts for the day. They arranged to do what they could the next day and postponed the departure they had planned for the next morning. Our travelers went to bed; all of them spent a sleepless night.

THE NEXT MORNING our friend arose quietly just after a splendid sunrise and sought to cool his heated blood in the open air. First he wandered some of the streets of the still barely stirring city where he had to observe the strange houses, squares, streets, every insignificant object with quiet attentiveness, because everything seemed to take on some melancholy connection with the picture of his friend. Each time he went around another corner he thought chance should guide him to Larkens. But there was not a soul he knew far and wide. The swallows chirped and swirled happily through the morning air, and Theobald could not but envy those fortunate creatures. How gladly he would have liked simply to sweep yesterday's apparition from his mind as an oppressive, dismal dream. In one of the tall street lamps the little night light was still burning, living past its measured time, to cast its strange hybrid light into the bright day; just so was Theobald's memory haunted by dismal remnants of that terrible night scene, which he found more incredible with every passing moment.

Impatience and fear finally drove him back to his hotel. How touchingly did Agnes meet him at the threshold with a shy greeting and kiss! How gently she inquired of him, sounding out his hopes and worries that she must not dare to dispel. So passed a tense and empty hour, and two and three went by without a soul appearing who might have brought news. Every time someone came up the stairs, Nolten felt his heart in his throat; it was incomprehensible that even Wispel did not put in an appearance; the unrest in which the three travelers consorted — taciturn, inactive, ill-humored — defies description.

Nanette had just taken up a book and offered to read something aloud, when suddenly they are all startled by an ever approaching tumult out on the stairs and hallway and leap from their chairs to see what is happening. The barber, out of breath, his voice shrill, bursts into the room, and, as he seeks in vain for the words to announce something horrible, the expression of undisguised pain and horror on the man's distorted face is truly horrific to behold for all present.

"You don't know yet?" he stammers — "holy merciful God! it's horrible — Joseph, there — Larkens, can you believe it — he has killed himself — last night — who could have thought such a thing — poison! he's taken poison — Go, Sir, just go, and see with your own eyes if you still doubt me! The police and the doctors and, what do I know, are already there, there's a crowd in front of the house and such an outcry that I felt quite unwell. I almost forgot about you from the shock of it all, then I ran as fast as my legs would carry me, and —"

Nolten had sunk to his chair in silence. Agnes reached out to console him, while Nanette broke the deathly silence that ensued by asking whether there was no hope of saving him.

"Oh, no, Mademoiselle!" is the stammered answer, "the doctors said, at the very least he died four hours ago. I can't repeat everything they were going on about. — O my dear sir, forgive me for what I said yesterday in such foolishness. You were his friend, you take his fate so much to heart, so save him from the gazes, from the hands of the doctors before they harm this poor body. I am a miserable, worthless dog of a scoundrel, I've so shamefully misused your friend and do not deserve to stand here before you, but may God damn me for eternity if I am without feeling now, if I could not endure death a hundredfold for this man, whose like the world shall never see again. And now they're to be allowed to treat him like a common sinner! If you'd just heard in what an unchristian way the medic was talking, this S. — I could have torn him to bits when he pointed his finger at the little bottle that had contained the potion and said, laughing, to another: 'The fool really wanted to make sure that the devil didn't meet him half way and send him back; I'll bet the vial there was full, but these louts measure everything by the tankard! — isn't that right, Hofrat, he who would be dead par force surely can't want to be dead in comparativo or superlativo?' And, as he spoke, that fat, all-knowing bigwig took a pinch from his golden snuffbox, so cold-blooded, so refined, that I — yes, believe me, that hurt Wispel worse than anything — Wispel has feelings too, just so you know it, I still have a heart, too!" And here the barber actually wept like a child. But now as he was about to go on with ready tongue to describe the dead man's appearance, the painter cut him off with an emphatic gesture, and, enraged, took Agnes in his embrace, sobbing loudly. "O Almighty!" he cried, rising from his chair and storming about the room wringing his hands, "for *that*, then, I had to come here! My poor, poor dear friend! *I*, yes, *I* have hastened his terrible resolve, my appearance was a signal for his fatal departure! But what unfortunate illusion made him think he had to flee from me! and so eternally, so without a loving word of farewell, of conciliation! Did I then look as though I were coming to drive him to despair? And if upon my brow he read the piteous question, why my Larkens had fallen so deep — well, as God is my judge, wasn't it natural that I should look at him that way? could I have greeted him with smiling face and open arms as though nothing had happened? could I have been ready for such a reunion? And yet, was I not long accustomed to accepting as well-known the unheard of when *he* did it? of excusing the inadmissible when *he* was its instigator? It surprised me, for moments a grievous doubt rose up in me, and in the next moments I called myself a liar: I am sure, my Larkens has remained true to himself and ever the same, his great heart, the deeply hidden noble diamond of his being, remained untouched by the slime in which the poor man lost himself!"

Even at the start of this impassioned self-recrimination the door had opened quietly, and meekly and with a silent greeting, a sealed letter in his hand, the gunsmith had entered without the painter's noticing him. Staring straight ahead, the peg leg stood over by the oven, and everyone noticed how, as Theobald was speaking his last words, Lörmer from time to time had raised his bushy eyebrows to shoot angry, glowing glances towards Nolten who, caught up in his misery, seemed to be speaking of the deceased and his accustomed environs in an almost defamatory way.

Scarcely had Nolten finished than the gunsmith came out calmly with the words: "Dear sir! It's quite right for the both of us that you are just now finishing of your own accord, for I felt as though I were standing on hot coals over here in the corner, since it could almost appear as if I merely wanted to be eavesdropping; but that's not my way, especially where the praise or shame of myself or one of my comrades is concerned, and that's just what you were talking about. With all due respect to your words, sir, you must have been a close friend of my good Joseph, and so I won't hold it against you. You will likely later come to realize that you are at present not so correctly informed of exactly how things stood with Joseph and his comrades. I should think he had no reason to be ashamed of his people. But we'll let that rest for now; first of all, it is my duty and obligation to hand over to you this document, for it is likely meant for you; they found it as it is, lying on the table in Joseph's parlor."

Eagerly, Theobald took the letter he was offered and hurried into the other room with it. When he returned after some time the others could see in his face a certain solemn peacefulness, he spoke more calmly and with better composure and was able in particular to pacify the insulted craftsman. In addition, he let the two comrades leave so that he could be alone with Agnes and his sister and reveal to them the most essential relationships of the whole matter. Often, he was interrupted by the pain, he stammered, his eyes aimlessly scanning the floor in confusion.

Of the content of the document that Larkens had left behind we have only the most general knowledge, since Nolten himself kept it secret. As far as we were able to learn, it was Larkens's brief, sober, and in fact, for the feelings of those left behind, conciliatory justification of the horrible act that he must have been planning in secret for some time and the execution of which had of course been hastened by Nolten's appearance, albeit not in a sense that implied any fault on Nolten's part. It would also be wrong to think that only the embarrassment of being surprised by Nolten had driven Larkens blindly to a rash decision, for in fact sufficient evidence later emerged to show how little his recent way of life, as strange as the choice might have been, could actually suffice to dishonor him. Conceivable is nonetheless the fact that, upon encountering his dearest friend, the unfortunate man was assailed with overwhelming force by the thought of his broken past and that he wanted to turn away once and for all from him with whom he could no longer hope in any respect to keep pace and from whose pure circle of good fortune the curse of is own fate seemed to ban him forever.

(Some years later we heard acquaintances of the painter assert the claim that the actor's secret passion for his friend's fiancée drove him to his desperate decision. We would be far from simply rejecting this tale, to which a statement by Nolten himself is said to have given rise, if it actually could be shown that Larkens — as, of course, is claimed — shortly after he had changed careers, saw Agnes at a public event, and unbeknownst to her, in Neuburg. — Thus while we refrain from deciding definitively on this point, we must all the more emphatically reject the harsh judgment of those who would like to accuse the unfortunate man of having perpetrated, even in death, yet another act of eccentric vanity.)

"Oh, if you knew," cried Theobald to Agnes, "what this man was to me, had I only but revealed to you what *you* too owe him, then you surely would not fault me for feeling a pain that knows no bounds!" Agnes did not dare to ask for now what he meant by these words, and she could not oppose him when he expressed the most restless desire to see the deceased for himself. At the same time, caring for the deceased's estate, for his friend's burial, became his most important duty. Larkens himself had given him several instructions and suggestions on this matter in writing, and Theobald had to conclude that his financial affairs were in very good order. First of all, he conferred with the magisterial authorities, and he believed that he immediately had to take possession of some papers.

By then it was late in the day, and so in something of a benumbed state he set out on the way to the place where the most sorry sight awaited him.

A boy led him through several narrow alleys to the house of a carpenter with whom Larkens had been officially employed for some months. The master carpenter, a dignified looking, quiet man, received him with considerable sympathy, answered the one question and the other with equanimity, and directed him down some stone steps to the lower floor by pointing him towards a door. Here our friend stood alone for some time with beating heart, without opening the door. Then he suddenly pulled himself together and entered a nicely tidied but otherwise meager chamber. No one was present. In one corner there was a low bed on which lay the corpse, completely covered with a sheet. Theobald, still from a distance, hardly dared a sidelong glance, his thoughts and feelings hardened as if to ice, and his only feeling at this moment was that he hated himself for the incomprehensible inner coldness that, in such moments, tends to be even more hard to bear than our most intensely expressed feelings of misery. Unable to bear this state any longer, he hurried to the bed, tore away the covering, and sank down upon the corpse, weeping loudly.

Finally, after it had already grown dark, Perse, the goldsmith, entered, bringing light. Theobald did not like being disturbed by a strange face, but he was impressed at once by the man's circumspect behavior and remained all the more so when the visitor revealed in noblest manner that he had his rightful place among the friends mourning the deceased, who, especially of late, had taken him much into his confidence. "I saw," he went on, "that this remarkable man had to be tormented by a profound sorrow, the cause of which he nevertheless kept carefully hidden; except that others could see many an indication of his excessive fear for his health, such as when he confessed to me himself that, aside from a certain fondness he might have had for the business, he had taken on a demanding manual labor such as carpentry mainly only to improve his physical strength. I could also see clearly how little need or necessity had led him to that pursuit, for he was surely a man of the finest gifts and talents; all the greater was my sympathy when I saw what bitterness his customary life caused him, how ill at ease he felt in our company, and that he was obviously suffering physically. And that can hardly have been otherwise, for according to his master he always took on tasks far

243

beyond his strength and often had to be restrained by force from doing so."
Here he uncovered the deceased's hands to show how they were hardened
and worn by hard labor. — At this point the door opened and there entered
a gaunt man of noble bearing from whom the goldsmith withdrew respectfully and whose quiet bow of greeting Nolten returned in like silence. He
took the stranger to be one of the authorities until Perse whispered to Nolten that the man was President von K*** and could not possibly have come
on official business. So the three of them stood about with no further explanation, each seeming to observe the corpse from his own perspective.

"Your pain tells me," the President began, after Perse had left, "how
close to you this dear man must have been. I cannot boast that my relationship to him was a more intimate one, yet my sympathy for this immense loss
is so genuine and heartfelt that I need not fear that my presence might disturb you —" "Oh, you are welcome here!" cried the painter, his innermost
soul revived by this unexpected overture, "I am a stranger here, I am looking
for consolation — and oh, how touched, how surprised I am to hear such a
voice, and from such a person, here in this corner, as dark as this unfortunate
man could have chosen in which to bury forever himself along with his entire worth and all the love and loyalty that he owed others."

The President's gaze rested some seconds in silence upon Theobald's
face before turning, deep in thought, back to the dead man.

"Is it possible?" he spoke at last, "do I see before me here the remains of
a man who bore within himself a world of jest and pleasure, who unfolded in
all their sense before our eyes bright magical gardens of springtime fantasy?
Oh, if an intellect that seemed like his to soar on the true wings of art above
the small troubles of life can so early turn a disgusted eye upon these commonplace doings, then what consolation remains for so many another who,
less gifted, drag on through the lowlands of this our earthly life? And if the
exceptional talent with which your friend delighted the world was itself not
as harmless as it seemed, if perhaps the cheerful flame of his spirit painfully
drew its nourishment from the finest oil of his inner self,[46] then who can tell
me why that nameless sorrow can in some moments bury all the manliness,
all the joy and strength of the soul in a timid sentimentality, yet at other
moments drive it to an anger that breaks all boundaries; who can tell me why
that homelessness of the spirit, why this yearning to wander and flee
through this world so rich in human beauty, must so often be the inherited
lot of those of such magnificent nature? — Yet for the riddle of such misfortune to be complete, the body too must play a helping role, providing,
in the absence of a genuine disease, an all the more hideous appearance
that wears down the poor soul with anxiety and totally bewilders its own
sense of itself!"

In such manner did the two men, tending to address more the corpse
than each other and often interrupted by long pauses, exchange their la-

ments and observations. Only at the very end, before they parted company, did the stranger, by giving his name, cause the painter to do likewise, as well as to name the hotel where that gentleman might seek him the next day. "For it is fitting," he said, "that after such an encounter we become better acquainted. Then you shall hear how chance only a few weeks ago revealed to me the remarkable existence of your friend, whom even to this day, as far as I know, not a single soul here knew. In the meantime it is my concern that tomorrow evening he can be accorded the final honor that we can show the dead without too much public attention, but rather by a company of worthy adherents of the arts. I have initiated tentative arrangements. But first I beg you for your own sake: do not linger all too long here in this sorrowful place. It is a man's finest prerogative and source of noblest pride that he know how to bear the inalterable with firm resolve. Sleep well. Give me your love! We shall meet again." The painter could not speak and, stammering, grasped the President's two hands.

When he found himself alone again, his tears flowed all the more, only now more quietly and with more comforting effect. He no longer felt so alone with his burden of pain, so horribly alien within these walls, in this city; indeed the sight of Larkens itself he no longer found to be so pitiful, just as if the deceased's shade would have to feel along with him the honorable respect in which he was still held.

Yet now Theobald felt a powerful urge to seek rest at the bosom of his beloved. He lit a night light for those holding the all-night vigil; involuntarily he said, half-aloud, a good night to his friend, and was already leaving the room when he found his way blocked by Lörmer, the gunsmith. The sight of that man had to awaken disgust, dread, and sympathy all at once. Frightfully inflamed by wine, staring vacantly, an ugly trace of a smile on his gaping mouth, in such a state was he about to enter the sacred shrine of death. Nolten, beside himself with pain and anger, pushes him back and snatches the key from the lock; Lörmer flies into a rage; the painter uses force and cannot prevent the monster from tumbling to the ground before him and banging his head on the floor. "I beg you," stammers Lörmer, as he tries in vain to get to his feet, not noticing that Nolten has already disappeared to report the scandal to the inhabitants of the house, "for the love of God! let me in! me! I am still the only man who can help him — you must realize, sir, he used at times to think quite highly of Lörmer, sir — do you see, I have this pocket watch from him — but it has stopped — We were on the closest of terms, my dear sir, the comic and I — Wasn't he always calling me his dear old beast? did he ever call anyone else that? and — — To the devil with all of you — I must see him, God won't help, and neither will the police — you haven't the devil of an idea whether a person indeed and in truth has snuffed it or not — shall I tell you something in confidence? He's lying in there cheerful and well and leading you all about by the nose. For he's a fellow, I tell you, who knows how to lead on the foolish. And — but — — if it were true —" (here he began to bawl) "if he wanted to break my heart and pack it in and leave his old peg-legged pal — if that's . . . — Jesus and Mary! Open up! open up! break down the door! I must confess to him — Let the devil take the Pope, priests, and bishops, the whole clergy! I want the comedian to hear my confession, even though he is a heretic — He must know all the sins I have committed against God and the world since I was confirmed! Open up! don't you hear? I'll bash this whole miserable building to ruins, I'll drum up such a Judgment Day that there'll be no doubt! — Old friend! my dear carpenter, let me in —" The lock gave way, and Lörmer stumbled down the few steps into the room where they found him lying unconscious at the foot of the bed.

THE NEXT MORNING A NOTE CAME from the President, inviting the painter and the women to a simple midday meal. Nolten welcomed this diversion especially for the girls' sake, whose deserted state — with Nolten required every moment to leave the house or to deal with documents — everyone much had to regret. Agnes and her behavior throughout all this was much to be praised. With all of her signs of sincere sympathy she exhibited the whole time a lovely, sensible calm; she even seemed more natural, more self-assured than likely had been the case in the course of the entire trip; not only the painter noticed it, but Nanette as well. Yet this strange transformation had its good reason, except that the girl was too modest to reveal it, or rather she was too shy to make mention of her "oddities" (as Theobald sometimes said) at a time when they were confronting frightening reality. Yet she too took very seriously what she now found advisable not to mention for now. For in the entire horrible turn of events with Larkens she saw nothing other than the certain fulfillment of her uncertain premonition, and thus she was better able to weep for an obvious misfortune that had taken place with a lighter heart than she was to anticipate a threatening calamity.

Nolten inquired of his host about the President's situation and learned that the gentleman, although on uneasy terms with his wife for years now, presided over one of the most respected homes in the community, but that he had recently, being a passionate man, had a falling out with the government and for the present resigned from office. He resided only rarely in the city and recently almost exclusively on his nearby estate.

Perse, the goldsmith, came to take care of some matters concerning the corpse. He related in passing that the barber, being suspected of having committed several thefts, had been confined to the tower since that morning. Yesterday in the public tavern he had, as a result of his change and regret, incriminated himself of having committed similar shameful acts against Larkens. The most malicious act that the ne'er-do-well had committed

246

against the actor was that he had taken considerable amounts of money to keep his silence about the man's true identity, this by threatening him daily with revealing everything. Theobald inquired at that point about the gunsmith and was able to understand from Perse's elaborate report that Larkens had shown some interest in that individual because he had a clever mind, but that such attention had been wasted because the actor's obvious intention of correcting and teaching him had merely fueled the fellow's arrogance, especially since the way Larkens went about doing it was too delicate by far. In addition, Larkens had made himself unforgettable not only to that small circle but to many poor people especially as an anonymous benefactor.

Midday had arrived, the girls dressed up, and Nolten ready to go with them. A daughter of the President received them most charmingly, and after some time her father appeared; otherwise no one from the family was present. The President's wife, with three other children — an older son and two daughters — was not expected to arrive from the country until evening, coming merely in order to exchange residences with her husband for some months.

While the President, until dinner was served, conversed enthusiastically with the painter, Margot joined the two women. She had always been her father's favorite and, because it was her inmost nature not to take sides, she formed a convenient mediating link between the two separate factions.

Dinner was served, and they took their seats. For the present, the conversation concerned only matters of more general interest. By the mutual but sensitively unspoken consent of those involved, the matter of solemn mourning was excluded from discussion for that hour. Yet for that reason the moment when feelings finally had their due was all the more dearly welcome. We must omit here so many a noteworthy word of mutual enlightenment about Larkens's peculiarities and gradual decline and tell instead in the President's own words the manner in which he came to know the actor.

"A quarter of a year ago, our local theater made an attempt — until then unheard of in all Germany — to stage Ludwig Tieck's comedies.[47] The idea originated with the renowned S***, who was a guest performer here for some months and was able to galvanize not so much the directorship of the theater but rather the higher circles of the educated public — for whom he held lectures — in support of that enthusiastic project.[48] After a very thorough preparation of our actors and after — by way of a series of other productions of a more usual nature — he had gained a very high degree of trust among all the theater lovers, Tieck's *Topsy-Turvy World* was finally announced. The few people who knew and appreciated this clever work claimed that, given the obtuseness not only of the public at large — which they had resigned themselves to disappoint — but also of the so-called cultured audience, the noble enterprise was bound to fail; indeed S*** himself is said to have predicted this, and people think that on this occasion he yielded too much, at great cost in part of the public at large and in part to his own reputation, to a personal whim. On the other hand his selflessness is to be admired, since it was obviously more important for him to glorify the genius of the poet in the eyes of the insightful than to use him as a foil for his personal art. Since at the same time the initiated did everything possible to awaken general expectations and to put one over on the philistines and make them confused in advance, these latter types, misled by the play's title, promised themselves a really action-packed theatrical spectacle and thus happily fell for the trap. The production, I may say, was masterful. But God forgive me, even today, when I think about the impression it made, I don't know how to express it. These faces, down in the pit and up in the galleries, you would have had to see! Tieck himself couldn't have more cleverly dreamed up the physiognomy of the mass audience as a performing player along with the various roles planted in the crowd. This involuntary self-persiflage, this five- and tenfold reflecting mirror of irony eludes human description. In my loge there was the Legation Councillor U., one of Tieck's warmest admirers; we spoke and laughed to our hearts' content during a long intermission (since for a quarter of an hour the director was despairing of whether to play on or to stop). During this wild tumult then, during all this humming and hissing, with shouts of bravo yet also much stomping and pounding, we heard next to us, separated only by a flimsy wire gate, a voice chattering away to someone in an uncommonly lively manner: 'Oh, just look, for heaven's sake, down there in the pit! and there! and here! the ridicule is hopping about everywhere like an army of fleas out of a sieve, at every turn and corner, here and there — Everyone is rubbing his eyes in order to see clearly, everyone wants to draw a flea out of his neighbor's ear and suddenly six more jump in on the other side — it's getting worse and worse! — a devil has turned every head — it's like a witches' Sabbath dream — it's as if everyone were sleepwalking — ladies and gentlemen compliment each other, greeting each other in their nightshirts, imagining they're at the grand assembly, saying: 'Were you at the topsy-turvy world yesterday, too? Thank God if we were now back home again' and so on — The old fop there from the chancellery, oh, how wonderful! he's offering a cheerful blonde his bonbon box with the mighty imperial seal wafers and assuring her they're very good against vapors and anxiety attacks. Here — just look — right under the chandelier — there stands a shopclerk in front of a young miss, lisping: 'Neapolitan linen in bulk? At once. How many yards would you like?' and he grabs his ear, pulls it out to an astonishing length, measures off a piece, and cuts it off. But don't you see that dandy by the third pillar from the orchestra pit? The way he passes his hand slowly over his forehead and suddenly embraces the poet: 'O my friend! I had such a beautiful dream tonight. I had a minutely small music box that I placed, you see, here, in my hollow tooth, I needed only to bite on it a bit and the whole *Magic Flute*, I tell you, the entire opera by Wolfgang Amadeus Mozart, played for three hours without a break. A lady standing next to me claimed it was Rataplan, the little drummer, that I was playing — Heavens! I said, I do know the bears and monkeys and these holy halls![49] Oh, it was divine — No! — But over there, I ask you — —' 'Allow me,' a bass voice at this point interrupted the rogue's talk in midstream, 'allow me at last to ask: are you trying to fool me with this nonsense, or other honest people?' 'Oh, not at all,' was the answer, 'neither of the two, I beg a thousand pardons — But what has happened to our neighbor? he is weeping bitterly — I beg your pardon, have you got a muscle cramp?' — At this moment the gate between us opens, and a long tearful face leans in with the pitiable words: 'Oh, dear gentlemen, is it possible that I could leave through your loge, get out of this asylum and into the fresh air? Or if that's not possible — then be so kind — only one question — What is the *indigo perfektum* of *obstupesco*, I am confused, have I turned into a mooncalf? the *perfectum indicativi* is what I meant to say — Oh, don't laugh — I am the most unfortunate man, I've long been the preceptor for Latin at the local school, I worked hard — and until now there was no problem, either, they were pleased with me — but for the last half-hour now, with this twisted, cursed stuff they're playing — I don't know — my memory — the most common words — I am testing myself from one moment to the next, the *examino memoriam meam* — I feel as if my schoolbag had a hole in it, a *rimulam*, at first only a small one but it's becoming bigger and bigger, I can even take my fist and — oh, horrors! It's all running by the bundle out of my boots, *praecepts fertur omnis erudito, quasi* a remnant of nature — O heavens, in half an hour I'll be totally emptied, down to the level of my worst elementary pupil — Let me out, out! I'll break through the fence —'

"The Legation Councillor and I were beside ourselves. But that person, enraged by our laughter, slammed the gate in our faces, and we didn't see him again for some time. We thought at the start it was a comic figure from the play. The Councillor swore in jest that it could be none other than Tieck himself. In the meantime, the last act began, and it went marvelously just like the first. The curtain fell. The stunned public pushed its way muttering and threatening to the doors; some wanted an explanation on the spot. 'Look at that,' the Councillor called out to me, 'an example, the first and the last for all of Germany, a warning for all theater directors who count on us having sense and good taste!' Suddenly a very calm voice at the gate answered with Caesar's words: 'Por ostento non ducendum, si pecudi cor defuit.' And at the same moment in pops that same preceptor face, but without the grimace it had on before and thus almost unrecognizable. 'Believe me gentlemen (for in the meantime I have recovered and had the most remarkable insight) this piece will be worshiped by our countrymen, and theater directors can without fear triple the cost of admission for such evenings to put up with the rabble. Think of me. Your servant.' While he was saying that, I seemed vaguely to recall that I'd seen this face somewhere before, I wanted to speak to him right away, but he had disappeared in the crowd. My good U. and I, after we'd recovered a bit from our astonishment, resolved to track this man down — if he were to stop anywhere else here, which we very much doubted — cost what it might. In vain we checked everywhere on the stairways and at the exits, we asked the people next to whom he was sitting, nobody knew anything about him. After eight days I had ceased thinking about the incident and had decided that the unknown man must have been from somewhere else. — Then one morning I am at the coffeehouse with several acquaintances. In passing, I tap my cigar at the open window and happen to cast a glance out into the street; a workman with boards under his arm is passing close by the house; perhaps my cigar ashes landed on him, but, at any rate, he looks up quickly, affording me a full view of his face, with an expression and movement of his body such as I've only seen one person do in my whole life, and — enough, in this moment I also knew who he was: the comic I had so admired five years ago in Moliere's *Le Misanthrope,* namely Larkens. Immediately I sent for him, without letting anyone know in the least what I was up to. He came, thinking someone wanted to hire him as a worker, and I went to him and led him to an empty room. There ensued, as you can well imagine, a very strange conversation, of which I say only that I acted less certain than I was, speaking only vaguely of a great similarity to a previous acquaintance so that, in the event that he would rather keep his secret, I could leave him the advantage of being able to deny it with no trouble. But here is where he showed his true mastery. Such an exquisitely perfect guild-member's face, such stolid toughness of bearing — no Flemish master could have painted his expression more realistically. One would have thought to be looking at a fellow whose brow was already taking on the casual easy bearing with which, come the peaceful evening with beer mug and bad tobacco, he would be offering up the scene to his comrades after he had seen fit to sharpen their curiosity sufficiently with some unnecessarily long barrage of fire. So now how could I have had the heart to spoil this incomparable man's game or keep questioning him? So I let him go, but of course couldn't say my 'Adieu, good friend, and don't take it amiss!' totally without a smile on my face. He saw it twitching around my mouth, turned around at the door, and said in a charming tone: 'I see clearly how the schoolmaster recently played a trick on me; I ask that His Excellency counts my present figure to the topsy-turvy world. Might I hope that this encounter remains between us, then I would be much indebted to His Excellency, and you have herewith my word of honor that there is nothing evil involved with my secret; but for now everything depends on my appearing what I would rather not be at all.' Now I hesitated no longer to welcome him by name. Since of course he found it embarrassing to carry on a discussion in his present attire, yet could not fail to notice my interest, he bade me fix a time and place where we could converse more conveniently, and with that he took his leave with a natural decorum that did him credit even in those clothes.

"Trying now to find an explanation for the whole strange incident, I was first tempted to believe that the artist had chosen to study lower life for a while first hand, even though the same purpose could surely have been served in a more comfortable way. When soon thereafter we met at my estate, he seemed inclined to allow me to persist in that belief; yet he was too honest a thinker not to at least hint at his true intention — of which he might have been ashamed — as a secondary motivation, and since I sensed as well his hypochondriac side from several details of his conversation I easily guessed that this must be the real reason. Naturally, I was happy to avoid that topic, but I found it striking that Larkens, whenever I guided the conversation towards art and related matters, showed only a distracted and forced interest. He consistently preferred to talk about practical or economic matters, even the most insignificant ones. With genuine pleasure he investigated my nursery and every type of farming implement; at the same time he would on occasion seek instruction from the gardener about these things and at times suggested improvements that he could have come upon neither in books nor by experience but only by way of his perceptive eye. We went on to meet, I regret to say, no more than three times; six days ago he dined with me for the last time."

The President was finished. A deep melancholy had descended upon every face, and no one wanted to speak. True, in the course of this narrative, at least in the middle of it, they had before them the living image of man who, albeit not in the purest and most happy sense, still, by way of the burning enthusiasm with which he was able to assimilate the highest manifestations of life and art, seemed to belong body and soul to this world, and thus they were able for some brief moments to forget completely that they were talking about someone deceased. Yet now the thought that in a few hours they would see his coffin lowered into the earth assailed their spirits with an unbearable pain and with a very special anxiety, and our friend felt pierced by a burning pain of impatient longing that he had never felt before. For a few seconds he could imagine to himself that the door would all at once open and someone would come in and explain with a friendly smile that it had all been a mistake, that Larkens would be here, fresh and healthy, without delay. But oh! there are no miracles and no almighty who can undo what has been done.

The President stepped quietly over to Theobald, laid his hand on his shoulder, and said: "My dear man! Now is the time that I approach you with a request, a truly heartfelt request that I have been pondering since yesterday evening and that surely you must not deny me. Stay with us a few days. We both have an undeniable need to bear and celebrate together the memory of our dear friend. We shall, as we calm ourselves, at the same time believe we are bringing his spirit to peace with itself. We must, if I may speak in such a manner, solemnly consecrate the ground to which he has consigned his unfortunate ashes, so that the earth can take the stranger in its motherly embrace. Once you have left us, then there is not a soul besides me who knew your Larkens and esteemed him as he deserves, and after all at least two should come together to sanctify the memory of one departed.[50] Yes, grant my request, don't ponder — give me your hand! Tomorrow we shall all ride out to my estate, resolved, sad, and pleased to be for each other what we can be."

Nolten let his gaze, tear-filled and full of friendship, glide over to rest upon Agnes, who then, as a sign of what she was thinking, fervently took hold of Margot's hand, who in turn, in loving response to that opinion, leaned over and kissed the two girls.

"Who could keep resisting here!" exclaimed Nolten. "Your goodness, dear man, is almost too much for me, yet I accept it, though humbly, in the name of our dear departed. — Our journey, my good children," he said to his party, "insofar as it was meant for pleasure, I had resolved since yesterday to cut short in any case, intending to proceed without delay to the place of our future residence and of my obligations. Unexpectedly now a third alternative has offered itself to us, which, even with its painful significance, promises us by far the greatest pleasure and the most charming haven."

A servant came and announced some gentlemen whom the President had invited to come at that hour. It was the director of the theater and three other artists, who were no less interested in Nolten than they were in the deceased, since the painter was long no stranger to them by reputation. The director had once been in personal contact with Larkens years ago. He wanted, at the behest of the President and thus with no objections from the clergyman, to say a few words at the graveside; Theobald had written down the necessary notes already that morning. They discussed some further matters pertaining to the ceremony.

By that time, it had grown quite late in the day, and its portentous twilight brought with its first death knell from the tower, slowly and solemnly, the last great weight of pain upon the breasts of our friends. The corpse had to be brought around before the house of the President, where then, as night fell, at exactly nine o'clock, the arranged escort would assemble and a torch-lit procession of artists and actors was to take up the corpse, while the rest of those marching and the carriages had been directed to wait there.

Nolten sought a moment to get away in order to take a last, quiet walk to the carpenter's house. There a crowd of curiosity seekers had already gathered in the narrow alleys, yet no one dared to follow him when the old master handed him the keys to the room far to the rear of the house. A white coffin, decorated with flowers, stood in the hallway. He encountered upon entering the aroma of costly incense. But he was most pleasantly surprised and touched by an adornment that an unknown hand had conferred upon the dead man. Not only was the body neatly wrapped in a fine, long shroud and black sash, but as well a large, dazzling white veil, richly stitched with silver, covered his countenance and allowed a green laurel wreath that had been placed on his high brow and even the features of his face to shimmer through.

The painter stood by the bed no longer than would suffice to allow that silent, drawn-out farewell — be it until they meet again or, oh! a parting for ever and eternity — to pervade the innermost depth of his soul and to fill every silent corner of his breast with this painful echo of love.

He heard footsteps in the hallway; he quickly tore himself away, jealously guarding this peaceful sight that he wanted to take with him for all times, that he might share it with no one else.

W E SEE A BRIGHT NEW DAY rise over the city and say of the evening before no more than that the entire ceremony proceeded to its conclusion with beauty and dignity.

This new morning — it was a Sunday — proceeded amidst packing and visits that Nolten had to make and return in the city. The extraordinary event had gained him a large number of partly curious, partly honest friends; one invitation followed the other, among them many honorable ones that he could not turn down. For that reason, they decided not to drive to the estate that evening as initially planned, but the next day. The President's family had in the meantime arrived in the city, and Nolten saw the President's wife briefly at her husband's side; yet for just that reason it was, with all possible civility on her part, still a rather frosty encounter. Nanette was present, and she could not marvel enough at the hollow affection that the refined couple displayed; afterwards she acted out for Agnes how they kissed each other and how elegantly the woman had lisped her phrases.

When Theobald addressed to the young mistress words of thanks for the funeral decorations accorded his poor friend — for he suspected that no one else involved could have been responsible — he learned that the veil was indeed from her, yet that the rest was from a noble lady who several years ago had seen the actor in some of his most outstanding roles. Margot uttered her name with respect and told how only a short time ago she had heard that very woman at a party telling with much good cheer about those performances.

Monday midday at last the friends departed the city, their spirits lightened. The Neuburg chaise with part of their baggage was to remain behind. Our party was divided between two of the President's coaches, the gentlemen by themselves in the one, the three women in the other.

After half an hour they could already see the castle before them, situated on a high plateau, at whose foot lay a small country town, its wayside signs announcing in advance, with many a roadside chapel along the way, with many a wooden cross, its Catholic population. The castle itself is an ancient building, massive and built of stone, consisting of two wings of equal length that join, at our point of approach, at a blunt angle so that the one wing lying more off to the side receded from view behind the other wing more and more the closer they came. The grave and dignified appearance of the whole lost little as a result of the modern, light brown facing. All over they could see protruding oriels and balconies, somewhat irregularly placed, but conveniently so, with an eye to affording a view into the distance. They drove into the castle courtyard, which to the rear is quite prettily enclosed by a semicircular avenue of chestnut trees, which, to the left and to the right, leads to the ends of the two wings. The middle of the semicircle embraces an octagonally closed lake with a fountain whose old-Frankish dolphin spouts sprayed their water in four directions. The avenue was broken by three straight paths that led out to the gardens situated immediately behind the avenue, with the middle of the three leading in a straight line to an attractive garden house.

The family inhabited only the two floors of the one wing of the entire castle, the upper floor occupied by the President, the lower one containing the rooms of his wife, where now the two girls and the young mistress were to be quartered. Everything there was, except for a few items, decorated according to more modern fashions. Of servants, women as well as men, there was no lack.

After the new guests had more or less settled in, they drank coffee in one of the many shrubbery alcoves in the garden and then strolled, once again divided into two parties, through the entire grounds. These were, while of considerable size, nevertheless smaller than they appeared to be from the inside, since trees and bushes obscured the view of the walls at every point.

Agnes and Nanette, their likeable friend between them, found themselves in a totally new element; yet with each quarter-hour they became more accustomed to its strangeness thanks to Margot's very obliging and unpretentious nature. In any case we now find time to speak of the President's daughter, and she merits our closer acquaintance. The most cheerful heart, paired with a sharp mind that, under the direct influence of her father, had come to embrace a variety of areas in the sciences that are usually more befitting only the masculine gender — doing so, one may quite boldly assert, with innate passion and without the slightest trace of pedantic coquetry — seemed sufficient qualities to balance off an outward appearance that had but little to appeal to the common eye — or, to put it more accurately, that had, in addition to much that was appealing, many an unpleasantly noticeable feature. Her figure was exceptionally beautiful, although only of moderate height; her head itself was of the most noble profile, and her oval face could not have been more delicately formed were it not for the protruding mouth and the snub nose; that was all paired with brown yet healthy skin and a pair of large, dark eyes. There were always, albeit only among the men, some who liked such a composition; they claimed that the contradictory parts of this face were fused in the most charming way by the full expression of soul into an indivisible whole. For that reason others had come to refer to those who admired Margot mockingly with the nickname "the African gourmets," and if certain widely revered beauties of the city did not find such interest very uplifting, they also found it irksome that it was precisely the cleverest lads who most liked to gather round the "African girl." The jokes made by the dandies of the partying circles were, for all that, a source of inexhaustible consolation to the jealousy of those women. For example, one lieutenant, who otherwise was not exactly renowned for his cleverness, had hatched out the most capital idea: you could notice upon closer exami-nation that the President's daughter had a fine moustache around her lips, which likely resulted from the fact that, as a small child, she had let herself be kissed by the bearded old grumblers, the Ciceros and Xenophones, and for-gotten to wipe her mouth clean. The nicest thing was that Margot was not bitter about such wretched jokes, even when she heard about them; she at-tended public amusements, to which it was more her mother than her own need that drove her, always with an uninhibited show of cheerfulness; she was even among the most merry at playing and dancing; but by treating both the well-meaning and the dubious in exactly the same way, she showed, without intending to do so, that she could do without either. Yet this inno-cent indifference, too, people interpreted either as heartlessness or as pride. Agnes and even her more frivolous sister-in-law adored the good creature with all their hearts, without even knowing her most splendid side.

The girls were sitting on a bench conversing when they saw a young per-son of about sixteen years of age, commonly but neatly dressed, carrying some small trees in an earthen pot and running their way along the broad path. As he passed, he gave them a quick curt nod without looking at them. The delicate features of his face, the boy's whole bearing attracted Nanette's attention, and Margot said: "He's the blind son of our gardener. You looked at him with sympathy, and that's how everyone reacts at first; they think he is suffering, but he is not; he considers himself the most fortunate person. We all love him. He helps his father and, once things are set up and ex-plained, takes care of a host of the gardening chores with an ease. He never sets a hand wrong, and not a single leaf ever breaks in his fingers, just as if objects had eyes of their own instead of him and cooperated with him of their own accord. This gives such a touching impression of the affection, of the unspoken harmony that exists between external nature and the nature of this unusual person. Since he became blind not at birth but at about the age of five, he can imagine colors and shapes, but it's amazing to hear him describe the color of certain flowers with great certainty but often completely wrongly as being this or that; he won't give up on his idea since he has preconceived it once and for all from some inexplicable instinct, mainly on the basis of the different aroma but then as well from the unique sound of the name. When he's wrong, one can let it pass, chance plays a role, and sometimes in the case of quite unknown flowers he has really been surprisingly accurate."

"But if," said Agnes, "there were any truth in that, then one should surely be able to have the gift of telling peoples' character from their voices or even from their names, for if it really were true that we created names for the flowers from a certain feeling or, how shall I say it? based on a natural similarity, then we humans would be poorly off compared to these children of spring who are surely, after all, baptized only after they are fully grown so that they are not done the injustice of being given a name that does not suit them, while we are given our names before we show even the least expression."

Margot was greatly pleased with this nice comment, and Nanette then chanced to recall the so-called language of flowers, out of which people for some time had been making proper little handbooks. "What I especially like about this theory is the fact that, with all its arbitrariness, we girls are able to determine and alter our feelings by way of the meaning that is assigned to a poor, unknowing thing, either because we have to credit the person who has presumed to assign something a fixed meaning once and for all with having some sense, or because a printed lie always has something more irresistible about it than any other lie."

"Or," added Margot, "because we are anxious that, with our repeated christening and rechristening, we shall bring about in that beautiful world a nasty confusion, with the result that the poor flowers ultimately won't want to make any more definite statements."

"Regarding the foolish thoughts I used to have about people's names — and still sometimes have — I cannot keep silent on this occasion," said Agnes. "Ought not the names that we are given as children, I thought, and even those that are less used, not have an influence on how people later go on to shape their inner lives and on how they relate to other people? I believe that a person's character takes on a special aura from his or her name."

"Such pleasant self-delusions," replied the young mistress, "can likely be avoided by no one who has any deep sense of character at all, and since they are as dangerous as they are appealing, we will not talk about them amongst ourselves."

Nanette had stepped off to one side and now returned with a small bouquet. While she was quietly arranging it, a comical thought seemed to pass through her mind and impart to her the irresistible urge to laugh out loud.

"What's that rascal thinking of?" asked Margot, "it concerns the one or both of us — so out with it!" "It's about you!" the girl laughed, "but it's nothing to take amiss. I was looking here for a flower that could suit your mind and your name, and now that Margot does in fact more or less mean Margarete it naturally occurred to me how frivolous it would have to seem, how stupid and inept, if someone were to honor you here with this *Gretchen in the bush*."[51] They all had a hearty laugh at this line of thought, which of course could not possibly have been any more tasteless.

"But seriously," said Nanette, expressing her heart's true feelings, "for you, dearest miss, I could probably search all summer, catalogue in hand, through the Imperial Gardens, before I finally encountered the flower worthy of your person or, as it's all one and the same, of your name." "Really?" laughed Margot, "so then I'll remain, at least until something else comes along, the good 'Gretel in the bush'! But as proof" (here she stood up and approached a round flower bed with blooming stems) "that I am luckier in finding things than you are, you naughty and beautiful girls, I shall stick this lovely rose in your hair, Nanette, while in Agnes's, on the other hand, I'll stick this blue blossom with its spicy vanilla aroma!"[52]

They now carried on with their joking, and the young mistress began again: "Good Henni we've forgotten completely, that's the blind boy, actually Heinrich. Since his aforementioned talents are to a certain degree two-sided, we must treat his other gifts with all the more justice. He has much mechanical skill and rare musical talent. In an empty chamber on the castle's left wing, which not long ago was set up as the previous owner's private chapel, there stands an organ that not a soul had looked at in a long time. It was in bad condition until Henni discovered it a year and a half ago. Then he had not a moment's rest until he had put the whole dusty, neglected works — the keyboards, pedals, and bellows, along with the missing or broken keys, clappers, and wires, whose number I'd guess may have run to one-hundred-and-one — back into working order. Often we could hear him working at night, pounding and sawing, and it was strange then to think of him there by himself, at work without any light there in that lonely chamber. But what no one would have believed he could do, in less than four weeks he had put everything in order. Some time you must, without his knowing about it, hear him fantasizing on the organ; he treats it in a manner all his own, and it would not be easy for another instrument to express this person's character so purely and completely. I had first briefly mentioned his piety as one of his strong points, yet after what has been said this will appear to you all the more true and special, and now I need to say all the less about it. — Playing the piano he had already learned on his own on an old piano that wasn't very good;[53] my father promised to give him a proper instrument for his birthday. When we are living in the city, I often leave the key in my piano and like to think that he indulges himself to his heart's content for a

257

brief hour while his mother is doing the cleaning. He recently praised my piano's tone so enthusiastically that he betrayed his own secret, he suddenly went blood red, and I would have gladly given much to go blind for a moment myself in order not to witness his embarrassment. There was nothing for me to do but invite him at once to try a sonata with me that he had heard my brother and me playing. Nothing gives him more pleasure than playing four-hand pieces. The piece I am talking about is one of the most difficult, yet we got all the way through with hardly an error."

T HE PRESIDENT WAS JUST standing with the painter on the right side of the castle when the girls came towards the courtyard; there the two men were talking about a certain architectural curiosity that we too must now accord a look. Namely, that right wing of the castle ended with a broad stone stairway, which formed a belvedere landing in front of the windows of the upper story and, equipped on all sides with a railing, led down a stone archway. With the last step at ground level, it led into a pretty little rose garden, which was enclosed in a quadrangle by a low, artistically wrought balustrade, looking on one side out onto the decline of the castle mountain while on the other side it led through an iron gate back onto the main avenue. That all was to be found in equal proportions on the other flank of the building, yet mostly done only in wood and for appearance's sake. The balcony and stairway were in bad repair and dangerous to use.

The party entered the house, and until dinner each did as he or she pleased. The President left his guests time to make themselves comfortable. Right at the outset he had explained to them the principle that there absolutely had to be, in addition to the hours of communal entertainment and direct contact with each other, a goodly portion of those moments that constitute what we might call the second, indirect, and certainly no less enjoyable portion of such sociability, where it is pleasant enough for all to know that they are together under *one* roof, able to encounter one another by chance, and likewise engage each other as the mood dictates. Our two women, who still felt something of a timidity towards their host, found such freedom to be especially welcome, the painter found it necessary in any case, and at once the President set an example by withdrawing for a brief hour to his study.

Mealtime gathered them all anew, and when at last they bade each other good night, each soul was astonished to think what immense providence had made it possible for such total strangers to find each other so that even today it seemed as though they had always known each other and had come together, never to part again.

After we have to this extent provided an idea of the situation of the people as well as of their domestic and natural environs, we hardly fear that our readers might expect from us a complete journal of the activities of the next days.

Whatever attractions outside of the castle area were to be reached by horse and wagon, and whatever the property of the President had to offer in the way of diversion — including a very large library — was sampled and enjoyed. The President loved the hunt, and although Theobald had neither the least bit of practice in nor even, until now, any taste for that pursuit, still, in his present state of mind, he came to appreciate and — with some luck in his first attempts — take great pleasure in the advantages of this mode of exercise in which body as well as soul experience a sustained and intense excitement. He returned home on one such evening in a noticeably excited state. The girls already had their fun with him when Margot claimed that a painter could likely not go through the most wonderful gallery of the rarest art works with greater interest than Nolten had shown in her father's gun room, where he had in fact stayed several hours. Surely, however, a collection of its like was not to be found far and wide. Rifles of all kinds, from the beginnings of the invention to the most recent examples of English and French craftsmanship, could be seen here in the finest order, displayed in five tall glass cabinets. The friends noted with a smile how Nolten selected a different flintlock for himself every time, for with each he hoped to have better luck, ultimately reaching for an old Turkish shooting iron that was indeed a fine and magnificent piece, yet not suited to the purpose and thus accompanied by the worst results.

Especially pleasant seemed the quiet hours they spent reading to each other every evening after dining. The painter had at the outset humbly suggested a text that they all found particularly welcome in two respects. Among the papers of which he had temporarily taken possession from Larkens's estate there chanced to be a thin, Italian quarto-volume containing *Rosmunda* by Rucellai,[54] of which the actor — in part on account of the rarity of the original Venetian edition, in part because he had pleasant memories bound up with it — had earlier spoken to him with special fondness and on one occasion told him that, as a fifteen-year-old boy, he had taken it and some other books out of his great uncle's collection, naturally without being able to understand it, but only because he found the beautifully gilt parchment cover so attractive. Some time later an expert had chanced to see the book in his possession and declared it to be an exceptional treasure; that made him curious about the content, this all the more so since his interest in dramas and tragedies flared up even then into a flaming passion. Then he had, to please Rosmunda, the unknown beloved, at once devoted himself to learning Italian with truly chivalrous zeal and, after he had gotten merely a taste of the language's sweetness, had had eyes and ears for nothing else. And in a short time too, as a second Almachilde (for such was the name of Rosmunda's lover and savior), he had completely conquered the poor princess.

While the piece was remarkable enough in its own right as a revered document of the beautiful beginnings of Italy's tragic theater, our circle, in memory of the man from whom they had it, approached the tragedy with a kind of reverence, although as they read and translated it there was no lack of merry comments, either because the translation at times tended to falter or because they could not help but find the essentially magnificent character of the poetry at times somewhat rough and woodcut-like. Aside from Agnes and Nanette, everyone knew the language; they took turns translating, but most of all they liked to see the book make its way back to Margot's hands, since she showed such exceptional skill in converting the verses to prose and usually had written out some scenes in advance in such a way that, since in fact the work's expression of strength, grandeur, and wholeness left nothing more to be desired, they all believed, even though everything had been rendered quite true to the original text, that they were hearing something quite new and seeing the poet being done justice in the original grandeur of his nature. Since the conclusion of the action was in some respects unsatisfying, Margot, in response to a felicitous suggestion by her father, helped out by inserting a short scene in which the reunion of the loving couple — which the poet had only hinted at but, for his higher purposes, not considered worth troubling with — was clearly motivated, in order to console the sensitively concerned reader. They regretted only that they had finished the reading so quickly, and since everyone's ear had been so charmed and captivated by the southern tones of the language, the President next proposed an Italian writer of novellas, whereas the painter would have preferred rhymed poems, and that, in fact, for a reason that he did not want to assert too vigorously. Namely he was enchanted by the way Margot read verses; he believed he had never heard such a pleasing sound from a native speaker, and although for some people it is counted a charming error if they are able to pronounce their r's only gutturally — as was precisely the case with the young mistress — this idiosyncrasy imparted extra zest to the charm of the foreign idiom. Agnes did not fail to notice with what pleasure friend Theobald focused on Margot's lips as she read, yet Agnes too was unable to resist the same charm.

As days went by the girls became acquainted with more and more of Margot's talents. Most of them came to light simply by chance and, far from playing at false modesty or from declining, in the arrogant conviction of her own mastery, to discuss certain topics with the unversed, she would instead explain at once the major concepts in the clearest way and, by way of the ease with which she treated everything, make the others believe that those matters were not at all as difficult as they first seemed. Once she even made the charming confession: "We women, when we are plagued with curiosity about the sciences, at times are merely cutting bait when we think we're fishing, and of course it's a consolation that the gentlemen of the philosophical discipline at times don't do any better — but look here," she exclaimed, and pushed aside the Spanish screen in the corner of a room to reveal a huge globe, "look, this is still one of my favorite activities where I can have solid ground under my feet. My father awakened my interest in it; he had the hollow wooden sphere covered with plaster and coated with fine white paint, I copy the most recent maps onto it and bit by bit make the trip around the entire world without ship or carriage. The one half will be finished soon, and here you can see the new world beginning to rise out of the empty ocean." Agnes marveled at the beauty and exactness of the drawing, the delicate script for the names, the broad wave of shading of the seas along the coastlines; but Nanette cried out: "If they just won't let women do anything else but the usual knitting, embroidering, ribbon painting, or sewing and related activities, then they surely ought not turn up their noses at this kind of work if I ever succeeded in doing it, for I would like to see the embroiderer who could do prettier stitching and netting than you, miss, have done with these latitudes and longitudes!"

At once Margot explained various details, and even though Nanette was always the one who grasped things most enthusiastically, understood them most quickly, and knew how to be most flattering, Margot still attended primarily to Agnes, albeit not directly, as she feared hurting her feelings by singling her out for instruction. In general her affection for the quiet girl had something special about it, one might even say passionate. It was rare to see the two together, even when they were out walking, without Margot having her arm around Agnes or her fingers intertwined with the girl's. At times, this intimacy, this incredible friendliness, embarrassed the simple child, leaving her at a loss as to how to behave, how to respond.

In the meantime, they had become quite well acquainted with the estate's environs and visited the city several times as well. Among other things, Theobald had to go there for the reading of Larkens's testament. There was a sizeable fortune. Without regard for distant relatives (though no close ones survived anywhere) the deceased first made some public donations, above all to his birthplace; then there were individual bequests for only a small number of friends, among them a lady whose name and identity Nolten alone learned. The latter and his bride were by no means forgotten. Remarkable in particular were the actor's express instructions that no one should take it upon himself to decorate his grave — wherever it might be — with any distinguishing marks of honor.

On that same evening, since these matters in the city had to be cleared up, a concert that all friends of music had long been discussing with great anticipation offered extremely rare enjoyment. It was Handel's *Messiah*. The painter found that staying over in town often cost a certain effort, since unavoidable diversions almost every time thwarted and disrupted the purity of his mood of mourning. But that evening he experienced, in the pious spirit

261

of one of the most magnificent pieces of music, the abundantly brimming echo of those feelings with which, coming directly from the grave of his beloved, he entered the concert hall. He had arrived late and had to content himself with the most modest seat, quite far from his company, in one of the most distant corners. Yet he could not have chosen a better one, for he deeply yearned to drink to the last drop and for himself alone the sweet sorrow of this hour. He longed to yield up his whole breast to the unrelenting storm of divinely sacred pain. — Late at night he drove home with the three women (the President had not come along) in the most beautiful moonlight. The masterpiece had had such an effect on all four that during their first quarter-hour back in the carriage it seemed as though they had taken a vow to forego all and any conversation about the concert; and when words were at last found they concerned almost exclusively their dear Larkens. The young mistress took this occasion to reveal herself for the first time more clearly from her emotional side, which at least for the painter was to some extent something new, since he had often tended to think that those qualities in her stood under the somewhat too strict and in any case too conscious control of her powerful reason. Yet the truth is: Margot, for all her usual vivacity, had always forbidden herself any bold expression of deep feelings, rather — such expression forbade itself, since her whole life long she had never had the companionship that her heart needed. It would not be easy to say what it was that actually could alienate such a fine person from childhood on from the feelings of other people or at least of those of her own gender. Yet she knew so little of the joy of friendship that she sensed only darkly her own impoverishment and that a totally new life, indeed a completely different understanding of her self, seemed to have begun in that moment when in Agnes she glimpsed perhaps the first feminine creature whom she could love from the bottom of her heart and by whom she wished to be loved. Nolten on this day read her right to the depths of her soul, although even now her words retained something that was reserved and anxious, such that she — and this was something unheard of — would falter as she spoke or even break off completely.

Arriving home, they all felt as though they had stepped out of the bright cloud of a holy and lovely dream and landed back on earth; yet each of them felt, inwardly so gently and happily stirred, that this evening would leave memorable traces both in their relationships to each other as well as in their individual lives.

THE PRESIDENT PLANNED TO TRAVEL at this time, and in fact on business, as he said; yet actually it was his intention to avoid the birthday celebrations of his wife. The painter and the girls had also been invited for propriety's sake, a courtesy they had to accept. The President was already gone when the message arrived that the festivities could not take place because the lady was not well. The likely reason was merely her irritation with her husband. Meanwhile, Margot drove into the city, yet promised to be back in the evening. So our people were left to themselves for a whole day, which seemed a pleasant enough change. They could think of themselves for that time as the lords of the estate. Nanette's rosy-hued humor enjoyed once again the greatest freedom; even Agnes claimed not to have lived such agreeable hours in ever so long a time, and Nolten at least took pains to dispel an untimely gravity that was weighing upon him. After dining the girls set about writing letters home. The painter, however, took a portion of his friend's posthumous papers into the garden.

It was a sultry afternoon. Nolten entered a so-called labyrinth. As we know, that is the term used in the old French art of gardening for certain carefully planned but apparently arbitrary arrangements of intertwined rows of hedges, with a single entrance that is hard to find again once one has gone some ways into the maze, because the many green chambers one encounters — they usually encircle each other in a spiral pattern and are connected with each other by countless entries — almost all resemble one another. The pathways are well kept, the hedge walls trimmed smooth with shears and usually open to the sky. The painter entered this pleasant shade, his mind occupied with thoughts, moving from cell to cell, and after long hoping in vain to reach the center he pursues one set direction and doing so soon arrives in a larger round chamber to which the various paths lead from all sides. Except for a small opening it is enclosed above by a vaulted arch of growth, and this gentle twilight, the seclusion of this small place, where hardly even the buzzing of a fly disrupted the deep midday silence, all completely suited the feelings of our friend. He sat down on a bench and opened the folder. There he found a variety of essays, mostly of a personal nature, poetry, brief diaries, fragmentary thoughts. Much of it seemed to concern Theobald himself; other pieces were totally incomprehensible, referring to earlier phases in Larkens's life. Especially inviting, however, was a thin green notebook with short poems, almost exclusively sonnets "To L.," very neatly written. Nolten guessed for whom they were written, for the deceased himself had spoken to him of an early love for the daughter of a clergyman. She was by all indications a wonderful girl who had died in the bloom of youth. Likely, the affair had occurred in the first years of Larkens's university studies; yet how sacred the memory of her had remained even in most recent times Theobald saw in part from the way Larkens spoke about the matter (which he did very rarely and then never without reserve) and in part from other indications that Theobald understood only now. For example, there lay in the delicately written pages a bright red ribbon with fine gold trim that from time to time, as Nolten clearly recalled, but always only on Fridays, the actor was wont to wear under his vest. The painter put the poems back, in order to enjoy them later with Agnes. Yet now he was mightily surprised and in fact startled by the inscription of another sheaf of papers. "Peregrina's Marriage to ***." A notation in the margin made clear who was meant; he thumbed through it and discovered, in all, an innocent fantasy about his early contact with Elisabeth. Long had it been the actor's accustomed need to take whatever briefly or at length captured his interest — the peculiarities of his close acquaintances, the entire lives of some friends — and impart to it by way of his imagination the ennobling embellishment of a magic gloss, to make it more his own and thus to enjoy it twofold. He did not tend to carry on this ennobling fraud to such a degree that it would have distorted or made distasteful the natural view of things and people; for example, he assessed Theobald's character in doing all this in the most sober fashion, and he pursued that fantastic pleasure with so little cost to friendship that he later took anxious care to hide all and any matters that could have had a negative effect in that respect on his emotional well-being. Thus he gave Theobald in particular no indication of his own affection for Elisabeth. Larkens was long concerned with that person's fate; yet aside from the memoirs, which the reader has already come to know and which held closely to the truth, he did not let Nolten see a single word of his other efforts along those lines. Without doubt Larkens had once intended to enlarge upon the story of the Gypsy on his own and take it into the realm of the fabulous. What the painter now held in his hands was in part premises for poems, in part completed pieces that, loosely and vaguely connected as seemed to befit a mythical composition, were ultimately to give full expression to a specific circle of life. Of course, this strange amplification of the facts — and they were wondrous in any case — occurred more in accordance with Larkens's own way of thinking than with Nolten's. The painter could take pleasure in the fiction as such, yet this sequence of strange images soon brought to bear upon him such an anxiety, unease, and depression that more than once he impatiently cast the pages aside.

In choosing to present a selection of some of the pieces here, we must, to aid the understanding of the first poem, mention a marginal notation that refers to a certain drawing that Nolten did when he was attending the school at ***, depicting Elisabeth in Asian costume with scenery to match; Larkens saw that sheet later and asked to have it, yet it was not included in the folder.

THE WEDDING*
(* meant to be spoken by the bridegroom)

> Adorned is now the pleasure hall;
> Bright lit, gay, in the soft summer night
> Stands the open garden pavilion;
> Like pillars, ascending,
> Richly entwined with leaves,
> The proud forms

Of six tamed, giant snakes,
Bearing, upholding the
Lightly latticed roof.

But still the bride waits modestly
In the chambers of the house.
At last the wedding train moves forward,
Bearing torches,
In solemn silence.
And in its midst,
On my left hand,
Black-clad, walks the bride so modest;
Beautifully folded, a scarlet scarf
Adorns her delicate head;
Smiling she walks on;
The feast's aroma already sweetens the air.

Later amidst the banquet's din,
We two stole aside,
Away, seeking the garden's shadows,
Where in the bush the roses glowed,
Where the moonbeams played about the lilies,
Where the trees dripped with evening dew.

And now, standing still, her gaze strange,
She stroked my temples with her finger:
At once I sank deep in slumber.
But strengthened by my wondrous sleep
I have awakened to days of bliss,
And I brought my strange bride into my house.

WARNING

The mirror of these loyal eyes so brown
Is like the reflection of inner gold;
Drawing it from within, so deep down,
There such gold might grow in sorrow, sacred, old.
To plunge into this night of your gaze,
O innocent child, you bid me yourself so bold;
Wanting that I inspire us two with burning breath —
Smiling you offer me in that cup of sin, my death.

PARTING FROM HER

A misdeed invaded the moon-lit gardens
Of a once sacred love,
With horror I found the long-past betrayal;
And with tearful gaze, yet cruelly,
I bade the slender
Enchanted girl
Go her way from me.
Ah, her brow so high,
— In which a lovely, sinful madness
Looked out through her dark eyes —
Was bowed, for she loved me.
But she departed in silence
Out into the grey,
Still world.

From that time on
My dreams were full of lovely melancholy,
As if woven in deep mist,
Left me never knowing how I was,
Ever yearning, full of blissful aching.

Oft in dreams I felt a curtain,
Dark and infinitely large,
Descend between me and the dark world.
Behind it I sensed a land of heath,
Behind it I heard the night wind howling;
The curtain's folds, too,
Soon began to stir in the storm
That passed behind it like a premonition,
Leaving me calm, yet fearful still,
As the heath storm grew ever quieter —
    Behold, there it was!

From a break in the curtain peered
Suddenly the magic girl,
A lovely sight, yet frightening.
Ought I not give her my hand,
Let her take it in her hand?
Did her eye not beg me,
Saying: I am back,
Returned from a far-off world!

AND AGAIN

Love, so true, is martyred at the stake,
And walks unshod, impoverished, left behind.
No resting place this suffering head can find;
With tears it bathes the wounds for its love's sake.

Alas, Peregrina did I thus find, the fair,
Like fever did her cheeks glow, blushing;
She laughed amidst the furious storms of spring,
With wild flower gardens woven in her hair.

What? I could once forsake such loveliness?
— Such past joys come doubled once again!
Come to my arms, come back to my embrace!

Alas, though, her look, her gaze of pain!
Loving and hating me she gives her kiss.
She turns away, and she'll not come again.

How strangely gripping Nolten finds this portrayal! how vividly he sees himself and Elisabeth even in this excessively colorful picture! and this nostalgia for the past, what a multifariously mixed thing it is in him! — At last he rises mechanically and will-less wanders here and there awhile in the dreamy confusion of the green shaded walkways. So enticing was the painful bewilderment of his soul, so thoroughly did he immerse himself in the magic gardens of his fantasy, that now, quite unexpectedly finding himself at the exit of the labyrinth, delivered once again unto the clear light of day, he experienced the most unpleasant awakening. In gloomy thought he steals about, here and there, and when at last Agnes, as the sun was setting, came happily from her writing desk to look for her beloved, she found him sitting alone on the settee of the large garden house. She was longing for the fresh air of evening and for relaxing conversation. Barely had they completed a few turns through the garden than they heard thunder in the distance, the storm headed their way. The gardener, who through these humid days had been sighing for rain, now came running — with Henni behind him — to the hotbed and the greenhouse, both loudly proclaiming their joy for the approaching blessing driven now nearer by powerful gusts of wind. The two lovers had stepped under the wooden roof of the belvedere; Nanette brought some chairs. They observed a two-staged weather system, its main body moving ahead towards the city, a lesser force at play behind the castle. The entire area had darkened quickly. Here and there they see flashes of lightning, the thunder crashing and rolling its anger majestically in the distance and wakening it there anew with a stronger crash. On the plain below it already seems to be raining heavily, while here above a muted quiet still prevails, the single drops of rain on the nearest chestnut tree barely audible as it lifts its broad leaves up to the railing of the balcony. But now here too the blessing bursts forth in all its might. — In such upheavals of nature the painter was once wont to feel himself inspired to high-spirited gaiety; and now too he was pleasantly caught up in the inspiring sight of the elements astir in such fiery passion, yet he remained still and pensive. Agnes understood his grief, and a few times she gently mentioned the name Larkens, yet she could coax no more from her silent lover than a sigh.

The skies had spent their rage, the rain ceased, here and there a star came out. The pleasant air, the dripping of the trees now revived, a gentle flare of summer lightning on the dark horizon now made the whole scene truly enticing. The young sister-in-law, in her restless way, had run off again to spend some moments with the young mistress's maid, a cheerful French girl in whom Nanette had discovered an inexhaustible trove of stories and jokes and a veritable chronicler of the court. Agnes tried to divine Nolten's thoughts, to dispel his silence with consolation. She recalled those words with which the painter, back at the hotel, in his first pain at hearing the news of Larkens's death, had let slip something to her about how she had to consider herself in some special way personally indebted to the deceased. Her questions about the matter Nolten had subsequently answered evasively and in as general terms as possible; this time too he passed over them quickly, and Agnes did not persist. But now she spoke with such complete calm, with such insight about the matter; now her simple words gave such a pure and certain understanding of the inmost workings of that unfortunate spirit that Theobald listened to her in wonder. Yet at the same time she hurt him, in all her innocence. For surely a feminine mind, even the most loving, had to have quite a different view of the basic moral substance of the thoughts and actions of a man like Larkens than did his closest friend, and Nolten was able quite easily to detect in the girl's reasoning, as gentle and heartfelt as it may have been, something that he felt was unfair to the deceased, without it being possible for him to hope to refute Agnes's viewpoint or even to dare to attempt to do so. "You don't know! you don't know him!" he finally exclaimed, full of passion, "this is impossible! Oh, if only you had seen him just once the way I saw him every day for those two years, then you would find another way to take his measure, or rather you would cast aside every other usual way of judging. Yes, dear heart" (he held back, thinking, and then exclaimed impatiently:) "Why keep it from you? what am I afraid of? O God, do I not owe it to him? You shall, Agnes, you must learn to love him! this is the moment to reveal to you the most touching secret. You are ready to hear this; give me your hand and listen to what now — believe me, dearest, now that we are so totally, so blissfully inseparable in possessing one another — can no longer frighten you. What then? Did the thunder that just now raged over your head with its violent blows leave us anything other than the

268

uplifting echo of its greatness, which now still reverberates through your expanded soul? and everywhere the traces of divine fruitfulness? the sweet, pure, cool air? We can speak calmly of what is past, without fear that it might then rise up against us with its old sorrow. Were it now daytime, then all around the scene would reflect the manifold splendor the sun! Yet let it be night! Let night consecrate my each and every word with a deep melancholy when I now speak to you of bygone times, when from the safe harbor of our present I now in reverence bless long-since weathered storms, here at your side, my only true love, you my dearest regained, yes, and now forever! Yes, into the blissful triumph of our hard-tested love I mix the gentle sorrow for the friend, who — as you will now hear — has guided us to this lovely goal.

"Agnes! take this kiss! now return it! Let that exchange stand for an oath that in your heart as in mine our union stands eternal and inviolable, exalted above all mistrust, ensuring that, whatever I might say, you shall not, with thoughts perhaps of past troubles, disrupt and spoil the freshly turned earth of our love.

"Someone else in my place would think it safest to be silent and secretive, but I find that impossible and cannot but despise it. Oh, and — is it not so? My Agnes will understand me! — What guilt of my own I have to confess, can, I know for certain, in a just heaven's eyes barely deserve to be called guilt; and yet so easily does vindicated reason fall prey to an uncertain conscience that in a thousand moments — and especially just when I drink deep draughts of the heaven of your love — I am assailed by the memory of my error as if of a crime. Indeed, if I otherwise understand myself rightly, then it is ultimately only this strange and heartfelt distress that drives me inexorably to this confession. I cannot rest until I have confided it unto your loving breast, until I hear from your lips the joyous news that I am for good and all absolved."

The painter did not notice how even these prefatory remarks made the poor girl tremble inside. In a few hurriedly blurted sentences he finally got out a part of his fateful confession. But suddenly his words die on his tongue. "Go on!" she says, her tone gentle and coaxing with feigned calm while, trembling, she kisses, then strokes, his hands. He wavers, clutching, as he falls, at an anxious swirl of thoughts; he cannot go back, he cannot move on; irresistibly it pushes him, tears at him; he can hold out no longer; with a convulsive start he lets himself fall. Now each word is like a dagger stabbing at Agnes's heart. Otto — the forged letters — the errant attraction to the Countess — he tells all, only the Gypsy he is so smart as not to mention.

He was finished. Gently he pressed her hand to his lips; but she, silent, cold, turned to stone, offers not the slightest sign of life.

"My child! O dear child!" he cries out, "have I said too much? have I? For God's sake, say something! What is it?"

269

She seems not to hear, as if closed off from all her senses. Only by touching her hand can he feel how strangely a recurring horror pulses through her body, as, lost in thought, she murmurs an unintelligible word. Before long she leaps impetuously to her feet — "Oh, misery! misery!" she cries, clapping her hands over her head, and dashes, pushing the painter vigorously away, into the house. Night falls upon his spirit — he follows her slowly, cursing himself and the moment.

M ARGOT DID NOT RETURN FROM the city until the next afternoon. She was surprised at having to note a striking change in mood among her guests. Discreetly she asked Nanette, yet that girl found herself in a state of the most alarmed uncertainty. Agnes was keeping to her room, remaining deaf to all inquiries, all entreaties, wishing to see no one. The young mistress hurries to her and finds her, fully clothed, lying on her bed, pencil in hand, thinking and writing. She is very taciturn, in all respects as if transformed, and so haggard her looks that Margot is shaken to her heart and willingly withdraws, not knowing what she is to think. Nanette assails her brother with questions, yet he exhibits only a quiet, gnawing despair. Too clearly does he see the full danger of his situation; he feels how in that moment the girl's heart is bleeding from a thousand old wounds torn open by his thoughtlessness; and now he is to stand and do nothing, as if shackled, leaving her to face her frightful madness alone and beyond help? he is not at once to break down the door that keeps him from her! Time and again he comes crawling to her threshold, but she does not open the door for him. At last his sister brings him a note from her; its content affords him some ambiguous consolation; she asks of him now only peace and patience. She was, Nanette told him, working on a rather long letter, but would not divulge to whom she was writing it.

The painter cannot but likewise take pen in hand. He offers up all that calm reason and whatever truest love can say in such an extreme case in tones to win her heart. He speaks to her as to a spoiled child playing ill, appealing with gentle reproach to her conscience, following each subtle rebuke with the most earnest vows, the most ardent protestations of his misunderstood affection.

In the evening the President arrived. Fortunately he encountered somewhat brighter faces than he would have a few hours earlier. The girls had reported to the painter that Agnes was calm and affable and had asked only that for today they still leave her to herself; she sensed — or rather she knew for sure and certain — that the coming night would resolve all her problems.

The President, who had much to tell them about, saw something of the distraction in the faces of his listeners and noticed Agnes was missing. "That's all right," he answered Nolten with a smile upon hearing him make light mention merely of a slight annoyance that he had caused, "as it should be! that is the most indispensable prenuptial ferment that gives the sweet juices their special tartness. You will find the wine of matrimony none the worse for it."

Dinner was over. They did not notice how late it had become. The two gentlemen sat conversing on the sofa. Nanette and Margot were reading in a small room that was only one doorway away from the room where Agnes was sleeping.

The men's discussion had turned in the meantime to an unusual topic. For the President had happened to speak of a nasty trick that the superstition of the folk and the cunning of a tenant had been able to put over on him. It concerned a very well-preserved house situated on a farm that he, as the landlord, had looked in on only yesterday. The house was rumored to be haunted, with the result that nobody wanted to live in it anymore. The tenant saw an advantage for himself in such foolishness, and he had long since thought of using the building for another purpose that the President would not allow, as a result of which the tenant was secretly doing what he could to increase the fear of those living in the house. The President now related with much relish how he had given all concerned a good straightening out and put an end to the matter, and this gave rise to a lively discussion about the belief in such occurrences and the degree to which reason and experience spoke for or against them. The painter found that it did not go against nature at all, but rather was quite in order, that some deceased people should communicate with the living in a variety of tangible ways. The President seemed in his heart to be far less averse to this view than he was willing to admit; perhaps as well he was intentionally playing the adversary to make the conversation more interesting.

"But I do want," he said at last, "to tell you a brief story, for the truth of which I myself can vouch. Yet I myself still cannot say for which of us it speaks best.

"I was living in England with a relative, a widow with no children. She had been married to her husband against both their wills; they lived together only a few months, and then he died after living abroad for some years. My sojourn in London coincided with the time when that attractive woman became engaged for a second time — and now quite decisively by choice — to a rich merchant from Germany. Religious zeal — the one thing that had made her so unhappy in her first marriage — combined this time with natural affection to constitute the essential bond between the two hearts. I still recall him quite well as a man of tall yet fine build, attractive, and of mysterious ways. He was a frequent guest in the widow's home; together they are said to have attended secret gatherings of a certain sect, whose tenets no one actually knew anything about, and, in short, he was her avowed fiancé; but no one understood why they did not proceed with the wedding that the family was sure would entail a celebration of the greatest splendor. In the

271

meantime he was compelled to make a very extended journey to North America on business, and people no longer doubted that he would quietly let their relationship come to and end; they felt sorry for his fiancée who, nevertheless, quite calmly and confidently watched as he embarked and sailed away and, as far as they could tell, soon began a lively correspondence with him. I was present on one occasion when a crate of special gifts arrived, which the Lady unpacked and laid out with festive pleasure, confiding to me as she did so that it was the dowry from her spouse. I did not understand that, and she offered no further explanation. Only later was I able to solve the riddle. It turned out that this unusual pair had agreed to be married in a highly mysterious and completely spiritual way. As they were separated by so many hundreds of miles of land and sea, they were to be blessed, each in his or her own house, at one and the same hour — here during the rise, there during the setting of the sun — by two special priests. So after the bride had quite secretly, dressed in her finest clothes and adorned with flowers picked in the garden towards dawn, prepared for the important act by praying through half the night, the clergyman appeared, accompanied by three fellow believers. A small salon was dimly lit, a table with two candles burning on it done up as an altar. Then when the minister came to that part of his liturgy where someone was to answer "Yes" in the name of the absent partner, one of the candles suddenly went out by itself, to the astonishment of those present and to the greatest alarm of the bride, whom for the time being they could console by claiming to see a promising sign for her in this chance occurrence; thus calmed she rose from her knees feeling a deep and mysterious bond with her beloved. When they then immediately left her, she mounted, as prescribed, a divan specially decorated for the matrimonial occasion and sprinkled with sweet perfumes, where she spent the entire morning behind shuttered windows. What manner of images occupied her dreams, whether she communed with the heavenly or with the worldly bridegroom, I cannot say — likely with both at the same time so that neither had cause to be jealous. But enough of this bizarre ceremony, whose all too artful sanctification of the sensual must shock everyone. What remains a surprise about it all is the fact that, later, news of the merchant's death arrived. He had, after a brief illness, died a few days before the wedding, in which he had, if one chooses to believe a poor wax candle, participated at least in spirit. And so what do you think of this manifestation of a deceased person, my dear painter?"

Theobald smiled and was about to answer when Margot and Nanette came running into the room, greatly agitated, and hastened to open a window that looked out on the garden avenue. "For God's sake, just listen," the young mistress called out to the two men, "what a strange song that is!" While the President, totally astonished, was arguing with the girls whether the voice was coming from inside or outside the garden, Nolten had stopped speechless in the middle of the room: he knew these tones, he suddenly saw the ruins of the Rehstock in his mind's eye and felt as if a fury's death chant were resounding prophetically in his ear; he drew his sister away from the window and bade her, with hastily confused words, go with him to see to Agnes. They found the girl's bedroom and bed empty. Crying out like a man in despair, he hurries down to the castle grounds. Servants with lanterns had already arrived there. The President indicated from the window the approximate direction from which the voice had come, for by now no more sound could be heard. The entire castle was in an uproar, and in the whole expanse of the gardens there were soon as many lights to be seen moving about as there were people to call out. The President himself was now eagerly helping search. It was a mild night, the sky overcast, not a breeze stirring the leaves. All the paths big and small, winding trails, walkways, arbors, pavilions, and greenhouses were soon searched in vain, while some climb over the walls and others hurry, without regard for the plants and flower beds, to shine light into the bushes and shadows. It is not long before the President's huntsman motions him away with a sad gaze, the painter and the women follow. A few paces from the house, directly under Agnes's windows, they see the dear child lying stretched out and motionless under some Weymouth pines in her white nightgown, her feet bare, her hair falling over the ground and her naked shoulders. Nolten sank to his knees beside the body, felt for breath, and, finding none, broke out into loud lament as he pressed the poor girl's hands to his hot lips. The others stood about, frightened, and by and by the lights gathered quietly around the unhappy site; an anxious silence prevailed while others hurried to fetch a litter and Margot wrapped the stricken girl's feet in her shawl. "Come now," said the President to Nolten, who was still crouching helplessly on the ground, "let us provide immediate aid with sense and resolve, your fiancée will soon open her eyes again!" And with that they carefully lifted the corpse-like body onto the cushions and were getting underway when a strange woman's voice, coming from the dense bushes right nearby, brought things to a sudden halt. Involuntarily Theobald clenched his fists when he saw the Gypsy's majestic figure step boldly into their midst; yet the presence of an unapproachable power seemed to hold all his strength in check.

As they carried Agnes away, accompanied by the concerned girls, Elisabeth said with calm gravity: "Wake the dear girl not! Release her spirit in peace so that it does not arrive in the nether regions of the night, like the frightened bird surprised that death came so soon. For otherwise her soul will return in agony to torment me and my friend; I fear her love continues to vie for him even in death. I am the chosen one! this man is mine! Yet he does not look at me, the fool! Leave us alone so that he can give me a friendly greeting!"

She approaches Theobald, who seizes her hand just as she is about to touch him gently and casts it away forcefully. "Out of my sight, intruder! hated, insolent specter, pursuing me with her curse wherever I go. Cursed forever and consigned to Hell be the day you met me for the first time! How I must atone for the fact that as an innocent boy I was drawn to you by the most sacred feeling, my sympathy captured by your misfortune; what shameful rage your sisterly affection has become, what devilish evil your feigned kindness! But I could know, childish, raving fool that I was, with whom I was dealing! — God in heaven! But this punishment is too harsh — misery upon misery, unheard of and unbelievable, descends on me. O you all, who gaze at me and this woman half with pity and half with degrading distrust, don't believe that my guilt is equal to the grief that unhinges my mind! The misery of this homeless woman you read upon her brow — and it has been the source of my overabundant sea of worry and confusion. A criminal I must not call her — she merited my sympathy, alas, and not my hatred! Yet who can remain tolerant, who can still be human, when merciful heaven expends its full force of cruelties?[55] What? Would it be a miracle if I were seized here on the spot by a raging madness that rendered me without feeling for the ultimate, the final thing that — oh, I see it drawing inexorably nearer! Why am I lamenting here? Why are we all standing here? and up there that angel is struggling between life and death — She is dying! She is dying! Shall I go to her? can I still save her? O follow me! — Where to? Here Margot is coming from her! Yes — yes, I can read it in her look — It has happened — Agnes, Agnes is no more! — Away! let me flee! flee to the ends of the earth —" Elisabeth holds him fast, in his immense pain he hurls a horrible oath at her, but with a cry she clings to his knees and he cannot move. The President turns away from the heart-rending scene. "Woe! Woe!" cries Elisabeth, "when my beloved curses me, then the star under which he was born trembles! Do you not recognize me? Dearest! recognize me! What has drawn me here? what has guided me all this way? Look upon these my bleeding feet! Love, you evil, ungrateful boy, was always driving me onward. In the glaring heat of the sun, through night and storm, through briars and swamp, love's yearning struggles on, inexhaustible, undying that meager bit of life, and takes pleasure in such sweet, such wild torment, and runs on, searching for the loathsome fugitive's traces from place to place until she finds him — and now she has found him — and there he stands and claims not to know her. Woe is me! how I hoped for a more joyous reception since I was so long lost to you and, dearest, you to me. So little does my heartfelt grief mean to you, and you drive me away like a mangy beast — but one that still licks its master's feet, that will not part from its master. — — You people, what does this mean? Why does no one help me to what is rightfully mine? Bear witness, O heaven, you holy firmament, that this boy belongs to me! He long ago swore so to me on the mountain where he found me. The

274

autumnal winds round the old walls heard the oath; and once each year the winds still speak of that happy day. I went back there, and they said: a lovely boy he was, had he only remained so pure! But only children are truthful. — Agnes, what does she mean to you? To her you could not keep your word; you yourself confessed it to her, that's what has made her ill, she told me of her sorrow that evening. And if you were untrue to her, well then, see, you were doubly so to me."

These last words struck the painter's heart like thunder. He raged against himself, and it was pitiful to see how this man, deaf to all reason that the President spoke to him, tore his hair in the true sense of the word and uttered words that can be forgiven only of despair. At last he sets out for the castle, the President, full of sympathy, hurrying after him. At his signal, some of the people are about to seize the mad woman, but, so fast that she seemed to have snatched it out of the air, she pulls a knife and brandishes it threateningly in her fist so that no one dares approach her. Then she stood quietly a long while and, with an indescribably painful gesture of farewell, reaching with both arms towards where Nolten had departed, she turned and vanished with reluctant tread into the darkness.

THE NIGHT PASSED QUIETLY. Agnes, even before the doctor arrived, had recovered quite quickly under the ministrations of so many tender hands. The young mistress and the sister-in-law did not part the entire night from her bedside; every hour Nolten had come to the door to hear how matters fared within. Since yesterday the girl had spoken hardly at all. In her almost uninterrupted slumber they heard only her occasional quiet whimpering. But in the morning she took her breakfast from Margot with a pleasing cheerfulness, insisting that she and Nanette lie down and rest, desiring nothing more than to be allowed to be by herself. Since they could not deny her that, they had someone stay in the adjoining room from which Agnes could be heard right away and, if need be, observed.

Nolten's desperate restlessness, as long as Agnes's condition remained unclear, cannot be described. He wandered through the castle and around the grounds, no different from a person who sees his death sentence approaching every moment. As he does so he tells himself that above all the President can expect a satisfactory explanation of the incident and that he also owes as much to himself and to his honor. Yet with the most noble consideration that man postpones such a discussion to a calmer point in time and readily grants Nolten the kindness of letting him first come to terms with himself on his own.

But alas, his sense and thoughts go numb at every turn; however he tries to turn and twist the frightening apparition of terror in himself, he cannot get to the bottom of these confusions; he takes the blame upon himself, for that evening when he shocked the poor soul so fatally and thus made her so susceptible for that woman's insane assault.

Unfortunately there were visitors that afternoon from the city, the gentlemen of the President's council with their wives and children. Nolten declined to attend; his sister did her loyal best to help Margot uphold the honor of the house.

Towards evening he found a favorable hour to give the President the explanation he had planned. When the President and the painter finally came back into the room after a long conversation in the garden, Margot saw that her father was noticeably moved; he did not want to speak; they sat down to dinner in silence, and afterwards they still did not want to part immediately; it was as though they all had need of each other, although no one seemed about to address or question anyone else. The girls rescued themselves from this stress in some unimportant work. The President saw a large packet of engravings, still unopened, lying nearby. It was Denon's magnificent collection on the French expedition to Egypt (he had brought it from the city for Nolten); they unpacked the pictures, but no one spent much time looking at them.[56]

Still weighing upon all was the terror of the previous evening; one moment they follow Elisabeth's fleeting form sympathetically on her dark paths; the next moment their thoughts stop once again at the lonely bedside of Agnes, who now seems cut off forever from the company by a strange dividing wall.

The President can no better than Nolten deny the fact that the girl is well on her way to letting a wrong idea totally destroy her. What her friends find so unbearable and frightful about that is the feeling that neither reason nor force nor persuasion can do anything here to bring about a reconciliation with Nolten; for this must be resolved, and in fact without delay, every moment sooner being, as with deadly poisoning, worth its weight in gold. But Agnes exhibited the most intractable aversion to her fiancé; they could not tell whether it was fear or disgust that she felt more. What effect Elisabeth had had they could not say, but they presumed it was very great; in any case two attempts that Theobald had made to gain access to his bride — first by imploring meekly, then by storming passionately — tended more to drive her to convulsions than to make her yield to his longing desire. So they had to leave the development of the matter to time and the fickle whim of chance.

The strangely embarrassed tension of the four people now sitting in the room isolated each of them in an unusual way. It was as if they were *unable* to talk at all, as if every sound, as in a vacuum, would have to disappear, powerless and inaudible, on their lips, indeed, as if an impenetrable fog kept one person from being fully aware of the other.

Nanette was the least constrained. She presented her views one by one. She found it so foolish that no one wanted to speak up and come quickly and boldly to the heart of the matter, that they did not plan some way to approach Agnes one way or another; she at least felt equal to the task of driving out the spirit in short order, whatever name it might bear, whatever corner it might be hiding in, if only she knew what they were dealing with, if only her brother would give her some sign. Their full attention was directed towards the President when he began to urge upon the company some rules of behavior regarding Agnes, the main thrust of which was that, no matter how hard they found it, they all had to suppress their feelings and act at all times as though nothing unusual had happened; they had to avoid acknowledging with word or deed the reason for her grief and seclusion; they were to make mention of Nolten to her at every available opportunity and in connection with the most everyday matters. The good man did not take into consideration that the women knew too little of the true facts of the situation to be able to see the sense of these rules completely. Nanette took a certain pleasure in observing the President under such critical circumstances. We shall express what the girl felt as she did so in the form of a general observation.

There are men whose very appearance immediately awakens in us the pleasing impression of complete trustworthiness. The predominance of a forceful, more negating than affirming nature, the integrity of a resolute character, even the special aura that rank and wealthy bestow upon them — all of this not only seems to make these men themselves masters of any adverse chance, but also works with its presence upon others, who are only vaguely aware of their benevolence, with the magic of a powerful talisman: right gladly would we like to see such a man of fortune involved even to a small degree in our own worries and dangers, for there is something not only assuring but also genuinely exciting about experiencing all at once, in a shared crisis, such a close human bond to a person who seems to be superior and inaccessible to us in every respect. The briefest word from such a man, the most insignificant consolation works wonders; indeed some even claim that at times simply physical contact with the softer hand, the softer garment of one of these noble personages has something irresistible about it, and that all the more so the less frequently it happens. This is what Nanette actually felt when, before, the President — as though he were adding the last ring to a chain of thoughts he had long been quietly pursuing — arose from his chair, his face somewhat gladdened, and, as he passed by, took the girl gently by the chin with a melancholy friendliness; she was so strangely touched by this small ray of light that for a second she thought all the trouble was at an end and everything was right again.

Now they parted. One person had to keep watch through the night, and the original arrangement of having Nanette and Agnes sleep in one room now proved useful.

THE PROFOUND PAUSE that had come about in the life of our company as the result of a terrible magic spell also marked the following days. Nanette and Margot had in the meantime been informed about what was at the root of the misfortune. Life in the castle had taken on another routine. It was no different than as if a deathly illness lay upon the house; everyone involuntarily avoided any kind of noise, even in places from where nothing could have easily disrupted Agnes's seclusion; it seemed it simply had to be that way, and, truly, whoever so much as looked at the painter, at his suffering renunciation, and read the dull pain in his sagging bearing believed he could not walk quietly and gently enough to honor, with every move, with every small consideration, the misfortune that in such cases demands a kind of respect from us. The President, however, took serious exception to this anxiousness, which infected even the servants; such an attitude, he claimed, had the worst possible influence on the ailing girl since it would only have to make her feel more and more justified in her imagined misery and right to sympathy.

In the meantime, they had gained more insights about Agnes. The girls were allowed unrestricted visits to her; but towards the young mistress alone, in spite of the sisterly love that Margot hoped would make them closer, she showed a distinct distrust. Agnes often left her room to go outside, as long as she could be assured of not encountering Theobald. But she was apparently not averse to seeing him now and then from a distance, and they even thought they noticed that she intentionally sought the opportunity to do so. For hours the President would read to her; she comported herself with great seriousness, yet was always pleasant and thankful. A reserve in her thoughts, a cunning evasiveness when one topic was discussed, could not go unnoticed; she was holding something back and seemed merely to be awaiting the right moment.

And this secret plan then came to light soon enough. One day the old gardener revealed to the President in all confidence that Agnes had pleaded with him to make it possible for her to leave the castle and travel to her home. She had made him all manner of promises and even very cleverly explained the way that his assistance could be kept totally secret. — Now, such a desire, discounting the secrecy, was not such an unforgivable thing, the painter had recently had the same thought for her; they discussed the matter seriously, and doubled their watchfulness.

One morning Nolten comes to the salon as usual for breakfast. When he enters, Nanette and Margot scatter, greeting him with their faces turned away, hiding their tears. "What has happened?" he asks full of apprehension, "what has happened to Agnes?" He wants to leave and see for himself, but at the same moment the President hurries in. "I am braced for anything" Nolten exclaims to him: "For heaven's sake, quickly! What has happened?" "Calm! Steady now! My dear friend, all is not lost yet. What we long had to fear, the earlier illness that you told me about, unfortunately seems to have returned — But brace yourself, oh, be a man! Just as it passed last time, so it will pass this time too." "No, never, not ever! She is the victim of my madness! And so that too now! Too horrifying! too ghastly! — What? and I am to stand by and watch? Am I to see all that with these eyes and still go on living? — Well, so be it! for that reason; the end is coming for both of us. I am expecting it, it's all well and good by me if someone comes to me tomorrow and says: Your fiancée is at rest, Agnes has died." He fell silent awhile and then rose up and, in the most impetuous outburst of anger and tears, not knowing what he wanted or what he was doing, wildly drew his sister to him — "Why are you just standing there? what are you gaping at?" "Sir, not that way! that is cruel!" cries Margot indignantly and protects the trembling girl, whom he has cast aside in a rage. "Oh," he cries out, striking his forehead with his fist, "why does no one rage against me? why am I standing here so quietly, so exhausted and miserable in my desolate ruination? Ha, if some bitter enemy were to throw my pain in my face, cast it at my feet! and berate me as the Godforsaken fool that I am, as the murderer I am, and pour salt and fire upon my wound — that should do me good, that should strengthen me —"

"We shall leave you to yourself, my friend," the President responded quite calmly, "wishing to show you in that way that we do not think we have to protect a man — and that's what I have taken you to be so far — from himself."

And so the painter now stood alone in the salon. It was the most terrible moment of his life.

When in a moment of our most unchecked misery we unexpectedly must confront a reproach from someone we respect, that is the most terrible chill we can ever experience. All at once you feel a deathly quiet within, and you see your pain, like a bird of prey when struck at its most daring height by a bolt of lightning, fall slowly from the sky and lie quivering half-dead at your feet.

The painter had thrown himself down on his chair. With cold observation he looked calmly into the depths of his inner self, much as we can watch at length as the sand runs out of an hourglass, where grain falls incessantly upon grain and slides and falls. He playfully picked apart his thoughts, one by one, smiling all the while. As he did so, he felt, time and again, his heart well up with a light and pleasant feeling, as though an angel of joy were just now gently, very gently unfolding its golden wings above him in order to appear to him incarnate.

Startled he looked up; he thought someone was coming, as if with soft, unshod tread, through the three rooms that opened one to the other. He stares in amazement — it is Agnes who is approaching him. She is barefoot, but otherwise not carelessly dressed; only one braid of her hair is hanging down in front, and she is holding the loose end to her chin, thoughtful and listening. An entire heaven full of pity seems to accompany her stealthy tread with a mute gesture of lament, and the folds of her dress sympathetically embrace her lovely form.

Nolten has stood up; yet he dares not move towards her; all his soul is holding its breath. The girl has approached the threshold of the salon where she stops and leans, in a comfortable and relaxed pose, her head upon the doorframe. She looks over at him attentively. The touching outline of her figure, so too the paleness of her face, are all the more attractive by the twilight of the green room, with its shutters closed against the sultry morning sun. As she observes him in this way she speaks only to herself: "He resembles him greatly, he has captured him well, one egg cannot look more like another, but one of the two is hollow." Then she said, loud and mocking, "Good morning, heath runner! Good morning, hellfire! Well, don't act like such a simpleton! Very well, very well! I am touched beyond words. He'll have a tip for his hocus-pocus. Just let him stay where he is — if you please, I can see it quite clearly, just keep twelve paces away at all times. What is his dear brown otter doing then? — haha, is it not so? My little finger tells me things too, every now and then. Well, I must move on. Short visits, that's the fashion in genteel circles. And let him not worry for my sake, we don't take such things so seriously."

She bowed and left.

When we — said a shaken Theobald to himself — when we chance to have a dream that is like what is really happening here, then the dreamer shakes himself in pain and calls out to himself: hurry, awaken, it will kill you! Quickly he turns the night side of his spirit to the true daylight — And even more! He resolutely reaches with his ghost arms through the thick wall behind which his body lies captive and miraculously unbolts the door for himself from outside. I have no heavenly wings sprouting from my shoulders to snatch me from this atmosphere of ever-looming deadly peril that is strangling me, for this is real, this is here, and no god will change it!

A S FAR AS THEY COULD TELL from Agnes's confused conversations, it appeared she had experienced a most unusual confusion of the identities of Nolten and Larkens; or rather, those two had in a certain way become one person in her mind. The painter she seemed to look upon as her beloved, but not at all in the form in which she beheld him. The letters of the actor she carried with her at all times as if they were a holy relic, and she awaited him at every moment with the quiet yearning of a bride, yet it was actually only Nolten again for whom she was waiting. We shall soon show more clearly what we mean by this.

In the meantime Agnes best liked to keep company with the blind boy, Henni; she called him her pious servant, had him do all kinds of errands, sang with him while he played the piano or the organ, talked him into accompanying her one place or the other, and she would usually guide him with her hand on his arm. People thought they were simply a brother-sister pair, so completely did they understand each other. For that reason, the President and Nolten lost no time to make clear to the young man certain rules in order that an appropriate conversation could guide her thoughts in the right direction. The good and sensible boy made that his main concern with all his soul. He proceeded most delicately and was so clever as to keep his intentions concealed. She herself had initiated the religious conversations so that he would really feel at home and with good cheer convey from the quiet treasure of his heart all that it knew on that theme. He was most happy when she could be guided on a topic to the point where she could continue talking about it on her own; and in fact she pursued the material not only at length and with relative consistency, but also in a way that made Henni marvel at the wealth of her thought, at the deep truth of her inner religious experience, which, to be sure, she may have drawn from her memories of her healthy state and presented more historically than as something that still guided her life; nevertheless her ability to recall these feelings so vividly was invaluable, just as the advantage of being able to strengthen those feelings and link new ones to them was welcome to the loyal Henni. She had some bizarre notions that were rooted in misunderstandings of biblical language that may have been her articles of faith since childhood and that then, unfortunately, though they had been suppressed during her more mature years, were now emerging again in foolishly expanded form, and these Henni had to combat quite urgently. In particular he had trouble with her false understanding of the faith in demons, because it was impossible for him to refute this tenet as one that was true of itself and based on scripture.

Yet he found it dismaying to a high degree whenever she, right in the midst of the most beautiful order, would fall into a glaring confusion of terms or all of a sudden change the subject completely.

That is what occurred once while they were sitting in their favorite spot, under the acacia tree in front of the greenhouse. She was reading from the New Testament. All at once she stops and asks: "And do you know why my dearest Theobald became an actor? I'll confide in you, but tell no one, especially not Margot, that little flatterer, she'll go and gossip it all to the liar, the heath runner. He's the one from whom my darling must hide. That's why he puts different clothes on, I tell you, every day a new shape so that the runner can't imitate him and doesn't know which of his many forms is the right one. A few years ago, Nolten came to me disguised as Cousin Otto; I didn't recognize him and made him very sad. I can never in all eternity forgive myself for that. But who knows everything about the actors! They can do simply everything. They're able to play dead, completely dead. Between us two, my darling did that too, to put an end to the liar's handiwork. I saw the corpse then, in the city. I tell you — you understand, you alone Henni! — the empty coffin is buried in the grave, only a few tattered shreds of clothes in it!"

She fell to thinking for a few seconds and then clapped her hands with joy: "O Henni! Sweet boy! in six weeks my bridegroom is coming and taking me away and we'll wed at once." She stood up and began, in the open place in front of Henni, to dance in the most charming way, taking hold of her dress here and there with her finger tips and singing as she danced. "If only you could see," she called to him, "how prettily I'm dancing! truly, you don't often see such pretty little feet. Birds of all types and colors come out to the nearest branches and look at me quite impertinently." She laughed mischievously and said: "I'm really just saying that because you always accuse me of being vain, I can't stand your preaching. But just wait, you still have to hear a bit of self-praise. But I'll let someone else speak for me." She took a letter from the actor from her sash and read:

"'But often I cannot call up your image, no matter how hard I try; I mean, the features of your face, even though I can imagine each one of them clearly enough, I cannot bring together so well. Then, again, in other moments, you are so close to me, near enough to touch with your every move! even your voice, especially when you laugh, comes so bright and natural to my ear. Your laughter! Why just that? Well, yes, the poets do indeed claim there's no melody more lovely than such a girlish giggle. A simile, dear child. In my youth, you know, I always had much to tell about elves. They are wont in the night to pass their time with all manner of lovely things, among other things with a little game of ninepins. This toy is made of the purest gold, and so when all nine fall they call it a golden laughter, because the sound when that happens is quite bright and happy. And just so, I imagine, is my darling laughing now.'

"Henni, what do you think of that? Fortunately I read so fast that you didn't even have time to become angry. Listen, when I was a child I had a schoolmaster who found an unusual method to break someone of the habit of reading too quickly; he would hand that person the book turned around so that it read right to left — 'So,' he would call out, 'now cut loose the horses! I will teach Hebrew on the side.' It's right that I think of him now — I beg you, alert your good father to the fact he's not supposed to say *djinese* gardenhouse any more, but *Chinese;* I'd be sorry if people were to make fun of him; that's already been quite a concern for me; today I even dreamed about it; I dreamed he gave me an explanation for it: 'Miss, I tend to alternate with that word, and with good reason: in the winter when every-

282

thing is frozen hard and stiff, I say *djinese,* but even by spring my G is getting softer, and in summer I am completely and totally *Chinese.*' And truly, that's what he is, too: he wears a queue. Seriously, I would really like to come up behind him some time with the scissors; it's really much too frivolous and old fashioned."

A maid ran across the path; Agnes turned her back on her angrily and said after she had gone by: "I don't feel at all well when I see Katie. Yesterday I heard her call out over to the wall to a farm boy: 'Did you know that the young miss visiting us has gone daft?' The silly, stupid girl. Who's crazy? No one is crazy. Providence is merciful. And that's why my morning prayer today went:

> Shower me neither
> With sorrow nor with joy,
> For in the middle
> Lies golden moderation.

Indeed, there is nothing better than contentment. Praise God, I have it; only one thing is missing, sadly, only one thing is missing!"

So she would often go on at length. And then when Henni, when the painter asked him a few times each day, had nothing more consoling to report, it almost broke the poor man's heart.

The doctors whom they consulted merely gave rules that were self-evident and, as well, given the girl's willfulness, hard to uphold. For example, she could be moved at no price to dine together with the others; and only when perchance they were all still sitting together in the dining room over desert, she would appear unexpectedly in the open doorway of a side room, calmly eyeing the circle, striking again a pleasant pose quite like the one we saw her assume earlier with the painter. But if Theobald tried to approach her, she would retreat without a sound and be less likely to come again.

In the meantime there had been renewed talk that it might perhaps be best simply to take her home. The suggestion was made to her with all due care by Nanette, yet instead of seizing the opportunity with both hands, as they expected, she thought it over seriously and then shook her head. It was as if she sensed her condition and was afraid of facing her father.

Someone suggested that either Nolten should absent himself completely or his fiancée should be made to believe that he was gone, since his presence obviously made her uneasy and gave daily sustenance to her delusions, whereas, if he went away, a desire for him might well stir within her, and if not, then they could ultimately use that occasion to introduce him to her formally as the true and awaited bridegroom, or let her, as if she were a child, make the happy discovery herself, as it were; if this trick succeeded and they were able to carry it off in bold and clever manner, then there was hope for a cure. — This view seemed not so far off the mark. Yet in the end Theobald claimed that he had to stay, she must see him from time to time, his calm, modest behavior, his look of silent worry would have a favorable effect on her. He did not care for artful ploys and deceptions; he thought that, if there was any hope at all, he would achieve a far more thorough and lasting cure his way.

But now we would consider it to be beneath the dignity of the topic and think that we were offending the feelings of our readers if we were to entertain them more extensively than necessary and in an embarrassing way with this girl's problems, however much charm her conversations, even in her lamentably disturbed state of mind, might still exhibit. For that reason we shall limit our depiction solely to what is intrinsic to an understanding the situation itself.

"Miss, you know Latin," she once said to Margot, "what is Latin for 'spark'?" "Scintilla," was the good-natured answer. "So, so: that's an exemplary word; there are proper sparks; but did you just quickly think of that? No matter, or rather: all the better; in the future, when I have something to say to you about the eyes of the man in question, when he is around I'll just say 'scintilla,' and then watch for the little green flame — Psst! Don't you hear? that's him stirring behind the oven screen — you see, he can make himself invisible — Aye, but you know that better than I do. And, Miss, when you make love with him again, it's all the same to me, but I've warned you." "What is that supposed to mean — Dear Agnes!" "Oh, you're in each other's arms when no one's around. I ask you, tell me, what is it like to kiss him? is he right horribly sweet? can you tell he's got the devil in him? — Miss, since it makes no difference to you whether he has other dalliances here and there besides you, I'll tell you about some of them right away; you can tease him about them: First there's a beautiful countess — noble, oh, so noble! See, this is the kind of manners she has —" (here she makes a gracious move through the room) "Have him on about it! But really you're all just being led on together. You don't want to believe that he's engaged to the Gypsy? If I wanted to, I could tell you the place where the promise was made and who blessed it, but proper Christians don't carry on about that sort of thing. In any case, now I'll have to go on a sleigh ride. Will you lend me your sable again?" Margot understood what she was talking about and gave her the garment. After a while she came out of her room all nicely dressed, like spring and winter, and went into the garden, to the carousel, where she usually sat down right away in one of the sleighs pulled by wooden horses. No one was allowed to spin the base; she claimed everything would get moving by itself if she looked for a while at the circle-jumping steeds and that it gave her a pleasant giddy feeling.

Nanette was sitting with her embroidery under the nearest tree. Soon Agnes joined her, urged her not to be sad, and promised her that her

284

brother would arrive soon and take them both away. "It's true, isn't it, we want to stay together? Your basically as fed up as I am with these false faces. Yes, yes, your eyes are gradually being opened. I noticed recently how you shuddered when that villain called you sister. Don't trouble yourself on his account, he can really do us no harm. — But now you're to see something lovely that will make you happy: Read these pages, you don't know the handwriting, but you do know who wrote it. They are my dearest treasure, more, more than gold and pearls and rubies! I have to sneak them away from the hellfire, he had stolen them from me. Be very careful with them and read them in total, reverent silence." She went away and left Nanette with the notebook of songs that we already mentioned as part of the actor's posthumous papers. Since these poems bore the title "To L." and one of Agnes's names was Luise, she claimed them as her own just as if Theobald had meant them for her. She had also found a silhouette among those pages and convinced herself that it was her image. They encountered her a few times holding two mirrors at angles to each other so she could compare her own profile with the silhouette.

Perhaps readers will take pleasure in seeing something of those poems, and in doing so, remembering the man who now, even in death as he once had in life, had come to occupy the heart of the unhappy child so intensely.

The sky it glows with springtime light so strong,
    The hill wells up to it, all longing,
    The frozen world, now blessed by love, is thawing,
And curls up round into the gentlest song.

When I my gaze now turn unto the hills
That round the valley of my love so misty range —
O heart, what can your pondering change,
That all the bitter strife of rapture might be still!

You, *love,* help dispel the magic spell
With which all nature torments now my heart!
And you, O *spring,* help now my love to bend!

Die out, O day! and let me by night grow well!
While you, gentle stars, your coolness do impart,
I to the abyss of contemplation would descend.

Tis true, my child, when you and I must part,
    Then longing is the comrade of my ways,
    Through mountains, forests, meadows, all the days
I'm driven by my lost, impatient heart.

Once in your arms! Oh, what joyful days!
But there, too, then my melancholy stirs,
I reel, as drunk, upon the heavenly stairs,
And time eludes me in a fleeting daze.

And so this heart, so easy stirred to plight,
Made anxious by too much of love's happiness,
Will here on earth know naught but restlessness;

Each pain dispels in the eternal light,
And all our teeming passions flow,
Rosy, like dreaming clouds, round our feet below.

When I, calmed by your gaze profound,
	In silence savor all your sacred worth,
	Then oft I hear the quiet gentle breath
Of the angel who is in you bound.

Then a surprised, a blissful smile I feel
Upon my lips, unless my dreams deceive,
And now I, to my heavenly content, perceive
My lone and boldest wish fulfilled by thee.

Then deep and deeper my mind raves,
I hear from distant reaches of God's night
The springs of fate in their melodious rush;

Upwards, entranced, I turn my gaze,
To heaven and the laughing stars so bright!
And kneeling, their bright song to hear, I hush.

Resplendent in silver dew blooms the young rose,
	Its gift from the gentle morn,
	Not knowing that to wilt it was born,
Not sensing each flower's last fate.

The eagle into endless heavens does fly,
In the glittering gold his eye does bask,
No fool, he'll not be the one to ask
If he might not collide with the sky.

Though one day youth's flower may pale and die,
Still the illusion was so dear
That we'll not renounce it before its time.

And like the eagle our love must fly:
Though all the world's gifts disappear,
Love may dare the flight beyond time.

A t forest's edge I lie some days so long
    To hear the cuckoo, there my watch I keep;
    He seems to lull the valley into sleep
With the peaceful steady beat of his sad song.

Then all is well, and my worst torment,
To harken to society's demands,
Here I have respite from those commands,
Where in my own way I may be content.

And if those fine folks only gave a thought,
To how poets all their time do spend
They would then still more envy me.

For the sonnet's ornate wreaths are wrought
As of their own accord in my hand,
While my eyes wander far and free.

In Holy Week

O Passion Week, you witness of sacred torment!
    So somber your mood midst these splendid spring days;
    You cast against the bright sun's newborn rays
The dark shadow of the cross upon the earth.

Silent you show your trappings of mourning,
While all around spring may blossom free
The violet fragrant 'neath the blooming tree,
And all the birds, so jubilant, singing.

O silence, you birds in the sky so blue!
All round the somber bells do ring,
And the angels their dirges now do sing,
O silence, you birds in the meadow's green hue!

You violets no curly locks shall adorn!
In a dark bouquet in my pious darling's hand
To the church you're bound, on the altar you'll stand
To honor Our Lord 'til your beauty is gone.

And if she then on pious thoughts does dwell,
And yearning in sweet love
Unite this world with heaven above,
Then let her think of me, of me as well!

I N THE MEANTIME, Agnes had taken a walk with Henni. She led him out
into the open fields without really saying where they were going — not an
unusual case, in which a third, reliable person would always follow unnotice-
ably at some distance. Agnes for some time had hardly taken off the lovely
velvet jacket, a gift from her supposed lover; she was wearing it now and
looked, despite some carelessness of her dress, very attractive in it. Conversing as usual, the two made it to the nearest woods and in the middle of it sat
down in a broad greensward surrounding a large, lone oak tree, which cast
its shade quite picturesquely over an open well. Agnes had occasionally heard
tell of this well as a noted curiosity. Indeed it is a vestige of pre-Christian antiquity worth seeing, its external features still well preserved. The round
stone wall stands approximately waist high above ground; its depth, though
it is partly caved in, remains considerable, such that one could drop a stone
in and count to sixteen at moderate speed before hearing it hit the water
down below. Its name, the "Alexis Well," came from a legend. Agnes insisted on hearing the saga in detail from Henni, and he narrated as follows:
   "Many hundreds of years ago, even before Christianity had become
widespread in German lands, lived a Count who had a daughter, Belsore,
whom he had promised in marriage to a Duke's son, Alexis by name. These
two loved each other truly and deeply; after a year, Alexis was to be allowed
to take her home. Yet before that, he had to go on an expedition with his
father, far away, to Constantinople. There for the first time in his life he
heard men preach of the Gospel of Christ, and this moved him and his father
to become better acquainted with this faith. They stayed a month in that city
and finally agreed joyfully that they would let themselves be baptized. Before
they traveled homewards, the father had two finger rings made by a Greek
goldsmith, with the sign of the cross embedded in each in precious jewels.
When they arrived home and the Count learned what they had done and
that his daughter was to become a Christian, his joy turned to anger and
venomous hatred; he vowed that he would rather kill his child with his own
hands before he would let such a one marry her, even though it might make
her a queen. Belsore was heartsick, especially since she was convinced, after
all that Alexis had told her about his new faith, that it was the only way for
her to find happiness. They secretly exchanged rings and vowed to be true
until death, whatever might happen to them. The Count gave Alexis time to
reconsider whether he might not want to denounce his error, in which case
he would then embrace him anew as his son-in-law. Yet the boy spurned this

288

outrageous offer, took leave of Belsore, and took up the wanderer's staff so that, humbly clad, he could travel about, now here, now there, as a messenger of the Gospel. Since he had always been able to speak wisely and forcefully and was also of pleasant appearance, his work was not without manifold blessings. Yet often, when he went his way so alone, spending his nights with the shepherds in the fields, with the colliers in the forest, and along with such discomfort also had to endure the mockery and scorn of the world, he was not safe from inner temptation and at times doubted whether he himself was in possession of the truth, whether Christ was the son of God and worthy that one renounce all things for him. He yearned, too, for Belsore, with whom he could long have been living in happiness and joy. In the meantime his wanderings had also led him into this area. Here, where the well is now, there is supposed to have been a deep cleft in the rocks with a spring nearby in which Alexis stilled his thirst. Here he prayed fervently to God for a sign that his was the true faith; yet he thought first to make himself more worthy of this grace by biding a year, during which time he would live peacefully at home with his father, the Duke, and turn his soul to religious matters. If in this time he grew no surer of his faith and returned then in the next spring to this same spot, then the rose tree should decide, to whose completely dead branch he now affixed Belsore's ring; if by that time the bush should bloom again and still hold fast the golden ring, then that should signal him that he had been on the right path to seeking his soul's salvation and that as well his love for his fiancée was pleasing to God. And so he now embarked upon his journey home. The Duke had remained during this time true to the Savior, and from Belsore Alexis received the same assurance by secret message. As much as this pleased him, he was still left with his own uncertainty; he was also aggrieved because the letter from his fiancée made it seem almost as if, despite her loyal affection for to him, she had still put his love somewhat behind her passionate love for the Savior. He could hardly wait until the year was over. When it was, he set out on foot, as he had vowed, on his way. He finds the forest again and knows the spot even from afar; he falls, before going any closer, to his knees and then hurries forward with anxious heart. Oh, wonder of wonders! Three roses he finds, the loveliest, hanging on the bush. But alas, the ring was missing. His faith thus told him that he had lost Belsore. Filled with despair he tears the bush from the ground and hurls it into the chasm. Immediately he regrets his misdeed; as a penitent he returns to his fatherland, most of whose inhabitants, through the efforts of the Duke, had already converted. Alexis sank into a dark melancholy; yet God did not abandon him; God gave him peace in His true word. Only on one point, regarding his love to the pious virgin, Alexis was not yet satisfied. A secret hope lived in him that he would have to find complete assurance back at that miraculous place. For the third time he makes his long pilgrimage and arrives at his goal without misfortune. Yet unfortunately he finds things there just as he had left them. With sorrow he recognizes the bare spot where he had uprooted the tree. No miracle happens, no prayer helps him find happy certainty. In such dire hopelessness night came upon him as he still lay stretched out on the rock that hangs over the chasm. In his mind he looked down deep into the darkness and pondered how the next morning he would wander on in God's name and send his dearest a letter of farewell. All at once he notices that far below on the calm surface of he water it is as if a gold and rose shimmer were flickering and flittering. At first he does not trust his eyes, yet from time to time the lovely light recurs. He begins to feel a happy presentiment welling up in him. As day approaches he climbs down the rock and, behold, the rose bush he had cast away had taken root, barely a hand's breadth above the water, and was quite gorgeously in bloom. Carefully Alexis detaches it, brings it up into the daylight, and finds, right at the same spot at which he had affixed the ring two years ago, fresh bark grown over it to hold the ring fast, with the bright gold barely shining out through a tiny slit. A year ago, had he not been so hasty and his faith in God greater, he would have had to notice it much more easily. How thankfully he now cast himself to the ground in prayer. With what tears did he kiss the bush that had, in addition to its many blossoming roses, a host of new buds. Gladly would he have taken it with him, yet he believed he had to replant it in the sacred spot where it had stood before. With much praise of God's omnipotence he returned to his father's home a transformed man. There he is received by a message at once of joy and sorrow: the old Count had died and, on his death bed, won over by the teaching of his daughter, had accepted Christianity and honestly regretted his harshness. Alexis and Belsore were united as a happy couple. The first thing they then undertook together was a pilgrimage to the miraculous spring, which they had built into a beautifully walled well. For many centuries it is said to have been in use, with bridal couples from far and wide in the area traveling there before their wedding to take a blessed drink from its clear waters, known as the rose drink; usually it was dispensed by a hermit pastor who lived here in the forest. That custom is long past, of course, yet many people, the shepherds and woodsmen, say that the rose-colored glow can still be seen at the bottom of the well on the eve of Good Friday and of Christmas."

Agnes looked at a protruding stone in the wall on which quite clearly three engraved roses and a cross were visible. Henni deduced from the story several lessons for the poor girl entrusted to his care; she paid little attention to them and soon drew him away from the place to climb a small peak nearby, its bare cone shape rising above the woods. "The wind is still blowing! I must sing the wind song; it is much in order today," Agnes called out as she hurried ahead.

They stood at the peak, and she sang the following verses in a free manner, as with each question and answer she altered her voice quite prettily and made lively motions in the air.

"'Gale wind, storm wind!
Here and there,
Tell me your home, oh where, oh where!'

'Child, we howl here
For many a year
Through the wide wide world,
And hope to learn
For an answer we yearn,
From the mountains and seas,
From heaven's clashing armies —
But they never can say;
Why, you're smarter than they,
If you can tell.
— But onward! Let's go!
Don't make us slow!
There will follow others,
They are our brothers,
Ask if they know.'
'Hold on! Abide!
A brief respite!
Tell where love dwells,
Its beginning, its end!'

'Oh, who could tell!
Roguish child,
Like the wind, it's wild,
Fleet and vibrant,
Resting never,
It lasts forever,
But never constant.
— But onward! Let's go!
Don't make us slow!
Over fields, forests, and meadows!
When your darling I see,
I'll greet her for thee;
Dear child, adieu!'"

Towards evening Agnes had gone to bed, exhausted; the President was by her for a while; all at once he came joyfully from her bedroom and hurriedly said to Theobald: "She wants to see you, go quickly!" He obeyed without delay; the others remained behind, and he closed the door behind him. Agnes was lying quietly on her side, resting her head on her arm. Meekly and with a friendly greeting he sat down on the chair beside her bed; in total calm, but in some doubt, she looked at him a long while; it seemed as though a pleasant memory were dawning on her that she was trying to match with his facial features. But her gaze becomes more heated and soft, her breathing quickens, her breast heaves, and now — as she covers her eyes with her left hand — she extends her right arm resolutely towards him, seizes his hand passionately, and presses it firmly to her bosom; the painter, before he can think, finds himself clasped to her neck and draws from her lips a glow to which the trepidation of the moment imparts an exciting thrill; insanity sparkles in triumph in her eyes; desperation presses that heavenly treasure, before it turns from him completely, into our friend's trembling arms one more time — yes, as he senses, for the last time.

But Agnes is already beginning to become restless and draw quietly away from his kisses; she raises her head anxiously: "What is whispering in you? what is speaking in you? I hear two different voices — Help! Oh, help! You devious Satan, be gone —! How I, oh, how I have been deceived! — oh, now it is over for me! — The liar will go and revile me to my beloved as if I weren't an honorable girl, as if I had knowingly and willingly kissed this monster — O Theobald, if only you were here so that I could tell you everything! I don't know how the serpent did it! or how they deranged my mind, me, your poor, naive, deserted child!" She knelt upright on the bed, weeping bitterly, with her hair loosed and tumbling down over her glowing cheeks. Nolten could not bear the sight, he hurried out, in tears: "Yes, just laugh up your sleeve and go and make fun of me to the others — it won't go on much longer than that, for it is godless, and the angels in heaven will have mercy on how you're tormenting a sick girl!"

The sister-in-law came in and sat down with her; they prayed: Agnes became more calm.

"Isn't it so?" she said afterwards, "a peaceful ending. That's really what everyone wants in the end; an easy death, nice and gentle, just as a boy's knee bends; where did I find an expression like that? I'm thinking of Henni; it would have to be good to die with him nearby."

She went on for a while in this tone, forgot it by and by, became more cheerful, ultimately even talkative, and in fact in such a manner that Nanette didn't like the sudden change. Agnes noticed this and actually seemed surprised herself and, ashamed and immediately, excused herself for her behavior in a way that clearly showed how lucid she could be in some moments: "You see," she said with the most lovely smile of melancholy, "I am just like the ship that has gone aground on a sandbank and can't be saved; that may well be unfortunate, but what can the poor ship do about it if in the mean-

292

time the red topsails still play their roguish game up there in the wind as through nothing had happened? Let things go as best they can. Not until the grass is growing over me will it be over."

THE PAINTER LEFT THE CASTLE the next day as early as possible: the President himself had advised him to do so and lent him one of his horses. They meant first to try it as an experiment for a few days to see how the girl would react if Theobald were out of her sight. He himself seemed uncertain, as he departed, about where he would go. For emergencies they decided on a third place where, if need be, they could leave a message for him. W*** was out of the question; just recently he had written there to postpone his arrival, not caring at heart whether they would permit his delay or whether it would ruin the whole arrangement.

The increased calm that the others are able to notice in Agnes gradually becomes, as soon as the object of her fear disappears, a quiet melancholy; her loquacity decreases. She is at times aware of her illness, and the smallest chance reminder of it, a word, a glance from those around her, can hurt her deeply. Striking in this respect is the following turn of events. The President, or rather Margot, had a large whippet that they called, because of its surpassing beauty, Merveille. The dog had previously not shown any disinclination towards Agnes, but for some time had clearly avoided her, actually slinking away when she came around. Without doubt this shyness had a natural cause, Agnes likely angered him without knowing it — but whatever it was, she herself seemed to believe that the animal sensed what was uncanny or sinister about her. She coaxed the dog in all possible ways, even with tears, and when nothing worked she gave up on him, vexed and dejected, without wanting to look at him anymore.

Recently, they noticed that she was no longer wearing her engagement ring. When they asked her why, she answered: "My mother took it." "But your mother is dead, are you claiming you've seen her then?" "No; but I still know that she took the ring away; I know the place where it is, and I have to go fetch it there myself. Oh, if only that were over with! It is a frightening place, but it can do no harm to a pious bride; a lovely angel will be standing there and will ask what I am seeking and hand it over to me. He'll also tell me right away where my beloved is and when he is coming."

Another time she let fall to Henni the following words: "Yesterday the thought came to me that, because Nolten has really been gone much too long, he's given up on me! And considered in the right light, you can't really blame him for that; what would he want with a fool like me? he would be taking on no end of trouble. And on top of that, O Henni — fading, fading, fading, everything is fading! Do you see how it's a good thing that there was no wedding; that's what I always thought. Now it may end when it will, for my maiden's wreath is safe at any rate, I'll take it to my grave. Between us, dear boy, I always hoped to go to heaven that way and no other. But first I've got to have the ring, I must be able to show it."

One more benign and pious scene should be recalled here, especially since it is the last that we have to tell of the girl's sad life.

At one point Nanette came bounding in with great haste and begged the young mistress and her father to follow her to the old chamber where the organ was, where, with the door slightly ajar, they could for a moment witness a musical performance by Henni and Agnes. So the three of them went quietly to the designated place and listened to a very touching song interwoven with the organ's flute tones. First the boy's voice, then the girl's voice predominated. It seemed to be old Catholic music. Wonderfully gripping in particular were the powerful verses of a Latin song of penitence in E-major. Here is only the beginning:

> Jesu benigne!
> A cuius igne
> Opto flagrare,
> Et te amare; —
> Cur non flagravi?
> Cur non amavi
> Te, Jesu Christe?
> — O frigus triste!*

*These lines are in fact to be found in a very old book of devotions that is now most likely out of print. They are inimitably beautiful; along with it we include, for some readers, a translation: "The fire of your love, / O Lord, how dear / I wanted to cherish it / I wanted to tend it / — Yet cherish it I did not / Tend it I would not, / Like ice was my heart, / — O pains of Hell!"

There followed still two more verses like that, after which Henni went into a long postlude, which then blended into a new song that expressed similar sentiments. Agnes sang this song alone, while the boy played.

> One love I know, and it is true,
> Was true since it first I did find,
> With a deep sigh it would ever anew,
> With a sigh it would ever anew,
> And consolingly with me bind.
>
> He who once with heavenly forbearance
> The bitterest draft of death did drink,
> Bore the cross and for my sin did penance,
> Till in a sea of grace it did sink.

And why does my sorrow still last?
Why do I still cringe in fear?
And ask, Lord, is the long night now past?
And: what can save me from death and sin, so dire?

O evil heart! yes, just confess,
Evil joy you've once more known;
Pious love, and loyalty's last trace —
Oh, that all is long since gone!

And that's why my sorrow still does last,
And why I still cringe in fear —
Watchman! Watchman! is the long night past?
And: what can save me from death and sin, so dire?

With the last words Margot threw her arms around Nanette's neck, weeping bitter tears. The President paced slowly back and forth. The organ music went on alone, as if in the harmony of infinite pain it could come to no end. At last all was silent. The door opened, a nice little girl, Henni's younger sister, who had been working the bellows, tiptoed out, departed quietly, and left the door open behind her. But then their eyes beheld a true picture of peace. For there sat the blind boy, leaning over, lost in thought, at the open keyboard, with Agnes, fallen into a light sleep, beside him on the floor, her head resting on his knee, a sheet of music in her lap. The evening sun broke through the dusty windowpanes, bathing the entire resting group in golden light. The large crucifix on the wall looked sympathetically down on them.

After the friends had looked on in silence for some time, they withdrew quietly, leaving the door slightly ajar.

THE NEXT MORNING Agnes was missing. Nanette had gotten up to find her bed empty and, filled with fear, raised the alarm at once. No one could understand at first how Agnes had been able to leaved the bedroom, since some time ago they had moved it, for a variety of reasons, from the lower to the upper floor, carefully locked the doors at night, and in fact found them locked that morning. But at a side window that led out onto the belvedere they discovered a long ladder among the trees; one of the garden workers, as he himself admitted, had placed it there the previous evening because Agnes had absolutely insisted on having a bird's nest that she had seen protruding from one of the gaps in the stone frieze above. Afterwards the ladder had been forgotten, which was without doubt what the girl had intended.

The morning hours flew by with frantic inquiries, endless deliberation, questions, messages sent and received. Within the castle's environs everything had been turned and turned again. Evening approached and still there was not the least news from any quarter, not the least hope. A false trail that came about as the result of a forester's erroneous statement gave rise to the longest delay.

The sun had gone down two hours before, and still all errands and messages remained fruitless. The friends were beside themselves. After midnight the last torchbearers returned, only the old gardener and even Henni were still out so long that they began to worry about them, too. No one in the castle thought of going to bed. The President posed the assumption that Agnes had taken some way towards her home and, depending on how early she had gotten underway, might already have had a considerable head start even before the searchers went out; he felt there was no reason to fear for her life; they could more likely expect that she would have been apprehended as suspicious along the way and that an official move was underway to deliver her back to her place of birth. Nanette imagined that in this case the unfortunate girl's arrival home in her father's house would be more frightening than anything. Yet if they could imagine her delivered, otherwise safe, into her father's arms, then from here on they could have new hope again. Yet with what heavy hearts they would have to anticipate the painter's return if nothing decisive should have happened by then! — Margot did not hold back from stating her suspicion that, this time too, the Gypsy had her ruinous hand in the game. All this they discussed and pondered, back and forth, until no other possibility seemed to remain, yet the worst no one dared think, let alone say. At last a glum silence ensued. In the various rooms here and there a forgotten candle still burned its pale light; the rooms themselves offered a picture of anxiety and destruction, for all things stood or lay about in disarray as everyone had left them yesterday morning in the first frightened hours. The castle clock let its morose chime be heard from time to time, from the grounds outside came the full, magnificent tones of a nightingale.

At a sign from the President they finally got up to go to bed. A group of the servants stayed awake.

Towards three in the morning, at the first grey light of day, the dogs in the courtyard gave sound but at once then fell silent again. Margot by then opens her window and sees in the pale dawn a number of men, among them the gardener and his son, standing at the castle gate with half-extinguished lanterns. A sudden premonition pierces the girl's heart, and she pulls the window shut with a loud cry, for it looked to her as though two of the people were struggling to carry their horrible discovery into the house. In the next moment she hears the clock from her father's bedroom. Everyone comes running, only half dressed, from far and near.

The lost girl had indeed been found, but unfortunately dead and beyond saving. An hour ago her corpse had been pulled, after much travail, out of the well in the forest. The gardener, alerted to the place by his son, had gone there when it was still late at night, and a glove he found there verified his suspicion. Immediately the old man had hurried to the nearest village to fetch men, tools, a rope ladder and hooks, as well as a surgeon.

The corpse, except for its soaked and torn clothes, showed only slight wounds; the snow-white face, around which the girl's hair lay in wet disarray, looked just as it always had; the half-opened mouth seemed to be smiling in pain; the eyes were shut tight. Obviously, falling head first, she had drowned; only one slight wound did they find, above her right temple. Remarkable too is the fact that she had found death while wearing the green jacket from Larkens, on which they had seen her yesterday busily but earnestly at work to alter a minor detail.

The surgeon made still one and then another futile attempt to find life. Of the boundless sorrow of all those gathered round we shall say nothing.

F OR NOLTEN THEY HAD SENT, but reached him with neither letter nor messenger. On the second day after the death of his fiancée he appeared unexpectedly, coming from the opposite direction. His whole bearing as he arrived, his strange reserve, his expression of drained resignation, his manner of greeting them were all such that he seemed already either to know or to suspect what had happened without wanting to hear any more about it. Accordingly he met a likewise awkward and taciturn reception. Nanette, who was not there when he first arrived, rushes to him with a loud cry as soon as she catches a glimpse of her brother's face. His appearance was not only pitiable but in fact frightening. He looked wild, sunburned, and many years older. His lifeless, glazed eyes betrayed not so much an intense pain as rather a weary surfeit of long suffering. The misfortune that the others still felt as something present in all its strength, seemed, from the look of him, to be something long past. He spoke only with difficulty and showed a strange, timid embarrassment about all that he did. He had, as they gradually learned from what he said, given himself over in the last six days to wandering about in various unknown areas, living, alone and without purpose, in his own grief; he'd scarcely even brought himself to write to Neuburg.

As now there was still no specific mention of Agnes and they had no idea how they should act with Nolten about it, everyone was more than a little surprised when he asked in all casualness when the burial was set and what plans they had along those lines. — With the same calmness he made his way on is own to the room were the dead girl lay. There he stayed, long and alone. Only in looking at her did he feel, fully and clearly, what he had lost, he wept bitterly when he returned to the others in the salon.

"Unfortunate, dear friend," the President now began, embracing the painter, "long ago somewhere I encountered the saying: we should continue hoping even when there is no more to hope for. Surely that is a magnificent phrase if only one chooses to understand it; once in a time of great need it awakened in my soul the most wonderful sense of solace, a shining golden glimpse of faith; and then one need only resolve to seize this faith with joy. Oh, that you might do this! A person whom fate holds so frighteningly in its iron grip, that person must surely be fate's favorite, and this cruel favor will some day reveal itself to be the eternal benevolence and truth. I have often found that those proscribed by heaven were its first saints. A baptism of fire has been visited upon you, and a higher life, more attuned to God, will from this hour on unfold in you."

"I can," Nolten responded after a brief pause, "I can if need be understand what you mean, and yet — misfortune makes me so weary that my dull ears but half perceive your kind words — oh, that slumber would fall upon me as heavy and muffling as mountains! That I knew nothing of yesterday, today, and tomorrow! That a deity would let this harried spirit fall back, gently cradling it in the void of old! — an immeasurable happiness — —!" He gave himself over to this thought for a moment, and then went on: "Yes, if only I had this first phase behind me! And yet who can be sure that the knot does not become entangled again *there*? — — O life! O death! Mystery upon mystery! Where we thought ourselves most sure to find sense or meaning, there it so seldom is, and where we sought it not, there it shows itself by half and in the distance, disappearing before we can seize it!"

A GNES'S BURIAL IS SET for Sunday morning.
The night before, Nolten is sleeping more peacefully than he had in some time. The good gardener has taken it upon himself to watch the night over the beloved corpse, accompanied by his son, and when the old man at last nods off, Henni is the only person awake in the castle. — The good boy was truly as if orphaned without his friend and mistress. He had become so close, so special to her, he had secretly nourished the hope — a hope of which he was now deeply ashamed — that God could perhaps have granted him the joy of leading the poor soul, with the power of the Gospel's word, back to recognition of her self, to the light of truth; all his striving and planning, all his prayers were ultimately aimed only at that goal, and how much more horribly than he ever could have feared was his devout trust deceived! — He holds and presses in his hands a dear, cold hand that he cannot see, lisping over it ardent words of blessing. He ponders the uplifting wisdom of Him in whom he believes with all his soul and before whose all-seeing eyes the book of time lies open, of Him who guides the hearts of people as He does the waters of the stream, of Him in whom we live and move and have our being.[57] He is startled for a moment of blissful shock when he realizes that what lies before him and to which he speaks with glowing tears is an unhearing nothing, a worthless illusion, and that the departed spirit, in much more lovely form, perhaps in this very hour is kneeling by the bright stream of paradise and, washing out its beclouded eye with pure clar-

ity, smiling in surprise and joy as it finds and recognizes itself once again.[58] — Henni stood up quietly, feeling a sweet unrest he had never known; he felt himself seized by an indescribable longing, yet this longing itself was only the overjoyed feeling, the incomprehensible sense of a heavenly future that awaited him, too. It was an unfriendly night, a violent storm rocking and swaying the high treetops, while up on the roof the weather vanes clashed in unison. The boy's wondrously aroused fantasy yielded itself to this tumult; exulting inwardly, he let the storm blow in his locks and listened rapturously to the hundred-voiced wind. He felt it was the sighing spirit chorus of the bound creature that was also impatiently awaiting a magnificent revelation.[59] His every thought and feeling was naught but a drunken song of praise to death, decay, and eternal rejuvenation. With force he must rein in the flight of his thoughts, mindful of the humbleness that dares not anticipate God. Yet, as he now returns to Agnes's mortal shell, he feels like someone who has gazed too long into the fiery sun and now sinks back into doubly painful blindness. Quietly he sits down and sets about finishing his wreath of roses and myrtles.

Meanwhile, after midnight, the painter is awakened by a strange sound that at first he thinks he had only dreamt, though soon he is able to convince himself that it is music that seems to be wafting over from the castle's left wing. It was as if someone were very solemnly playing the organ, but then again it sounded like a completely different instrument, always coming only in fragments, with longer and shorter pauses, one moment unpleasantly harsh and glaring, the next moment gentle and touching. Perplexed he leaps out of bed, uncertain what he should do, where he should turn first. He listens and listens, and — again these same incomprehensible tones! Throwing on his dressing gown, he walks quietly on stocking feet out his door and steals, groping along the wall with his hands, down the dark hallway until he approaches the room where the gardener and Henni are. He calls for light, and the gardener hurries out, surprised to see the painter there at so late an hour. Since at this point neither father nor son claim to have heard anything but the varying howl of the wind that is buffeting the house harder on this side, Nolten left, apparently calmed, taking the light with him but not letting anyone accompany him back to his room.

Hardly a minute had gone by when the old man and Henni heard the tones described above quite clearly, immediately followed by a loud crash and a loud scream.

Barely have they reached the old chapel, barely has the father glimpsed, only three paces away, the painter lying sprawled lengthwise in the open doorway without sign of life, than Henni, clinging in fear to his father and not letting him go, calls out "Stop, father, stop! for God's sake don't you see — there in the chamber —"

"What?" shouts the old man impatiently, since the boy is holding him back, "so let me go, then! Here, in front of us, lies what frightens me — the painter, lifeless, on the floor."

"But there — he's standing there, too, and — oh, look, someone else —"

"Are you out of your mind? you're blind! what's wrong with you?"

"As surely as God lives, I see!" the boy went on quietly, his voice choked with fear as he keeps pointing towards the far end of the chamber, to the organ, where the gardener can see nothing; he wants only to aid the painter, past whom Henni is looking. "Father! now — now — they are stealing towards us — Horrors! O flee —" Here his voice fails, and he faints, clinging to the arm of his father, who now raises a desperate cry for help. From all sides, people come running, shouting, the President himself arriving among the first, and the surgeon already at hand, having not left the castle in these last days; he hurries from Nolten to Henni, then from Henni to Nolten. They carry them both away, everyone wants to help, with advice, with keeping watch; they get in each other's way, tripping and pushing, so the President sends them all away except for a few. A horseman gallops off to the city to fetch the other doctor while the one present, a calm, able man, continues to proceed by the rules with liniment and warm towels, the dreadful odor of the most potent medicines already filling the room. With Henni there is no danger, although he has not yet fully returned to consciousness. With Nolten even after hours of effort, both art and hope fail. Humbly the surgeon expressed his doubts, and when at last the medic arrived he declared after his third look that no more trace of life was to be found.

WHILE AGNES'S ILLNESS AND DEATH had aroused the greatest attention and warmest sympathy in the area, this new calamity called forth in peoples' minds genuine panic, especially since no adequate explanation was evident. Since at any rate some violent fright had to have been the cause, the painter's state of exhaustion from worry and despair led people to assume that, in this case, imagination, as many other examples show, had done its worst. The doctors were of this opinion, as was the President. Yet in the castle there was also, depending on the extent to which people chose to accord certain circumstances a frightening significance, no lack of other suspicions, which, at first only quietly hinted at and either smiled upon or strictly forbidden by those of reason, soon nevertheless gained more consideration and in the end tacit credence.

Nolten's sister could not be long shielded from the misfortune, it cast her down as if it were her own death. Margot held to her loyally, yet to be sure there was little or nothing here in the way of consolation.

Henni is well again, at least outwardly. He seems to be brooding over a monstrous experience that he cannot master. He sits immobile, his vacant stare swallowing up his real pain. He is at a loss with impatience as soon as people ask him about his behavior yesterday; he flees contact with the others, but fear immediately frightens him back to his family.

The President, hoping for some new insight into the sad events, commands the boy, in the presence of the gardener, to speak. But even then, still in a halting manner and with a kind of defiant reluctance that was quite unusual in the gentle boy, Henni, at first very tersely but then with ever growing emotion, offered a confession that visibly left the President somewhat at a loss as to how he was to take it.

"Last night," so Henni spoke in reply to the President's question, "when I ran to the chapel with my father in response to the noise that we heard in the main hallway — the door was open and the lantern outside in the hallway threw a bright light into the chamber — I saw far back by the organ a woman standing, like a shadow, and facing her only a short distance away a second shadow, a man in a dark cloak, and this was Herr Nolten."

"Strange boy!" the President responded, "how can you claim to have seen this, then?"

"I can say nothing but that it had become light before my eyes, and I could see, and that is as sure as the fact that now I can no longer see."

"That woman" — the President now asked slyly, "can you compare her to anyone?"

"At that time I could not yet do so. Not until today did I have to think of the strange, mad woman, so I had her described to me and I cannot deny the similarity."

"But Herr Nolten, how could you recognize him so quickly?"

"My father pointed down to the ground and, as he did so, called the man lying there the painter; only then did I notice that this man lying in front of us and the other man standing over there were totally alike and one and the same man."

"Why do you say the woman was like a 'shadow'?"

"That's just how it seems to me; and still the faces and expressions and the color of the clothing were clearly different. When the two embraced and were about to go arm in-arm to the door, then they simply curved, like a column of smoke, around the wooden pillar that stands in the middle of the chamber."

"Arm in arm, you say?"

"Close, holding each other close; she started it; he did as she did, sadly, and as if being forced. And then — but O almighty God! how am I to express, how can I express what no tongue can say and what surely no one will believe and that no one can believe, least of all coming from me, from me, poor boy that I am?" He drew a deep breath and then went on: "They slipped silently over the threshold, he glided away over his likeness, indifferent, as if no longer knowing himself. Then all at once he casts an eye on me, oh, an eye full of misery! and yet such a sharp, penetrating gaze! and he hesitates as he walks, looks at me and moves his lips as if unable to speak — then I could no longer stand it, and from here on I know nothing more to say."

The President spared the young person any further questions, calmed him, and recommended to father and son that they keep the matter to themselves, giving to understand as he did so that he thought there was nothing more to it than a huge self-delusion. But the old gardener seemed very serious and inwardly attributed even to his master a different opinion than he had just now chosen to state.

A FTER THE TWO CORPSES WERE CONSIGNED to the earth in the Catholic cemetery of the nearest village — albeit with the aid of a Protestant clergyman — that noble-minded man, the President, who above all had succeeded in seeing to it that this last duty was discharged with all desirable dignity and with a stately procession, immediately made arrangements to offer up yet another sacrifice to friendship and love of mankind. He could allow neither that the poor surviving sister of the painter undertake alone so sorrowful a journey home as she now faced, nor that the forester should hear of the loss of his two children other than from the lips of the host whose house had become the innocent site of such dire fates.

Thus the President was soon sitting in the coach with Nanette and Margot. He had already quietly decided for himself that the girl, if it should please her and her family, return with him to his estate so that he might see to her future happiness. This idea had actually started with Margot, and she barely resisted coaxing Nanette's to accept.

The pain of the old man in Neuburg transcends all expression; yet the personality of the noble guest did not fail to have its beneficial effect.

While the President was still in Neuburg a letter from the Hofrat arrived at the forester's house, addressed to Nolten and with the express request that it be forwarded to him as quickly as possible. The forester opened it, read it, and handed the page to the President in silent surprise. The letter read as follows:

"I have just learned from a friend the cruel blow that has been dealt you with the death of your beloved bride. The full circumstances and all contributing factors I have learned as well. Your misfortune, which corresponds so closely to my own and which in fact truly stemmed from the unhappy legacy of my existence, has shaken me profoundly and now forces me to speak.

"How often, when you were still amongst us, did my heart burn to embrace you and confide! How my secret pressed and pained me! But — what can one say — fear, whimsy, shame, cowardice — I could not do so, I postponed the revelation from one day to the next, dreading having to find again in you, in the son of my brother, my second self, my entire past, and having to go through that labyrinth again, if only in conversation, in recollection!

"Since your departure I have been, as God is my witness, justly punished for such selfishness with a remarkable longing to see you, my most worthy friend! Yet now I am honestly and truly thirsting to see you; we have very, very much to tell each other. My thoughts run as follows: for such demanding activity as would now await you in W*** you might well have little heart; thus you will all the more easily accept the fact that there, as letters inform me, certain people, in response to your delay, are busy casting you in a bad light. We will, I should think, outflank those very people and lose nothing by it. Listen to my suggestion: the two of us live together! be it here or, even better, in some small place where we can live nice and quietly, just as befits two people, at least one of whom no longer cares about the world's opinion, and the other, as far as I know, has always had a strong desire to retreat with his art into a hermit-like life. For my part, I have only a few years to live. But how happy I would be if I could pass on whatever may still be vital in me to you, my nephew. Yes, let us salvage our ruins from life's shipwreck! I'll act as if I were still a young man. With pride and melancholy let it be said that we are two branches of the same tree that a flash of lightning has split, with the loss, perhaps, of a lovely laurel wreath. You must still save that laurel, and I shall help you do so.

"You see, we truly belong together, as twin brothers of fate! Gods both friendly and hostile have joined us together with three-fold bonds of iron — a strange drama to show the world if we were to choose not to withhold it; but that's a long way off; the grave shall one day cover our misery no better than we will keep this secret between us now, wouldn't you say? — But come! so come at once!

"In closing, one more small request: that among others you always let me keep the name by which in *** you came to know my humble person.

"But you may call me what I am:

Your loyal uncle
Friedrich Nolten,
Hofrat."

The President could have fallen over in a faint with astonishment. He had heard about this relative from Theobald as the deceased father of Elisabeth, and now — he thought he was dreaming.

The two men looked at each other a long time in silence and gazed down into an immeasurable abyss of fate.

The President stayed another day and then, much moved, departed. It was natural for Nanette not to leave the old forester alone. Later the two, upon the Hofrat's insistent urging, went to live with him in a third town out in the countryside not far from Neuburg. The uncle had become almost distraught when he heard that his nephew had died and that his confession had not even reached him! With greater calm did he receive the news of the death — likely only days before Theobald's — of his insane daughter. They had, as the President announced immediately upon his arrival home, found her dead on the public highway some miles from his estate, where she had doubtless simply succumbed to exhaustion. — Her father had known about her miserable existence for years. He had previously made some attempts, in secret, to find her a proper family to live with, but, once deprived of her accustomed freedom, she began, like her mother before her, to fade visibly, resorting repeatedly and with great cunning to flight — and since, as well, her melancholy nature, an innate legacy of her mother, seemed incurable, they ultimately stopped taking the trouble to bring her back.

It remains only to mention that Countess Armond, long ill and otherwise cut off from all the world, was nevertheless, through her contact with the Hofrat, secretly concerned with Nolten's fortune right to the last and survived his fate by only a few months.

Notes

[1] Publius Papinus Statius (ca. 45–96 A.D.) was a Roman poet. Tillsen has had his strange visitor depict a scene either from his *Thebais* (91), an epic about Oedipus's quarreling sons, or from his *Achilleis*.

[2] Jassfeld has described one painting based on a sketch by Nolten — the water nymph and satyr presiding over the kidnapped youth — plus the second sketch of the churchyard concert. He does not describe the second sketch he mentions, but it is likely the "Sacrifice of Polyxena," which Tillsen in the meantime has done in oil and exhibited. Given the context of "sacrifice," that Polyxena is most likely the Polyxena of the *Iliad* and of Euripides' *The Trojan Women*. She was Hector's sister, whom the Greek generals, at the behest of Achilles' ghost — he was enamored at the sight of the Trojan princess — sacrifice on Achilles' tomb. Nolten likely saw Giambattista Pittoni's version of Polyxena's sacrifice during his time in Italy.

[3] The barber Wispel — his name in either language evoking lisping, whispering, and wispiness — is an invention of Mörike's based on a character that he used to perform for the amusement of his fellow seminarians in Tübingen. Wispel is also the only figure from the novel that Mörike portrayed graphically.

[4] "Hofrat" can be translated as 'Privy Councillor' but has been left in its original throughout. Contrary to some opinions (Tscherpel) he appears later, referred to as 'the eccentric old Hofrat,' at one of the Countess's gatherings later in Part One (page 44) and then plays a more prominent role through Part Two, eventually, in the final episode, revealing himself to be Theobald Nolten's uncle, the painter and Gypsy adventurer, long-lost and presumed dead Friedrich Nolten.

[5] Nolten's thoughts of Constanze here — her face as the expression of the angel breathing within — recur verbatim late in Part Two in the first stanza of the third sonnet "To L," which Agnes finds in Larkens's posthumous papers (see page 286). This invites questions about the degree of closeness and collaboration linking Nolten and Larkens — and the fictive narrator.

[6] 'King Richard' here refers to the title figure of Shakespeare's *Richard III.* The Duke of Friedland is General Wallenstein, title hero of Schiller's great historical tragedy of 1799.

[7] The relationship of Nolten here to his actor friend's imaginative inventions is typically unwitting and obtuse, a tendency that leads to trouble with the "Orplid" intermezzo. Here Larkens invents a scenario that most of the audience takes to be merely a satire on "boisterous students," but that may in fact have, in the 1820s and 30s, incendiary political content — inasmuch as it seems to reflect on the deflated power and significance of the students and intellectuals who once, from 1813 to the Wartburg Festival (1817), exerted considerable influence on liberal politics of the day. With the intervening events involving Karlsbad and Metternich, that once great body of students and intellectuals might be seen to have been reduced by some chimney-sweeping acts of pedagogical control, censorship, and propaganda, with various plans for a united and remapped Germany, with dreams of one crowned head presiding

over several broken crowns, with basic lessons in matters Grecian — the horrible costs of that 1828 revolution — playing an obvious role in helping to divert the interests of that group towards matters of religion and the church.

[8] Ludvig Holberg (1684–1754) was a Danish writer who, starting in the early 1720s, made major contributions to the new Danish National Theater with comedies ranked with those of Molière, his portrayals differing from those of the French master by depicting main comic characters totally dominated by delusion, detached from reality.

[9] One of three major unsolved mysteries in the novel (see also notes 19 and 55) is Larkens's motivation for steering his young friend away from Constanze. He is said to be concerned with ensuring that Theobald does not court ruin and waste his energies in dissolute affairs as he himself did (e.g. pages 131–32). But that does not explain why he so strongly favors Agnes and abhors Constanze. Readers might be expected to speculate that a drive to exert greater control over Nolten is in play.

[10] Herbert Meyer (Mörike, V 231) points out that talk of the "language of the flowers" was a popular social entertainment in Mörike's day, resulting in several "handbooks" on the topic. Late in Part Two, it becomes a matter of conversation among Agnes, Nanette, and Margot (see page 256).

[11] The use of the definite article here indicates that '*the* eccentric Hofrat' (emphasis added) in this episode and then at the outset of Part Two is, contrary to some assumptions (see Tscherpel 80–81), the same person as the "Hofrat" who converses with Leopold and plays cards with Larkens in the episode beginning on New Year's Eve in the Spanish Court.

[12] Tillsen is referring to two Vestris, father and son, both great dancers of the eighteenth and nineteenth centuries. Gaetano Vestris (1729–1808) once proclaimed himself to rank with Frederick the Great and Voltaire as one of the three greatest men of his day. He in turn taught dancing to his son, Auguste (1760–1842), considered the greatest dancer of his time.

[13] The reference is to Shakespeare's drama *King John,* Act IV, Scene 1, the confrontation between young Prince Arthur and his would-be murderer, Hubert.

[14] A *double entendre* stems from the fact that the German word used here for a painter's brush, "der Pinsel," is also commonly used for "simpleton" or "nincompoop." The phallic symbolism of scarpello and brush then imparts a treble dimension to the word play. The "Italian sculptor" pronounces himself ready to take on a German painter, a German simpleton, and to raise his own instrument against a simple and ineffectual German painter's tool.

[15] The original contains the following footnote at this point: 'Sunclock — that is what they called the three specially arranged stone obelisks that, with the shadow they cast, were supposed to have served the original inhabitants as a kind of sundial.'

[16] Ludwig Bauer's Orplid-based drama *Der heimliche Maluff* reveals that the mythical inhabitants of this mountain area in Orplid were subjects of King Maluff called the "Schmettens."

[17] Unique in the entire "Orplid" piece, this 'Water Lily Lake' corresponds with a real locality in Germany, the "Mummelsee" in the northern Black Forest. It figures

prominently in saga and legend, also in a Mörike poem, "Die Geister am Mummelsee" ('The Ghosts of Lily Lake').

[18] With Constanze keeping the manuscript at this point, it becomes hard to understand how, in the ensuing episode, the King can be said in the meantime to have read it and passed it on to the Duke for further study.

[19] The second of three major mysteries in the novel (see notes 9 and 55) is the exact motivation for Constanze's disturbingly vengeful decision to render Nolten up to arrest and investigation. The text carefully suggests that she does not simply turn angry at feeling he has betrayed her with another woman; but it merely hints that she could be much more disturbed by an act of betrayal involving two men.

[20] The use of the term "Wahlverwandtschaften" ('elective affinities') is a direct allusion to Goethe's 1811 novel of that title. Herbert Meyer (Mörike, V, 208) points out that the introduction of Leopold ('Leopold — as we shall call the young traveler'; page 12) also evokes that same novel, which introduces its male protagonist as 'Eduard — as we shall call a wealthy Baron.' Mörike's shifting of the phrase from main male protagonist to a secondary figure invites speculation as to parodic intent.

[21] Herbert Meyer (Mörike V) notes numerous specific echoes of Goethe's works (*Meister, Elective Affinities*) — or, for example, the designation of the "Orplid" intermezzo as 'phantasmagorical' recalling the Helena act of *Faust II* (see also S. S. Prawer's article). Noteworthy too are evocations of various Romantic stories, especially here in this "notebook" inlay. Here, for example, the Zulima encounter of the fourth chapter of Novalis's *Heinrich von Ofterdingen* is recalled, where the title hero is given the mysteriously inscribed medallion by the beautiful singing girl from the Holy Lands. The same sequence of a mountain encounter with an exotic singing woman offering a mysteriously carved artifact — plus the father's prohibitive intervention — also echoes Ludwig Tieck's *Der Runenberg* ('Rune Mountain').

[22] Philomela is the figure of Greek legend, saddened to melancholy in a love triangle with King Tereus of Thrace and his wife, Procne, who was her sister. All three are turned into birds by the gods, Philomela, in Latin versions, into a nightingale.

[23] William Hogarth (1694–1764) was an English painter and engraver whose aesthetic theories and practice influenced German thinkers since Lessing and whose works underwent a renaissance in the 1830s. The reference to him here by the Hofrat is a salient example of the text's tendency to make specific reference to a figure whose ideas and works are evoked elsewhere in the novel — other examples being Tieck, Novalis, Lichtenberg, and Goethe. Above all Roland Tscherpel (esp. 76–84) has argued that Mörike was well versed in Hogarth's ideas, which turned away from rigid divisions in modes of art in favor of provocative combinations of the grotesque and the beautiful, the comic and the sublime.

[24] This sentence is a translation of a central clause in Psalm 4:4 in the Lutheran Bible ("Erkenne doch, daß der Herr seine Heiligen wunderlich führet"). The equivalent (Psalm 4:3) in both the Kings James and the Douay version is quite different.

[25] Trying to put as happy a face as possible on his deception of two "lovers," Larkens is alluding to Shakespeare's *A Midsummer Night's Dream*.

[26] Cupido dirus is a 'cruel' or 'terrible' Eros (Amor or Cupid), a frequent characterization in classical literature. Anteros, in later classical mythology, was the brother, also often playmate and adversary of Eros.

[27] Ariadne is the wife of the Greek god Bacchus; since Bacchus becomes Liber in Roman mythology, Ariadne becomes Libera.

[28] 'Forest devil' here is a direct translation of "Waldteufel," according to Herbert Meyer (Mörike, V 224) a sixteenth-century Germanization and Christian restyling of "satyr" or "faun," the two terms coinciding in Goethe's poem "Satyros oder Der vergötterte Waldteufel" ('Satyros or The Deified Forest Devil').

[29] The forester is quoting Psalm 77:6–7 of the Lutheran Bible. Although he uses his Bible's "Saitenspiel" (literally a 'stringed instrument'), his quotation has been translated using 'harp' instead. The King James Bible shares with the Lutheran Bible many references in Psalms to awakening to praise God with, singly or severally, a "harp," "psaltery," or "instrument of ten strings," the latter being closest to "Saitenspiel" (cf. Psalms 33:2, 57:8, 71:22, 92:3, and 144:9), but its version of Psalm 77:6–7 refers to no musical instruments. The translation here favors 'harp' over 'instrument of ten stings' because the latter usage seemed potentially misleading, implying crossbow perhaps instead of the rifle or gun of which the forester speaks ("Büchse"). Also, following the forester's reference to "harp," the translation ('I commune with my heart . . . .') adheres to the King James version's Psalm 77:6.

[30] Georg Christoph Lichtenberg (1742–1799) was a leading natural scientist of his day and writer of great genius and wit, much admired by Mörike. Mentioning his name briefly here, the text calls attention to its subsequent homage to Lichtenberg's pithy and trenchant opposition, echoed in the later description of Margot, the daughter of President von K*** (page 254–55), to the physiognomical theories of Johann Caspar Lavater (1741–1801), a popular pseudo-science that proposed to deduce and categorize the true self of the individual according to facial features, profile, skull shape. The presence of Lichtenberg's name and thoughts at these points in the text also signals that there may be more than coincidence behind Mörike's choice of "Nolten" for his protagonist's surname. "Nolten" is also the name of a figure in Lichtenberg's "Zum Andenken der Verstorbenen" ('In Memory of those Deceased'; 1769). The fact that Lichtenberg's Nolten was a gunsmith takes on significance in the light both of the dubious relationship of Mörike's Nolten men to firearms and shooting and of the later role of the figure Lörmer, likewise a gunsmith.

[31] Novalis is the pen name of Friedrich von Hardenberg (1772–1801), a leading poetic and philosophical talent among the Early German Romantics in the late 1790s, author of Hymnen an die Nacht ('Hymns to Night') and the novel fragment Heinrich von Ofterdingen, as well as several philosophical and poetic fragments and the cycle of Geistliche Lieder ('Spiritual Songs'). The brief mention of him here suggests that the echoes of his Ofterdingen that emerge with the "notebook" about Nolten's youth are no coincidence. Herbert Meyer (Mörike, V 225–26) astutely surmises that the Baron is referring here to an aphoristic fragment by Novalis that Mörike, well acquainted with the poet's works, would have encountered in an 1826 edition of his writings compiled by Novalis's fellow Early Romantics, Ludwig Tieck and Friedrich Schlegel, namely the following: "Die Kunst, auf eine angenehme Art zu

befremden, einen Gegenstand fremd zu machen und doch bekannt und anziehend, das ist die romantische Poetik" ('The art of estranging in a pleasant manner, of making an object strange yet still known and attractive — that is romantic poetics'; cf. Novalis, *Schriften,* Volume 3, ed. P. Kluckhohn and R. Samuel, 685).

[32] 'Italian flowers' are artificial flowers, so called because of their popularity in Italy since medieval times. They enjoyed great popularity in the Biedermeier era as decorative bouquets.

[33] Amandus is alluding here to the altercation between Lazarus's sisters Martha and Mary in Luke 10:41f., where Martha is "cumbered" with household chores while her sister Mary sits at Jesus' feet.

[34] The original contains the following footnote at this point: 'The short description of this area reflects as nearly as possible the actual landscape. The point singled out here is in Württemberg in the county of Nürtingen, nearby the parish Groß-Bettlingen.'

[35] The original contains the following footnote at this point: 'To forestall possible misunderstanding, since this story deals with a specific place, it should be born in mind that neither such a memorial nor even this saga exists there, the author having drawn his inspiration for them from the real name of the hill in question.'

[36] This account of the various tales told and evoked is doubly indebted to Gottfried August Bürger (1747–1794), the reference here to ghost brides to his ballad "Lenore," the preceding tale of the rope ladder hooking the moon's horn to one of his tales about Baron von Münchhausen. In the Münchhausen tale, it is a bean plant that hooks the moon, and there is no giant named Floemer or Flömer.

[37] Nolten had early on assured Larkens that he had received, from certain honorable personages in Neuburg, "friendly" letters warning him of Agnes's possible disloyalty (38). He had declined then to state who had written those letters, but a comment by the narrator (59) and a later, silent exchange between him and the Baron (295–96) indicate that the Baron's judicious warnings had played a role in Nolten's misjudging the girl. This disclosure, however, sustains the reader's uncertainty and raises the possibility that Nolten, in making his earlier case against Agnes, was also guided by gossip from sources less reliable than the Baron. Throughout, the confusions and vagaries involving alleged, forged, unread, and misread letters are part of the text's critical self-reflection on the reliability of written texts.

[38] Literally, the forester tells Nolten that the 'slipper' ("Pantoffel") from the 'bad girl' suits him well, a humorous reference to the German term "Pantoffelheld" (literally 'slipper hero' or 'hero in slippers'), which remains a commonly used colloquialism for a dominated or "henpecked" husband. The translation replaced "slipper" with "apron" in order to convey the basic meaning without confusion.

[39] The earlier reference to Georg Christoph Lichtenberg (page 205 and note 30) subverts the assumption that Mörike's protagonist only by chance shares his surname with a gunsmith in Lichtenberg's "Zum Andenken der Verstorbenen" ('In Memory of the Deceased'; 1769). This Nolten-gunsmith link draws attention to the text's emphasis on the problems that Mörike's Nolten men have with guns and shooting: the father with his foolishly abusive use of his shooting instrument to tyrannize the women of his household with his little "tube" (page 146), the son with his marked

contrast to fellow adventurers and artists (Raymund and Young Volker), as well as to his older male mentors (the forester, the Baron, and President von K***), as inept in his choice and use of such weapons (page 259). In this context, the gunsmith Lörmer must be considered in his function as a mirror of Nolten: like him a wanderer for some reason disrupted and hampered in his professional progress, like him a comrade and protégé of Larkens, like him a man convinced that some higher fate has numbered his days.

[40] Translating the original's "Joseph, der Tischler" as 'Joseph the Carpenter' has a distinct appeal, in that it would help to convey Larkens's tendency to self-glorifying histrionics and role play by evoking the designation of Jesus' father in Matthew 18:55 as a "carpenter" — a possible, if not optimal, translation of "Tischler." However, since Mörike differentiates Larkens's Joseph as "Tischler" from the Lutheran Bible's Joseph as "Zimmermann," the translation here as 'Joseph the Joiner' avoids imposing a link that the original has chosen not to make.

[41] To "read someone the Levites" was a common German phrase for lecturing someone sternly on the rules and prescriptions of behavior, referring to Leviticus, the third book of the Old Testament (the 'Third Book of Moses' in the Lutheran Bible). While the common phrase usually used the plural "Levites," referring to the many rules, Perse here corrects the phrase to the singular, referring to the entire book.

[42] The joy of finding his watch has given Lörmer the power to speak exotic tongues, not only French but Kalmukian, the language of a people who originated in Mongolia and, in the thirteenth century, split into two groups, the one, the Kalmuks, settling along the Volga.

[43] Lörmer had earlier (page 236) mentioned a ticking or knocking "Holzwurm" residing in his peg leg — literally a 'wood-worm' but translated here as 'woodworm beetle' because it is in fact a member of the beetle family, the "Klopfkäfer" (literally 'knock beetle') or *anobium pertinax,* which can infest wood and make an audible knocking or ticking sound. Here he refers to it by its more common German name, the "Todtenuhr" (modern German "Totenuhr"), literally 'death clock,' so called because its eerie ticking sound was taken to be a portent of death.

[44] A "Titus" or "Tituskopf" (literally 'Titus-head') was in Mörike's day a hair style consisting of tight, frizzy curls, its name derived from stone busts of the Roman Emperor Titus wearing such a head of ringlets. In post-Napoleonic times it became the most fashionable hair style among women.

[45] "Joko" is a reference to Philipp Taglioni's ballet *Danina oder Jocko, der brazilianische Affe* ('Danina or Joko, the Brazilian Monkey'), frequently performed, from 1826 on, at the Stuttgart *Hoftheater* (music by Peter von Lindpaintner).

[46] Herbert Meyer (Mörike, V 230) recognizes this phrase as an allusion to Goethe's *Apprenticeship of Wilhelm Meister,* where, in VIII, 8, Mignon's lively gratitude seems "die Flamme zu seyn [. . .] die das Öl ihres Lebens aufzehrte" ('to be the flame that consumed the oil of her life').

[47] Ludwig Tieck (1773–1853) was, with Friedrich Schlegel and Novalis, a central figure among the Early Romantics in Berlin and Jena, active and prolific at that time in many genres. He collaborated with his friend Wilhelm Heinrich Wackenroder to

produce the seminal Romantic work *Herzensergießungen eines kunstliebenden Kloster-bruders* ('Heart Outpourings of an Art-Loving Friar'; 1797). His own artist novel, *Franz Sternbalds Wanderungen* ('Franz Sternbald's Wanderings'; 1798), was first taken to be a work by Goethe; he wrote seminal Romantic *Kunstmärchen* ('artistic fairy tales') such as *Der blonde Eckbert* ('Eckbert the Fair'; 1797) and *Der Runenberg* ('Rune Mountain'; 1803); and his Early Romantic dramas — *Der gestiefelte Kater* ('Puss in Boots'; 1797) and *Die verkehrte Welt* ('Topsy-Turvy World'; 1798) — are tours de force of Romantic irony and metadrama.

[48] Herbert Meyer suggests (Mörike V, 230) that Mörike is thinking here of actor and director Carl Seydelmann, active in the Stuttgart Hoftheater from 1829 to 1837, although there is no evidence that Seydelmann ever thought of staging Tieck's comedies.

[49] *Rataplan, der kleine Tambour* ('Rataplan [= rat-a-tat], the little drummer') was a popular revue by Ferdinand Pillwitz. The 'bears and monkeys and these holy halls' refers to Mozart's *Magic Flute*.

[50] The President's comment here evokes Matthew 18:20: "where two or three are gathered together in my name, there am I in the midst of them."

[51] "Gretchen im Busch" ('Gretchen in the bush') is one common name for the *nigella damascena*, also known as "Jungfer im Grünen" ('virgin in the green'), and in English often "devil in the bush" or "love in the mist." Exactly why it is tasteless to associate Margot with a flower so named is not immediately apparent; perhaps it implies some association with an apparent virgin secretly capable of mischievous, devilish love.

[52] Herbert Meyer (Mörike, V 232) suggests that the *Heliotropium peruvianum* is the flower referred to here.

[53] Margot actually uses the term "Pantalon" to refer to what is probably an old fashioned piano of some sort. That term is derived from the name Pantaleon Hebenstreit (1667–1750), who in the 1690s developed from the dulcimer a musical instrument known as the "Pantaleon" or also "Klöppelklavier" ('mallet piano'), a harpsichord-sized, enlarged dulcimer, in which the strings were struck with hammers. It influenced the development of the pianoforte in the early eighteenth century.

[54] The original refers to "Rosemonde" by "Ruccelai," whereas the author is generally referred to as Giovanni Rucellai (1475–1525), a Florentine courtier and dramatist, whose tragedy *La Rosmunda* appeared in Sienna in 1525.

[55] A third major mystery of the text (see notes 9 and 19) is the time and cause of Theobald's turn against Elisabeth. The notebook account of his adolescent encounter with her mentions a solemn oath and portrays him saddened by her absence and never encountering her again. But what has happened to turn him so vehemently against her while making no attempt at contact, communication, or clarification?

[56] Dominique Vivant Denon (1747–1825), draftsman, engraver, author, also diplomat, art collector, and general director of the Napoleon Museum (now the Louvre) from 1802–1815. He accompanied Napoleon to Egypt, an undertaking that resulted, in 1802, in his *Voyage dans la Basse et Haute Égypt*.

[57] The last part of Henni's reflections ("in welchem wir leben . . ." = 'in whom we live . . .') quotes Acts 17:28.

[58] The "bright stream of paradise" evokes Genesis 2:10, replacing "Eden" with "paradise."

[59] This vision of the bound creature evokes Romans 8:19.